STEFAN ZWEIG was born in 1881 in Vienna, into a wealthy Austrian-Jewish family. He studied in Berlin and Vienna and was first known as a poet and translator, then as a biographer. Zweig travelled widely, living in Salzburg between the wars, and was an international bestseller with a string of hugely popular novellas including *Letter from an Unknown Woman*, *Amok* and *Fear*. In 1934, with the rise of Nazism, he moved to London, and later on to Bath, taking British citizenship after the outbreak of the Second World War. With the fall of France in 1940 Zweig left Britain for New York, before settling in Brazil, where in 1942 he and his wife were found dead in an apparent double suicide. Much of his work is available from Pushkin Press.

STEFAN ZWEIG

BEWARE
OF PITY

Translated from the German by
Anthea Bell

PUSHKIN PRESS

LONDON

Pushkin Press
71-75 Shelton Street,
London WC2H 9JQ

Original text © S Fischer Verlag
English translation © Anthea Bell 2011

Foreword © Nicholas Lezard 2011

Beware of Pity first published in German as
Ungeduld des Herzens in 1939.

This translation first published in 2011

This edition published in 2013

003

ISBN 978 1 908968 37 1

Set in 10.5 on 14 Monotype Baskerville
by Tetragon, London

Printed in Great Britain by CPI Group (UK) Ltd, Croydon, CR0 4YY

www.pushkinpress.com

BEWARE
OF PITY

Contents

When Stefan Zweig, forced into a peripatetic life because of the rise of Nazism, arrived in New York in 1935, he was persistently asked to make a statement about the treatment of the Jews in Germany. He refused to be drawn out, and said in correspondence that his reason was that anything he said would probably only make their situation worse. Similarly, when staying in London, he found that while he loved the English way of not getting too het up about things, their civility and general decency, he found the regular denunciations of the Third Reich a little too much—he felt that they lost force by repetition.

To which one might have countered—one couldn't say often enough that the Third Reich was evil incarnate. And one would have thought that Zweig, Jewish himself, and fully aware that his books were being burned in university quads all over Germany (and that, given he was probably the most popular author in the world at the time, would have been quite an impressive conflagration in brute terms of scale), might have had more to say publicly on the subject.

Similarly, *Beware of Pity*, completed in 1938, and composed over a period of years before the outbreak of the Second World War (there are eleven extant—extant, mind—volumes of notes and drafts which attest to Zweig's painstaking work on this, his only full-length novel), itself very pointedly has almost nothing to say about contemporary times—on the surface, at least. On the surface it is the story of a young Austrian cavalry officer, Anton Hofmiller, who befriends a local millionaire, Kekesfalva, and his family, but in particular the old man's crippled daughter, Edith, with terrible consequences.

Well, it almost has nothing to say about the times it was written in. Which means that it has something to say about it; obliquely, and passed across your eyes quickly, like a Hitchcock cameo. But the novel's very flight from pressing concerns is in itself significant. Of course, Zweig's temperament was pretty influential here—following Hitler's rise to power, the first project Zweig embarked upon was a biography of Erasmus, which he described as "a quiet hymn of praise to the anti-fanatical man," or, in other words, in direct but non-violent opposition to the loathsome qualities that were becoming deemed desirable, indeed compulsory, in society at large. But sometimes evasiveness isn't a straightforward matter of wanting to keep out of trouble, or stick up for virtues which are in danger of being trampled.

One of the earliest writers to note what Freud was doing, Zweig took on board early the lesson that directly dealing with terrible things is not necessarily the way the mind works. His stories are full of characters poisoned by things left unsaid, or situations misread. We tell ourselves stories about what is going on; but sometimes these are the wrong stories. In one of his earlier stories, *Downfall of the Heart* (whose original title—*Untergang eines Herzens*—is a proleptic echo of the German title of *Beware of Pity*—*Ungeduld des Herzens*, or "the heart's impatience") a self-made businessman succumbs to a terrible decline after seeing, or imagining he has seen, his daughter sneaking out of a man's hotel room in the middle of the night. And in *Beware of Pity* we have a hero who makes a habit of getting things wrong. "Since this seems to be the day for making wrong diagnoses … " says the admirable Dr Condor at one point in the novel, but it is the "hero" (and I had better start using inverted commas around that word, for reasons our "hero" would most certainly approve of) who keeps making wrong diagnoses. There is the terrible *gaffe* he makes which sets the whole terrible train of events in motion (it's a small train, admittedly, but big enough to cause havoc); there is his initial impression that Kekesfalva is a genuine venerable Hungarian nobleman, that Condor is a bumpkin and a fool; and, in one splendidly subtle piece of writing, in which an interior state of mind is beautifully translated into memorable yet familiar imagery, he imagines himself to be better put together than Condor, when they walk out in bright moonlight on the night of their first meeting:

And as we walked down the apparently snow-covered gravel drive, suddenly we were not two but four, for our shadows went ahead of us, clear-cut in the bright moonlight. Against my will I had to keep watching those two black companions who persistently marked out our movements ahead of us, like walking silhouettes, and it gave me—our feelings are sometimes so childish—a certain reassurance to see that my shadow was longer, slimmer, I almost said "better-looking", than the short, stout shadow of my companion.

This has a ring of interior psychological veracity, which shows just how sharply Zweig could pay attention to his characters' inner workings. And if, as Henry James said, a novelist is someone upon whom nothing is lost, then we have in Zweig's "hero" here, a man on whom everything is lost. In more than one sense of the phrase.

When we first meet Hofmiller, though, it is not the eve of the First World War, when the events described in *Beware of Pity* take place, but on the eve of the Second, explicitly, in 1938, when the framing narrator—a famous novelist whom we might as well assume to be Zweig himself—is briefly introduced in a café to Hofmiller by a well-meaning "hanger-on" (who could also, possibly, be said to be a mischievously unflattering self-portrait of another aspect of Zweig's personality. He was known for that kind of thing). Hofmiller is a famously decorated soldier, but he obviously treats his decoration—the highest military order Austria can offer, her equivalent of the Victoria Cross—with disdain bordering on contempt, and only speaks to the framing narrator when they meet accidentally at a dinner party later on.

And it is at this moment that we should realise that the message of the book is not only its ostensible one—that pity is an emotion that can cause great ruin (although this aspect of the book is given greater weight in English, because of its title in translation, the message is delivered firmly and frequently enough in the course of the work)—it is that we must not judge things by appearances. He may be entitled to wear the Order of Maria Theresia but he can tell you that, in his instance at least, what others might regard as courage is actually the result of a monumental act of cowardice.

Stefan Zweig was hugely famous throughout the world as a writer of novellas and short stories, as well as popular histories and biographies, so it is remarkable that he only wrote one full-length novel. It has led some commentators to suggest that in this instance he overstretched himself, that he became prolix, or, more charitably, that *Beware of Pity* is actually two novellas of unequal length stitched together. The latter suggestion is certainly worth consideration (how Kekesfalva got his loot is certainly a story in itself), but *Beware of Pity* is the length it is because it has to be (and, as with all Zweig's writing, it zips along almost effortlessly, like a clear-running stream; it doesn't read as though it could do with much trimming). The loop back in time that Zweig is taking us on has to be accounted for; it has to take time. He said himself that the impulses behind the novel were not only nostalgia—itself one of the most powerful of narrative impulses, as anyone who has even heard of Proust knows—but pity—pity specifically directed at Lotte, his secretary, with whom he was having an affair, and who was to become his second wife (and with whom he would successfully undertake a suicide pact in a hotel room in Petrópolis, Brazil). Make of that what you will. He wanted this to be the Great Austrian Novel, and so a certain scope was demanded of him.

And he had to go back to pre-1914. For that was when everything began to go wrong. In his story *The Invisible Collection,* first published in 1927, a collector of rare prints who has gone blind is deceived by his family—they have sold his valuable collection bit by bit in order to feed themselves, and him, during the disastrous inflation that followed the First World War, and have replaced the prints with blank paper of the same dimensions and thickness. When he strokes the blank sheets the narrator notes his happiness: "Not for years, *not since 1914*, had I witnessed an expression of such unmitigated happiness on the face of a German … " (Italics mine.)

It is a scene of such potent and telling symbolism that it verges, tremulously, on the corny. But that is not to gainsay its validity and power. The Great War ruined and erased everything, and reduced the past almost to a state as if it had never been. Zweig's portrait of pre-war Vienna, *The World of Yesterday*, is a long lament for a vanished world, tantamount to a suicide note. Interestingly— in fact, very interestingly indeed—he does not, in *Beware of Pity*, allude to, or make any real use of, the atmosphere of stifling sexual repression that animates 'Eros Matutinus', one of the best chapters of *The World of Yesterday*, in which Zweig acknowledges there were some very significant aspects of genteel society the world was right to discard. In fact, if anything, the return to the values of 1913 is tacitly endorsed, albeit in a complex and ambiguous fashion, when Hofmiller discovers, to his horror, that Edith has sexual desires.

But *Beware of Pity* ends with a note of almost bitter disillusionment. (Not to mention the reader's relief at having finally climbed out of an emotional tumble-dryer, which is just the effect Zweig wanted his best work to have.) In fact, if it didn't sound so off-putting, *Disillusionment* could be a perfectly plausible title for the novel (to go with Zweig's other one-word titles for some of his novellas—*Amok*, *Confusion* or *Fear*). But disillusionment is, though often painful—and *Beware of Pity* has moments of high melodrama that, over seventy years on, still have the power to make one put one's free hand over one's mouth as one reads—a very necessary process. And it is a very useful kind of Bildungsroman in which it is not only the chief character who learns something by the end of it, but the reader, too.

NICHOLAS LEZARD 2011

AUTHOR'S NOTE

A SHORT EXPLANATION may perhaps be necessary for the English reader. The Austro-Hungarian Army constituted a uniform, homogeneous body in an Empire composed of a very large number of nations and races. Unlike his English, French, and even German *confrère*, the Austrian officer was not allowed to wear mufti when off duty, and military regulations prescribed that in his private life he should always act *standesgemäss*, that is, in accordance with the special etiquette and code of honour of the Austrian military caste. Among themselves officers of the same rank, even those who were not personally acquainted, never addressed each other in the formal third person plural, *Sie*, but in the familiar second person singular, *Du*, and thereby the fraternity of all members of the caste and the gulf separating them from civilians were emphasized. The final criterion of an officer's behaviour was invariably not the moral code of society in general, but the special moral code of his caste, and this frequently led to mental conflicts, one of which plays an important part in this book.

STEFAN ZWEIG

There are two kinds of pity. One, the weak-minded, sentimental sort, is really just the heart's impatience to rid itself as quickly as possible of the painful experience of being moved by another person's suffering. It is not a case of real sympathy, of feeling with the sufferer, but a way of defending yourself against someone else's pain. The other kind, the only one that counts, is unsentimental but creative. It knows its own mind, and is determined to stand by the sufferer, patiently suffering too, to the last of its strength and even beyond.

INTRODUCTION

"To him that hath, more shall be given." Every writer knows the truth of this biblical maxim, and can confirm the fact that "To him who hath told much, more shall be told." There is nothing more erroneous than the idea, which is only too common, that a writer's imagination is always at work, and he is constantly inventing an inexhaustible supply of incidents and stories. In reality he does not have to invent his stories; he need only let characters and events find their own way to him, and if he retains to a high degree the ability to look and listen, they will keep seeking him out as someone who will pass them on. To him who has often tried to interpret the tales of others, many will tell their tales.

The incidents that follow were told to me almost entirely as I record them here, and in a wholly unexpected way. Last time I was in Vienna I felt tired after dealing with a great deal of business, and I went one evening to a suburban restaurant that I suspected had fallen out of fashion long ago, and would not be very full. As soon as I had come in, however, I found to my annoyance that I was wrong. An acquaintance of mine rose from the very first table with every evidence of high delight, to which I am afraid I could not respond quite so warmly, and asked me to sit down with him. It would not be true to say that this excessively friendly gentleman was disagreeable company in himself; but he was one of those compulsively sociable people who collect acquaintances as enthusiastically as children collect stamps, and like to show off every item in their collection. For this well-meaning oddity—a knowledgeable and competent archivist by profession—the whole meaning of life was confined to the modest satisfaction of being able to boast, in an offhand manner, of anyone whose name appeared in the newspapers from time to time, "Ah, he's a good friend of mine," or, "Oh, I met him only yesterday," or, "My friend A told me, and then my friend B gave it as his opinion that … " and so on all through the alphabet. He was regularly in the audience to applaud the premieres of his friends' plays, and would telephone every leading actress next morning with his congratulations, he never forgot a birthday, he never referred to any poor reviews of your work in the papers, but sent you those that praised it to the skies. Not a disagreeable man, then—his warmth of feeling was genuine, and he was delighted if you ever did him a small favour, or even added a new item to his fine collection of acquaintances.

However, there is no need for me to say more about my friend the hanger-on—such was the usual name in Vienna for this particular kind of well-intentioned parasite among the motley group of social climbers—for we all know hangers-on, and we also know that there is no way of repelling their well-meant attentions without being rude. So I resigned myself to sitting down beside him, and half-an-hour had passed in idle chatter when a man came into the restaurant. He was tall, his fresh-complexioned, still youthful face and the interesting touch of grey at his temples made him a striking figure, and a certain way of holding himself very upright marked him out at once as a former military man. My table companion immediately leapt to his feet with a typically warm greeting, to which, however, the gentleman responded with more indifference than civility, and the newcomer had hardly ordered from the attentive waiter who came hurrying up before my friend the lion-hunter was leaning towards me and asking in a whisper, "Do you know who that is?" As I well knew his collector's pride in displaying his collection, and I feared a lengthy story, I said only a brief, "No," and went back to dissecting my Sachertorte. However, my lack of interest only aroused further enthusiasm in the collector of famous names, and he confidentially whispered, "Why, that's Hofmiller of the General Commissariat—you know, the man who won the Order of Maria Theresia in the war." And since even this did not seem to impress me as much as he had hoped, he launched with all the enthusiasm of a patriotic textbook into an account of the great achievements of this Captain Hofmiller, first in the cavalry, then on the famous reconnaissance flight over the river Piave when he shot down three enemy aircraft single-handed, and finally the time when he occupied and held a sector of the front for three days with his company of gunners—all with a wealth of detail that I omit here, and many expressions of astonishment at finding that I had never heard of this great man, decorated by Emperor Karl in person with the highest order in the Austrian Army.

Reluctantly, I let myself be persuaded to glance at the other table for a closer view of a historically authentic hero. But I met with a look of annoyance, as much as to say—has that fellow been talking about me? There's no need to stare! At the same time the gentleman pushed his chair to one side with an air of distinct displeasure, ostentatiously turning his back to us. Feeling a little ashamed of myself, I looked away from him, and from then on I avoided looking curiously at anything, even the tablecloth. Soon after that I said goodbye to my talkative friend. I noticed as I left that he immediately moved to the table where his military hero was sitting, probably to give him an account of me as eagerly as he had talked to me about Hofmiller.

That was all. A mere couple of glances, and I would certainly have forgotten that brief meeting, but at a small party the very next day it so happened that I again found myself opposite the same unsociable gentleman, who incidentally looked even more striking and elegant in a dinner jacket than he had in his casual tweeds the day before. We both had some difficulty in suppressing a small smile, the kind exchanged in a company of any size by two people who share a well-kept secret.

23

...ognised me as easily as I did him, and probably we felt the same
amusement in thinking of the mutual acquaintance who had failed to
throw us together yesterday. At first we avoided speaking to one another,
and indeed there was not much chance to do so, because an animated
discussion was going on around us.

I shall be giving away the subject of that discussion in advance if
I mention that it took place in the year 1938. Later historians of our
time will agree that in 1938 almost every conversation, in every country
of our ruined continent of Europe, revolved around the probability or
otherwise of a second world war. The theme inevitably fascinated every
social gathering, and you sometimes felt that fears, suppositions and hopes
were being expressed not so much by the speakers as by the atmosphere
itself, the air of those times, highly charged with secret tensions and
anxious to put them into words.

The subject had been broached by the master of the house, a lawyer
and self-opinionated, as lawyers tend to be. He trotted out the usual
arguments to prove the usual nonsense—the younger generation knew
about war now, he said, and would not stumble blindly into another
one. At the moment of mobilisation, guns would be turned on those
who had given orders to fire them. Men like him in particular, said our
host, men who had fought at the front in the last war, had not forgotten
what it was like. At a time when explosives and poison gas were being
manufactured in tens of thousands—no, hundreds of thousands—of
armaments factories, he dismissed the possibility of war as easily as he
flicked the ash off his cigarette, speaking in a confident tone that irritated
me. We shouldn't always, I firmly retorted, believe in our own wishful
thinking. The civil and military organisations directing the apparatus of
war had not been asleep, and while our heads were spinning with utopian
notions they had made the maximum use of peacetime to get control of
the population at large. It had been organised in advance and was now,
so to speak, primed ready to fire. Even now, thanks to our sophisticated

propaganda machine, general subservience had grown to extraordinary proportions, and we had only to look facts in the face to see that when mobilisation was announced on the radio sets in our living rooms, no resistance could be expected. Men today were just motes of dust with no will of their own left.

Of course everyone else was against me. We all know from experience how the human tendency to self-delusion likes to declare dangers null and void even when we sense in our hearts that they are real. And such a warning against cheap optimism was certain to be unwelcome at the magnificently laid supper table in the next room.

Unexpectedly, although I had assumed that the hero who had won the Order of Maria Theresia would be an adversary, he now spoke up and took my side. It was sheer nonsense, he said firmly, to suppose that what ordinary people wanted or did not want counted for anything today. In the next war machinery would do the real work, and human beings would be downgraded to the status of machine parts. Even in the last war, he said, he had not met many men in the field who were clearly either for or against it. Most of them had been caught up in hostilities like a cloud of dust in the wind, and there they were, stuck in the whirl of events, shaken about and helpless like dried peas in a big bag. All things considered, he said, perhaps more men had fled into the war than away from it.

I listened in surprise, particularly interested by the vehemence with which he went on. "Let's not delude ourselves. If you were to try drumming up support in any country today for a war in a completely different part of the world, say Polynesia or some remote corner of Africa, thousands and tens of thousands would volunteer as recruits without really knowing why, perhaps just out of a desire to get away from themselves or their unsatisfactory lives. But I can't put the chances of any real opposition to the idea of war higher than zero. It takes far more courage for a man to oppose an organisation than to go along with

25

the crowd. Standing up to it calls for individualism, and individualists are a dying species in these times of progressive organisation and mechanisation. In the war the instances of courage that I met could be called courage en masse, courage within the ranks, and if you look closely at that phenomenon you'll find some very strange elements in it—a good deal of vanity, thoughtlessness, even boredom, but mainly fear—fear of lagging behind, fear of mockery, fear of taking independent action, and most of all fear of opposing the united opinion of your companions. Most of those whom I knew on the field as the bravest of the brave seemed to me very dubious heroes when I returned to civil life. And please don't misunderstand me," he added, turning courteously to our host, who had a wry look on his face, "I make no exception at all for myself."

I liked the way he spoke, and would have gone over for a word with him, but just then the lady of the house summoned us to supper, and as we were seated some way apart we had no chance to talk. Only when everyone was leaving did we meet in the cloakroom.

"I think," he said to me, with a smile, "that we've already been introduced by our mutual friend."

I smiled back. "And at such length, too."

"I expect he laid it on thick, presenting me as an Achilles and carrying on about my order."

"Something like that."

"Yes, he's very proud of my order—and of your books as well."

"An oddity, isn't he? Still, there are worse. Shall we walk a little way together?"

As we were leaving, he suddenly turned to me. "Believe me, I mean it when I tell you that over the years the Order of Maria Theresia has been nothing but a nuisance to me. Too showy by half for my liking. Although to be honest, when it was handed out to me on the battlefield of course I was delighted at first. After all, when you've been trained as a soldier and

26

from your days at military academy on you've heard about the legendary order—it's given to perhaps only a dozen men in any war—well, it's like a star falling from heaven into your lap. A thing like that means a lot to a young man of twenty-eight. All of a sudden there you are in front of everyone, they're all staring at something shining on your chest like a little sun, and the Emperor himself, His Unapproachable Majesty, is shaking your hand and congratulating you. But you see, it's a distinction that meant nothing outside the world of the army, and after the war it struck me as ridiculous to be going around as a certified hero for the rest of my life, just because I'd shown real courage for twenty minutes—probably no more courage, in fact, than ten thousand others. All that distinguished me from them was that I had attracted attention and, perhaps even more surprising, I'd come back alive. After a year when everyone stared at that little bit of metal, with their eyes wandering over me in awe, I felt sick and tired of going around like a monument on the move, and I hated all the fuss. That's one of the reasons why I switched to civilian life so soon after the end of the war."

He began walking a little faster.

"One of the reasons, I said, but the main reason was private, and you may find it easier to understand. The main reason was that I had grave doubts of my right to be decorated at all, or at least of my heroism. I knew better than any of the gaping strangers that behind that order was a man who was far from being a hero, was even decidedly a non-hero—one of those who ran full tilt into the war to save themselves from a desperate situation. Deserters from their own responsibilities, not heroes doing their duty. I don't know how it seems to you, but I for one see life lived in an aura of heroism as unnatural and unbearable, and I felt genuinely relieved when I could give up parading my heroic story on my uniform for all to see. It still irritates me to hear someone digging up the old days of my glory, and I might as well admit that yesterday I was on the point of going over to your table and telling our

27

loquacious friend, in no uncertain terms, to boast of knowing someone else, not me. Your look of respect rankled, and I felt like showing how wrong our friend was by making you listen to the tale of the devious ways whereby I acquired my heroic reputation. It's a very strange story, and it certainly shows that courage is often only another aspect of weakness. Incidentally, I would still have no reservations about telling you that tale. What happened to a man a quarter-of-a-century ago no longer concerns him personally—it happened to someone different. Do you have the time and inclination to hear it?"

Of course I had time, and we walked up and down the now deserted streets for some while longer. In the following days, we also spent a great deal of time together. I have changed very little in Captain Hofmiller's account, at most making a regiment of hussars into a regiment of lancers, moving garrisons around the map a little to hide their identity, and carefully changing all the personal names. But I have not added anything of importance, and it is not I as the writer of this story but its real narrator who now begins to tell his tale.

BEWARE
OF PITY

T HE WHOLE AFFAIR BEGAN with a piece of ineptitude, of entirely accidental foolishness, a faux pas, as the French would say. Next came my attempt to make up for my stupidity. But if you try to repair a little cogwheel in clockwork too quickly, you can easily ruin the whole mechanism. Even today, years later, I don't know exactly where plain clumsiness ended and my own guilt began. Presumably I never shall.

I was twenty-five years old at the time, a lieutenant serving in a regiment of lancers. I can't say that I ever felt any particular enthusiasm for the career of an army officer, or a special vocation for it. But when an old Austrian family with a tradition of service to the state has two girls and four boys, all with hearty appetites, sitting around a sparsely laid table, no one stops for long to consider the young people's own inclinations. They are put through the mill of training for some profession early, to keep them from being a burden on the household. My brother Ulrich, who had ruined his eyesight with too much studying even at elementary school, was sent to a seminar for the priesthood, while I, being physically strong and sturdy, entered the military academy. From such chance beginnings the course of your life moves automatically on, and you don't even have to oil the wheels. The state takes care of everything. Within a few years, working to a preordained pattern, it makes a pale adolescent boy into an ensign with a downy beard on his chin, and hands him over to the army ready for use. I passed out from the academy on the Emperor's birthday, when I was not quite eighteen years old, and soon after that I had my first star on my collar. I had reached the first stage of a military career, and now the cycle of promotion could move automatically on at suitable intervals until I reached retirement age and had gout. I was to serve in the cavalry, unfortunately an expensive section of the army, not by any wish of my own but because of a whim on the part of my aunt Daisy, my father's elder brother's second wife. They had married when he moved from the Ministry of Finance to a more profitable post as managing director of a bank. Aunt Daisy, who was both rich and a snob, could not bear to think that anyone who happened to be called Hofmiller should bring the family name into disrepute by serving in the infantry, and as she could afford to indulge her whim by making me an allowance of a hundred crowns a month, I had to express my humble gratitude to her at every opportunity. No one, least of all I myself, had ever stopped to wonder whether I would enjoy life in a cavalry regiment, or indeed any kind of military service. But once in the saddle I felt at ease, and I didn't think much further ahead than my horse's neck.

In that November of 1913, some kind of decree must have passed from office to office, because all of a sudden my squadron had been transferred from Jaroslav to another small garrison on the Hungarian border. It makes no difference whether I give the little town its real name or not, for two uniform buttons on the same coat can't be more like each other than one provincial Austrian garrison town is to another. You find the same ubiquitous features in both: a barracks, a riding school, a parade ground, an officers' mess, and the town will have three hotels, two cafés, a cake shop, a bar, a run-down music hall with faded soubrettes whose professional sideline consists of dividing their affections between the regular officers and volunteers who have joined up for a year. Army service means the same sleepy, empty monotony everywhere, divided up hour by hour according to the old iron rules, and even an officer's leisure time offers little more variety. You see the same faces and conduct the same conversations in the officers' mess, you play the same card games and the same games of billiards in the café. Sometimes you are quite surprised that it has at least pleased the Almighty to set the six to eight hundred rooftops of these small towns under different skies and in different landscapes.

But my new garrison did have one advantage over my earlier posting in Galicia—a railway station where express trains stopped. Go one way and it was quite close to Vienna, go the other and it was not too far from Budapest. A man who had money—and everyone who served in the cavalry was rich, even and indeed not least the volunteers, some of them members of the great aristocracy, others manufacturers' sons—a man who had money could, with careful planning, go to Vienna on the five o'clock train and return on the night train, getting in at two-thirty next morning. That gave him time for a visit to the theatre and a stroll around the Ringstrasse, courting the ladies and sometimes going in search of a little adventure. Some of the most envied officers even kept a permanent apartment for a mistress in Vienna, or a pied-à-terre. But such refreshing diversions were more than I could afford on my monthly allowance. My only entertainment was going to the café or the cake shop, and since cards were usually played for stakes too high for me, I resorted to those establishments to play billiards—or chess, which was even cheaper.

So one afternoon—it must have been in the middle of May 1914—I was sitting in the cake shop with one of my occasional partners, the pharmacist who kept his shop at the sign of the Golden Eagle, and who was also deputy mayor of our little garrison town. We had long ago finished playing our usual three games, and were just talking idly about this or that—what was there in this tedious place to make you want to get up in the morning?—but the conversation was drowsy, and as slow as the smoke from a cigarette burning down.

At this point the door suddenly opens, and a pretty girl in a full-skirted dress is swept in on a gust of fresh air, a girl with brown, almond-shaped eyes and a dark complexion. She is dressed with real elegance, not at all in the provincial style. Above all she is a new face in the monotony of this godforsaken town. Sad to say, the elegantly dressed young lady does not spare us a glance as we respectfully admire her, but walks briskly and vivaciously with a firm, athletic gait past the nine little marble tables in the cake shop and up to the sales counter, to order cakes, tarts and liqueurs by the dozen. I immediately notice how respectfully the master confectioner bows to her—I've never seen the back seam of his swallow-tailed coat stretched so taut. Even his wife, that opulent if heavily built provincial Venus, who in the usual way negligently allows the officers to court her (all manner of little things often go unpaid for until the end of the month), rises from her seat at the cash desk and almost dissolves in obsequious civilities. While the master confectioner notes down the order in the customers' book, the pretty girl carelessly nibbles a couple of chocolates and makes a little conversation with Frau Grossmaier. However, she has no time to spare for us, and we may perhaps be craning our necks with unbecoming alacrity. Of course the young lady does not burden her own pretty hands with a single package; everything, as Frau Grossmaier assures her, will be delivered, she can rely on that. Nor does she think for a moment of paying cash at the till, as we mere mortals must. We all know at once that this is a very superior and distinguished customer.

Now, as she turns to go after leaving her order, Herr Grossmaier hastily leaps forward to open the door for her. My friend the pharmacist also rises from his chair to offer his respectful greetings as she floats past. She thanks him with gracious friendliness—heavens, what velvety brown eyes, the colour of a roe deer—and I can hardly wait until she has left the shop, amidst many fulsome compliments, to ask my chess partner with great interest about this girl, a pike in a pond full of fat carp.

"Oh, don't you know her? Why, she is the niece of ... "—well, I will call him Herr von Kekesfalva, although that was not really the name—"she is the niece of Herr von Kekesfalva—surely you know the Kekesfalvas?"

Kekesfalva—he throws out the name as if it were a thousand-crown note, and looks at me as if expecting a respectful "Ah yes! Of course!" as the right and proper echo of his information. But I, a young lieutenant transferred to my new garrison only a few months ago, and unsuspecting as I am, know nothing about that mysterious luminary, and ask politely for further enlightenment, which the pharmacist gives with all the satisfaction of provincial pride, and it goes without saying does so at far greater length and with more loquacity than I do in recording his information here.

Kekesfalva, he explains to me, is the richest man in the whole district. Absolutely everything belongs to him, not just Kekesfalva Castle—"You must know the castle, it can be seen from the parade ground, it's over to the left of the road, the yellow castle with the low tower and the large old park." Kekesfalva also owns the big sugar factory on the road to R, the sawmill in Bruck and the stud farm in M. They are all his property, as well as six or seven apartment blocks in Vienna and Budapest. "You might not think that we had such wealthy folk here, but he lives the life of a real magnate. In winter, he goes to his little Viennese palace in Jacquingasse, in summer he visits spa resorts, he stays at home here only for a few months in spring, but heavens above, what a household he keeps! Visiting quartets from Vienna, champagne and French wines, the best of everything!" And if it would interest me, says the pharmacist, he will be happy to take me to the castle, for—here he makes a grand gesture of self-satisfaction—he is on friendly terms with Herr von Kekesfalva, has often done business with him in the past, and knows that he is always glad to welcome army officers to his house. My chess partner has only to say the word, and I'll be invited.

Well, why not? Here I am, stifling in the dreary backwaters of a provincial garrison town. I already know every one of the women who go walking on the promenade in the evenings by sight, I know their summer hats and winter hats, their Sunday best and their everyday dresses, always the same. And from looking and then looking away again, I know these ladies' dogs and their maidservants and their children. I know all the culinary skills of the stout Bohemian woman who is cook in the officers' mess, and by now a glance at the menu in the restaurant, which like the meals in the mess is always the same, quite takes away my appetite. I know every name, every shop sign, every poster in every street by heart, I know which business has premises in which building, and which shop will have what on display in its window. I know almost as well as Eugen the head waiter the time at which the district judge will come into the café, I know he will sit down at the corner by the window on the left, to order a Viennese melange, while the local notary will arrive exactly ten minutes later, at four-forty, and will drink lemon tea for the sake of his weak stomach—what a daring change from coffee!—while telling the same jokes as he smokes the same Virginia cigarette. Yes, I know all the faces, all the uniforms, all the horses and all the drivers, all the beggars in the entire neighbourhood, and I know myself better than I like! So why not get off this treadmill for once? And then there's that pretty girl with her warm, brown eyes. So I tell my acquaintance, pretending to be indifferent (I don't want to seem too keen in front of that conceited pill-roller) that yes, it would be a pleasure to meet the Kekesfalva family.

Sure enough—for my friend the pharmacist was not just showing off—two days later, puffed up with pride, he brings a printed card to the café with my name entered on it in an elegant calligraphic hand and gives it to me with a flourish. On this invitation card, Herr Lajos von Kekesfalva requests the pleasure of the company of Lieutenant Anton Hofmiller at dinner on Wednesday next week, at eight in the evening. Thank Heaven, I am not of such humble origins that I don't know the way to behave in these circumstances. On Sunday morning, dressed in my best, white gloves, patent leather shoes, meticulously shaved, a drop of eau de cologne on my moustache, I drive out to pay a courtesy call. The manservant—old, discreet, good livery—takes my card and murmurs, apologetically, that the family will be very sorry to have missed seeing Lieutenant Hofmiller, but they are at church. All the better, I tell myself, courtesy calls are always a terrible bore. Anyway, I've done my duty. On Wednesday evening, I tell myself, you'll go off there again, and it's to be hoped the occasion will be pleasant. That's the Kekesfalva affair dealt with until Wednesday. Two days later, however, on Tuesday, I am genuinely pleased to find a visiting card from Herr von Kekesfalva handed in for me, with one corner of it turned down. Good, I think, these people have perfect manners. A general could hardly have been shown more civility and respect than Herr von Kekesfalva has paid me, an insignificant officer, by returning my original courtesy call two days later. And I begin looking forward to Wednesday evening with real pleasure.

But there's a hitch at the very start—I suppose one should be superstitious and pay more attention to small signs and omens. There I am at seven-thirty on Wednesday evening, ready in my best uniform, new gloves, patent leather shoes, creases in my trousers ironed straight as a knife blade, and my batman is adjusting the folds of my overcoat and checking the general effect (I always need him to do that, because I have only a small hand mirror in my poorly lit room), when an orderly knocks vigorously on the door. The duty officer, my friend Captain Count Steinhübel, wants me to go over to join him in the guardroom. Two lancers, probably as drunk as lords, have been quarrelling, and it ended with one hitting the other over the head with the stock of his rifle. Now the idiot who suffered the blow is lying there bleeding and unconscious, with his mouth open. No one knows whether or not his skull is intact. The regimental doctor has gone to Vienna on leave, the Colonel can't be found, so Steinhübel summons me to help him in his hour of need, damn his eyes. While he sees to the injured man, I have to write a report on the incident and send orderlies all over the place to drum up a civilian doctor from the café or wherever there's one to be found. By now it is a quarter to eight, and I can see that there's no chance of my getting away for another fifteen minutes or half-an-hour. Why in Heaven's name does this have to happen today of all days, when I'm invited out to dinner? Feeling more and more impatient, I look at the time. Even if I have to hang around here for only another five minutes, I can't possibly arrive punctually. But the principle that military service takes precedence over any private engagement has been dinned into us. I can't get out of it, so I do the only possible thing in this stupid situation, I send my batman off in a cab (which costs me four crowns) to the Kekesfalva house, to deliver my apologies in case I am late, explaining that an unexpected incident at the barracks … and so on and so forth. Fortunately the commotion at the barracks doesn't last long, because the Colonel arrives in person with a doctor found in haste, and now I can slip inconspicuously away.

Bad luck again, however—there's no cab in the square outside the town hall, I have to wait while someone telephones for a two-horse carriage. So it's inevitable, when I finally arrive in the hall of Herr von Kekesfalva's house, that the big hand of the clock on the wall is pointing vertically down; it is eight-thirty instead of eight, and the coats in the cloakroom are piled on top of each other. The rather anxious look on the servant's face also shows me that I am decidedly late—how unlucky, how really unlucky for such a thing to happen on a first visit.

However, the servant—this time in white gloves, tailcoat and a starched shirt to go with his starchy expression—reassures me; my batman delivered my message half-an-hour ago, he says, and he leads me into the salon, four windows curtained in red silk, the room sparkling with light from crystal chandeliers, fabulously elegant, I've never seen anywhere more splendid. But to my dismay it is deserted, and I clearly hear the cheerful clink of plates in the room next to it—how very annoying, I think at once, they've already started dinner!

41

Well, I pull myself together, and as soon as the servant pushes the double door open ahead of me I step into the dining room, click my heels smartly, and bow. Everyone looks up, twenty, forty eyes, all of them the eyes of strangers, inspect the late-comer standing there by the doorpost feeling very unsure of himself. An elderly gentleman is already rising from his chair, undoubtedly the master of the house, quickly putting down his napkin. He comes towards me and welcomes me, offering me his hand. Herr von Kekesfalva does not look at all as I imagined him, not in the least like a landed nobleman, no flamboyant Magyar moustache, full cheeks, stout and red-faced from good wine. Instead, rather weary eyes with grey bags under them swim behind gold-rimmed glasses, he has something of a stoop, his voice is a whisper slightly impeded by coughing. With his thin, delicately featured face, ending in a sparse, pointed white beard, you would be more likely to take him for a scholar. The old man's marked kindness is immensely reassuring to me in my uncertainty; no, no, he interrupts me at once, it is for him to apologise. He knows just how it is, anything can happen when you're on army service, and it was particularly good of me to let him know; they had begun dinner only because they couldn't be sure whether I would arrive at all. But now I must sit down at once. He will introduce me to all the company individually after dinner. Except that here—and he leads me to the table—this is his daughter. A girl in her teens, delicate, pale, as fragile as her father, looks up from a conversation, and two grey eyes shyly rest on me. But I see her thin, nervous face only in passing, I bow first to her, then right and left to the company in general, who are obviously glad not to have to lay down their knives and forks and have the meal interrupted by formal introductions.

For the first two or three minutes I still feel very uncomfortable. There's no one else from the regiment here, none of my comrades, no one I know, not even any of the more prominent citizens of the little town, all the guests are total strangers to me. Most of them seem to be the owners of nearby estates with their wives and daughters, some are civil servants. But they are all civilians; mine is the only uniform. My God, clumsy and shy as I am, how am I going to make conversation with these unknown people? Fortunately I've been well placed. Next to me sits that brown, high-spirited girl, the pretty niece, who seems to have noticed my admiring glance in the cake shop after all, for she gives me a friendly smile as if I were an old acquaintance. She has eyes like coffee beans, and indeed when she laughs it's with a softly sizzling sound like coffee beans roasting. She has enchanting, translucent little ears under her thick black hair, ears like pink cyclamen flowers growing in dark moss, I think. Her bare arms are soft and smooth; they must feel like peaches.

It does me good to be sitting next to such a pretty girl, and her Hungarian accent when she speaks almost has me falling in love with her. It does me good to eat at such an elegantly laid table in so bright and sparkling a room, with liveried servants behind me and the finest dishes in front of me. My neighbour on the left speaks with a slight Polish accent, and although she is built rather on the generous scale she too seems to me a very attractive sight. Or is that just the effect of the wine, pale gold, then dark red, and now the bubbles of champagne, poured unstintingly from silver carafes by the servants with their white gloves standing behind us? No, the good pharmacist was not exaggerating. You might think yourself at court in the Kekesfalva house. I have never eaten so well, or even dreamt that anyone *could* eat so well, so lavishly, could taste such delicacies.

More and more exquisite dishes are carried in on inexhaustible platters, blue-tinged fish crowned with lettuce and framed by slices of lobster swim in golden sauces, capons ride aloft on broad saddles of piled rice, puddings are flambéed in rum, burning with a blue flame; ice bombs fall apart to reveal their sweet, colourful contents, fruits that must have travelled halfway round the world nestle close to each other in silver baskets. It never, never ends, and finally there is a positive rainbow of liqueurs, green, red, colourless, yellow, and cigars as thick as asparagus, to be enjoyed with delicious coffee!

A wonderful, a magical house—blessings on the good pharmacist!—a bright, happy evening full of merry sound! Do I feel so relaxed, so much at ease, just because the eyes of the other guests, to my right and my left and opposite me, are also shining now, and they have raised their voices? They too seem to have forgotten about etiquette and are talking nineteen to the dozen! Anyway, my own usual shyness is gone. I chatter on without the slightest inhibition, I pay court to both the ladies sitting next to me, I drink, laugh, look around in cheerful high spirits, and if it isn't always by chance that my hand now and then touches the lovely bare arm of Ilona (such is the name of the delectable niece), then she doesn't seem to take my gentle approach and then retreat in the wrong spirit, she is relaxed and elated like all of us at this lavish banquet.

I begin to feel—while wondering if it may not be the effect of the unusually good wine; Tokay and champagne in such quick succession?—I begin to feel elated, buoyant, even boisterous. I need only one thing to crown my happiness in the spell cast over my enraptured mind, and what I have unconsciously been wanting is revealed to me next moment, when I suddenly hear soft music, performed by a quartet of instrumentalists,

44

beginning to play in a third room beyond the salon. The servant has quietly opened the double doors again. It is exactly the
kind of music I would have wished for, dance music, rhythmical
and gentle at the same time, a waltz with the melody played
by two violins, the low notes of a cello adding a darker tone,
and a piano picking out the tune in sharp staccato. Music,
yes, music, that was all I still needed! Music now, and perhaps dancing, a waltz! I want to move with it, feel that I am
flying, sense my lightness of heart even more blissfully! This
Villa Kekesfalva must indeed be a magical place where you
have only to dream of something and your wish is granted.
So now we stand up, moving our dining chairs aside, and two
by two—I offer Ilona my arm, and once again feel her cool,
soft, beautiful skin—we go into the salon, where the tables
have been cleared away as if by brownie magic, and chairs
are placed around the wall. The wooden floor is smooth and
shiny, a mirror-like brown surface, waltzing is the apotheosis
of skating, and the lively music played by the invisible instru-
mentalist next door animates us.

I turn to Ilona. She laughs, understanding me. Her eyes have
already said "Yes", and now we are whirling round the room,
two couples, three couples, five couples moving over the whole
dance floor, while the older and less daring guests watch or talk
to each other. I like dancing, I may even say I dance well. Closely
entwined, we skim the floor. I think I have never danced better
in my life. I ask my other neighbour at dinner for the pleasure
of the next waltz. She too dances very well, and leaning down
to her I smell the perfume of her hair and feel slightly dizzy.
Oh, her dancing is wonderful, it is all wonderful, I haven't felt
so happy for years. I hardly know what I am doing, I would
like to embrace everyone, say something heartfelt, grateful to

them all, I feel so light, so elated, so blissfully young. I whirl from partner to partner, I talk and laugh and dance, and never notice the time, carried away by the torrent of my pleasure.

Then I suddenly look up and happen to see the time. It is ten-thirty—and I realise, to my alarm, that I have been dancing and talking and amusing myself for almost an hour but, great oaf that I am, I haven't yet asked my host's daughter to dance. I have only danced with my two neighbours at dinner and two or three other ladies, the ones I liked best, entirely neglecting the daughter of the house! What uncivil behaviour, what a slight to her! I must put that right at once!

I am shocked, however, to realise that I cannot remember exactly what the girl looks like. I bowed to her only briefly when she was already seated at table, all I recollect is the impression of fragile delicacy that she made on me, and then the quick, curious glance of her grey eyes. But where is she? She is the daughter of the house, surely she can't have left the party? I look uneasily at all the girls and women sitting by the wall; I see no one like her. Finally I step into the third room where, hidden behind a Japanese screen, the quartet is playing, and breathe a sigh of relief. For there she is—yes, I am sure of it—delicate, slender, sitting in her pale-blue dress between two old ladies in the corner of this boudoir, at a malachite-green table with a shallow bowl of flowers on it. Her head is slightly bowed, as if she were entirely absorbed in the music, and the deep crimson of the roses in the bowl makes me notice the translucent pallor of her forehead under her heavy light-red hair. But I have no time for idle gazing. Thank God, I think fervently, now I've tracked her down, and I can make up for being so remiss.

I go over to the table—the music is playing merrily away— and bow to indicate that I am asking her to dance. She looks at me in startled surprise, her lips still half open, interrupted in the middle of what she was saying. But she makes no move to rise and go with me. Didn't she understand? I bow again, and my spurs clink softly. "May I have the pleasure of this dance, dear young lady?"

Something terrible happens next. She had been leaning slightly forward, but now she flinches abruptly back as if avoiding a blow. At the same time the blood rushes into her pale cheeks, the lips that were half open just now are pressed hard together, and only her eyes keep staring at me with an expression of horror such as I have never seen in my life before. Next moment a paroxysm passes right through her convulsed body. She braces herself on the table with both hands, making the bowl of roses clink and jangle, and at the same time something hard, made of wood or metal, falls from her chair to the ground. Both her hands are still clutching the table, which sways, her childlike body is shaken again and again, but all the same she does not run away, she only clings even more desperately to the heavy tabletop. And again and again that shaking, those tremors run from her cramped fists all the way up to her hairline. Suddenly she bursts into sobs, a wild, elemental sound like a stifled scream.

But the two old ladies are already with her, to right and left, one on each side, holding her, caressing her, speaking soothing, reassuring words to the trembling girl. Her convulsed hands relax, drop gently from the table, and she falls back into her chair. However, the weeping goes on, even worse than before, like a rush of blood, like a surge of hot vomit rising in her throat it keeps bursting forth. If the music drowning the sound of it out from behind the screen were to stop for a moment, even the dancers in the next room would hear her sobbing.

I stand there, horrified, bewildered. What exactly has happened? Baffled, I stare at the two old ladies as they try to calm the sobbing girl. Now, as she begins to feel ashamed of her outburst, she has laid her head on the table. But she still breaks into fresh tears again and again, wave after wave of them shaking her slender body up to her shoulders, and each of these abrupt fits of weeping makes the glass and china clink. As for me, I stand there at a loss, my thoughts frozen like ice, with my collar constricting my throat like a burning cord.

"I'm sorry," I finally stammer in an undertone, and while both ladies are busy with the sobbing girl—neither of them spares me a glance—I retreat, feeling dizzy, into the hall beyond. No one here seems to have noticed anything yet. Couples are circling with verve on the dance floor, and I have to hold on to the doorpost, because the room is going round and round before my eyes. What happened? Have I done something wrong? My God, did I drink too much and too fast at dinner, did I drink enough to stupefy me and make me commit some silly blunder?

The music stops, the couples move apart. The district administrator who is Ilona's partner relinquishes her hand with a bow, and I immediately hurry over to her and make the surprised girl go over to the window with me. "Please help me! For Heaven's sake, help me, explain!"

Obviously Ilona was expecting me to whisper something amusing to her when I took her aside, for suddenly her glance is unfriendly. I must have looked either pitiable or alarming in my agitation. My pulse beats fast as I tell her everything. And strange to say, she cries out with the same sheer horror in her eyes as the girl in the other room.

"Are you out of your mind? … Don't you know? … Didn't you notice? … "

"No," I stammer, shattered by these fresh and equally incomprehensible signs of horror. "Didn't I notice *what*? And I don't know anything—this is the first time I've been in this house."

"But didn't you see that Edith is … is lame? Didn't you notice her poor crippled legs? She can't drag herself two paces without crutches, and then you … you callous … " (here she quickly suppresses some angry term for me). "Then you ask the poor girl to dance … oh, how dreadful! I must go straight to her."

"No"—and in my desperation I clutch Ilona's arm—"just a moment, one moment … you must give her my apologies for everything. I couldn't guess … I'd only seen her sitting at the dinner table, just for a second … please explain that … "

But Ilona, with anger in her eyes, has already freed her arm and is on her way to the other room. I stand in the doorway of the salon, my throat tight, the taste of sickness in my mouth. All around me there is dancing, couples circling on the floor, chattering voices as the guests talk and laugh in a carefree way that is suddenly more than I can bear. Another five minutes, I think, and everyone will know about my folly. Five more minutes, and then scornful, disapproving, ironic glances will be cast at me from all sides, and tomorrow the story of my rough, clumsy behaviour, passed on by a hundred mouths, will be the talk of the whole town, delivered at back doors with the milk, retold in the servants' quarters, reaching the cafés and offices. Tomorrow my regiment will know about it.

At that moment, as if through a mist, I see the girl's father. He is crossing the salon with a rather anxious expression—does he know already? Is he on his way towards me? No—oh, if I can only avoid him now! I am suddenly in panic terror of him,

49

of everyone. And without really knowing what I am doing, I stumble to the door leading into the front hall, and so out of this infernal house.

"Are you leaving us already, sir?" asks the surprised servant, with a look of respectful incredulity.

"Yes," I reply, and take fright to hear the word come out of my mouth. Do I really want to leave? Next moment, as he takes my coat off the hook where it is hanging, I realise that by running away now I am committing another stupid and perhaps even more unforgivable offence. However, it is too late to change my mind. I can't suddenly hand my coat back to the servant as he opens the front door for me with a little bow, I can't go back into the salon. And so there I am all of a sudden, standing outside that strange, that accursed house, with the cold wind in my face, hot shame in my heart, and breathing as convulsively as if I were being choked.

That was the unfortunate act of folly with which the whole story began. Today, with my blood less agitated and after an interval of many years, when I conjure up the memory of the stupid incident that set everything else in motion I cannot help seeing that I stumbled into this misunderstanding entirely innocently. Even the cleverest and most experienced of men could have committed the faux pas of asking a lame girl to dance. But at the time, under the immediate impression of those first horrified reactions, I seemed to myself not just a hopeless fool but a villain, a criminal. I felt as if I had whipped an innocent child. With a little presence of mind, after all, the entire misunderstanding could have been cleared up. But I realised, as soon as the first gust of cold air blew in my face outside the house, that by simply running away like a thief in the night, without even trying to apologise, I had made it impossible to retrieve the situation.

My state of mind as I stood there outside the house is beyond description. I heard no music on the other side of the lighted windows; perhaps the musicians had stopped for a rest. In my overwrought sense of guilt, however, I immediately and feverishly imagined that the dancing had stopped because of me, and everyone was now crowding into the little boudoir next to the salon to comfort the sobbing girl—all the guests, men, women and girls, were unanimously waxing indignant over the conduct of the dastardly man who had asked a crippled girl to dance, only to run away like a coward after committing his offence. And tomorrow—I broke out in a cold sweat; I could feel it under my cap—tomorrow the entire town would know about my disgrace, would be talking about it, passing on the gossip. I saw them all in my mind's eye, my comrades, Ferencz, Mislyvetz, above all Jozsi the regimental joker, I imagined them coming up to me, smacking their lips with relish. "Well, Toni, what a way to behave! Let you off the leash, and you'll put the whole regiment to shame!" The mockery and talk would go on for months in the officers' mess; when old comrades sit at table together they go back over every idiotic act ever committed by one of us again and again, for ten, twenty years, every folly is immortalised, every joke set in stone. Even today, sixteen years after the event, they still tell the sad story of Captain Volinski, who came back from Vienna to boast of meeting Countess T in the Ringstrasse and visiting her in her apartment that very first night. Two days later the newspaper printed the scandalous story of her maid's dismissal for her confidence tricks, making herself out to be the Countess for the purpose of her own amorous adventures—and what was more, the would-be Casanova had to spend three weeks being treated by the regimental doctor. A man who has once looked ridiculous in the eyes of his comrades remains ridiculous for ever; they never forget and never forgive. The more I pictured it, the more I thought about it, the more absurd ideas came into my fevered mind. At that moment it seemed to me a hundred times easier to exert a little quick pressure on the trigger of my revolver than to suffer the infernal torments of the next few days, that helpless waiting to find out whether my comrades had yet heard of my folly, whether the whispering and grinning had already begun behind my back. I knew myself only too well; I knew I would never have the strength to withstand the mockery and scorn and tittle-tattle once it began.

I don't remember how I got home that evening. All I recollect is that the first thing I did was to fling open the door of the cupboard where I kept a bottle of slivovitz for visitors and tip two or three half-full tumblers of it down my throat, to dispel the horrible sensation of my rising nausea. Then I threw myself on the bed, fully dressed as I was, and tried to think. But delusions in the dark are like hothouse flowers; they grow faster and with more tropical luxuriance. Confused and fantastic, they shoot up in the warm ground into bright creepers that choke your breath, forming with the speed of dreams and chasing the most absurd fears through the overheated brain. Shamed for life, was all I could think, a social outcast, mocked by my comrades, the talk of the whole town! I would never leave my room again, I could never again venture out into the street for fear of meeting one of those who knew about my crime (for that night, under extreme nervous strain, I felt that my sheer stupidity was a crime, and I myself would be the butt of mockery, a subject of universal derision). When I finally fell asleep, it can have been only a shallow, restless sleep in which my anxiety went on working feverishly.

For as soon as I open my eyes I see the girl's angry, childish face there before them again. I see her quivering lips, her hands convulsively clutching the table, I hear the sound of falling wood and now, in retrospect, realise it must have been her crutches, and I am overwhelmed by a stupid fear that the door might suddenly open, and her father—black coat trimmed with white braid, gold-rimmed glasses, neat little goatee beard—will march into my room. In my alarm I jump up. And as I stare at my own face, damp with the sweat of night fears and anxiety, I feel like punching the nose of the fool reflected in the pale mirror.

But luckily day has dawned, footsteps clatter up and down the corridor, carts pass along the cobblestones outside. And once the windowpanes let in light you think more clearly than slumped in the ominous darkness that conjures up phantoms. Perhaps, I say to myself, it's not all so terrible after all. Perhaps no one noticed. *She* did, of course—she will never forget, never forgive, that poor pale, sick, lame girl! And then a good idea abruptly flashes through my mind. I hastily comb my untidy hair, fling on my uniform and run past my surprised batman Kusma, who calls frantically after me, in his poor Ruthenian German, "Lieutenant, sir—Lieutenant, coffee ready is."

I run down the barracks stairs and race past the lancers lounging half-dressed around the yard. I've gone by them so fast that they don't even have time to stand to attention. Next moment I'm out of the barracks gate, running (in so far as it is proper for a lieutenant to run) straight to the florists' shop on the town-hall square. In my haste I had entirely forgotten that the shops aren't open at five-thirty in the morning, but fortunately Frau Gurtner sells not just flowers, real and artificial, but also vegetables. A cart delivering carrots is standing half-unloaded at the shop door, and as I knock vigorously on the window I can already hear her making her way downstairs. Once in the house, I make up a story—yesterday, I say, I entirely forgot that today some dear friends are celebrating an anniversary. We leave barracks in half-an-hour's time, and I would like to have flowers sent at once. So flowers, please, the finest that she has! At once the stout florist, still in her bed jacket and slippers with holes in them, shuffles along to open her shop and show me her crown jewels, a large bunch of long-stemmed roses. How many would I like? All of them, I say, all of them! Just as they are, simply tied together, or would I rather have them in a pretty basket? Yes, yes, a basket. All that's left of my month's pay will go on this lavish order, and at the end of the month I shall have to deny myself supper and the café for a few days, or else borrow some money, but at the moment I don't mind that, I am even glad that I shall have to pay a high price for my folly. All this time I still feel a perverse desire to punish myself severely for being a fool twice over, I want to pay dearly for my own double blunders.

But now surely all would be well again? The finest of roses, well arranged in a basket, sure to be sent off at once! However, Frau Gurtner runs down the street after me in desperate pursuit. Where are they to go, then? The gentleman hasn't told her who the flowers are for. Oh no, idiot that I am three times over now, in my agitation I forgot! To the Villa Kekesfalva, I say, and just in time, thanks to Ilona's dreadful outburst, I remember my poor victim's first name; they are for Fräulein Edith von Kekesfalva.

"Of course, of course, the Kekesfalvas," says Frau Gurtner proudly. "Our best customers!"

And another question, just as I am turning to hurry off again—didn't I want to write a word to go with them? Write a word? Ah, yes! The name of the sender! The giver of the gift! How else is she to know where the flowers come from?

So I go back into the shop again, take out a visiting card and write on it, "A plea for forgiveness." No—impossible! That would be a fourth mistake—why remind anyone of my folly? But what else can I put? "With genuine regret"—no, that won't do either. She might think I was sorry for her. Better not to write anything at all.

"Just put the card in with them, Frau Gurtner, only my card."

Now I feel better. I hurry back to barracks, swallow some coffee, and get through my hour's drill as best I can, probably more nervous and distracted than usual. But in the army it's not particularly unusual for a lieutenant to come on duty with a hangover in the morning. Think how many come back from a night on the tiles in Vienna so exhausted that they can hardly prop their eyes open, and fall asleep on a trotting horse. In fact it suits me very well to be occupied in giving commands, inspecting the men, and then riding out. To a certain extent action takes my mind off my troubles, although my uncomfortable memories are still churning away inside my head, and there's a lump in my throat like a sponge soaked in bitter gall.

But at midday, just as I am going over to the officers' mess, my batman runs after me with an urgent cry of, "*Panje* Lieutenant!" He is holding a letter, an oblong envelope, English notepaper, blue and delicately perfumed with a finely traced coat of arms on the back. The address is in thin, steeply angular handwriting, a lady's hand. I swiftly tear the envelope open and read:

Thank you so much, Lieutenant Hofmiller, for the beautiful flowers, which I really do not deserve. They have given me great pleasure, and still do. Please come to tea with us any afternoon you like. There is no need to give advance notice. I am—unfortunately!—always at home.

Edith v K

Delicate handwriting. I involuntarily remember the slender, childish fingers braced against the table, the pale face suddenly glowing crimson, as if claret had been poured into a glass. I read the few lines again once, twice, three times, and breathe a sigh of relief. How discreetly she glosses over my folly! How skilfully and at the same time tactfully she refers to her affliction: "I am—unfortunately!—always at home." I could not have been more elegantly forgiven. There is no tone of offence at all in her note. A weight falls from my heart. I feel like a defendant in court who expects to be given a life sentence, but the judge rises to his feet, puts on his cap, and announces, "Not guilty." Of course I must soon go out there to thank her. This is Thursday—so I will pay a call on Sunday. Or no, Saturday would be better!

But I do not stick to my decision. I am too impatient. Under pressure from my own uneasiness, I want to know that I have atoned for my offence, I want to be rid of the discomfort of uncertainty as soon as possible. I am still under the nervous strain of fearing that someone in the officers' mess, the café or some other place will start talking about my faux pas. "Now, do tell us about that evening in the Kekesfalvas' house!" To which I can then reply coolly and with supercilious ease, "Delightful people! I was there again yesterday, taking tea."

Then, I think, everyone will see that I've had no trouble in making amends. Oh, to draw a line under the whole wretched affair, to get it over and done with! And in my nervous state I suddenly decide the very next day, Friday, while I am strolling on the promenade with my best friends Ferencz and Joszi, to pay my call at once. I abruptly take my leave of my slightly startled comrades.

It really is not a particularly long way out there, a walk of half-an-hour at the most if you go at a good pace. Five tedious minutes through the town first, then along the rather dusty country road that also leads to our parade ground; when our horses go that way they know every stone and every bend, so that you can loosen the reins. About halfway along this road, where you come to a little chapel on a bridge, a narrow avenue shaded by old chestnut trees branches off to the left. This avenue is more or less private, with few people going along it either on foot or in a carriage, and a small stream winding its way at a comfortable pace runs beside it.

But strange to say, the closer I come to the little castle, when the white wall around it with the ornamental iron gate are in sight, the more my courage fails me. Just as when you are approaching the dentist's door you look for an excuse to turn back before ringing the bell, I now want to make my escape quickly. Did it really have to be today? Shouldn't I consider that Fräulein von Kekesfalva's letter had settled the whole embarrassing business for good? I instinctively slow down; there is still time for me to turn back. Making a detour is always a welcome notion when you shrink from arriving at your destination, so I leave the avenue and turn off into meadows, crossing the little stream on a rickety plank bridge. First I will make a circuit of the villa outside its wall.

The house behind the high stone wall proves to be an extensive, single-storey late baroque building, painted Schönbrunn yellow in the old Austrian style, with green shutters at the windows. Separated from it by a yard, a few smaller buildings stand close together, obviously to accommodate the servants, the estate's management staff and the stables. They extend a little way into the large park, of which I saw nothing on that first visit by night. Only now do I notice, looking through the oval bull's-eye openings in the mighty wall, that the Kekesfalva house is not a modern villa, as the furnishing of the interior made me think at first, but a country house, a traditional gentleman's residence, the kind of place I had seen now and then in Bohemia when I was riding past on manoeuvres. The most striking feature is its remarkable rectangular tower, slightly reminiscent in shape of an Italian campanile, rising as if it did not really belong here, perhaps all that remains of an old castle that may have stood here long ago. Now, in retrospect, I do remember seeing this strange watchtower quite often from the parade ground, although in the belief that it was the tower of some village church. Only now do I notice that it does not have the usual ornamental little topknot of churches in these parts, and the curious rectangle has a flat roof that may be used as a sun terrace or perhaps an observatory. However, the more aware I become of the old feudal nature of this landed estate, passed on from father to son, the less easy in my mind I feel. To think that I had to make such an unfortunate first appearance here of all places, where they must set great store by etiquette!

But finally, after concluding my circuit of the house and finding myself approaching the wrought iron gate again from the other side, I pull myself together. I walk up the gravel path between trees pruned to stand ramrod straight, lift the heavy, chased bronze knocker that, in the old way, serves instead of a doorbell here, and bring it down. At once the manservant appears—strange to say, he does not even seem surprised by my unannounced visit. Without asking questions, or taking the visiting card I have ready to offer him, he asks me, with a civil bow, to wait in the salon; the ladies, he says, are still in their boudoir but will be with me directly, so it seems there is no doubt that they will receive me. He leads me on like an expected visitor, and feeling uncomfortable again I recognise the salon wallpapered in red where couples danced, and a bitter taste in my throat reminds me that the boudoir with the fateful corner must be next door.

At first, however, cream-coloured double doors delicately adorned with gilt decoration hide the view of the scene of my folly, which is still clearly present to me, but after a few minutes I hear chairs being moved behind that door, whispering voices, some kind of restrained coming and going that indicates the presence of several people. I try to employ the wait in studying the salon: opulent Louis XVI furniture, old tapestries to right and left, and between the glass doors leading straight out into the garden old pictures of the Canal Grande and the Piazza San Marco. Even though I knew little of such things, they look to me valuable. To be sure, I can distinguish nothing of these artistic treasures very clearly, for I am listening intently at the same time to the noises in the room next door. There is a quiet clink of plates in there, a door creaks, now I also think I hear the irregular, dry tapping of crutches on the floor.

At last a still-invisible hand pushes the two halves of the double door apart from the inside. Ilona comes towards me. "How nice of you to come, Lieutenant Hofmiller." And she is already leading me into the room I know only too well. The lame girl is sitting in the same corner of the boudoir, on the same chaise longue behind the same malachite-green table (why are they staging a scene that was so painfully embarrassing for me again?), with a full, heavy white fur rug draped over her lap—obviously I am not to be reminded of "that occasion". With a friendly manner no doubt rehearsed in advance, Edith greets me with a smile from her invalid's position in the corner. But this first meeting is still an alarming encounter, and from her self-conscious way of offering me her hand across the table, clearly with a little effort, I realise at once that she thinks so too. Neither of us succeeds in bringing out the first words to draw us together.

Fortunately Ilona casts another question into the difficult silence. "What can we offer you, Lieutenant Hofmiller, tea or coffee?"

"Oh, just as you like," I reply.

"No, no—whatever *you* would rather have, Lieutenant Hofmiller! Please don't stand on ceremony, it makes no difference to us."

"Well, coffee then, if I may," I decide, glad to hear that my voice is reasonably steady.

Clever work on the part of the dark-haired girl to bridge the first tense moments with such a down-to-earth question. But how inconsiderate of her to leave the room next moment to go and give the servant her orders! It means that I am left alone with my victim, which is awkward. Now would be the time to say a few words, to make some kind of conversation, any kind. But I feel as if I have something stuck in my throat, and my eyes must betray my embarrassment, because I dare not look towards the sofa in case she thinks I am staring at the fur covering her paralysed legs. Luckily she proves calmer and more composed than I am, and begins talking with a certain nervous vivacity that I now notice in her for the first time.

"Oh, do sit down, Lieutenant Hofmiller! Move that armchair up. And why not take off your sword—we're at peace, aren't we?—and put it down there on the table, or on the windowsill, wherever you like."

I move an armchair over, rather formally. I still can't meet her eyes without awkwardness. But she energetically helps the conversation to get going.

"And I must thank you again for the lovely flowers … they are really wonderful. Just see how beautiful they look in that vase. And then … then … I must also apologise for my stupid loss of self-control. I behaved so badly … I couldn't sleep all night, I was so ashamed of myself. You meant it so kindly … and how could you have any idea? What's more"—and here she suddenly utters an abrupt, nervous laugh—"what's more, you guessed my most private thoughts … I was sitting, on purpose, where I couldn't see the guests dancing, and just as you came up to me I had been wishing so much that I could join in … I adore dancing. I can watch others dancing for hours—watch so closely that I can sense every movement far within me—really, every movement. And then it's not someone else dancing, I'm dancing myself, turning and bending, yielding, letting myself be carried away, swaying to the rhythm of the dance. Perhaps you can't even guess how foolish I can be. But I did dance well as a child, I loved dancing—and now, whenever I dream, it's dancing I dream of. Silly as it sounds, I dance in my dreams, and perhaps it's a good thing for Papa that … that *this* happened to me, or I would have run away from home to be a dancer. I'm passionate about dance, I think it must be wonderful to use your body, your movements, your whole self to fascinate hundreds and hundreds of people every evening, seizing their imagination, uplifting them … and by the way, to show you how

61

stupid I am, I collect pictures of the great ballerinas. I have them all: Saharet, Pavlova, Karsavina. I have photographs of them posing in all their roles. Wait, I'll show you ... over there, they're in that box over by the hearth—that Chinese lacquered box." Her voice was suddenly sharp with impatience. "No, no, no, there on the left beside the books ... oh, how clumsy you are! Yes, that's it." I had finally found the box and was bringing it over to her. "Look, that one, the one on top, it's my favourite picture, Pavlova as the dying swan ... oh, if I could only travel and go to see her perform. I think it would be the happiest day of my life."

The door behind us through which Ilona disappeared begins to move slightly on its hinges. Hastily, as if caught in a guilty act, Edith snaps the box shut with a sharp, dry sound. When she tells me, "Not a word to the others about what I've been saying!" it sounds like an order.

It is the white-haired manservant with the neatly trimmed side whiskers, reminiscent of Emperor Franz Josef's, who carefully opens the door. Behind him comes Ilona, pushing in a lavishly laden tea trolley on rubber wheels. She pours tea and coffee, sits down with us, and I immediately feel safer. The enormous angora cat who has slipped soundlessly into the room with the tea trolley, and begins rubbing around my legs with friendly familiarity, provides a welcome subject for comment. I admire the cat, an exchange of questions and answers begins—how long have I been here, how do I like the garrison, do I know Lieutenant So-and-So, do I often go to Vienna? Soon we have fallen easily into light conversation. After a while I even venture to cast a few sidelong glances at the two girls, so very different from each other. Ilona is already a grown woman, sensuously warm, full-breasted, opulent, healthy; beside her Edith, half child and half young girl, maybe seventeen years old, maybe eighteen, seems somehow immature. A strange contrast—a man would want to dance with Ilona and kiss her, but to spoil Edith as an invalid, caress her with care, protect and above all soothe her, for she seems very restless. Her face is never for a moment still; now she looks right, now left, sometimes her attitude is tense, then she leans back again exhausted, and she speaks as nervously as she moves, always disjointedly, always staccato, never stopping to pause. Perhaps, I think, this restlessness and lack of self-control is a way of compensating for the forced immobility of her legs, or perhaps a constant slight fever speeds up her gestures and her speech. But I do not have much time to observe her, for she is good at drawing attention to herself with her rapid questions and the light volatility of her remarks. To my surprise, I become involved in a stimulating and interesting conversation.

It lasts for an hour, perhaps as long as an hour and a half. Then the shadow of a figure coming from the salon suddenly falls on me. Someone is approaching cautiously, as if afraid of disturbing us. It is Kekesfalva.

"No, no, don't get up," he says, pressing me back into my chair as I am about to rise respectfully to my feet, and then he leans down to his child and drops a quick kiss on her forehead. Once again he is wearing his black coat with its white braid trimming and an old-fashioned cravat; indeed, I never saw him wearing anything else. He looks like a doctor, his eyes discreetly watching behind gold-rimmed glasses. And like a doctor at a patient's sickbed, he sits down cautiously beside the lame girl. Curiously enough, as soon as he comes into the room it seems more melancholy. The anxious way he sometimes looks sidelong at his child, affectionately scrutinising her, inhibits our earlier easy discussion, casting a shadow over it. Kekesfalva himself soon senses our self-consciousness, and tries to broach a new subject of conversation. He asks about the regiment, the Captain, enquires after the former colonel, who is now a divisional commander in the War Ministry. He seems to have been surprisingly well informed about our affairs for years, and I don't know why, but I feel that there is a certain purpose behind the way he lays special emphasis on his close acquaintance with every high-ranking officer in the regiment.

Ten more minutes, I am thinking, then I can unobtrusively take my leave, when there is another quiet knock at the door. The manservant comes in, as quietly as if he were barefoot, and whispers something in Edith's ear. She flares up angrily.

"Tell him to wait. Or no, tell him to leave me in peace today. I want him to go away, I don't need him."

Her vigorous protests embarrass us all, and I stand up with a painful sense of having outstayed my welcome. But she snaps at me as angrily as at the servant.

"No, don't go away! This really doesn't matter."

There is a touch of incivility in her imperious tone, and her father seems to be aware of the awkwardness, for he reproves her—"Now now, Edith … "—with a helpless expression of distress on his face.

At this she herself realises, perhaps because of his dismay, perhaps because I am standing there so uneasily, that she has lost her temper, for she suddenly turns to me.

"Forgive me. Josef really could have waited instead of bursting in like that. It's just that my daily tormentor is here, the masseur who does stretching exercises with me. Sheer nonsense, one, two, one, two, up, down, down, up. It's supposed to make me

64

better some day—our good doctor's latest idea, and a totally unnecessary nuisance. Pointless, like everything else."

She looks challengingly at her father, as if blaming him. The old man, embarrassed (he is ashamed of her in front of me), leans over to her.

"But child ... do you really think that Dr Condor? ... "

However, he stops, because the corners of her mouth have begun to twitch, and her delicate nostrils are quivering. Her lips had looked just the same at our fateful first encounter, and I fear another outburst. However, she suddenly blushes and murmurs with more docility, "It's all right, there's no point in it, but I'll go. Forgive me, Lieutenant Hofmiller. I hope you will come to see us again soon."

I bow, and am about to take my leave, but she has already had second thoughts.

"Or no, do stay and keep Papa company while I go off, quick march!" She snaps those last two words in sharp, staccato tones, like a threat. Then she picks up the little bronze bell standing on the table and rings it—only later do I notice similar bells all over the house, placed on tables within easy reach for her, so that she can always summon someone without having to wait. The bell rings, shrill and sharp. The manservant, who has discreetly made himself scarce during her outburst, reappears at once.

"Help me," she orders him, throwing off the fur rug. Ilona bends down to whisper something to her, but Edith, visibly annoyed, snaps an angry "No!" at her friend. "I only want Josef to support me," she adds. "I can manage on my own."

What follows is a painful sight. The servant bends over her and, with an obviously practised grip, lifts her slight body with his two hands under her armpits. As she stands upright, both her own hands holding the back of her chair, she sizes us all up,

65

one by one, with a challenging look. Then she reaches for the crutches that were hidden under the rug, presses her lips firmly together, braces herself on the crutches and—click-clack, click-clack—trudges, sways, forces herself forward, stooping like a witch, while the servant is on the alert behind her with his arms outspread, ready to catch her at once if she slips or if her feet give way under her. Click-clack click-clack, a step and then another, and as she moves there is the faint clinking, grinding sound of metal and tautly stretched leather. I dare not look at her poor legs, but she must be wearing devices of some kind on her ankle joints to support her. My heart contracts as if an icy hand had closed around it at the sight of her setting out on this forced march, for I immediately understand her obvious purpose—she won't let anyone help her to walk or take her out of the room in a wheelchair; she wants to demonstrate her crippled condition to all of us, and me in particular. Out of some mysterious, desperate desire for revenge, she wants to torment us with her own torment, complaining of her fate not to God but to us, the hale and hearty. In itself, this dreadful challenge makes me feel—and feel a thousand times more strongly than her earlier outburst when I asked her to dance—how much she must suffer from her helplessness. At last, after what seems an eternity, she has gone the few steps to the door, swaying back and forth, forcibly shifting the full weight of her slender, shaking body from one crutch to the other as she flings herself forward between them. I cannot bring myself to look straight at her even once. The mere hard, sharp click of her crutches as she pushes herself along, the grinding, dragging sound of the braces supporting her joints, accompanied by the low gasping she makes in her physical effort upsets and agitates me so much that I feel my heart thudding against the fabric of my uniform. She has already left the room, but I still listen, holding my breath, as the dreadful sound grows softer, finally dying away on the other side of the closed door.

Not until a welcome silence has descended do I dare to look up again. The old man, as I notice only now, has risen quietly to his feet and is staring intently out of the window—rather too intently. As the light is in front of him, I can make out only his shadowy outline, but the shoulders of his bowed figure are shaking. He himself, her father, who sees his child torment herself like that daily, he too is shattered by the sight.

All is perfectly still in the room between the two of us. After a few minutes his dark figure finally turns and comes unsteadily over to me, as if he were walking over a slippery surface.

"Please don't blame the child for being a little brusque, Lieutenant Hofmiller. You don't know how she has been tormented all these years … always some new treatment, and progress is so terribly slow that I can understand her impatience. But what are we to do? We must try everything, we have to."

The old man is standing beside the abandoned tea trolley. He does not look at me as he speaks. Standing very still, he keeps his eyes, almost hidden by their grey lids, bent on the trolley. As if in a dream he puts his fingers into the sugar bowl and takes out a cube, which he turns this way and that, staring at it pointlessly and then putting it down again, with something of the demeanour of a drunk. He still cannot look up from the tea trolley, as if something on it held him spellbound. Abstractedly, he touches a spoon, picks it up, and then speaks again, apparently to the spoon.

"If you knew what the child used to be like! Upstairs and downstairs all day long, running up and down steps and through all the rooms, oh, she terrified us. At the age of eleven she was riding her pony full tilt in the meadows, no one could keep up with her. We often feared for her, my late wife and I, she was so reckless, so high-spirited and agile, everything came so easily to her. You felt she had only to spread out her arms to be able to fly … and the accident had to happen to her, of all people … "

The parting in his sparse white hair is bent lower and lower over the table. His nervous hand is still fiddling with all the items strewn around the tea trolley, not a spoon now but a pair of sugar tongs, and he traces curious round runes on the trolley with the little tongs. I know it is out of shame and embarrassment; he is afraid to look at me.

"And yet it's still so easy to make her happy. She can rejoice like a child at the least little thing. She will laugh at the silliest joke and immerse herself enthusiastically in a book—I wish you could have seen how delighted she was when your flowers arrived, and she felt free of her fear that she had offended you. You have no idea how intensely she feels everything, far more strongly than the rest of us. I know very well that she is more distressed than anyone else when she knows she has lost control of herself. But how can anyone … how *could* anyone exercise such self-control? How can a child always be patient when progress is so slow, hold her tongue when God has inflicted such a blow on her, and she has done nothing to deserve it … she never hurt a soul!"

He was still staring at the imaginary figures traced with the sugar tongs in the empty air by his trembling hand. Suddenly he put the tongs down with a little clink, as if alarmed. It was as if he were waking up, and only now realised that he was speaking not to himself alone but to a total stranger. In a very different voice, wakeful if dejected, he awkwardly began to apologise.

"Forgive me, Lieutenant Hofmiller, what must you think of my unburdening myself to you, telling you our troubles? It was only that … it just came over me, I wanted to explain … I wouldn't like you to think too badly of her, I wouldn't want you to—"

I don't know how I found the courage to interrupt the awkwardly stammering voice and go towards him. But suddenly I took the old man's hand—the hand of a perfect stranger—in both of mine. I said nothing. I just held his cold, bony hand as it instinctively flinched, and pressed it firmly. He stared at me in surprise, the lenses of his glasses glinting, and behind them an uncertain gaze gently and shyly sought mine. I was afraid he would say something now, but he did not. His round black pupils grew wider and wider, that was all, as if they were brimming over. I myself felt the rise of an emotion that I had never known before, and to escape it I quickly bowed and left.

Out in the front hall, as the manservant was helping me into my coat, I suddenly felt a draught of air behind me. Without even turning to look, I knew that the old man had followed me and was standing in the doorway, feeling a need to thank me. But I did not want to be put to shame. I acted as if I didn't notice him there behind me. Quickly, my pulse beating fast, I left that house of tragedy.

Next morning—with a pale mist still hanging over the houses, and the shutters over the windows all closed so that good citizens can sleep soundly—our squadron rides out to the parade ground as it does every day. First we cross the cobblestones, uncomfortable going for the horses; at a brisk walking pace, my lancers, still drowsy from sleep, stiff and morose, sway in their saddles. Soon we have gone down the four or five streets to the broad main road, where we change pace to a light trot, and then we turn off right to the open meadows. I give my squadron the command "Gallop!" and away go the horses, snorting in unison. They know the soft, green, broad fields, clever animals; there is no need for us to urge them on now, we can hold the reins loosely, because as soon as they feel the pressure of their riders' thighs the horses will be off as fast as they can go. They too feel the pleasure of excitement and physical relaxation.

I am in the lead. I am passionately fond of riding. I feel a rush of blood rising from my waist as it carries the warmth of life circulating through my relaxed body, while cold air whistles around my face. Wonderful morning air; you can still taste last night's dew in it, the breath of the turned soil, the scent of fields in flower, and at the same time you are surrounded by the warm, sensuous moisture from the horses' nostrils as they breathe out. I always love this first morning gallop that does the lethargic, still sleepy body such good, shaking it up, snatching away drowsiness like a dull mist. Instinctively, my parted lips drink in the air rushing by as a sense of being weightless carries me forward and my chest expands. "Gallop! Gallop!" I feel that my eyes are brighter, my senses livelier, and behind me the men's swords clink in a regular rhythm, the horses snort, there's a soft squeal and squeak from the saddles, the beat of hoofs falling in time. This swift group of men and horses is a single centaur-like body, carried away by the same verve. On, on, on, gallop, gallop, gallop! Oh, to ride like this to the ends of the earth! With the secret pride of being master and creator of this pleasure, I sometimes turn in the saddle to look back at my men. And suddenly I see that the faces of all my fine lancers have changed. Gone is their heavy Ruthenian air of morose depression, they are wide awake now, the drowsiness wiped from their eyes as if it were soot. Aware that I am observing them, they straighten themselves in the saddle and smile back, in response to the pleasure in my own gaze. I sense that even these dull-witted peasant lads are full of the joy of swift movement, a dreamlike anticipation of human flight. All of them feel as blessed as I do in the animal pleasure of youth, in exerting and releasing their strength.

But then I suddenly order them, "Haaalt! Trot!" Surprised, they all rein in their horses with a sudden jolt. As if an engine had been sharply braked, the whole column falls into the more sedate pace of a trot. They glance at me, slightly puzzled, for they know me well, and my delight in riding headlong, and we usually race across the meadows at a rapid gallop until we reach the area marked off as a parade ground. But I feel as if a strange hand had suddenly seized my reins; I have remembered something. I must unconsciously have caught sight of the rectangular white wall around the Kekesfalva villa on the rim of the horizon over to the left, the trees in its garden, the tower on the roof, and a thought has flashed into my mind—perhaps someone is watching you from there! Someone whose feelings you hurt with your pleasure in dancing, and you may be hurting them again now with your pleasure in riding. Someone immobilised by her lame legs who may be envying you for racing away as light as a bird in the air. At least, suddenly I am ashamed of my good health, my ability to gallop full tilt, intoxicated by speed; I am ashamed of my all too physical pleasure as if it were a privilege that I do not deserve. Slowly, at a heavy, lethargic pace, I get my disappointed men trotting through the meadows after me. I can tell, even without looking at them, that they are waiting in vain for a command to send them galloping away again.

It is true that, at the same moment as this strange inhibition affects me, I know that such self-chastisement is stupid and pointless. I know there is no sense in denying myself a pleasure because it is denied to others, forbidding myself enjoyment because someone else is unhappy. I know that, in every second when we are laughing and cracking silly jokes, somewhere or other another human being is breathing stertorously on his deathbed, I know that misery lies hidden behind thousands of windows and men and women go hungry, that there are hospitals, stone quarries and coalmines, that countless drudges work themselves to the bone in factories and offices, countless prisoners do forced labour at every hour of the day, and it does none of them any good in their hour of need for another man to torment himself for no good reason. I realise that if you were to begin thinking in detail of all the misery present in the world at one and the same time, you would never be able to sleep, and all laughter would die in your throat. But theoretical, imagined suffering is not what distresses a man and destroys his peace of mind. Only what you have seen with pitying eyes can really shake you. In the middle of my passionate elation I had thought I suddenly saw, as close and natural as if in a vision, that pale, distorted face as she dragged herself through the salon on her crutches, at the same time hearing their click-clack and the squealing and clinking of the hidden devices on her poor joints. I have reined in my horse as if in alarm, without thinking about it. It is useless for me to say now, in retrospect—what good are you doing anyone by adopting this stupid, heavy trotting pace instead of the thrill and excitement of a gallop? For all that, a blow has struck some part of my heart lying close to my conscience, and I no longer feel bold enough to enjoy my own strong, free, healthy physical pleasure in life. Slowly and apathetically, we trot as far as the outskirts of the parade ground, and only when we are entirely out of sight of the villa do I pull myself together. Nonsense. I think, stop wallowing in sentimentality! And I give the order, "Forward—at the gallop!"

It began with that one sudden moment when I reined in my mount. That was what you might call the first symptom of my strange case of poisoning by pity. First I felt only vaguely—as you do when you are ill and wake feeling bemused—that something had happened or was happening to me. Until now I had lived a carefree life in my own narrowly circumscribed circle, I had thought only of what seemed important or amusing to my comrades and my superior officers; I had never taken a personal interest in anything, nor had anyone taken such an interest in me. I had never been deeply moved by anything. My family circumstances were well-ordered, the course of my professional career was all marked out and subject to rules and regulations, and my carefree attitude—as I realise only now—had made my heart thoughtless. Now, all of a sudden, something had happened to change me—nothing outwardly visible, nothing of any apparent importance. But that one angry look, when I had seen hitherto unsuspected depths of human suffering in the lame girl's eyes, had split something apart in me, and now sudden warmth was streaming through me, causing mysterious fever that seemed to me inexplicable, as his illness always does to a sick man. All I understood of it at first was that I had broken out of the charmed circle within which I had lived at my ease until now, and I was on new ground which, like everything new, was both exciting and disturbing. For the first time I saw an abyss of feeling open up, and in some way that, again, I could not explain, the prospect of exploring it, plunging into it, seemed enticing. Yet at the same time instinct warned me against giving way to this rash curiosity. "That's enough," it warned me. "You have apologised, you've settled the whole stupid business." But then another voice whispered, "Go there again! Feel that shudder, that sense of fear and tension run down your spine once more." To which the warning voice replied, "Don't do it. Don't force your way in, don't intrude. You foolish young man, you don't know how to deal with such an excess of emotion, and you'll only make worse mistakes than you did that first time."

To my surprise, the decision was taken out of my own hands, for three days later I found a letter from Kekesfalva on my table asking if I would care to dine with them on Sunday. The only guests this time were to be gentlemen, including Lieutenant Colonel von F of the War Ministry, to whom he had mentioned me, and of course his daughter and Ilona would also be particularly pleased to see me after dinner. I am not ashamed to admit that, diffident as I then was, I was very proud of this invitation. So I had not been forgotten, and that remark about Lieutenant Colonel von F even seemed to suggest that in this discreet way Kekesfalva (out of a sense of gratitude that I immediately understood), was trying to make me a friend who would be useful in my military career.

And sure enough, I had no reason to regret my instant acceptance of the invitation. It was a very pleasant evening, and as a junior officer of whom no one in the regiment took much notice, I felt that I met with special and unusually warm treatment from these older, more sophisticated gentlemen. Obviously Kekesfalva had made a point of drawing me to their attention. For the first time in my life, a superior officer was treating me without any of the condescension of his higher

74

rank. Was I happy with my regiment, he asked, what were my prospects of promotion? He encouraged me to get in touch with him if I came to Vienna, or let him know if there was anything else I needed. Another of the guests, a cheerful, bald-headed notary with a kindly, shining moon face, invited me to his house, the director of the local sugar factory kept turning to ask my opinion—this was a very different kind of conversation from our talk in the officers' mess, where I had to respond with great deference to any remark by a superior officer! I felt a pleasant sense of confidence sooner than might have been expected, and after half-an-hour I was already talking entirely at my ease.

Once again the two servants waiting at table handed round wonderful dishes previously known to me only by hearsay and from the boasting of more prosperous comrades: chilled caviar—delicious; it was the first time I had tasted it—venison pie, pheasants, and all accompanied by those wines that so pleasingly delighted the senses. I know it's stupid to be impressed by such things. But why deny it? As an insignificant young lieutenant, unused to indulgence, I felt a positively childish vanity to be eating at so lavish a table with such distinguished older men. Good heavens, I kept thinking, good heavens, I wish Vavreschka could see this, and that pasty-faced volunteer who's always showing off about the magnificent dinners he's had at the Hotel Sacher in Vienna! They ought to be in a house like this some day, then their eyes would widen and their jaws would drop. Ah yes, if those envious fellows could see me sitting here at my ease, with the Lieutenant Colonel from the War Ministry raising his glass to me, if only they could see me in friendly discussion with the director of the sugar factory, and hear him say, meaning it, "I'm surprised to find you know so much about all this."

Then black coffee is served in the boudoir, cognac is brought in large, chilled, balloon-shaped glasses, and once again that kaleidoscope of liqueurs is on offer. So, of course, are the fat cigars with showy bands around them. In the middle of the conversation Kekesfalva leans over to me and asks discreetly whether I would rather join the card party or talk to the ladies. The latter, of course, I am quick to say, because I am not entirely happy with the idea of risking a rubber with a Lieutenant Colonel from the War Ministry. If I were to win it might annoy him; if I were to lose, there went my budget for the rest of this month. Moreover, I remind myself, I have only twenty crowns in my wallet at the most.

So while the card table is set up in the room next door, I sit down with the two girls, and strange to say—is it the wine, or does my good mood transfigure everything before my eyes?— they both strike me as particularly pretty today. Edith doesn't look as pale, sallow and sickly as last time I saw her—perhaps she has applied a little rouge, or is it really just her animation that brings the colour to her cheeks? Whatever the answer, the tense, nervous twitch of that line around her mouth is gone, and so is the arrogant lift of her eyebrows. She is wearing a long pink dress, with no fur or rug to hide her lame legs, and yet it seems to me that in our present cheerful mood none of us is thinking of 'that'. In Ilona's case, I even suspect, from the way her eyes are flashing, that she is slightly tipsy, and when she throws back her beautiful white shoulders, laughing, I have to move away if I am to resist the temptation of touching her bare arms as if by chance!

Even the dullest of men would not find it hard to talk agreeably with a cognac inside him, warming him very pleasantly, with the smoke of a fine fat cigar delicately tickling his nostrils, with two pretty, lively girls beside him, and after such a succulent dinner. I know that I can generally tell a story well unless my wretched tendency to shyness overcomes me. But this time I am on particularly good form, and I talk with genuine vivacity. Of course I tell only silly little stories, the latest incident to have happened at the barracks, for instance how our colonel wanted to send an express letter off by the fast train to Vienna last week before the post office closed, summoned one of our lancers, a typical rustic Ruthenian lad, and impressed it upon him that the letter must go off to Vienna at once, whereupon the silly fellow runs straight off to the stables, saddles his horse, and gallops down the road to Vienna. If we hadn't been able to get in touch by telephone with the garrison nearest to ours, that idiot really would have spent eighteen hours riding the whole way. I am not, Heaven knows, taxing myself and my companions with words of great wisdom, just telling everyday anecdotes, tales of the barracks square both old and new, but to my own amazement they amuse the two girls enormously, and both are kept in fits of mirth. Edith's laughter is particularly high-spirited, with a pretty silvery note that sometimes breaks into a descant, and her amusement must be genuine and spontaneous, for the thin, translucent porcelain skin of her cheeks shows more and more colour, a touch of good health and even beauty lights up her face, and her grey eyes, usually rather sharp and steely, sparkle with childlike delight. It is pleasant to look at her when she forgets her crippled body and her movements are easier, freer, her gestures less constrained, she leans back in a perfectly natural way, she laughs, she drinks, she draws Ilona to her and puts an arm around her shoulders. In fact, the two girls are really enjoying my trifling anecdotes. Success in storytelling always gratifies the storyteller. I recollect a great many stories that I

77

had forgotten long ago. Although I am usually rather timid and awkward, I find new courage in myself. I laugh with the girls, and make them laugh. The three of us sit comfortably together there in the corner like high-spirited children.

And yet as I crack joke after joke, apparently entirely absorbed in our cheerful little company, I am half aware of a gaze resting on me. It comes from above the frame of a pair of glasses, that glance, it comes from the card table, and it is a warm, happy expression that increases my own happiness yet further. In secret (I think he is ashamed of it in front of the others) and very cautiously, the old man is peering at us from time to time over his cards, and once, when I catch his eye, he gives me a confidential look. At that moment his face has the concentrated, radiant glow of a man hearing music.

This goes on almost until midnight, and not once does our cheerful conversation flag. Once again we are served something delicious to eat—excellent sandwiches—and surprisingly, I am not the only one to fall upon them. The two girls help themselves as well, and they too are drinking a good deal of the fine, heavy, dark old English port. But finally we have to wish one another goodnight. Edith and Ilona shake hands with me as they would with an old friend, a dear, reliable comrade. Of course I have to promise them to come again soon, perhaps tomorrow or the day after tomorrow. Then I go out into the hall with the three other gentlemen. The car is to take us home. I fetch my own coat while the manservant is busy helping the Lieutenant Colonel into his. Then, as I fling the coat on, I suddenly feel someone trying to help me; it is Herr von Kekesfalva, and while I resist, horrified—how can I let him play the part of a servant, an old gentleman helping a callow lad like me?—he comes close to me, speaking in a whisper.

"Lieutenant Hofmiller," says the old man shyly, low-voiced. "Oh, Lieutenant Hofmiller, you have no idea, you can't imagine how happy it has made me to hear the child laugh properly again. She has no pleasures usually, but today she was almost back to what she was in the old days when … "

At this moment the Lieutenant Colonel approaches us. "Well, shall we be off?" he says, addressing me with a friendly smile. Of course Kekesfalva does not venture to contradict him, but I feel the old man's hand stroking my sleeve, stroking it very, very lightly and timidly, as you might caress a child or a woman. There is infinite liking and gratitude in the hidden, surreptitious nature of this shy touch; I sense such mingled happiness and despair in it that I am deeply moved once again, and as I go down the three steps to the car with the Lieutenant Colonel, bearing myself with proper military deference, I have to take care that no one notices my bemused state of mind.

I could not drop off to sleep at once that evening; I was too excited. Slight as the cause of that might seem to outward view—an old man's hand touching my arm with affection, nothing more—that single restrained sign of fervent gratitude had been enough to flood my heart to overflowing. I had sensed more pure yet passionate feeling in that touch than I had known before, even from a woman, and it bowled me over. Young as I was, this was the first time in my life that I had been aware of having helped someone else, and I was astonished to think that an insignificant, ordinary young officer like me, still uncertain of himself, really had the power to make someone so happy. To account for the intoxicating emotion that I felt in that abrupt discovery, perhaps I ought

79

to explain, and indeed remind myself, that ever since childhood nothing had weighed on my mind more than my conviction that I was an entirely superfluous person, of no interest at all to anyone else, or at the best a matter of indifference to others. At cadet school and then the military academy, I had always been one of those average students who attracted no attention, never one of the popular or especially privileged young men, and it was the same in the regiment. I was therefore absolutely convinced that if I suddenly suffered a fatal accident, say I fell off my horse and broke my neck, my comrades might perhaps say, "What a shame about him," or, "Poor old Hofmiller," but by the time a month was up no one would really miss me. It had been just the same with the relationships I struck up with a couple of girls in the two garrisons where I had been stationed. There was a dentist's assistant in Jaroslav, and in Vienna Neustadt just south of the capital I used to go out with a little seamstress. On Annerl's day off we would go to her room, I gave her a little coral necklace for her birthday, we exchanged the usual loving words, and she probably genuinely meant them. But when the regiment was stationed elsewhere we had both been quick to console ourselves. For the first three months we wrote the obligatory letters to one another from time to time, and then found other partners, and the only difference was that in tender moments she said Ferdi to her new friend instead of Toni. All over and forgotten. So far, however, and I was now twenty-five years old, I had never felt that I was the cause of any strong, passionate emotion, and at heart all that I myself expected and wanted of life was to do my duty properly and not incur disapproval.

But now the unexpected had happened, and I examined myself with surprise and curiosity. Did I, an ordinary young man, really have power over other people? I had hardly fifty crowns in the world, and could I make a rich man happier than any of his friends? Could I, Lieutenant Hofmiller, help and console someone else? If I sat talking to a crippled, disturbed girl for an evening or two, did my presence really brighten her eyes, make her face come to life, and bring light to the whole gloomy house?

In my agitation I walked so fast through the dark streets that I felt quite warm. I wanted to fling my coat open as my heart expanded in my chest. For a new, second and even more intoxicating notion unexpectedly mingled with my astonishment—the thought that it was so easy, so incredibly easy to make these people my friends. And what exactly had I done? I had shown a little sympathy, I had spent two evenings in the house—two cheerful, animated, lively evenings—and was that really enough to do it? Then how stupid it would be to spend all my leisure time sitting apathetically in the café playing dull games of cards with my tedious comrades, or strolling up and down the promenade. Well, there'd be no more of that tedium from now on, no more wasting my time so stupidly! I would go to the café less often, would stop playing tarot and billiards, draw a firm line under all those ways of killing time that did no one any good and merely stupefied my own mind. I would rather go and visit the sick girl, I would even make preparations beforehand so that I always had something new and amusing to tell her and Ilona, we would play chess or indulge in some other agreeable pastime together. In itself, my resolve to make myself useful to others from now on aroused a kind of enthusiasm in me. I felt like singing, I felt like doing something ridiculous in my elation. Only when we know that we mean something to other people do we feel that there is point and purpose in our own existence.

So it was that over the next few weeks I spent my late afternoons, and usually my evenings as well, at the Villa Kekesfalva. Soon those friendly hours of talk became a habit, even an indulgence that had a touch of danger in it. But how enticing it also was for a young man who, from his boyhood years, had been passed from one military institution to another to find a home so unexpectedly, a home after his own heart instead of cold barrack rooms and the smoke-filled officers' mess. When the day's duties were over, and I strolled out to the villa, my hand was hardly on the knocker before the manservant was opening the door to me with a cordial expression, as if he had seen me coming through a magical peephole. Everything showed clearly and affectionately how naturally I was regarded as part of the family; special attention born of familiarity was taken of all my little weaknesses and preferences. The brand of cigarettes that I particularly liked was always there; if on my last visit I had happened to mention a book that I would like to read some day, there was a copy—new, but with the pages carefully cut—lying as if by chance on the little stool; a certain armchair opposite Edith's chaise longue was always regarded as 'my' place—small, trifling things, all of them, but perfectly calculated to warm a strange room pleasantly with a sense that I was at home, to cheer and raise the spirits imperceptibly. I sat there more confidently than I ever did among my military comrades, talking and joking just as the fancy took me, perceiving for the first time that any form of compulsion binds the real powers of the mind, and the true qualities of a human being come to light only when he is at ease.

But something else, something much more mysterious also contributed, unconsciously, to the fact that the time I spent daily with the two girls made me feel so elated. Ever since I had been sent off, a mere boy, to the military academy, and thus for the last ten or fifteen years, I had been living in an exclusively masculine environment. From morning to night, from night to first thing in the morning, in the dormitory at the military academy, in tents when we were on manoeuvres, in the officers' mess, at table and on the road, in the riding school and the lecture hall, I had never breathed the odour of any but male companions, first boys, then adolescent lads, but always men—men accustomed to energetic gestures, their firm, loud footsteps, their deep voices, the aura of tobacco about them, their free and easy ways, sometimes verging on vulgarity. To be sure, I liked most of my comrades very much, and could hardly complain if they did not feel quite so warmly about me. But that atmosphere lacked something to lighten it, it did not contain enough ozone, enough exciting, intriguing, electrifying force. And just as our excellent military band, in spite of its rhythmical verve, played nothing but music for brass—hard, cold, down to earth, intent on nothing but keeping time, lacking the tender and sensuous tone of stringed instruments—so even our most cordial regimental occasions had none of that muted fluidity that the presence or even the mere proximity of women adds to any social gathering. Even at the time when we fourteen-year-olds paraded through the town two by two in our smart cadet uniforms, when we met other young lads flirting with girls, or talking to them easily, we had felt, with vague longing, that we were being forcibly deprived of something by spending our youth in barracks while we did our training, something that our contemporaries took for granted daily in the street, on the promenade or the skating rink, in the dance hall—they were entirely at their ease in the company of girls. Shut away behind bars as we were, we used to stare at those girls in their short skirts as if they were magical beings, and dreamt of a single conversation with a girl as something unattainable. One doesn't forget such deprivation. Later adventures, fleeting and usually cheap, with all kinds of obliging females, were no substitute for these boyish dreams, and although I had now slept with a dozen women, the awkwardness and stupidity that afflicted me in company when I happened to meet a young girl made me feel that long deprivation had ruined me for natural, straightforward social intercourse, and it would be denied to me for ever.

And now, suddenly, the boyish wish, to which I had never admitted, for friendship with young women instead of only with my bearded, uncouth, masculine comrades was granted in full. Every afternoon I sat, cock of the walk, between the two girls. The clear femininity of their voices did me good physically—I don't know how else to put it—and for the first time, with almost indescribable happiness, I enjoyed losing my timidity with young girls. It only heightened the particular pleasure of our relationship that Edith's special circumstances ruled out the crackling electrical contact that is usually inevitable when young people of different sexes are together alone for any length of time. Any of the sultry possibilities that otherwise make a tête-à-tête at dusk so dangerous were wholly absent from our long hours of conversation. At first, to be sure, and I readily admit to this, Ilona's full lips, ripe for kissing, and plump arms, the Magyar sensuousness evident in her graceful movements had intrigued me in very pleasantly. Several times I had to keep my hands firmly under control to resist the desire to draw this soft, warm girl with her laughing black eyes to me and kiss her at length. But for one thing Ilona had told me in the early days of our acquaintance that she had been engaged for two years to a young man training to be a notary in Becskeret, and now was only waiting for Edith to be restored to health or at least improving before she married him. I guessed that Kekesfalva had promised Ilona, the poor relation, a dowry if she would stay until then. Moreover, we would have been guilty of brutality and perfidy to indulge in little kisses or hand-holding without being really in love, behind the back of Ilona's companion whose plight was so touching, and who was fettered to her wheelchair. So that original hint of intriguing sensuality quickly died down, and what affection I was able to feel was turned more and more on the helpless Edith, for in the mysterious chemistry of emotions pity for an invalid imperceptibly begins to go hand in hand with affection. Sitting beside the lame girl, cheering her up with conversation, seeing her thin, mobile mouth calmed by a smile—if she gave way to a violent impulse and made an impatient gesture, I could shame and mollify her with a touch of my hand and received a look of gratitude from her grey eyes—such little familiarities in a friendship of the mind with this defenceless, helpless girl made me happier than passionate adventures with her friend Ilona would have done. And thanks to these quiet revelations I discovered—how much better I had come to know myself in these few days!—tender areas of emotion wholly unknown to me before, emotions at which I had never guessed.

Unknown, tender areas of emotion—but dangerous all the same! For despite every effort, a relationship between a healthy man and a sick woman, the former free, the latter a prisoner, cannot stay in perfect equilibrium for ever. Unhappiness makes people vulnerable and constant suffering makes them unjust. In the same way as there is an ineradicable awkwardness between a creditor and a debtor, because one inevitably gives and the other takes, a sick person always nurtures a secret irritability and is ready to flare up at any visible sign of concern. I had to be always on my guard against crossing the barely perceptible line beyond which sympathy, instead of being soothing, injured the easily wounded girl even more. Spoilt as she was, she demanded on the one hand to be served like a princess and pampered like a child, but next moment such thought for her feelings could turn her bitter, because it made her even more clearly aware of her own helplessness. If you moved the stool closer to her, for instance, to spare her as far as possible the effort of reaching for her book or her cup, she might snap, with flashing eyes, "Do you think I can't pick something up for myself if I want to?" And just as a caged animal will sometimes pounce on its usually kindly keeper for no apparent reason, now and then the lame girl was overcome by a malicious desire to wreck our carefree mood by showing her claws, suddenly calling herself a "poor wretched cripple". At such tense moments I really had to summon up all my strength to avoid being unjust to her and her aggressive reaction.

But to my own astonishment, I kept finding that I had that strength. Once you have gained some understanding of human nature, further understanding of it seems to grow mysteriously, and when you are able to feel genuine sympathy for a single form of earthly suffering, the magic of that lesson enables you to understand all others, however strange and apparently absurd they may be. So I did not let Edith's occasional irritable moments of rebellion lead me astray, on the contrary. The more unjust and painful her outbursts were the more they shook me, but I also gradually came to understand why my arrival was so welcome to her father and Ilona, and my presence to the whole household. In general a long illness wears out not just the invalid but the sympathy of others—strong feelings cannot be prolonged indefinitely. Edith's father and friend certainly sympathised deeply with the poor impatient girl, but by now they were suffering from exhaustion and resignation. They saw the sick girl *as* a sick girl, her lame legs as a fact, they always waited with eyes lowered until her brief nervous outbursts had died down. But they were no longer as startled by them as I always was. I, on the other hand, the only one to whom her suffering always meant a new moment of deep emotion, was soon the only one before whom she felt ashamed of her loss of control. When she flared up angrily, I had only to say a word of gentle reproof—"Oh, my dear Fräulein Edith!"—and she would cast her eyes down obediently. She blushed, and you could see that she would have liked to run away from herself if only her feet did not root her to the spot. And I could never say goodbye without hearing her say, in a certain pleading tone that went straight to my heart, "But you'll come again tomorrow, won't you? You're not cross because of all the silly things I said today, are you?" At such moments I felt a kind of strange astonishment that I, who had nothing at all to offer but my genuine pity, had so much power over other people.

But it is in the nature of youth to be over-excited by every new discovery, and once a feeling carries you away you can't get enough of it. A strange transformation began to take place in me as soon as I discovered that my empathy for others was a force that did not just arouse my own pleasurable sensations, it had a beneficial effect on others as well. Since I had first allowed this new ability to feel for other people into my mind, it seemed as if a toxin had entered my blood stream and made it warmer, redder, swifter, pulsating more strongly. All at once I could no longer understand the dull state in which I had lived to no purpose until now, as if in indifferent grey twilight. A thousand things that I had previously passed by unheedingly now aroused me and occupied my mind.

As if that first insight into someone else's suffering has opened a sharper, more knowledgeable eye in me, I am now aware of details everywhere that interest me, inspire enthusiasm in me or move me. And as our whole world, street by street and room by room, is full of sad stories, is always flooded with terrible misery, my days are filled with expectant interest. For instance, when trying out new horses I catch myself unable to strike a refractory mount a heavy blow on the crupper without guiltily feeling the pain that I have inflicted, and the welt left on the horse burns on my own skin. Or my fingers curl instinctively when our choleric riding master punches a poor Ruthenian lancer in the face for saddling his mount in a slipshod way, and the fellow stands to attention, hands in line with his trouser seams. The other men standing around are all staring or laughing foolishly, but I, and only I, see how the dull-witted fellow's lashes grow damp over his eyes, which are downcast in shame. In the officers' mess I suddenly can't stand the jokes about clumsy or unskilful comrades; since beginning to understand the pain of that defence-less, powerless girl I feel angry with any brutality and ready to spring to the defence of those who cannot defend themselves. For example, I notice that the woman in the tobacconist's where I always buy my cigarettes holds the coins she is given strikingly close to the round lenses of her glasses, and I immediately wonder in concern if she is developing a cataract. Tomorrow, I think, I will ask her a few cautious questions, and perhaps ask Goldbaum, our regimental doctor, if he would examine her. And it occurs to me that the volunteers have made a point recently of cutting little red-headed K dead, and I recollect a piece in the newspaper about his uncle, imprisoned for fraud (how can he help what his uncle is like, poor lad?). I deliberately sit down with him at table in the mess and strike up a long conversation, sensing at once, from his grateful expression, that he understands I am doing it only to show the others how unjust and loutish their treatment of him is. Or I intervene on behalf of one of my men whom the Colonel would otherwise have told off for four hours' fatigues. I enjoy this new pleasure of mine daily, trying it out more and more often. And I tell myself that from now on I will help everyone and anyone as much as I can. I will not lapse into lethargy and indifference again! I will heighten my faculties by giving myself, I will enrich myself by becoming a brother to everyone else, I will feel sympathy for everyone and understand the suffering of others. And my heart, surprised by itself, trembles with gratitude to the sick girl whose feelings I unwittingly hurt, and whose suffering has taught me this creative magic of pity.

Well, I was soon roused from these romantic feelings, and a rude awakening it was. It happened like this. We had been playing dominoes at the Villa Kekesfalva one afternoon, and then fell into cheerful conversation and passed the time in such a lively mood that none of us noticed how late it was. At last, at eleven-thirty in the evening, I looked at the time and hastily took my leave. But as Edith's father accompanies me out into the hall, we hear a buzzing and humming outside like a hundred thousand bumblebees. A positive cloudburst is drumming down on the porch roof. "The car will take you home," Kekesfalva assures me. I protest that there's no need; I really dislike the idea of the chauffeur being roused now, at eleven-thirty, to get dressed again and take out the car he has already put in the garage, just for me. (All this empathising and thinking of other people is entirely new to me, and I have learnt to do it only in the last few weeks.) But after all, it is tempting to think of being whisked home in an upholstered, well-sprung car in such filthy weather, instead of trudging along the muddy road for half-an-hour in my thin patent-leather shoes, dripping wet, so I give in. The old man insists on going to the car with me himself and putting a rug over me. The chauffeur turns the starting handle, and soon I am on my way home at a fast pace through the drumming of the rain.

It is wonderfully comfortable and pleasant to be driven along in this car as it glides silently along the road. But now—the journey has been magically fast—as we are making for the barracks I tap on the pane between me and the chauffeur and ask him to stop in the square outside the town hall. I would rather not drive up to the barracks in Kekesfalva's elegant vehicle! I know it doesn't look good for an insignificant lieutenant to drive up in state like an archduke in a fabulous car, helped out by a liveried chauffeur. The top brass don't like such ostentation, and in addition instinct has been advising me for some time to keep my two worlds as far apart as possible—the luxury of the Villa Kekesfalva, where I am a free man, independent and indulged, and my other world of military service, where I have to keep my head down, where I'm a poor devil who is greatly relieved when there are only thirty days in the month before my money runs out, not thirty-one. Unconsciously, I don't want the others to know about my real life, and indeed I sometimes don't know myself which *is* the real Toni Hofmiller, the one in barracks or the one at the Kekesfalvas' castle, the Hofmiller out there or the Hofmiller stationed here.

At my request, the chauffeur stops in the town-hall square, two streets away from the barracks. I get out, turn up my coat collar and am about to cross the wide square. But just at that moment the storm breaks again with redoubled fury, and the wind blows rain straight into my face. Better to wait in the entrance to a building for a few minutes before walking back to the barracks. Or perhaps the café is still open, and I can sit in shelter there until the heavens have finished pouring the contents of their largest watering can over us. The café is only six buildings away, and I'm glad to see the gaslight glowing faintly behind the streaming wet windowpanes. My comrades may still be at their regular table in there, a good opportunity to make up for various omissions. It's high time I kept them company again. Yesterday, the day before, all week and all last week too, I've been away from our regular table. They'd be justified in feeling annoyed with me; if you're going to be unfaithful you should at least observe the proprieties.

I lift the latch. At the front of the café the lights are already extinguished to save on expense, the newspapers lie around open, and Eugen the waiter is cashing up for the night. However, I can still see light and a glint of shiny uniform buttons in the card room at the back. Sure enough, there they are, the usual card-players, Jozsi the first lieutenant, Ferencz the second lieutenant, and the regimental doctor Goldbaum. It looks as if their game finished long ago, and now they are just lounging around in the torpor typical of the café. I'm familiar with it, it sets in when no one wants to go to the trouble of standing up. It's a real stroke of good luck for them when my appearance rouses them from apathy.

"Hey, if it isn't Toni!" Ferencz announces to the others, and, "What a great honour for our humble home!" declaims the regimental doctor, quoting Schiller. We often accuse him of suffering from chronic quotationitis. Six sleepy eyes blink cheerfully at me. "Hello there!"

I'm glad they are pleased to see me. They're good fellows, I think. They don't think any worse of me for staying away from them all this time without any apology or explanation.

"A black coffee," I tell the sleepy waiter who comes wearily over, and I pull out a chair with the inevitable, "Well, what's the latest news?" that opens all our gatherings.

Ferencz's smile stretches his broad face, making it even broader, his twinkling eyes almost disappear into his rosy apple cheeks, his doughy mouth opens.

"The very latest news," he says with that slow grin of his, "is that your distinguished self has condescended to put in an appearance here again."

And the regimental doctor leans back in his chair and begins reciting, this time turning to Goethe's ballad 'The God and the Dancing Girl', "Mahadöh, lord of the earth—when he came down here below—assumed a form of human birth—here to share our joys and woe."

All three of them are looking at me with amusement, and I get a sinking feeling in the pit of my stomach. Better start talking myself, I think, before they ask where I've been all this time and where I've just come from. But before I can get a word in Ferencz is winking and nudging Jozsi.

"Look at that, will you?" he says, pointing at my feet under the table. "How about that? Patent-leather shoes in a downpour like this, and those smart clothes! Our friend Toni has found a home from home! I hear they really live it up at the old Manichaean's place! Five courses every evening, so the pharmacist says, caviar and capons, genuine Bols and the best

92

of cigars—unlike our pigswill at the Red Lion. I tell you what, we've all underestimated our Toni, he knows which side his bread is buttered!"

Joszi joins in at once. "A little short on good comradeship, though, our Toni. Yes, Toni, I suppose you don't think of telling the old boy up there, 'Hey, old fellow, I have a couple of good friends, smartly turned out, splendid chaps, they don't eat with their knives, why don't I bring them along?' No, not he, let the rest of 'em drink sour Pilsner and eat the same old beef goulash! A fine sort of friend he is, I must say! All for him, nothing for the rest of us! Did you at least bring back a nice fat Upmann cigar? If so you're forgiven, for now."

They all three roar with laughter. My blood suddenly rises from my collar to my ears. How the devil could Jozsi guess that Kekesfalva really did put one of his excellent cigars in my pocket as I was leaving—he always does! Is it sticking out between the two buttons on the breast of my coat? I just hope they don't notice anything! Embarrassed, I force a smile.

"Oh, of course, an Upmann! Won't you be happy with anything less? I can offer you one of our ordinary cigarettes." And I open my cigarette case and hold it out to him. At the same moment my hand suddenly jerks back—the day before yesterday happened to be my twenty-fifth birthday, and somehow or other the two girls had worked that out. When I took the napkin off my plate at dinner, I felt something heavy folded into it—a birthday present of a cigarette case. But Ferencz has already noticed my new acquisition—the least little thing is a great event in our closed circle.

"Hello, what's that?" he growls. "Something new!" He simply takes the cigarette case from my hand (what can I do to stop him?), feels it, examines it, and finally weighs it up in the palm of his hand. "Hey, seems to me," he says, leaning over the table to the regimental doctor, "seems to me this is the genuine article. Take a look, will you? Your worthy papa deals in such items, right? You'll know more about them than I do."

Dr Goldbaum, who is indeed the son of a goldsmith in Drohobycz, puts his pince-nez on his rather fleshy nose, picks up the cigarette case, weighs it in his own hand, examines it from all angles and taps it expertly with a knuckle.

"Yes, the genuine article," is his final diagnosis. "Pure gold, hallmarked and damn heavy. We could fill the entire regiment's teeth with this. Price range around seven to eight hundred crowns."

After delivering this verdict, which startles me, too (I had honestly thought it was just gilt), he hands the case on to Jozsi, who treats it with much more respect than the other two (how highly we young men think of anything valuable!). He looks at it, inspects his reflection in it, feels it, finally opens the clasp and says in surprise, "Hello—there's an inscription! Hey, listen to this! 'To our dear friend Anton Hofmiller on his birthday. Ilona and Edith.'"

All three are now staring at me. "Good heavens," says Ferencsz at last, "you choose your friends well these days. My respects! You'd have got a brass matchbox from me at the most."

My throat feels tight. Tomorrow the whole regiment will hear the embarrassing news of the gold cigarette case, my birthday present from the Kekesfalvas, and everyone will know the inscription by heart. "Let's have a look at that showy cigarette case of yours," Ferencz will say in the officers' mess, to show off, and I shall have to show it to the riding master, the Major, maybe even the Colonel. They'll all weigh it up in their hands, estimate its value, grin knowingly at the inscription, and then, inevitably, there'll be questions and jokes, and I can't be uncivil to my superior officers.

In my anxiety to put an end to this conversation quickly, I say, "Well, does anyone fancy another game of cards?"

But at once their kindly grins become loud laughter. "Ever heard the like of that, Ferencz?" says Jozsi, nudging him. "Wants a game of cards now, at half-past midnight, when the place is about to close!"

And the regimental doctor leans back lazily, very much at his ease. "Lucky fellow, doesn't have to take any notice of the time of day!"

They go on laughing at this poor joke for some time, but the waiter Eugen is civilly pointing out that it's time he closed. Police regulations. We leave—the rain has stopped—and walk back to barracks together, where we shake hands and say goodnight. Ferencz claps me on the shoulder. "Good to have you back." And I can tell that he really means it. So why was I so angry with them? They're all decent fellows without a trace of envy or malice in them. And if they laughed at me a little, they bore me no ill will.

They certainly didn't bear me any ill will, good fellows that they were—but with their silly marvelling and whispering they irretrievably destroyed my sense of security. For before this happened my curious relationship with the Kekesfalvas had increased my self-confidence wonderfully. I had felt, for the first time in my life, that I was the one with something to give, the one offering help. Now I realised how others saw this relationship, or rather how any outsider, unaware of all the hidden convolutions, would inevitably see it. What could strangers know about the subtle desire to show pity to which I had fallen prey—I can't think how else to put it—as if it were some dark passion? They were bound to suppose that I had made myself at home in that gener- ously hospitable house only to curry favour with the rich, save the price of an evening meal, and get presents. And they really don't mean ill, I think; they're my friends, they don't grudge me a warm place to sit, fine cigars to smoke. Undoubtedly—and this is just what irks me—they see nothing in the least wrong or dishonourable in my allowing such people to make much of me, because cavalry officers like us, as they see it, do a moneybags like Kekesfalva honour by sitting at his table. There was not the slightest disapproval in the way Ferencz and Jozsi admired the gold cigarette case—on the contrary, it even made them feel a certain respect for my ability to get such things out of my pa- trons. But what annoys me so much now is that I am beginning to feel uncertain about myself. Am I really just sponging on the Kekesfalvas? As an officer, a grown man, can I allow myself to be courted like this and keep every evening free? The gold cigarette case, for instance—I ought never to have accepted it, any more than I should have accepted the silk scarf they gave me recently when it was stormy weather outside. A cavalry of- ficer doesn't let people put cigars in his pocket to take home, and what's more—for God's sake, I must talk Kekesfalva out of this tomorrow—there's the business of the horse! Only now do I remember that the day before yesterday he was murmuring something to the effect that my bay gelding (for which of course I was paying by instalments) was not in very good shape, and he was right there. But his idea of lending me a three-year-old from his own stud farm, a famous former racehorse that would do me credit, really won't do. Yes, "lend", I understand what he means by that! Just as he has promised Ilona a dowry, only to keep her as companion to poor Edith, he wants to buy me too, pay me cash down for my sympathy, for my jokes, my social skills! And idiot that I am, I nearly fell for it, without noticing that I was degrading myself to the status of a sponger!

Then I tell myself that this is nonsense, and remember, moved, how the old man caressed my sleeve, how his face always brightens as soon as I come through the door. I remember the warm fraternal friendship between me and the two girls; they certainly are not watching to see if I drink a glass too many of the good wine, and if they do notice any such thing then they are just glad that I feel at my ease with them. Nonsense, pure nonsense, I keep telling myself. That old man feels more for me than my own father does.

But what use is all this persuading and encouraging myself now that I have been knocked off balance? I can tell that the lip-smacking astonishment of Jozsi and Ferencz has destroyed my peace of mind. Do you really go to see these rich people, I ask myself suspiciously, only out of sympathy, out of pity? Isn't there a good deal of vanity and self-indulgence in it as well? I have to clear this up. And for a start I decide to visit less regularly from now on. Tomorrow I won't go to see the Kekesfalvas in the afternoon as usual.

So I stay away next day. As soon as duty hours are over I stroll off to the café with Ferencz and Jozsi. We read the paper and begin the usual game of taroc. But I play my cards shockingly badly, because right opposite me a round clock is fitted into the panelling on the wall. Four-twenty, four-thirty, four-forty, four-fifty. Instead of paying attention to the game, I am counting down the time. At four-thirty I am usually approaching the villa, where tea will be ready and waiting, and if I'm even fifteen minutes late they'll be wondering why, asking each other, "What's happened to him today?" My punctual arrival has already become such a habit that they expect it, as if it were an obligation. I haven't missed a single afternoon for two and a half weeks, and they are probably looking as uneasily at the time as I am, waiting and waiting. Wouldn't it be proper for me at least to telephone and explain that I won't be coming? Or maybe better, I could send my batman with the message …

"Come on, Toni, your play is a disgrace today. Watch what you're doing, can't you?" says Jozsi in annoyance, looking at me quite angrily. My absence of mind has cost him, as my partner, a game. I pull myself together.

"Look, can I change places with you?"

"Of course, but why?"

"I don't know," I say, untruthfully. "I think all the noise in here is putting me off my stroke."

It is really that I don't want to see the clock as the minutes tick steadily by. My nerves are on edge, my ideas keep scattering hither and thither, I wonder again and again whether I ought not to go to the telephone and apologise. For the first time I begin to realise that true sympathy can't be turned on and off like an electric switch, and when you really share someone else's fate it means giving up some of your own freedom.

But damn it all, I snap at myself, I'm not in duty bound to spend half-an-hour trudging out there every day. And in line with the secret law of transference, whereby a man who feels annoyed unconsciously takes his annoyance out on perfectly innocent parties, like a billiard ball speeding this way and that, I turn my irritation not on Jozsi and Ferencz but on the Kekesfalvas. Let them wait for me in vain for once! Let them see that I'm not to be bought with presents and kind attentions, that I don't turn up on the dot like the masseur or the gymnastics instructor. I'm not going to set a precedent, I won't be bound to a habit, or tied down in any way. So in my stupidly defiant mood I sit in the café for three and a half hours, until seven-thirty, solely to prove to myself that I am entirely free, I can come and go as I please, and the Kekesfalvas' good food and fine cigars are a matter of indifference to me.

At seven-thirty we leave together. Ferencz plans to stroll on the promenade. But as soon as I have followed my two friends out of the café, I catch a glance from someone I know in passing. Wasn't that Ilona? Of course—even if I hadn't admired her dark red dress and broad-brimmed panama hat with the ribbon around it only the day before yesterday, I'd have recognised her from behind by the graceful way she sways from the waist as she walks. But where is she going in such haste? She's not strolling along like a girl out to join the others on the promenade, she is in a hurry—I must go after the pretty bird, however fast she flutters!

"Excuse me," I say, leaving my surprised comrades rather abruptly and hurrying after the red dress on its way down the street. For I really am delighted by the coincidence of seeing Kekesfalva's niece in my military world for once.

"Ilona, Ilona, stop, stop!" I call after her. She is walking remarkably fast, but finally she does stop, without seeming in the least surprised. Of course she noticed me before when she passed me.

"How splendid to meet you here for once, Ilona. I've been wishing for some time that I could walk around this town where we're stationed with you. Or would you rather go into the cake shop we both know so well?"

"No, no," she murmurs, rather awkwardly. "I'm in a hurry, they expect me at home."

"Well then, they'll have to wait five minutes more. If the worst comes to the worst and you risk being made to stand in the corner, I'll give you a note to excuse you. Come along, don't look at me so sternly."

I would like to take her arm, for I am genuinely glad to meet Ilona, the more striking of the two girls, in this other world of mine, and if my comrades see me with such a pretty girl all the better! But Ilona herself seems ill at ease.

"No, I really must go home," she says hastily. "The car's already waiting over there." And sure enough, the chauffeur salutes me respectfully from where he is waiting in the square outside the town hall.

"Well, at least let me escort you to the car."

"Of course," she murmurs in curious agitation. "Of course ... and by the way ... why didn't you come to see us this afternoon?"

"This afternoon?" I ask, deliberately slowly, as if I have to search my memory. "This afternoon? Oh yes, such a silly thing happened this afternoon. The Colonel was buying himself a new horse, and we all had to go with him to inspect the animal and try its paces." (In fact this incident had happened a month ago. I'm a very bad liar.)

She hesitates, about to say something in reply. But why is she tugging at her glove, why is she tapping her foot so nervously? Then she suddenly, hastily says, "Won't you at least come back with me now, and have dinner with us?"

Stick to your decision, I quickly tell myself, don't give way. Hold out at least for a single day! So I sigh regretfully. "What a pity, I'd be delighted to come. But today's no good, the regiment has a social gathering this evening and I must be there."

She looks at me sharply—curiously, she now has exactly the same impatient line between her brows as Edith—and says nothing, whether out of deliberate incivility or embarrassment I don't know. The chauffeur opens the car door for her, she slams it and then asks me, looking out of the window, "But will you come to see us tomorrow?"

"Yes, certainly." And the car is driving away.

I am not very pleased with myself. Why this curious haste on Ilona's part, that awkwardness, as if she were afraid of being seen with me, and why her swift departure? What's more, out of mere courtesy I ought to have asked her to give my regards to Edith's father, I should have sent a kind message to Edith, what have they done to harm me? On the other hand I am quite pleased to have shown some reserve. I did hold out. Now at least they can't think that I am trying to force my company on them.

Although I have told Ilona that I will visit at the usual time next afternoon, to be on the safe side I telephone beforehand to say I'm coming. Better to observe the forms of etiquette—you're safe with them. I want to make it clear that I am not descending on anyone as an unwanted guest, from now on I will always ask whether my visit is expected, and whether I will be welcome. Not that I really need to doubt it this time, because the front door is already open, the manservant is waiting there, and as soon as I am inside the house he eagerly lets me know that "The young lady has gone up to the roof terrace on top of the tower and would like you to join her there, sir." And he adds, "I don't think you have ever been up to the terrace, sir. The beautiful view will amaze you."

Old Josef was right about that. I really never had been on the roof terrace of the tower before, although that curious and puzzling building had often interested me. Probably, as I mentioned before, it was originally the corner tower of a castle that had long ago been demolished or fallen into ruin (even the girls didn't know its previous history). This solid, square structure had stood empty for years and was used as a storehouse. In her childhood, and to her parents' terror, Edith had often climbed the rather decrepit ladder to the loft at the top, where bats fluttered drowsily among old junk, and thick clouds of dust and decay rose with every step taken over the rotten old floorboards. But the child, with her liking for fantasy, had chosen this useless place, with an unimpeded view from the dirty windows into the distance, as her own hideout, her play world, for the very reason that it *was* mysteriously useless. After the accident, when she could not hope ever to climb up to that high romantic lumber room again with her paralysed legs, she felt numb. Her father often watched as she looked up bitterly at the beloved paradise of her childhood, now a paradise lost.

To give her a surprise, while Edith was away for three months at a sanatorium in Germany, Kekesfalva commissioned a Viennese architect to convert the old tower, and lay out a pleasant terrace with a good view at the top. When Edith was brought back in the autumn, with hardly any improvement at all in her condition, the rebuilt tower already had a lift fitted, as broad as those installed in the sanatorium, and so the sick girl was able to ride up to her beloved lookout post in her wheelchair at any time. The world of her childhood was unexpectedly restored to her.

It is true that the architect, working in some haste, had thought less of observing consistency of style than of technical convenience. With its geometrically straight lines, the uncompromising form that he had imposed on the precipitous old four-square tower was better suited to a dockyard or a power station than the pleasingly elaborate baroque structure of the rest of the little castle, which probably dated from the reign of Maria Theresia. However, it turned out to fulfil Herr von Kekesfalva's expectations; Edith was delighted by the terrace, which so unexpectedly freed her from the narrow, monotonous confinement of her sickroom. It was her own lookout post, and up there she could see, through a pair of binoculars, the wide, flat landscape and everything that went on around the house: seed time and hay-making, business and social occasions. Back in the world again after being shut away from it so long, she could spend hours on this vantage point, looking at the railway down below where trains merrily chugged across the landscape like toys, puffing out little curls of smoke. No vehicle coming up the avenue escaped her notice, and I learnt later that she had watched many of our regimental exercises on horseback and parades through a telescope. But out of a strange kind of jealousy she kept this remote terrace to herself, a private world where guests in the house were not allowed, and only the faithful Josef's spontaneous enthusiasm told me what a special distinction it was to be invited to this usually inaccessible stronghold.

He wanted to take me up in the lift that had been installed; you could see how proud he was that working this expensive means of transport was solely his own prerogative. But I declined the offer as soon as he told me that a little spiral staircase wound its way up to the roof terrace, with daylight falling through openings in the walls on each floor. I immediately thought how pleasant it would be to see the landscape dropping further and further below as I went up from landing to landing, and indeed, each of those narrow, unglazed windows offered a new enchanting view. A hot, clear, windless day lay over the summer countryside like a golden web. Smoke rose from the chimneys of the scattered houses and farms, standing almost motionless in the air. You could see thatched cottages with the inevitable storks' nests on their rooftops, every outline showing against the background of the steel-blue sky as if it had been cut out with a sharp knife; you could see duck ponds glittering like polished metal outside barns. And among them, in the pale fields of ripening crops, you saw tiny, Lilliputian figures, dappled cows grazing, women pulling out weeds and washing clothes, heavy wagons drawn by oxen, little carts moving quickly among the neat patchwork of the arable land. When I had climbed about ninety steps, the view embraced the Hungarian plain all around as far as the slightly hazy horizon, where a blue strip might perhaps be the Carpathians, and on the left was our little garrison town, with its buildings huddled close together and the onion dome of its church. I could easily make out our barracks, the town hall, the school, the parade ground, and for the first time since being transferred to the garrison here I was really aware of the quiet charm of this remote part of the country.

But I cannot give myself up to contemplation of this pleasant scene just now, for I have reached the terrace on the flat roof, and I must prepare to greet the lame girl. At first I can't see Edith at all; the broad back of the comfortable wicker chair in which she is sitting is turned to me and, like the colourful curve of a seashell, hides her thin body entirely. I guess where she is only from the table beside the chair, which is laden with books and the gramophone with its lid up. I hesitate to approach too suddenly; I might perhaps disturb her if she is resting or dreaming. I walk around the square of the terrace so that I can approach her from in front. However, on moving carefully forward, I realise that she is asleep. Her slender form has been comfortably settled with a soft rug over her feet, and her oval childlike face, framed in pale-red hair, rests on a white pillow, turned slightly sideways. The sun, already sinking, lends her complexion a look of golden, glowing health.

Instinctively I stop and make use of this hesitant, waiting moment to examine the sleeping girl as if she were a picture. At our frequent meetings I have never really had a chance to look at her properly, because like all who are sensitive, or indeed over-sensitive, she unconsciously resists such a gaze. Even if you happen to look her in the face during a conversation, that little line of annoyance instantly appears between her brows, her eyes dart quickly back and forth, her lips twitch nervously; she never for a moment shows you her profile at rest. Only now that she lies there with her eyes closed, motionless and unresisting, can I really contemplate that face (and doing so feels improper, like theft). Her features are rather angular, as if still unfinished; it is a face where child, woman and invalid mingle in a very attractive way. She is breathing gently through her lips, which are slightly open as if she were thirsty, but even this tiny effort makes her childishly small breasts rise and fall, and it has exhausted her, her pale face in its frame of red hair is laid back on her pillows. I move cautiously closer. The shadows under her eyes, the blue veins at her temples, the rosy translucence of her nostrils show

105

what a thin, colourless protection her alabaster skin offers from the outside world. How sensitive she must be, I think, when the nerves throb so close to the surface, unprotected, how infinitely she must suffer with such an elfin body, light as thistledown, a body that seems made for swift running, for dancing, hovering in the air, and yet is cruelly chained to the hard, heavy earth! Poor, captive creature—once again I feel the hot springs of pity welling up from inside me. It is a painfully tiring and at the same time wildly exciting sensation that overcomes me every time I think of her unhappiness; my hand trembles with longing to caress her arm gently, bend over her and, as it were, pluck the smile from her lips if she wakes up and recognises me. A need for tenderness, mingling with my pity whenever I think of her or look at her, makes me go closer. But I do not want to disturb the sleep in which she escapes from herself and her physical reality. It is wonderful to be close to the sick when they are asleep, when all anxieties lie at rest inside them, when they have forgotten their frailty so entirely that a smile sometimes settles on their half-open lips like a butterfly settling on a leaf—a strange smile that does not really seem to be their own, and will be banished as soon as they wake up. What divine mercy, I think, that at least in sleep the crippled and mutilated know nothing about the form or perhaps the formlessness of their bodies, that in a gently deceptive dream at least their bodies appear to them beautiful and regular, that at least in the world of sleep, surrounded by the dark, suffering invalids can elude the curse to which they are physically chained. What strikes me most are her hands, lying crossed on the rug, long hands with shadowy veins, fragile joints and pointed, bluish nails—delicate, bloodless, helpless hands, perhaps strong enough to stroke small animals, pigeons and rabbits, but too weak to hold and grasp anything firmly. Much moved, I wonder how she can defend herself against real suffering with such helpless hands. How can she fight for anything, hold and keep it? And I am almost repelled by the thought of my own hands, firm, heavy, strong and muscular hands that can control the most intractable horse with a pull on the reins. Against my will, my eyes are now drawn to the rug, a shaggy, heavy rug, much too heavy for this bird-like creature, weighing down on her bony knees. Under that impervious covering lie her helpless legs—I don't know whether they are crushed, crippled or simply deprived of strength, I have never had the courage to ask—but they are strapped into those steel and leather devices. At every movement, I remember, those cruel contraptions hang heavy as a ball and chain round her feeble joints; delicate and weak as she is, she always has to carry their horrible clinking and grinding about with her. You feel that to her, of all people, running, hovering, swinging through the air would be more natural than walking!

I involuntarily shudder at the thought, and so strongly does the tremor run through me, all the way to the soles of my feet, that my spurs too move and clink. That silvery, clinking chime can only have been a tiny, barely audible sound, but it seems to have penetrated her shallow sleep. Still breathing irregularly, she does not open her eyes yet, but her hands are beginning to wake up. They fall apart, stretching and tensing as if the fingers were yawning. Then her eyelids flutter, in search of something, and her eyes look blankly around her.

Suddenly they catch sight of me, and instantly become fixed. A mere glance has not yet made the connection with conscious thought and memory. But then she shakes herself and is fully awake. She has recognised me, and blood, pumped from her heart all at once, rushes to her cheeks in a crimson wave. Once again, it is like pouring red wine suddenly into a crystal glass.

"How stupid," she says, drawing her brows sharply together, and nervously clutching the rug, which has slipped, closer to her, as if I had taken her by surprise lying there naked. "How stupid of me! I must have fallen asleep for a moment." And already—I know how to tell which way the wind is blowing with her by now—already I see her nostrils twitching slightly. She looks at me, a challenge in her eyes.

"Why didn't you wake me up at once? It's not fair to watch people when they're asleep! Everyone looks ridiculous sleeping."

Sorry that my concern for her has annoyed her, I try to gloss it over with a silly joke. "Better to look ridiculous asleep than ridiculous awake," I say.

But she has already straightened up in the chair, bracing both hands on its arms. The line between her brows is deeper now, and I see that stormy fluttering and flickering around her lips. She darts a sharp glance at me.

"Why didn't you come to see us yesterday?"

This attack comes out of the blue so unexpectedly that I can't answer at once. But she is already going on, like an inquisitor, "You must have had some special reason just to leave us waiting. Otherwise you would at least have telephoned."

Idiot that I am, I ought have seen that question coming and prepared an answer in advance. Instead, I shift awkwardly from foot to foot, coming up with the now stale excuse of the new horse that had to be inspected. At five, I say, I was still hoping to be able to get away, but then the Colonel wanted to show us all his new mount, and so on and so forth.

Her unwavering grey gaze, stern and sharp, is fixed on me. The thicker I lay on the circumstantial detail, the more suspicious it becomes. I see her fingers nervously tapping the arms of her chair.

"I see," she finally replies in a harsh, chilly tone. "And how does this touching tale of a new horse to be inspected end? Did the Colonel decide to buy his brand new mount or not?"

I realise that I have veered dangerously off course. She slaps the table with the glove she has removed from her hand once, twice, three times, as if to work off the restlessness of her joints. Then she gives me a dark look.

"Let's not have any more of these tall stories! Not a word of them is true. How dare you expect me to swallow such nonsense?"

Her empty glove comes down on the top of the table harder and harder. Then, with a decided movement, she flings it far away from her.

"None of this drivel is true! Not a single word! You never went to the riding school. You weren't inspecting any new horse. You were in the café at half-past four, and as far as I'm aware you don't have to ride a horse to get there. So don't pretend! Our chauffeur happened to see you still there playing cards at six o'clock."

I'm still at a loss for words. But she brusquely interrupts herself.

"Anyway, why shouldn't I call a spade a spade? Do you expect me to play hide and seek because you tell lies? I'm not afraid to tell the truth. Just so that you know—no, it wasn't purely by chance that our chauffeur saw you in the café. I sent him specially to ask what was wrong with you. I thought you might be ill or something else had happened to you when you didn't even telephone, and … oh, for all I care you can think my nerves are all on edge, but I can't bear being kept waiting, I simply cannot bear it … that's why I sent our chauffeur to ask about you. But at the barracks he found out that Lieutenant Hofmiller was in perfect health and sitting in the café over a game of taroc, so then I told Ilona to find out why you were snubbing us like that, maybe something had offended you yesterday ... I know I'm not always responsible for what I say when I lose control in my silly way. Well, there you are, *I'm* not ashamed to confess my failings to you. And then you come up with such stupid excuses—can't you feel how shabby it is to lie in that wretched way among friends?"

I was going to reply—I think I even had the courage to tell her the whole tale of Ferencz and Jozsi. But she snaps at me, "No more inventions, please ... no new lies, I can't bear any more. I get told so many lies that I feel quite sick. People are always coming up with lies from morning to night. 'Oh, you look so well today, you're walking very well, wonderful, you're much, much better!' Always the same soothing, sugary stuff all day long, and no one notices it choking me. Why don't you say, straight out: 'I didn't have either the time or the inclination to visit you yesterday'? We haven't taken out a monopoly on your time, nothing would have pleased me more than if you'd just phoned to tell me, 'I'm not coming out to see you today, we're going to have a good time strolling about the town.' Do you think I'm so silly that I can't understand how boring it must be for you sometimes, acting the Good Samaritan here day after day, do you think I don't realise that a grown man would rather go riding or walk about on his own strong legs instead of feeling bound to a stranger's armchair? There's only one thing that I simply can't bear, and that's excuses and deceit and lies—I'm sick and tired of them, sick and tired. I'm not as stupid as you all think, I can bear to hear the truth. You know, a few days ago we engaged a new Bohemian maid to do the dishes and scrub the floors because our old maid-of-all-work had died, and on her very first day, before she'd had a chance to talk to anyone yet, she sees me being helped into my chair with my crutches. She drops her scrubbing brush in horror, crying out loud, 'Oh, dear Jesus, what a misfortune, oh, how sad! Such a rich, distinguished young lady, and a cripple!' Ilona went for the good woman like a spitfire, she was all for having the poor soul dismissed and turned out. But I was *glad*, her horror did me good because it was honest, because it's only human to take fright when you see something like that unexpectedly. I gave her ten crowns at once, and she went straight off to church to pray for me. I felt glad of it all day, genuinely glad to know for once what a stranger *really* feels on seeing me for the first time. But the rest of you, you always think you ought to 'spare me' with your false delicacy of feeling, you imagine that your wretched consideration for me does me good ... do you think I don't have eyes in my head? Do you think that, hidden behind all your chattering and stammering, I don't sense the same discomfort, the same horror as that good, that genuinely *honest* soul? Do you all think I don't notice you suddenly catching your breath when I pick up my crutches, hastily talking on so that I won't notice—as if I didn't see through you all with your sugary-sweet talk, valerian pills to soothe me, oh, it's all so slimy and disgusting! I know just how you all breathe a sigh of relief when you can close the door behind you and leave me lying there like a dead body, do you think I don't? I know exactly how you instantly sigh, 'Oh, poor child,' and at the same time you're very pleased with yourselves for so generously giving up an hour or so of your time to the 'poor child'. But I don't want any sacrifices.

I don't want any of you feeling in duty bound to serve me up my daily dose of your pity—I couldn't care less about your wonderful sympathy!—once and for all, I don't want pity. If you want to come and see me, then come, and if you don't want to then don't! But be honest about it, don't tell me tales of new horses to be tried out! I can't … I just can't stand the lies and your revolting attempts to spare me, I can't bear it any more!"

As she utters these last words she sounds absolutely beside herself, her eyes burning, her face pale. Then her tension suddenly dies down. As if exhausted, she lets her head fall against the back of the chair, and gradually blood comes back into her lips, which are still quivering with emotion.

"There now," she says very quietly, as if ashamed of herself. "Well, I had to say it sometime, and now I have! We won't talk about it any more. Give me a cigarette, will you?"

And now something strange happens to me. I am usually in reasonably good control of myself, and I have firm, steady hands. But this unexpected outburst has shaken me so much that I feel as if I were the one paralysed; never in my life has anything upset me so badly. With difficulty, I get a cigarette out of my case, hand it to her and strike a match. But as I hold the match to the cigarette my fingers are trembling so badly that I cannot keep it straight, and the little flame flickers and goes out. I have to strike a second match, and this one too wavers in my trembling hand before I light the cigarette with it. However, she must have noticed my obvious clumsiness, shaken as I was, for now she asks me, quietly, in a very different, an amazed and concerned voice, "Oh, what's the matter? You are trembling. What … what has upset you? What is it?"

The little flame of the match has gone out. I am sitting there in silence, and she murmurs, moved, "But how can you mind my stupid talk? Papa is right about you—you really are a ... a very unusual person."

At that moment I hear a slight humming sound behind us. It is the lift coming up to the roof terrace. Josef opens it and out steps Kekesfalva with the shy, somehow guilty manner that for no good reason always seems to weigh him down as soon as he approaches his invalid daughter.

I stand up quickly to greet the new arrival. He nods to me self-consciously, and immediately bends down to kiss Edith's forehead. Then a remarkable silence descends. Everyone in this house seems to know instinctively all there is to know about everyone else; the old man must certainly have felt a dangerous tension between his daughter and me, and now he stands there uneasily, eyes cast down. I can tell that he would like to make his escape again at once. Edith tries to help.

"Just think, Papa, this is the first time Lieutenant Hofmiller has seen the terrace."

"Yes, it's really beautiful up here," I say, and instantly I am painfully aware of making a shockingly banal remark, and my voice falters again. To ease the general awkwardness, Kekesfalva leans over the wicker wheelchair.

"I'm afraid it will soon be too cold here for you. Why don't we go down?"

"Yes, let's," says Edith. We are all glad to find a few unimportant things to do to distract our minds: packing up the books, putting Edith's shawl around her, ringing the bell, for a bell stands ready here, as on every table in this house. Two minutes later the lift is humming on its way up, and Josef wheels the lame girl in her chair over to the lift shaft.

"We'll be down in a few minutes," says Kekesfalva, waving affectionately to Edith. "Perhaps you'd like to get ready for dinner. I can walk a little longer in the garden with Lieutenant Hofmiller."

The manservant closes the door of the lift, the wheelchair containing the crippled girl goes down as if into a crypt. The old man and I have turned away. We are both silent, but suddenly I feel him hesitantly coming closer to me.

"If you don't mind, Lieutenant Hofmiller, there's something I would like to discuss with you … that's to say, something I want to ask you. Perhaps we could go over to my office in the estate-administration building … only if it's not a nuisance to you, of course. Otherwise … otherwise, naturally, we can walk in the park."

"Why, it would be an honour, Herr von Kekesfalva," I reply. At this moment I hear the lift humming as it comes up again for us. We ride down in it, walk across the yard to the estate management building, and I notice how cautiously Kekesfalva steals along close to the wall, how small he makes himself look, as if afraid of being caught out in some misdemeanour. Involuntarily—I can't help it—I walk behind him with an equally quiet, cautious tread.

At the far end of the long, low estate-management building, which could do with a new coat of whitewash, he opens the door into his office. It proves to be not much better furnished than my own room in the barracks: a cheap, well-worn desk with its wood beginning to rot, stained old wicker chairs, a few old documents, lists or tables that obviously haven't been consulted for years up on the wall, pinned over the shabby wallpaper. And the musty smell also reminds me of our own office in the barracks. Even at first glance—and how much I have learnt in these few days—I realise that this old man heaps every luxury and comfort on his child, while spending as little as a tight-fisted farmer on himself. As he walks ahead of me, I also see for the first time how shiny the elbows of his black coat are with wear; he has probably had it for ten or fifteen years.

Kekesfalva pushes a big chair upholstered in black leather over to me—it is the only comfortable chair in the office. "Sit down, Lieutenant Hofmiller, do please sit down," he says, with a certain affectionately pressing note in his voice, and before I can prevent it he takes one of the rickety wicker chairs for himself. Now we are sitting close together and he could, should begin on what he wants to say. I am waiting impatiently, as I'm sure anyone can understand, because what can this rich man, this millionaire, have to ask of me, an indigent army lieutenant? However, he keeps his head bowed as if intent on examining his shoes. I hear only the heavy, difficult breathing from his narrow chest.

At last Kekesfalva raises his head, and I see beads of sweat standing out on his brow. He takes off his clouded glasses, and without that glittering protection his face immediately looks different, more naked, so to speak, more wretchedly tragic. His eyes, as so often with the short-sighted, appear much duller and wearier than behind the lenses that amplify his vision. And the sight of the slightly reddened rims of his eyelids makes me think that this old man sleeps little, and poorly. Once again I feel that warm surge of emotion—an emotion that I now know to be pity. All at once I am facing not the rich Herr von Kekesfalva, but an old man weighed down by cares.

And now he begins, in a whisper, "Lieutenant Hofmiller"—his husky voice will not obey him yet—"I want to ask you a great favour. I know very well that I have no right to trouble you; after all, you hardly know us … and you can always say no … of course you can say no. Perhaps it's presumption on my part, and I am importuning you, but I have had confidence in you from the first. You are a good, a helpful person, one feels that straight away. Yes, yes, yes"—I must have been shaking my head—"you *are* a good person. There's something about you that makes others trust you, and sometimes … sometimes I feel as if you were sent to us by … " Here he hesitated, and I felt he was about to say "by God" but could not quite find the courage to do so. "Sent to us," he continued, "as someone to whom I can speak honestly … and it's not so very much that I want to ask you, but here I go talking on and on, and I haven't even asked if you will listen to me."

"But of course I will."

"Thank you … you know, in old age one has only to set eyes on someone to know him inside out. I know what a good person is like, I know that from my wife, God rest her soul. That was the first tragedy, when she died and I lost her, and yet today I tell myself that perhaps it was better for her to know nothing about our child's tragic misfortune. She could never have borne it. You know, when it happened five years ago … at first I couldn't *believe* that it would last so long. How can you imagine a child running about and playing, active as a spinning top like all the other children … and suddenly that's all over, all over for *ever*? And then we all grow up feeling such respect for doctors … you read in the papers about the miracles they can work, how they can sew up hearts and transplant eyes, so people say … we laymen are bound to feel sure, don't you

116

agree, that in that case they can do what sounds so simple, they can make a child … a child born healthy, a child who's always been healthy … they can soon make her better again. So at first I wasn't so very much alarmed, because I never for a moment *believed* that God could do such a thing, that he would strike down a child, an innocent child, for ever … if he had struck *me* down, well, my legs have carried me around for long enough. Why would I need them any longer? And then I wasn't a good person, I have done many bad things, I have … oh, what was I saying just now? Yes … yes, if I'd been struck down I would have understood it. But how can God miss his target so badly, how can he hit the wrong, the innocent person … and how can a man like me understand why a living creature, a child, is suddenly to have her legs *deadened* because of some tiny thing, nothing? A bacillus, the doctors said, thinking that meant something. But it's only a word, an excuse, and the other side of the coin is real, a child lying there with her limbs suddenly paralysed so that she can't even walk, she can't move, and there was I standing helplessly watching … I *can't* understand that."

With a brusque movement, he wiped the sweat from his damp, untidy hair with the back of his hand. "Of course I asked all the doctors … and if I heard of any really famous doctor then we consulted him … I asked them all to come here to me, and they lectured me and talked Latin and discussed the case and gave advice, one tried this and the other that, and then they said they hoped, they thought, and they took their money and went away, and everything was still the same as before. Or rather, something was rather better, indeed considerably better. She had always had to lie flat on her back the whole time before, and her whole body was numbed … now at least her arms and her upper body are normal, and she can walk alone using her crutches … so when I say rather better, no, I mustn't be unjust, I should say it was much better then. But none of them could really help her, they all shrugged their shoulders and advised patience, patience, patience … Only one of them has persevered with her, and that's Dr Condor … I don't know if you've ever heard of him. You're from Vienna."

I had to say no, I had never heard the name.

"Of course, how could you know him? You're a healthy man, and he's not one to go around all puffed up. He's not a university professor, not even a lecturer. And I don't think he has a very flourishing practice … that's to say, he doesn't *want* a large practice. He's a very individual, unusual man … I don't know that I can really explain it to you. He's not interested in the ordinary cases that any run-of-the-mill physician can treat, he's interested only in the difficult ones, the cases that the other doctors pass by with a shrug of their shoulders. Of course, uneducated as I am, I can't claim that Dr Condor is a better doctor than all the others … I only know he's a better *man* than the rest of them. I first met him when … when my wife … and I saw how he fought for her life. He was the only one who wouldn't give up until the last minute, and that was when I realised how he lives and dies with every one of his patients. He has … I don't know if I'm expressing it well … he has a kind of passion to be stronger than the illness. He's not like the others, the doctors whose only ambition is to get their fees and be professors and get awarded distinctions. He doesn't think of himself, he thinks of others, of those who are suffering … oh, he's a wonderful man."

The old man was in the grip of his enthusiasm; his eyes, weary only just now, were shining.

"A wonderful man, I assure you, and he never lets anyone down. To him, every case is a duty ... I know I can't put it very well, but it's as if he feels guilty if he can't help someone—personally guilty, I mean, and that's why ... You probably won't believe this, but I swear it's true—the one time he didn't succeed in what he set out to do ... he'd promised a woman who was going blind that he would cure her, and when she really did go blind he married her, imagine it, a young man marrying a blind woman seven years his senior, not beautiful and with no money, a hysterical creature who's a burden on him now, and not at all grateful ... Well, doesn't that show what kind of man he is? So you'll understand how glad I am to have found someone like him ... a man who looks after my child as devotedly as I do. I've left him a legacy in my will. If anyone can help her, then he will. God grant he does, God grant he does!"

The old man had both hands clasped as if in prayer. Then he moved a little closer to me.

"So now please listen, Lieutenant Hofmiller. You remember I wanted to ask you something. I've told you already what a sympathetic man Dr Condor is ... but you'll see, you'll understand ... it's *because* he is such a good man that I'm anxious, I'm always afraid, you see, that he may not be telling me the truth out of consideration for me, not the whole truth. He's always consoling me, promising me that my child is sure to get better, she'll be cured some day, but whenever I ask him more closely when, how much longer it will be, he avoids answering and just says: 'Patience, patience!' But I need to be certain ... I'm an old man, a sick man, I have to know whether I shall live to see it and whether she will get well at all, *really* well. Believe me, Lieutenant Hofmiller, I can't live like this any longer ... I have to know if she is certain to get

119

better, and when it will be … I have to know, I can't bear this uncertainty any more."

He stood up, overwhelmed by his emotion, and took three firm and rapid steps over to the window. I knew him by now; whenever tears rose to his eyes, he resorted to that brusque turning away. He didn't want pity either—he was very like her! At the same time, his right hand was feeling clumsily in the back pocket of his sombre black coat, crumpling up a handkerchief as he brought it out, and then pretending that he only wanted to mop the sweat from his brow with it. But in vain; I saw his reddened eyelids only too clearly. He paced up and down the room once, twice; the crumbling floorboards groaned under his tread, or was it he who was groaning, an old man also in decline? Then he took a deep breath, like a swimmer about to push off.

"Forgive me, I didn't mean to speak about it … where was I? Oh yes … Dr Condor will be coming from Vienna again tomorrow, he telephoned to say so … he regularly comes to visit us every two or three weeks to examine her … if I had my way I wouldn't let him leave us again at all … he could live in this house, I'd pay him anything he wanted. But he says he needs a certain distance to … now what was I going to say? I know … so anyway, he's coming tomorrow, and he will examine Edith in the afternoon. He always stays for dinner in the evening, and goes back to Vienna on the night express. And so I was thinking, suppose someone happened to ask him entirely by chance, someone who's a total stranger and has no personal interest in it, someone he doesn't know at all, suppose that person were to ask him quite … quite by chance, as you might ask about a mere acquaintance … were to ask how bad her paralysis really is, does he think the child will ever be entirely cured … *entirely* cured, do you hear? And how long does he think it will take … I have a feeling he won't lie to you; he doesn't have to spare you. He can tell you the truth with an easy mind … with me, perhaps something keeps him from it. I'm her father, I'm a sick old man, and he knows it would break my heart … But of course you mustn't let him guess that you have been talking to me about it … you must mention it *entirely* by chance, as you might ask any doctor … will you … would you do that for me?"

How could I refuse? The old man was sitting in front of me, eyes swimming with tears, waiting for me to say yes as if waiting for the last trump to blow on Judgement Day. Of course I promised to do as he wanted. He impulsively reached both hands out to me.

"I knew it … I knew it when you came back, and were so good to the child, after … well, you know, then I knew at once—this is a man who will understand me … he and no one else will ask him for me and … I promise, I swear to you, no one will know about it before or afterwards, not Edith, not Condor, not Ilona … only I will know what a service, what a great service you have done me."

"But Herr von Kekesfalva, it's nothing … it's only a small thing for me to do."

"No, it's not a small thing … it will be a great, a very great service that you do me. And if … "—he bowed his head slightly, and his voice too was lowered—"if there's ever anything that I can do for you in return … perhaps you have … "

I must have made a startled movement (was he actually thinking of paying me?), for he was quick to add, in the disjointed manner typical of him in moments of strong emotion, "Oh, don't misunderstand me … I only mean … I don't mean anything material … just that … I think … well, I have good connections … I know a great many men in the ministries, including the War Ministry … and these days it's always good to have someone you can count on, that was all I meant, of course … A moment may come for everyone when … well, that was all … all I wanted to say."

The shy awkwardness with which he offered me his hands put me to shame. All this time he had not once looked straight at me, but down at his own hands as if speaking to them. Only now did he look up uneasily, feel for the glasses he had placed on the desk and put them on with trembling fingers.

"Perhaps it would be better," he murmured, "if we went over to the house now, or … or Edith will notice what a long time we've been away. I'm afraid we've had to be terribly careful with her since she's been ill. She seems to have … to have sharper senses than other people, somehow. Even in her room she knows about everything going on in the house … she guesses everything almost before you've finished putting it into words, so she could end up … well, that's why I suggest we go over before she suspects anything."

We went over to the house, where Edith was already waiting in her wheelchair in the salon. When we came in she turned her keen grey gaze on us as if to read what the two of us had been talking about in our rather awkwardly lowered eyes. And as we did not give her any hint of it, she remained strikingly monosyllabic all evening, absorbed in her own thoughts.

I had told Kekesfalva that it was "only a small thing" to do as he wished and ask the doctor, whom I did not yet know at all, as unselfconsciously as possible about the lame girl's prospects of a cure, and if you looked at it from the outside I really had undertaken to make only a modest effort. But I can hardly describe how much this unexpected request meant to me personally. Nothing increases a young man's self-assurance, nothing encourages the formation of his character so much as to find himself unexpectedly facing a task that he must perform entirely on his own initiative and by his own powers. Naturally I had already shouldered responsibility, but it had always been of a military nature, just something that I had to do as an officer on the orders of those who outranked me, and within a closely circumscribed sphere of influence, for instance commanding a squadron, taking charge of a transport of material, buying horses, settling quarrels between the men. All these orders, however, and the task of carrying them out were only what was usual. I had written or printed instructions, and if I was in any doubt I had only to ask an older and more experienced comrade for advice before doing exactly what I was expected to do. Kekesfalva's request, on the other hand, was an appeal not to the soldier in me but to the essence of my character, of which I myself was still uncertain. I had not yet discovered my powers and their limitations. For Kekesfalva, a relative stranger, to appeal to me in his time of need, out of all his friends and acquaintances, was more gratifying than any praise I had yet received in my military career from any of my fellow soldiers.

But this sense of gratification went hand in hand with a certain dismay, for it showed me once again how shallow and casual my sympathy had been so far. How could I have visited this house for weeks on end without asking the most natural and obvious question of all—will that poor girl be crippled for life? Could the art of medicine not find a way to cure her disabled limbs? I felt dreadfully ashamed of myself; not once had I asked Ilona, Edith's father, or our regimental doctor that question. I had fatalistically accepted her paralysis as a fact, and the anxiety that had haunted her father for years now struck me with the force of a bullet. Suppose this doctor of his could really cure the child of her malady? Suppose those pathetic, helpless legs could stride out freely again, suppose that poor creature, abandoned by God, could run about easily once more, upstairs, downstairs, to the sound of her own happy laughter! The idea was intoxicating; it was delightful to imagine the two of us, or three of us, riding out together over the fields, to see her welcoming me at the door of the house instead of waiting for me in the room where she was a prisoner, to think of her going for walks with me. I was impatiently counting the hours until I could find out her chances from the doctor I had never met, counting them even more impatiently, perhaps, than Kekesfalva himself. Nothing in my own life had ever been so important to me.

So I arrived next day earlier than usual, after specially requesting extra leave of absence. This time Ilona received me on her own. The doctor from Vienna had come, she told me, he was now with Edith, and today he seemed to be giving her a particularly thorough examination. He had already been here for two and a half hours, and afterwards Edith would probably be too tired to join us, so I would have to make do with only her, Ilona's, company—that was to say, she added, if I had nothing better to do.

This remark told me, to my delight (for sharing a secret with only one other person always flatters one's vanity) that Kekesfalva had not said anything about our agreement to Ilona. However, I did not let my gratification show. We passed the time playing chess until, after quite a long time, I heard the footsteps I had been impatiently awaiting in the next room.

124

At last Kekesfalva and Dr Condor came in. They were in the middle of animated conversation, and I had to exert great self-control not to show a certain consternation, for my first impression of this Dr Condor was a great disappointment. Whenever we meet someone after hearing many interesting things about him, the imagination goes to work conjuring up a visual image in advance, recklessly lavishing romantic notions culled from memory on the stranger. In imagining a brilliant doctor such as Kekesfalva had described, I had resorted to the usual physical features that an average theatrical director and make-up artiste would use to present such a physician on stage: an intellectual face, a sharp and penetrating eye, elegant bearing, sparkling and witty conversation—we always fall hopelessly prey to the delusion that nature endows the particularly gifted with a particularly striking appearance. I felt a painful jolt of surprise, then, when I found myself unexpectedly bowing to a stocky, rather stout gentleman, short-sighted and with a bald patch, wearing a crumpled grey suit dusted with cigarette ash and with his tie carelessly arranged. Instead of the keen diagnostic gaze I had expected, a casual and rather sleepy glance was turned on me from behind cheap, steel-rimmed pince-nez. Even before Kekesfalva had introduced me, Condor was offering me a small, moist hand, and then he turned straight to the table where all the equipment for smoking stood to light a cigarette. He stretched, almost lazily.

"Well, there we are. And I might as well confess at once, my dear friend, that I'm hungry as a hunter and would be glad if we could have something to eat soon. If it's too early for dinner, maybe Josef could find me something to nibble—a sandwich, whatever's available." Then, sinking at his ease into an armchair, he added, "I always forget that there's no dining car on the afternoon express … yet another instance of typical Austrian inefficiency." Then he interrupted himself with an "Ah, excellent!" as the manservant came through the double doors of the dining room. "And my regards to your cook as well. What with all the chasing around I never managed to snatch any lunch today."

As he spoke he went over to the table, sat down without waiting for the rest of us, tucked his napkin into his neck and began drinking soup—rather too noisily for my liking. He did not say another word to either Kekesfalva or me during this urgent operation. There seemed to be nothing on his mind but the food, and at the same time his short-sighted eyes were turned to the wine bottle.

"Excellent—a fine Szamorodni Tokay, the 'ninety-seven vintage too! I remember that from last time. It's worth rattling out here on the train for your Tokay alone! No, Josef, don't pour it yet. I'll take a glass of beer first … yes, thank you."

Emptying the glass of beer at a single draught, he began helping himself lavishly from the dish quickly served up, and then slowly munched with relish. As he seemed to be ignoring the rest of us, I had plenty of time to observe him from one side as he feasted. Disappointed, I saw that this man, so enthusiastically praised to me, had the most ordinary, fleshy face imaginable, like a full moon pitted with little dimples and craters, a potato-shaped nose, a double chin, ruddy cheeks with a dark five o'clock shadow, a short, thick neck—exactly the sort of man known in Viennese dialect as a *Sumper*, a jovial, outspoken *bon viveur*. He sat there eating at his leisure in exactly the *Sumper* way, his waistcoat creased and half unbuttoned, and gradually the ponderous persistence of his munching came to irritate me—perhaps because I remembered how very civil to me the Lieutenant Colonel and the sugar manufacturer had been at this same table, or perhaps because I rather doubted whether a man who ate and drank so copiously, holding his wine up to the light before gulping it and smacking his lips, would be able to give me a precise answer to such a discreet question as I had to ask.

"Well, and what's the local news here? How does the harvest look? Not too dry these last few weeks, not too hot? I read something about that in the paper. And what about the factory? Are you members of the sugar cartel putting up the price again?" Condor sometimes interrupted his rapid chewing and munching with such casual and, I may say, nonchalant questions, queries that called for no real answer. He appeared to overlook my presence entirely. I had heard a good deal before about the typical offhand manner of medical men, but I began to feel a certain anger in the company of this coarse if well-meaning physician. In my annoyance, I said not a word.

However, he was not in the least disturbed by our presence, and when we finally moved into the salon, where black coffee was waiting ready for us, he sat down with a grunt of pleasure in, of all places, Edith's armchair, which was fitted with all kinds of special comforts like a swivelling bookcase and ashtrays, and had adjustable arms. Annoyance makes one sharp-sighted as well as bad-tempered, and I could not help noticing with a certain satisfaction, as he lolled there at his ease, that his legs were short, with socks flopping around his ankles, and his paunch was flabby. To demonstrate how disinclined I was to get to know him any better, I moved my chair so that my back was turned to him. However, he seemed entirely indifferent to my ostentatious silence and the nervous way old Kekesfalva kept pacing around the room and plying him with cigars, matches and cognac. Condor helped himself to no fewer than three expensive imported cigars from the box, placing two in reserve beside his coffee cup. Well as the deep chair fitted itself to his form, it still did not seem to be comfortable enough for him. He shifted and fidgeted about until he had found the best position in it. Only when he had drunk his second cup of coffee did he sigh with satisfaction, like an animal that has eaten its fill. Repellent, I told myself, repellent. Then he suddenly stretched out his legs and cast Kekesfalva an ironic glance.

"Well, St Laurence, on tenterhooks there on your gridiron? I suppose you won't let me enjoy my good cigar because you can't wait for me to deliver my report! But you know me by now, you know I don't like to mix medicine and mealtimes—and I really was too hungry and too tired. I've been on my feet since seven-thirty this morning, and I felt as if my head and my stomach were both left drained dry. Well now"—here he drew slowly on his cigar, blowing rings of grey smoke—"well now, my dear friend, let's get to the nub of it! Everything is going very well. Walking exercises, stretching exercises, she's doing just as she should. Perhaps there's a very, very slight improvement compared to last time. As I say, we can be satisfied. Only"—and he drew on the cigar again—"only in her general state of mind … in what you might call the psychological side of her … I thought that today … please don't be alarmed, my dear friend … I thought she was rather different today."

In spite of Condor's warning Kekesfalva looked very alarmed indeed. The spoon he was holding in his hand began to tremble.

"Different? What do you mean? Different in what way?"

"Well, different means different … I didn't say worse, my dear friend. Impute nothing to me and infer nothing from what I say, in the words of the great Goethe. Just now I don't know

128

myself exactly what's the matter with her, but … but there's something wrong."

The old man was still holding the spoon, and clearly didn't have the strength to put it down.

"What … *what* is wrong?"

Dr Condor scratched his head. "I wish I knew! Anyway, don't worry. We are speaking in purely academic terms, with no beating about the bush, so let me say again, straight out—it's nothing in her illness that has changed, it's something in herself. Something was the matter with her today, and I don't know what. For the first time I had a feeling that she was somehow evading me." He drew on the cigar again, and then glanced once more at Kekesfalva with his quick-moving little eyes. "You know it's best for us to go about this perfectly honestly. We have no need to pretend to each other, we can show our cards. Well … my dear friend, please tell me clearly and honestly, have you, in your eternal impatience, consulted another doctor? Has someone else been examining or treating Edith since I last saw her?"

Kekesfalva reacted as if he had been accused of some monstrous crime. "For God's sake, doctor, I swear on my child's life—"

"Yes, well, never mind swearing," Condor quickly interrupted him. "I believe you without that. So that was my question— peccavi! I was wide of the mark—a wrong diagnosis, anyone can make one, however academically distinguished. Stupid of me … and yet I could have sworn that … Well, then it must be something else. Strange, though, very strange. May I? … " He poured himself a third cup of black coffee.

"Yes, but what is it about her? What's different? What do you think it is?" the old man stammered. His lips were dry.

"My dear friend, you really do make it hard for me. There's nothing for you to worry about, I give you my word on that again, my word of honour. If there were the prospect of anything serious, you surely don't think I'd say so in front of a stranger … forgive me, Lieutenant Hofmiller, I don't mean to be unfriendly, it's just that … well, I wouldn't talk about it from this chair while drinking your good cognac, my friend, and it really is excellent."

He leant back again, and closed his eyes for a moment.

"Yes, it's hard to say off the cuff just what's different in her, because it lies at the upper or lower limit of what can be put into words. But if I suspected at first that some other doctor had been involved in treating her—and really I don't think so now, Herr von Kekesfalva—then it was because for the first time communication between Edith and me wasn't working properly today. We couldn't make contact in the normal way … wait a minute, maybe I can put it more clearly. I mean, during treatment that lasts for any length of time a certain very distinct contact builds up inevitably between the doctor and his patient … it may even be going too far to call it a contact, a word that ultimately implies 'touch', and thus something physical. In that relationship confidence mingles in a curious way with distrust, working against each other, attraction and repulsion, and of course that mingling will be different from one occasion to the next—but we are used to that. Sometimes the patient seems different to the doctor, sometimes it's the other way round. Sometimes the two of them can communicate with no more than a glance, sometimes they find themselves talking at cross purposes … yes, these oscillations are very strange; one can't grasp them, let alone assess them. Perhaps a comparison will express it best, although there's a risk that it will be only a rough comparison. Well—let's say that with a patient it's as if, when you have been absent for a few days and you come back and go to your typewriter, it appears to work in exactly the same way as usual. But all the same, you feel, from a certain something you can't quite pin down, that someone else has been using it while you were away. Or to take you as an example, Lieutenant Hofmiller, no doubt you can tell from the behaviour of your horse if another man has borrowed it for a couple of days. There's something not quite right in the animal's attitude, you have somehow lost perfect control over it, and probably you can't say exactly why you notice that precisely because the differences are so infinitesimally small ... I know these are very rough comparisons, for the relationship of a doctor to his patients is of course far more subtle. In fact, and I don't mind telling you this, I would be in great difficulty if I were to try explaining exactly what has changed in Edith since the last time I saw her. But there's something going on, something has changed in her, and it annoys me that I can't work out what."

"But how ... how does this change show in her?" gasped Kekesfalva. I saw that none of what Condor said could reassure him, and there was a damp gleam on his forehead.

"How does it show? Well, in small things, in imponderables. I noticed as soon as we started the stretching exercises that she was resisting me. Before I could try really examining her she was in revolt. 'Nonsense, it's all just the same as usual,' she said, but normally she would wait impatiently for me to say what I thought. And then, when I suggested certain exercises, she made stupid remarks such as, 'Oh, that won't do any good,' or, 'We won't get anywhere like that.' I'll admit that such comments have no importance in themselves—they're the result of petulance or nervous tension—but never before, my dear friend, has Edith said anything like that to me. Well, perhaps it was just bad temper, the kind of thing that can happen to anyone."

"But you didn't find any change in her for the worse … did you?"

"How many times do I have to give you my word of honour? If the least little thing were wrong, I would be as anxious a physician as you are a father, and as you can see I am not in the least anxious. On the contrary, I'm not at all displeased to find her putting up resistance to me. Admittedly your little daughter is acting more irritably, with more recalcitrance and impatience than a few weeks ago—and she's probably giving you a hard time of it as well. But on the other hand, such rebellion indicates a certain strengthening of her will to live and get better—the more strongly and normally an organism begins to function, the more determined it is, of course, to be finally done with its infirmity. Believe me, we doctors are by no means as happy with our 'good', docile patients as you may think. They're the ones who do least to help themselves. We can only rejoice to find a patient putting up energetic, even angry resistance, because curiously enough this apparently senseless reaction sometimes has a more beneficial effect than any of the medicines we, in our wisdom, prescribe. So let me repeat, I am not at all worried. If we were to try a new course of treatment for her now, for instance, we could expect her to make every effort to co-operate. Indeed, perhaps this would be the right moment to call on the psychological forces that play such a large part in her case. I don't know," he added, raising his head and looking at us, "whether you entirely understand what I mean."

"Of course," I instinctively said. It was the first remark that I had made directly to him, and indeed what he said seemed to me clear and sensible.

But the old man still sat there transfixed and motionless. He was staring straight ahead, his eyes empty. I realised that he did not in fact understand any of what Condor was trying to explain because he didn't want to. Because his mind and all his fears were set on the crucial question—will she get better? Will she get better soon? And if so, when?

"What course of treatment do you mean?" He was stammering disjointedly, as usual when he was agitated. "What new cure? … You spoke of a new cure of some kind … What new course of treatment do you want to try?" (I noticed at once how he clung to the word "new", because it suggested to him new hope.)

"Leave it to me, my dear friend, to decide what I will try and when—don't press me, don't keep trying to achieve something that can't be done by force! Your own 'case', as we doctors unattractively put it, is the worst of my anxieties. We'll have to do something about that."

The old man looked at us, silent and depressed. I saw him forcing himself not to ask yet another of his insistent questions. Condor himself must have felt some of that silent stress, because he suddenly got to his feet.

"And that's enough for today, don't you think? I have told you what I think, anything else would be nothing but nonsense and drivel … even if Edith proves more irritable than usual in the near future, don't take alarm, I'll soon find out what's behind it. All you have to do is refrain from pestering her with your own distress and anxiety. Oh, and another thing—do take good care of your own nerves. You don't look to me as if you are getting enough sleep, and I'm afraid that with all your fretting and worrying you'll do harm to your own health. You can't inflict that distress on your child. You'd better start by going to bed early this evening—take a few valerian drops before you fall asleep, and then you'll feel well rested in the morning. There, that's the end of my prescription for today! I'll finish smoking my cigar, and then I'll be off."

"Are you really … are you really leaving already?"

Dr Condor was firm about it. "Yes, my dear friend, that's enough for today! I have one last patient to see this evening, he's rather run down, and I prescribed him a good walk. As you can see, I've been out and about since seven-thirty today, I spent all morning at the hospital—a curious case, that one, but let's not talk about it. Then I was in the train, and then here, and even we doctors need to get fresh air in our lungs now and then to clear our heads. So please don't offer me your car today, I'll walk to the station. There's a wonderful full moon. Of course I won't deprive you of Lieutenant Hofmiller's company, and if you want to stay up this evening in spite of my medical advice then I'm sure he'll keep you company a little longer."

But at once I remembered my mission. No, I said firmly, I had to be on duty early next morning, and had been thinking of leaving for some time. "So if you don't object, let's walk back to the town together."

And now, for the first time, I saw Kekesfalva's ashen glance light up. My task! The question! The answer I was to find out! He too had remembered.

"I'll go straight to bed, then," he said, with unexpected docility, but giving me a surreptitious and meaning look behind Condor's back. It wasn't necessary; even without such a reminder I felt the pulse in my wrist beating strongly against my cuff. I knew that this was the moment for me to do as Kekesfalva had asked.

Condor and I involuntarily stopped as soon as we were on the top step of the little flight of steps outside the door of the house, for the front garden was an amazing sight. During the hours that had been spent in earnest discussion indoors, it had not occurred to any of us to look out of the window, but now a transformation scene surprised us. A huge full moon stood overhead, a shining, polished silver disc in the middle of the starlit sky, and as the breeze, warm from the sunny day, blew mild summer air into our faces a magical winter seemed to have descended on the world in that dazzling moonlight. The gravel looked white as freshly fallen snow between the neatly pruned trees that cast their dark shadows on the open path, and the trees themselves seemed to be holding their breath, standing now in the light and now in the dark, like alternating mahogany and glass. I cannot remember ever feeling moonshine as haunting as here in the total peace and stillness of the garden, drenched in the icy light of the moon, and the spell it cast was so deceptive that we instinctively hesitated to set foot on the shining steps as if they were slippery glass. And as we walked down the apparently snow-covered gravel drive, suddenly we were not two but four, for our shadows went ahead of us, clear-cut in the bright moonlight. Against my will I had to keep watching those two black companions who persistently marked out our movements ahead of us, like walking silhouettes, and it gave me—our feelings are sometimes so childish—a certain reassurance to see that my shadow was longer, slimmer, I almost said "better-looking", than the short, stout shadow of my companion. That superiority—I know that it takes courage to admit to such naivety—slightly increased my self-confidence. A man's state of mind is always influenced by the most curious coincidences, and the smallest outer factors can increase or decrease his sense of security.

We had reached the wrought-iron gate without speaking a word. In closing it we necessarily had to look back. The facade of the house looked as if it were painted with bluish phosphorus, and in the dazzling moonlight we couldn't see which of the windows were still lit from within and which only on the outside. Nothing but the sharp sound of the gate latching broke the silence. As if encouraged by that earthly sound in the midst of the ghostly silence, Condor turned to me and said, as much at his ease as I could have hoped, "Poor old Kekesfalva! I've been reproaching myself all this time. Of course I know he would have liked to keep me there for hours, asking me hundreds of questions, or rather the same question hundreds of times. But I couldn't take any more. It's been a long day, patients from morning to night, and none of them cases that are making any progress."

By now we were walking down the avenue, where the moonlight filtered through the shadowy canopies of the trees meeting overhead. The snowy-white gravel shone all the more brightly in the middle of the path, and we both walked along that bright channel of light. I felt too respectful to Condor by now to reply, but he didn't seem to notice.

"There are days when I just can't take any more of his persistence. You know, the patients aren't the hardest part of a doctor's life; we learn to get along with them, we work out a technique. And after all, if patients complain and ask questions and press you for answers, it's part of their condition, like a high temperature or a headache. We expect them to be impatient from the start, we're prepared for that and armed against it, and every one of us has soothing phrases and white lies on the tip of his tongue, just as he can prescribe sleeping pills and painkillers. But no one makes our lives more difficult than the relations who intervene, unasked, between doctor and patient, and always want to know 'the truth'. They act as if no one else in the world were ill at the moment but this one invalid, and there's no one else to be treated anywhere. I really don't mind Kekesfalva's constant questions, but you know, if impatience becomes a chronic condition sometimes the doctor's own patience lets him down. I've told him ten times over that I have a severe case in Vienna, it's a matter of life or death. And although he knows that, he keeps telephoning day after day, urging and urging me, trying to force some words of hope out of me. At the same time, as his doctor, I can see how bad all this stress is for him. In fact I'm far more concerned about him than he knows, far, far more. It's as well that he doesn't know how poor the prospects are."

I was alarmed. So the prospects were poor? Frankly and spontaneously, Condor had told me what I was supposed to be worming out of him. I said, in great agitation myself, "Forgive me, doctor, but I'm sure you'll understand how anxious that makes me feel ... I had no idea that Edith was in such a bad way."

"Edith?" Condor turned to me in surprise. He seemed to notice, for the first time, that he had been talking to someone else. "What do you mean—Edith? I never said a word about Edith ... you've entirely misunderstood me. No, no, Edith's condition is the same as ever ... I am sorry to say, but yes, the same as ever. However, I'm concerned about *him*, Kekesfalva, increasingly concerned. Hasn't it struck you how much he's changed in these last few months? How ill he looks, how he's getting worse every week?"

"Well ... of course, I can't judge that. I've had the honour of knowing Herr von Kekesfalva only for a few weeks, and ... "

"Oh, I see. Forgive me … then of course you couldn't have seen the change … But I've known him for years, and speaking for myself I was genuinely horrified when I happened to look at his hands today. Have you noticed how translucent and bony they are? You know, when a doctor has seen the hands of many dead people, it's always distressing to see that particular bluish colour on a living hand. And then—I don't like to see him so quickly moved to emotion. His eyes fill with tears at the least little thing, the slightest new fear drains the colour from his face. It's particularly alarming to see a man who used to be as thrusting and energetic as Kekesfalva giving up like that. I'm afraid it doesn't bode well when hard men suddenly turn soft—I don't even like to see them become kindly. It shows that something's wrong, something inside them has given way. Of course, for some time I've intended to give him a thorough examination—only I just don't trust myself to broach the subject to him. Because my God, suppose I start him thinking of himself as ill now, let alone thinking that he might die and leave his crippled child behind … well, I don't like to imagine it! He's undermining his own health anyway by all that brooding of his, his headlong impatience … no, no. Lieutenant Hofmiller, you misunderstood me. I'm far more worried about him than Edith … I'm afraid the old man won't last much longer."

I was devastated. I had never thought of that. At the time I was twenty-five years old, and I had never seen anyone close to me die. I couldn't immediately take in the idea that a man with whom I had just been sitting at table, a man I had been talking to, drinking with, could be lying cold in his shroud tomorrow. At the same time a slight, sudden pang at my heart told me that I really had become fond of the old man. Moved and awkward about it as I was, I wanted to say something, anything.

"That's terrible," I said, still feeling bemused. "That would be really terrible. Such a distinguished, generous, kind man—in fact the first genuine Hungarian nobleman I've ever met … "

But here a surprising thing happened. Condor stood still so abruptly that I instinctively stopped as well. He stared at me, the lenses of his pince-nez gleaming as he brusquely turned his head. Only after taking a deep breath once or twice did he ask, in astonishment, "A nobleman? A genuine nobleman at that? Kekesfalva? Forgive me, my dear sir … but do you mean that seriously? I mean about his being a genuine Hungarian nobleman?"

I didn't entirely understand the question. I just had a sense of having said something foolish, and I replied, in embarrassment, "Well, I can't judge that kind of thing for myself, but Herr von Kekesfalva has always shown his kindest, most distinguished side to me … and in the regiment we've always had the Hungarian gentry described to us as particularly arrogant. But … I … I never met a kindlier man … I … I … "

My voice died away. I sensed Condor still examining me with a careful, sidelong look. His round face shone in the moonlight, the lenses of his pince-nez looked larger than life, and I could see the searching glance behind them only indistinctly. It gave me the uncomfortable feeling of being a scrabbling insect placed under a very strong magnifying glass. Facing each other now in the middle of the country road, we would have presented a curious sight to any passer by, but the road happened to be entirely empty.

Then Condor lowered his head, began striding on again, and muttered, as if to himself, "Well, you really are an oddity—forgive me, I don't mean it in any bad sense. But it really is odd, you must admit, very strange … you've been going to the house for some weeks, I hear. And you're living in a small town, a kind of chicken coop full of cackling fowls at that, and you still think Kekesfalva is a great magnate. Haven't you ever heard any of your comrades make certain … well, let's not say derogatory remarks, but haven't you just heard hints that he's not really one of the old nobility? You must have been told something."

"No," I said firmly, feeling anger rise in me (it is not pleasant to be described as an oddity and very strange). "I'm sorry, but I have heard no such imputation. I have never discussed Herr von Kekesfalva with any of my comrades."

"How curious," murmured Condor. "How very curious. I always thought he was exaggerating in what he said about you. And since this seems to be my day for making the wrong diagnosis, I'll admit frankly that his enthusiasm made me slightly suspicious. I couldn't really believe that you were such a regular visitor because of your faux pas in asking Edith to dance, and then you kept going back purely out of pity for her, out of sympathy. You've no idea how the old man has sometimes been exploited, and I had made up my mind (why shouldn't I tell you?) to find out what really draws you to that house. I was thinking—either this is a fellow—how can I put it politely?—a fellow with ulterior motives for trying to fleece the old man, or else he must have the feelings of a very young man, because only the very young are so strangely attracted to tragedy and danger. That instinct of theirs, by the way, nearly always does them credit, and your feelings didn't deceive you—Kekesfalva really is an unusual man. I know exactly what can be said against him, and all that struck me as rather funny—do please forgive me—was to hear you describe him as a nobleman. But you may believe me—I know him better than anyone else around here—there is nothing for you to be ashamed of in showing such friendship to him and his poor child. Whatever you may yet hear, don't let it mislead you; it bears no relation to the touching and remarkable character that Kekesfalva is today."

As he walked on, Condor said this without looking at me. It was some time before he slowed down. I felt that he was thinking something over, and I did not want to disturb him. We walked on side by side in total silence for four or five minutes; a cart came towards us, and we had to step aside. The rustic driver stared curiously at the strange couple we made, a lieutenant beside a small, stout gentleman in pince-nez, the two of them walking together along the road in silence so late at night. We let the cart go past, and then Condor suddenly turned to me.

"Listen, Lieutenant Hofmiller. Matters half finished and hints half dropped are never a good idea. All the evil in the world comes from doing things by halves. Perhaps I've let slip too much already, and I wouldn't like to offend you when your attitude is so generous. But I've also made you too curious not to ask other people about what I have just said, and I am afraid I can't help fearing that you will not get very accurate information. After all, it's impossible to keep visiting a house without really knowing what the people who live in it are like—and if you heard such rumours you probably couldn't visit them in future in your former easy way. So if it would really interest you to know a little more about our friend, Lieutenant, then I am entirely at your service."

"Yes, of course I'd like that."

Condor took out his watch. "A quarter to eleven. That gives us two good hours. My train doesn't leave until twenty-past one. But I don't think that such stories can be told out in the road. Perhaps you know a quiet place somewhere, a place where we could talk in peace."

I thought about it. "I'd suggest the Tyrolean Wine Bar in Erzherzog Friedrichstrasse. It has little private boxes, like the boxes in a theatre, where we wouldn't be disturbed."

"Excellent! That sounds just right," he replied, and he quickened his pace again.

Without another word, we walked all the way down the road into town. Soon the first houses were lining our route in the bright moonlight, and fortunately we met none of my comrades in the already deserted streets. I don't know why, but I would have felt awkward to be asked next day who my companion had been. Ever since becoming so strangely entangled with the Kekesfalva family, I had been anxiously hiding any thread in the tangle that might lead others to the labyrinth which, I felt, was enticing me into new and ever more mysterious depths.

The Tyrolean Wine Bar was a comfortable little tavern with a slightly raffish air about it. Standing in a rather secluded position in a crooked, old-fashioned alley, it was really part of a second- or third-rate inn, an establishment that was particularly popular in our military circles because of the understanding way the clerk at the reception desk would diligently forget to ask guests who wanted a room with a double bed—sometimes in the middle of the day—to fill in the registration form required by police regulations. Further assurance of privacy for those indulging in trysts of long or short duration was the convenient fact that, to reach those love nests, you didn't have to draw attention to yourself by coming through the main entrance (for there are a thousand eyes on the watch in any small town), but could make your way at your leisure straight from the bar to the stairs, and thus reach your discreet destination. While the inn itself might be a place of dubious repute, there was no fault to be found with the good Terlaner and Muscatel wines served in the bar downstairs. The townsfolk sat comfortably here every evening at the heavy wooden tables, which were graced by no tablecloths, earnestly or casually discussing the usual kind of local and world affairs over several jugs of wine. Around the rectangular common room of the bar itself, usually frequented by the humbler sort of topers who were only after the wine and each other's down-to-earth company, there was a gallery a step higher up consisting of 'boxes', separated from each other by thick, soundproof wooden partitions which were also, unnecessarily, adorned with pokerwork and drinking mottoes. Thick curtains cut the eight boxes off from the room in the middle, so that each could almost claim to be a *chambre séparée*, and to some extent served the same purpose. If the officers or gentlemen volunteers serving a year in the garrison wanted to amuse themselves, undisturbed, with a couple of girls from Vienna, they would reserve one of these boxes, and rumour had it that our colonel, usually a strict disciplinarian, had expressly approved this sensible measure because it kept civilians from seeing too much of his young men's moments of off-duty relaxation. Discretion also reigned in the internal arrangements of the inn. On express orders from the proprietor, a man called Ferleitner, the waitresses in their Tyrolean costume were strictly forbidden ever to raise the sacred curtains over the boxes without clearing their throats loudly first, or to disturb the military gentlemen in any other way unless they were summoned by a bell, so that the dignity of the army and its pleasures were both preserved.

In the annals of the Tyrolean Wine Bar, one of these boxes cannot often have been booked purely so that its occupants could talk undisturbed. But I would have found it embarrassing to be disturbed as I listened to Dr Condor's promised revelations by the greetings of any of my comrades who came in, or their curious glances, or by having to get to my feet and salute smartly on the appearance of a superior officer. Even the prospect of walking through the common room of the bar with Condor made me feel uncomfortable—what jokes would there be tomorrow if I was seen seeking privacy with this stout stranger?—but I was relieved to see, on entering the place, that the boxes were deserted, not surprising when the end of the month is near in a small garrison town like ours, and the officers are eking out their pay. No one from the regiment was there, and we had our choice of any of the boxes.

Obviously to avoid any further intrusion by the waitress, Condor immediately ordered two litres of white wine, paid for them at once, and gave the girl such a generous tip that she disappeared with a grateful, "Your good health, sir!" The curtain was drawn down, and after that all we could hear, and then only very indistinctly, was a few loud words or a laugh from the tables in the middle of the room. We were secure in our cell, and could not be overheard.

Condor poured wine into the tall glasses, first for me and then for himself. A certain deliberation in his movements told me that he was working out in advance what to tell me, and perhaps what not to tell me as well. When he turned to me, however, the drowsy, ponderous manner that had previously irked me was entirely gone, and there was a look of concentration in his eyes.

"Well, we'd better begin at the beginning, and we can leave the aristocratic Herr Lajos von Kekesfalva right out of it at this point, for that gentleman didn't even exist yet. There was no owner of a large estate in a black coat and gold-rimmed glasses, no nobleman or business magnate. There was only a narrow-chested, sharp-eyed little Jewish boy in a poverty-stricken village on the border between Hungary and Slovakia. His name was Leopold Kanitz, but I believe he was generally known as Lämmel Kanitz."

I must have given a start of surprise, or shown astonishment in some other way. I thought I was prepared for anything—but not this. However, Condor went on, matter-of-fact and smiling.

"Yes, Kanitz, Leopold Kanitz, I can't help that. It was only much later that, at the request of a government minister, the name was so sonorously made to sound Magyar and provided with the noble particle *von*. You may not have remembered that after living here for a long time, a man with influence and good connections can get himself a new identity, have his name Magyarised, and sometimes even have the noble *von* added into the bargain. After all, you're a young man, there's no reason why you should know what a great deal of water has flowed along the River Lajtha since the time when that sharp-eyed, clever little Jewish lad was holding horses for the local farmers, or guarding their carts while they drank in the tavern, or carrying baskets home for market women in return for a handful of potatoes.

"So Kekesfalva's father, or I should say Kanitz's father, was no magnate but an indigent Jew with long ringlets at his temples, the tenant landlord of a roadside tavern selling spirits just outside the little place. The woodcutters and carters would stop there to fortify themselves with a glass—or several—of strong schnapps before or after braving the frosts of the Carpathians. Sometimes the liquid fire went to their heads too quickly, and then they would smash chairs and glasses. It was in one such fight that Kanitz's father got the blow that killed him. A few farmers coming home from market dead drunk started a brawl, and when the landlord tried to separate them, in defence of his sparse furnishings, a giant of a man flung him into a corner so hard that he lay there groaning. After that he kept spitting blood, and a year later he died in hospital. He left no money, and the boy's mother, a capable woman, provided for herself and her small children by working as a washerwoman and midwife. She also went from door to door as a hawker, and Leopold carried her packs on his back. In addition he scraped a few kreuzers together by any means he could; he helped the shopkeeper as an errand boy, he carried messages from village to village. At an age when other children are still playing happily with their marbles, he knew the price of everything, where and how to buy and sell, how to make himself first useful and then indispensable. He also found time to get some education. The rabbi taught him to read and write, and he grasped the principles so quickly that at thirteen he could already act as clerk to an advocate, and for a few kreuzers he would do accounts and make out tax returns for the local grocers. To save on lamplight— every drop of oil was a great expense in that poverty-stricken household—he would sit by the light in the signal box—the village had no railway station of its own—studying the torn newspapers that other people had thrown away. The community elders were already nodding their heads approvingly and prophesying that the lad would do well for himself.

"How exactly it was that he left the Slovakian village and came to Vienna I don't know. But when he turned up in these parts at the age of twenty he was already agent for a well-regarded insurance company, and his tireless industry allowed him to do many little business deals in addition to his official job. He became what they call a 'factor' in Galicia, someone who deals in everything, acts as a go-between, and builds bridges between supply and demand.

"At first he was merely tolerated. But soon people began to notice him, even to need his services. He knew about everything, he knew the way of the world in general. If there was a widow who wanted to get her daughter married, he would instantly set up shop as a marriage broker; if there was a man planning to emigrate to America who needed information and papers, Leopold would get them for him. He also dealt in old clothes, watches and clocks, and antiques; he gave estimates of the value of land, goods and horses and saw the subsequent deals through, and if an officer needed someone to stand surety for him, Kanitz would fix it. His knowledge and his sphere of influence expanded in parallel to each other year after year.

"With such tireless and persistent energy you can earn good money, but real fortunes are made only when there is a particular connection between income and expenditure, takings and outgoings. This was the other secret in the rise of our friend Kanitz—in all those years he spent almost nothing, apart from supporting a whole series of relations and helping his brother to study. The sole major purchase he had made for himself was a black coat and that pair of gold-rimmed glasses you know, which won him a reputation as a scholar among the local rustics. But long after he had become prosperous, he was still modestly describing himself as just an agent, to be on the safe side. Agent is a wonderful word, and can cover any number of contingencies. What Kekesfalva hid behind it was the fact that he had long ago ceased to be a mere go-between; he had now become a financier and entrepreneur. It seemed to him far more fitting and important to be rich than to be considered rich (as if he had read Schopenhauer's *Parerga and Paralipomena*, with its wise remarks on what we are and what we make ourselves out to be).

"In my view, however, it takes no special philosophical approach to work out that a man who is not only industrious but also clever and thrifty will sooner or later make money, nor is that cause for wonder and admiration. We doctors know that at crucial moments a man's bank account is not much use to him. What has really impressed me about our friend Kanitz is his positively daemonic determination at that time to increase his knowledge at the same time as his fortune. All those nights spent on railway journeys, every free moment in a carriage, in the inns where he stayed, on the road, he was reading and studying. He taught himself all the legal textbooks of commercial law and trade law, so that he could be his own lawyer; he followed the auctions in London and Paris like a professional antique dealer, and was as well versed in all financial investments and transactions as a banker. So it naturally turned out that his businesses gradually assumed a grander style. From working for small tenant farmers he moved on to leaseholders, from leaseholders to the great aristocratic estate owners; soon he was arranging the sale of entire harvests and forests, he was supplying factories, founding consortiums, and finally he was also commissioned to deliver certain supplies to the army. And now his black coat and gold-rimmed glasses were often to be seen in the waiting rooms of government ministries. But still—and at that time he already owned property worth perhaps a quarter of a million or half a million crowns—people here thought Kanitz a mere unimportant agent, and went on greeting him in a very offhand way in the street—until he pulled off his great coup, and all of a sudden Lämmel Kanitz became Herr von Kekesfalva."

At this point Condor interrupted himself. "Well, what I've told you so far is known to me only at second hand. This last story, however, I have from Kekesfalva himself. He told it to me on the night of his wife's operation, when we were sitting in a room in the sanatorium from ten in the evening until dawn, waiting for news. From here on I can vouch for every word. At such moments, no one tells lies."

Condor slowly and thoughtfully took a small sip of wine before lighting another cigar—I think his fourth that evening, and I took note of his constant smoking. I was beginning to understand that the deliberately stolid, jovial manner he assumed as a medical man, along with his slow speech and apparently casual attitude, were a special technique allowing him to think and perhaps to observe at his leisure. Three or four times he put the cigar to his full lips, drawing on it slowly, while he watched the smoke rise with almost dreamy fascination. Then he suddenly gave himself a brisk shake.

"The story of how Leopold or Lämmel Kanitz became Herr von Kekesfalva and master of a landed estate begins in a passenger train from Budapest to Vienna. Although by now he was forty-two years old, and there were strands of grey in his hair, our friend still spent most of his nights travelling—the thrifty like to save time as well as money—and I don't suppose I have to point out that he always went third class. He was an old hand at travelling by night, and had long ago worked out a technique for it. First he would spread a Scottish tartan rug that he had once picked up cheap at an auction over the hard wooden seat, then he carefully hung up his inevitable black coat on the hook provided, to spare it wear and tear, put his gold-framed glasses away in their case, took a soft old dressing gown out of his canvas travelling bag—he never went to the expense

of buying a leather suitcase—and finally crammed his cap well
down over his forehead to keep the light out of his eyes. Then
he would settle back into the corner of the compartment, used
as he was to falling asleep where he sat, for little Leopold had
learnt as a child that you can spend the night asleep without
the comfort of a bed.

"This time, however, our friend did not drop off to sleep,
because there were three other men in the compartment, discussing the business they had been doing. And when people
talked business, Kanitz couldn't help pricking up his ears. His
avid desire to learn had persisted through the years, like his
wish to make money. They were bound together as if by an
iron screw, like the two parts of a pair of pincers.

"In fact he had been very close to dozing off, but the phrase
that roused him, like a warhorse hearing the trumpet sound,
was a number. 'Guess what, the lucky bastard made sixty thousand crowns at one fell swoop, and through his own ridiculous
folly too!'

"What sixty thousand crowns? Whose sixty thousand crowns?
Kanitz was wide awake at once, as if icy water had been dashed
in his face to rouse him from sleep. Who had made sixty thousand crowns, and how did he do it? Kanitz had to find out. Of
course he took care not to let his three fellow travellers notice
that he was listening. In fact he pulled his cap a little further
down on his face, so that his eyes were entirely hidden in its
shadow, and the others would think him asleep. At the same
time he cunningly used every jolt of the railway carriage to
move slightly closer to them, so as not to miss hearing a single
word in the noisy rattle of the wheels.

"The young man speaking with such animation, the man
whose indignant trumpet call had alerted Kanitz, turned out to

be a clerk in a Viennese lawyer's chambers, and his amazement at his employer's huge stroke of luck lent him eloquence.

"'And he'd made the most shocking mess of the whole business! He arrived in Budapest a day late on account of a piddling little case that earned him maybe fifty crowns, and by the time he did get there the silly goose had been well and truly taken in. It was all going without a hitch—watertight will, trustworthy Swiss witnesses, two impeccable medical opinions stating that Princess Orosvár was in full possession of her wits at the time of signing it. The whole darn bunch of great-nephews and pseudo-relations by marriage wouldn't have inherited a penny, in spite of the scandalous insinuations their lawyer managed to get into the evening papers, and my bone-headed boss was so sure of himself that because the hearing wasn't until Friday, back he goes to Vienna to see his silly little case through, thinking no harm. But while he was gone, that wily scoundrel Wiezner, lawyer for the other side, gets at her, pays her a friendly visit, and the idiotic woman goes into hysterics—*Oh, but I don't want such a terrible lot of money as all that, I only want to be left in peace!*' He mimicked a woman's voice speaking with some kind of north German accent. 'Well, she's left in peace now and no mistake, and the rest of 'em are left, entirely unnecessarily, in possession of three-quarters of her inheritance. Without waiting for my boss to arrive, the idiot woman signs a settlement, the most ridiculous settlement you ever set eyes on. That one stroke of the pen cost her a cool half million.'

"And now, Lieutenant Hofmiller, pay attention," Condor continued, turning to me. "All the time this oration was in progress our friend Kanitz was curled up like a hedgehog in the corner, saying nothing, cap well down over his eyebrows, drinking in every word. He realised right away what it was all about, because at the time the Orosvár trial—I've changed the family's name, the real one is too well known—that trial was making the headlines in all the Hungarian newspapers, and it was really an amazing business; I'll give you just a brief summary.

"Old Princess Orosvár, stinking rich even before she arrived from the Ukraine, tough as old boots and evil-minded as they come, had survived her husband by a good thirty-five years … Ever since her two children, the only ones she had, died of diphtheria on the same night she had heartily hated all the other Orosvárs for being alive while her children were dead. It seems to me perfectly possible that she lived to the age of eighty-four purely out of spite and malice, to keep her impatient nephews and great-nieces from inheriting her fortune. When one of her would-be heirs tried to visit, she refused to see him; even the friendliest letter went straight into the wastepaper basket unanswered. Misanthropic and cranky as she was after the death of her husband and children, she never spent more than two or three months a year at Kekesfalva, and no one came to see her there. The rest of the time she travelled around the world, living the high life in Nice and Montreux, where she got dressed and undressed, had her hair done, had her nails manicured and her face painted, read French novels, bought a great many clothes, and went from shop to shop bargaining and haggling like a Russian market woman. Of course the one person she would tolerate near her, her companion, didn't have an easy time. The poor soft-spoken woman had to feed and groom three bad-tempered pinschers and take them for walks every day, she had to play the piano to the old Princess, read aloud to her, and put up with savage scolding for no reason at all. There were times when the old lady drank a few glasses of cognac or vodka too many, a habit she had brought from the

Ukraine with her, and it's credibly reported that then she actually used to beat the unfortunate companion. The massive figure of the old Princess with her heavily painted pug face and her dyed hair was a familiar sight in all the luxury resorts, in Nice and Cannes, in Aix les Bains and Montreux. She was always talking at the top of her voice, never mind whether anyone was listening to her, she would abuse waiters like a fishwife, and she made faces at anyone she didn't like. And wherever she went on her terrifying promenades, the companion followed her like a shadow—always walking behind her with the dogs, never beside her. She was a slim, pale, blonde woman with frightened eyes, and you could see she was constantly ashamed of her mistress's overbearing ways, while at the same time fearing her like the Devil incarnate.

"At the age of seventy-eight, staying at the hotel in Territet that also enjoyed the custom of Empress Elisabeth, Princess Orosvár suffered a bad attack of pneumonia. How the news travelled from Switzerland back to Hungary remains a mystery. But without any mutual consultation the old lady's relations came swarming in, booked out the hotel, pestered the Princess's doctor for news, and waited and waited for her to die.

"However, bad temper kept her going. The old dragon recovered, and on the day when they heard that the convalescent was coming downstairs to the hotel foyer for the first time, the impatient relations moved out. All the same, Princess Orosvár had heard about the arrival of her ostentatiously anxious heirs. Spiteful as she was, she began by bribing waiters and chambermaids to tell her everything her relations said. It was all true. The would-be heirs had fought furiously with each other over who should get Kekesfalva, who should inherit Orosvár, who was to have the pearls, who the Ukrainian estates and the grand town house in Ofnerstrasse. That was the first shot fired in the battle. A month later she received a letter from a Budapest broker by the name of Dessauer, saying that he could not extend the term of his loan to her nephew Deszö unless he, Dessauer, had her written assurance that the aforesaid nephew would be one of her heirs. Princess Orosvár sent by telegraph for her own lawyer from Budapest, drew up a new will with him, and did it—for spite can open your eyes—in the presence of two doctors who explicitly certified that the Princess was in full possession of her intellectual faculties. The lawyer took this will back to Budapest with him, and it stayed sealed in his chambers for six years, because the old lady was in no hurry to die. When it was finally opened it came as a great surprise. It named as sole heiress the companion, one Fräulein Annette Beate Dietzenhof from Westphalia, whose name thus struck terror for the first time into all the old woman's relations. She was to get Kekesfalva, Orosvár, the sugar factory, the stud farm, and the town house in Budapest. The old Princess left her Ukrainian estates and her cash there to her home town in the Ukraine, to pay for the building of a Russian church. None of her relations was to inherit so much as a button, as she explicitly and maliciously stated in the will, on the grounds that 'they couldn't wait for me to die'.

"So now there was a full-blown scandal. The family raised hell, flocked to their lawyers, and the lawyers made the usual appeals against the will. The Princess had not been in her right mind, they said, because she had made it while she was suffering from a severe illness, and as in addition she had been pathologically dependent on her companion there could be no doubt, said the lawyers, but that the latter, through cunning suggestion, had distorted the sick woman's true wishes. At the same time they tried to inflate the story into an affair of national importance. Were Hungarian estates that had been owned by the Orosvár family since the time of Árpád to fall into the hands of a foreigner, a Prussian woman, while what remained of the old lady's fortune went to the Orthodox Church? Column upon column of the newspapers was devoted to the subject. But in spite of all the fuss kicked up by those involved, the family had a weak case. They had already lost it on two points—first, it was their bad luck that both doctors were still living in Territet, and confirmed once again that the Princess had been fully responsible for her actions when she made her will. And second, other witnesses had to admit under cross-questioning that while the old Princess had been cranky in her last years, her mind had been as sharp and clear as ever. All legal tricks and attempts at intimidation failed; the chances were a hundred to one that the royal court of appeal would not overturn earlier decisions in favour of Fräulein Dietzenhof.

"Kanitz, of course, had read about the case himself, but he listened closely to every word, for he was passionately interested in the financial affairs of others as object lessons, and moreover he knew the Kekesfalva estate himself, from his days as an agent in those parts.

"'As you can imagine,' the clerk was telling his friends, 'my boss was left stewing in his own juice, furious with the stupid woman for being fooled like that. She'd already put it in writing that she gave up all claim to Orosvár and the town house in Ofnerstrasse, and was happy to be fobbed off with the Kekesfalva estate and the stud farm. That cunning fellow Wiezner had obviously impressed her mightily by promising that she'd have no more trouble with the courts now, and the old lady's natural heirs would even be generous enough to pay her own lawyer's costs.

Well, in law it would still have been possible to contest this set-tlement. After all, it had not been signed before a notary, only in front of witnesses, and that greedy gang the old woman's family could easily have been starved out. They didn't have a penny to their names to enable them to drag the whole thing out by more and more appeals to new authorities. Of course it was my boss's duty to tell them so and contest the agreement in the interests of the heiress. But the gang knew how to get around him—they offered him a fee of sixty thousand crowns, no questions asked, not to make any more trouble. And since he was so angry anyway with his stupid client, who had let herself be wheedled out of a fortune of a good round million in half-an-hour's talk, he declared the settlement valid and pocketed his cash—sixty thousand crowns, what do you say to that, for letting his client ruin her whole case by his own stupid decision to go to Vienna? Well, we all need luck, and it looks as if the good Lord sends even the greatest fool luck in his sleep! So now she has nothing left of that legacy of a million but Kekesfalva, and if I know her sort she'll soon make such a mess of things that she'll throw that away too!'

"'Do what with it?' asked one of the other men.

"'Throw it away, I bet you! She's sure to do something stupid! And anyway, I've heard that the sugar cartel would like to take the factory off her hands. I believe the chairman of the board is coming from Budapest to see her the day after tomorrow. And I understand there's a man called Petrovic would like to lease the estate—he used to manage it—but maybe the sugar cartel will take that over as well. They have plenty of money, there's talk of a French bank—didn't you read about it in the newspaper?—wanting to prepare the ground for a merger with Bohemian industries … '

"Here their conversation turned to general subjects. But our friend Kanitz had heard enough to set his ears burning. Few people knew Kekesfalva as well as he did; he had been there twenty years earlier to give an estimate of the house contents for insurance purposes. He also knew Petrovic, in fact he knew him very well from his early days doing business deals. Through his, Kanitz's, agency that apparently upright character had invested considerable sums of money—acquired by annually lining his own pockets from the management of the estate—in securities offered by one Dr Gollinger. Most important of all to Kanitz, however, was this—he remembered the cupboard of Chinese porcelain very clearly, along with a number of jade figurines and silk embroideries acquired by Princess Orosvár's grandfather, who had been Russian ambassador to Peking. As the only person aware of their immense value, Kanitz had tried, on behalf of Rosenfeld in Chicago, to buy them from the Princess in her lifetime. They were very rare objects, worth perhaps two or three thousand pounds each. Of course the old lady had no idea of the high prices that had been paid in America for East Asian art during the last few decades, and had sent Kanitz off with a flea in his ear, saying she wasn't letting anything out of her hands, and he could go to the devil. If those pieces were still in the house—Kanitz trembled at the mere thought—he might be able to get them really cheap if the place was changing hands. It would be best, of course, to make sure he had the right of first refusal for the entire inventory of the house contents.

"Our friend Kanitz pretended to be suddenly waking up—his three fellow travellers had been talking about other subjects for some time now—yawned elaborately, stretched, and took out his watch. The train would be stopping here in this town, where you are stationed yourself, Lieutenant Hofmiller, in half-an-hour's time. He quickly folded up his dressing gown, put on his usual black coat, and tidied himself up. At two-thirty in the morning he got out of the train, went to the Red Lion, had himself shown to a room, and I don't have to point out that like every military commander before a battle where the outcome is uncertain he slept poorly. At seven o'clock—he didn't want to waste a moment—he got up and marched down the avenue along which we have just come to reach the little castle. I must get there first, he was thinking, I must get there before anyone else. I must deal with it all before the vultures from Budapest arrive! Now for some fast talking to get Petrovic to let me know at once if there's going to be a sale of the house contents. If necessary I'll join him in bidding for them all, and make sure I get the *objets d'art* when it comes to dividing them up between us.

"Few of the domestic staff had been kept on after the Princess's death, so Kanitz could easily steal up to the house and take a good look around. A handsome property, he said to himself, and in excellent condition too, the shutters freshly painted, the walls attractively colour-washed, a new fence—oh yes, Petrovic knows why he's had all these repairs done, thinks Kanitz, he pockets a good commission on every bill that comes in. But where, our friend wonders, is he? The front door at the porch of the house turns out to be locked, there's no one stirring in the yard where the estate management buildings stand, however hard he knocks—damn it, has the man already taken himself off to Budapest to settle everything with that fool of a Dietzenhof woman?

"Kanitz goes impatiently from door to door, calling out, clapping his hands—no one, not a soul. At last, cautiously looking in through the side door, he sets eyes on a woman in the conservatory. He can see her through the panes, watering flowers—at last, someone who can give him information. Kanitz taps sharply on the glass. "Hello," he calls, clapping his hands to attract attention. The female busy with the flowers starts in alarm, and it is some time before, as timidly as if she has done something wrong, she approaches the door. Blonde, slender, no longer young, wearing a plain dark blouse and a cotton apron, she is now framed in the doorway, still holding the half-open garden scissors.

"Rather impatiently, Kanitz snaps at her, 'You certainly take your time! Where the devil's Petrovic?'

"'Who?' asks the thin young woman with a surprised expression. She instinctively retreats a step, hiding the garden scissors behind her back.

"'Who? How many men called Petrovic are there around here? I mean Petrovic the estate manager!'

"'Oh, I'm sorry … Herr Petrovic the estate manager … well, I haven't seen him yet myself. I believe he's gone to Vienna … but his wife said she hopes he'll be back before evening.'

"Hopes, hopes … thinks Kanitz angrily. I'll have to wait until evening. Kick my heels in the hotel for another night. More unnecessary expense, and no idea what will come of it.

"'So stupid! Today of all days the man has to be out,' he mutters in an undertone, turning back to the woman. 'Can I look round the place in the meantime? Does someone have the keys?'

"'The keys?' she repeats blankly.

"'Yes, the keys, for God's sake!' (Why is she havering like this, he wonders. Probably been told by Petrovic not to let anyone in. Well—all I have to do is give this frightened woman a tip.) And Kanitz immediately adopts a jovial tone, speaking with a Viennese accent.

"'There now, not so scared, miss! I ain't about to rob you. I just fancy a little look around. So how about it … you got them keys or not?'

"'The keys … well, of course I have the keys,' she stammers. 'But … I don't know when Herr Petrovic the manager … '

"'Like I said, your friend Petrovic don't need to be with me. So no more fooling about, miss. Know your way around the house, do you?'

"The woman's awkwardness becomes even more obvious. 'I think … yes, I think I can say I know my way around it.'

"An idiot, thinks Kanitz. What useless domestic servants Petrovic's been hiring! He orders, in a loud voice, 'Let's get a move on, then. You think I got all day?'

"He goes ahead, and she actually follows him, meek and uneasy. At the front door she hesitates again.

"'For God's sweet sake, open that door!' Why does the woman act so stupid, he wonders, so awkward? As she takes the keys out of the thin, shabby leather bag she is carrying, he asks, to be on the safe side, 'What's your position in this house, eh?'

"Intimidated, the woman stops, and blood rises to her cheeks. 'I'm … ' she begins, and then corrects herself at once. 'I mean I used to be … I was the Princess's companion.'

"It is our friend Kanitz's turn to catch his breath (and I assure you it was hard to throw a man of his stamp off balance). He involuntarily takes a step back.

"'You're … you're never Fräulein Dietzenhof, are you?'

"'Yes,' she replies in alarm, as if she had been accused of some misdemeanour.

"If there was one thing to which Kanitz had been a stranger all his life, it was embarrassment. But in that one second he was horribly embarrassed, as he realised that he had run

160

headlong into the legendary Fräulein Dietzenhof, the heiress of Kekesfalva. He immediately changed his tune.

"'I'm so sorry,' he stammers, dismayed, and he is quick to take his hat off. 'I'm so sorry, my dear young lady … But no one told me you had arrived already … I had no idea … do please excuse me … I … I came only … '

"He stops short, because now he has to think up something plausible.

"'It was only about the insurance … you see, I was here several times years ago, when the late Princess was still alive. Unfortunately I never had a chance of meeting you then, dear lady … Yes, it was only about the insurance … just to see whether the house contents are still intact … It's our duty to check up on such things. But there's no great hurry.'

"'Oh, please, please … ' she says in alarm. 'I don't know anything about such matters. Perhaps you'd better discuss it with Herr Petrovic.'

"'Of course, of course,' says our friend Kanitz, who still hasn't quite recovered his presence of mind. 'Of course I'll wait to see Herr Petrovic.' (Why explain any more, he asks himself.) 'But maybe, if it's not too much trouble for you, dear lady, I could just take a quick look around the castle, and then it would all be dealt with in no time. I don't suppose anything much has changed in the furnishings and other contents.'

"'No, no,' she says hastily, 'nothing at all has changed. If you'd like to make sure of that for yourself … '

"'You're too kind, dear lady,' says Kanitz, bowing, and they both go into the house.

"His first glance in the salon is for the four Guardis, the Venetian scenes that you know yourself, and next door, in what is now Edith's boudoir, he checks the glass-fronted cupboard of

Chinese porcelain, the tapestries and the little jade figurines. What a relief! It's all still there. Petrovic hasn't stolen anything from indoors, the stupid fellow has confined himself to oats, clover and potatoes, and to seeing that his own domain is kept in repair. Meanwhile Fräulein Dietzenhof, obviously fearing to disturb the strange gentleman as he looks nervously around, throws open the closed shutters. Light floods in, and there is a view through the tall French windows far out in the park. I must get into conversation, thinks Kanitz, mustn't neglect her. Make friends with her, he tells himself.

"'A lovely view of the park,' he begins, taking a deep breath. 'What a wonderful place to live!'

"'Yes, lovely,' she obediently agrees, but something about the way she echoes him doesn't sound whole-hearted. Kanitz senses at once that, intimidated as she has been, she has forgotten how to disagree with anyone frankly, and only after a while does she add, by way of explanation, 'Of course the Princess never felt quite at her ease here. She was always saying the flat countryside made her melancholy. She really liked only the sea, and the mountains. It was too isolated for her here, and the people … '

"Here she catches herself up again. Go on, Kanitz reminds himself, talk to her, keep the conversation going.

"'But I hope you're going to stay with us now, dear lady?'

"'I—stay here?' She instinctively raises her hands as if to fend off something undesirable. 'Here? Oh no, no! What would I do in this big house all by myself? No, I'll be leaving just as soon as everything's been settled.'

"Kanitz gives her a cautious sidelong glance. How small and thin she looks standing in this large room, the unhappy owner of the whole place! She is rather too pale and too unsure of herself, or she could almost be described as pretty. That long, delicate face with its downcast eyelids is like a landscape seen in rain. Her eyes themselves are a soft cornflower blue, warm and gentle, but she dares not turn their radiance on anyone—instead they keep retreating behind their lids again. Kanitz, a good observer, immediately sees that here is someone whose will has been broken. She has no backbone any more, he can twist her around his little finger. So he must make conversation, talk to her! And with a frown of sympathy on his brow, he makes further enquiries.

"'But what will become of this handsome property? A place like this needs management, firm management!'

"'I don't know. I really don't know.' She speaks very nervously. Her whole frail body expresses uneasiness, and in that one moment Kanitz realises that this woman, used to dependency for years, will never have the courage to make an independent decision, and is more alarmed by her inheritance than glad of it. She feels the anxiety of it lying like a heavy burden on her slender shoulders. He thinks at lightning speed. Not for nothing has he learnt all about buying and selling in the last twenty years, urging a sale or alternatively showing reluctance. You have to encourage the buyer and discourage the seller, that's the way for an agent to proceed, and he immediately strikes the requisite note of discouragement. Make it seem onerous to her, he thinks, and in the end I'll be able to lease the estate from her in one swift operation and get in ahead of Petrovic. Perhaps it's lucky after all that the manager is in Vienna today. He immediately assumes a regretfully sympathetic manner.

"'Yes, you're quite right! A large property always means trouble. You never get any rest, you have to deal with the management and domestic staff on a daily basis, and then there are running battles with the neighbours, not to speak of taxes and the expense of lawyers! Whenever people feel there's a bit of property and money about, they'll try to cash in. You find you're surrounded by enemies, however little ill will you bear them. It just can't be helped, there's nothing for it—wherever there's a smell of money about then, sad to say, very sad to say, everyone proves to be a thief. You're quite right; a property like this has to be ruled with a rod of iron, or you'll never succeed. You have to be born to that kind of thing, and even so it's a ceaseless battle!'

"'Oh yes!' She sighs deeply, and he can see that she is remembering something that makes her shudder. 'People are dreadful, dreadful when it comes to money. I already knew that!'

"People? What does Kanitz care about people? Why should he care whether they act well or badly? He just wants to lease this estate as quickly as possible and on the most favourable possible terms. He listens to her, nods politely, and as he listens and nods he is working out, in another corner of his brain, how to fix it as fast as he can. I could found a consortium to take on the lease of Kekesfalva, the whole of it—the arable land, the sugar factory, the stud farm. Then it can be sublet to Petrovic for all I care, he thinks, so long as I can keep my hands on the house contents. First and foremost I must see about leasing the place at once—put the fear of God into her and she'll accept whatever she's offered. She's never earned money, she doesn't deserve to get much of it. While every nerve and fibre of his brain is working at top speed, his lips go on uttering apparently sympathetic commonplaces.

"'And the legal quarrels are the worst of it—however much you may like a quiet life, you find you can't avoid those eternal quarrels. That's what has always put me off buying any kind of property. Legal proceedings the whole time, lawyers, negotiations, court cases and scandals ... no, better to live quietly with a sense of security and none of all that trouble. You might think yourself well off with an estate like this, but really you're just plagued by other people the whole time, never a moment's real peace and quiet. In itself, of course, this castle is a wonderful place … such a fine old property, wonderful … but you'd need the strongest nerves and an iron fist to run it, or it will never be anything but a constant burden.'

"She is listening to him with her head bowed. Suddenly she looks up with a heavy, heartfelt sigh. 'Yes, a terrible burden … if only I could sell it!'"

At this point Dr Condor stopped suddenly. "Here I have to interrupt myself, Lieutenant, to explain what that brief sentence meant to our friend. I've already said that Kekesfalva told me this story on the worst night of his life, the night of his wife's death, and thus at one of those moments that come only two or three times in anyone's life—one of those moments when even the most cunning deceiver feels a need to reveal himself to another human being as he truly is, as he might before God. I can still see him as we sat downstairs in the sanatorium waiting room. He had moved close to me, and was talking quietly, intently, as a great flow of words poured out. I felt that he was telling this whole long tale to make himself forget that his wife was dying upstairs, he was numbing himself by talking on and on. But at this point in his narrative, when Fräulein Dietzenhof said, 'If only I could sell it!' he suddenly stopped. Think of it, Lieutenant— fifteen or sixteen years later, the memory of that moment when the unsuspecting young woman, almost an old maid already, confessed so impulsively that she just wanted to sell Kekesfalva quickly, as quickly as possible, moved him so strangely that he turned quite pale. He repeated it two or three times, probably with exactly her own intonation: 'If only I could sell it!' For the Leopold Kanitz of that time had seen at once, with his quick perception, that the deal of his life was falling into his hands, and he had only to hold on to it. He could buy this fine estate himself, not just lease it. And as he hid his inner turmoil under a show of unruffled conversation, ideas were chasing each other headlong through his mind. I must buy it, of course, he thought, before Petrovic intervenes, or the chairman of the sugar factory board from Budapest. I mustn't let go of her, I must make sure she can't go back on her word. I'm not leaving here until I am master of Kekesfalva. And at the same time, with that mysterious ability to pursue two trains of thought at once that is often given to us at moments of great tension, he was thinking one thing to himself and purely *for* himself, while at the same time telling her the opposite in tones of calculated, slow deliberation.

'"Sell it … yes, of course, dear lady, one can always sell anything, everything. Selling is easy, but the trick of the thing is to sell *well*. It all depends on selling on good terms. You'd need to find an honest purchaser, someone who knows this countryside, knows the land and the people … someone with connections, certainly not one of those lawyers who'd want to drag you unnecessarily into court cases … and then, an important consideration in this particular case, you should sell for cash down. You'd need to find someone who wouldn't tie up the purchase price in bonds and promissory notes, because then you'd be at odds with your buyer for years to come … no, you want to sell on secure terms and at the right price.' At the same time he was doing calculations in his head—I can go up to four hundred thousand crowns, or four hundred and fifty thousand at the most. After all, there are those pictures, they'll be worth fifty thousand, maybe even a hundred thousand in themselves. There's the house, the stud farm ... I'd have to see if they're encumbered in any way, and find out whether anyone else has already made her an offer ... Suddenly he pulled himself together and forged ahead.

"'Do you, dear lady—forgive me for asking an indiscreet question—do you have a rough idea of the price you should ask? I mean, are you thinking of a certain sum?'

"'No,' she replied, at a loss, looking at him with dismay in her eyes.

"Damn! Not good, thought Kanitz, not good at all! Negotiating with sellers who don't name a price is always more difficult. They go hither and thither asking for advice, and everyone they ask makes an assessment and gets his word in. If I give her time to ask other people's opinions I'm lost. But even as this inner turmoil shook him, his lips talked tirelessly on.

"'However, you must surely have come to *some* conclusion of what you would ask, dear lady ... after all, buyers would also want to know whether the property is encumbered, and if so to what amount. Encumbered by any mortgages, I mean.'

"'Mort ... mortgages?' she repeated. Kanitz realised at once that this was the first time in her life she had heard the word.

"'I mean, some rough assessment of the estate's value must have been made ... if only for the purposes of inheritance tax. Didn't your lawyer—forgive me if I seem to be intruding, but I really would like to be able to advise you honestly—didn't your lawyer mention any figure?'

"'My lawyer?' She seemed to be dredging up a sombre memory of something. 'Yes, yes, wait a minute ... yes, the lawyer did write to me. It was something about an estimate ... yes, you're right, because of taxes, but … but it was all in Hungarian, and I don't know Hungarian. That's right, I remember now, my lawyer wrote to say I ought to get it translated, and—oh, my God!—in all the turmoil I quite forgot. I must have put all the documents in my bag over there … I mean in the management building, that's where I'm staying. I couldn't sleep in the room that used to belong to the Princess … But if you would really be kind enough to go over there with me, I'll show you all the papers … that is … '—and here she suddenly stopped short— 'that is if I'm not troubling you too much with my affairs … '

"Kanitz was trembling with excitement. All this was going his way at dreamlike speed—she herself wanted to show him the files, the estimates, and that would finally give him the upper hand. He bowed respectfully.

"'But my dear Fräulein Dietzenhof, it would be a pleasure for me to advise you. And I may claim, without exaggeration, to have some experience in these matters. The late Princess,' he added, lying outrageously, 'always turned to me when she needed financial information. She knew that my sole interest was to advise her to the best of my ability …'

"They went over to the administration buildings. Sure enough, all the papers to do with the inheritance had been stuffed into a briefcase, all the correspondence with her lawyer, the documents about inheritance tax, a copy of the agreement she had signed with the other heirs. She nervously leafed through these documents, and Kanitz, breathing heavily as he watched, found his own hands trembling. At last she unfolded a sheet of paper.

"'I think this must be the letter.'

"Kanitz took the sheet of paper, which had an enclosure in Hungarian clipped to it. It was a short note from the Viennese lawyer. 'As my Hungarian colleague has just informed me, his

connections have enabled him to get a particularly low estimate of the late Princess's estate, with a view to inheritance tax. In my opinion this estimated value corresponds to about one third and in the case of many items even only a quarter of the real value.'
His hands trembling, Kanitz picked up the list of estimates. Only one part of it interested him—the Kekesfalva property. It was estimated at one hundred and ninety thousand crowns.

"Kanitz turned pale. The sum, he worked out, tallied with his own calculations—Kekesfalva would be worth exactly three times this artificially low estimate. The real value, then, would be six hundred thousand to seven hundred thousand crowns—and the lawyer didn't even know about the Chinese porcelain. How much was he going to offer her now? The figures danced and blurred before his eyes.

"But the voice beside him asked, very anxiously, 'Is this the right paper? Can you understand what it says?'

"'Of course,' said Kanitz, pulling himself together. 'Yes, indeed. Well … the lawyer has written telling you that the estimate for Kekesfalva is a hundred and ninety thousand crowns. Of course, that is only the estimated value.'

"'Estimated value? Forgive me … but what does estimated value mean?'

"And now for some quick sleight of hand, now or never! Kanitz forced himself to breathe calmly. 'The estimated value … well, the estimated value is always an uncertain, a very dubious figure, because … because the official estimate never corresponds entirely to the real sale value. You can never be sure … I mean, you can never rely *for certain* on receiving the full estimated value … in some cases of course you may get it, in some even more, but only in certain circumstances … this kind of procedure, selling to the highest bidder, is always something of a game of chance. The estimated value, after all, is nothing but a kind of reference point, and of course a very vague one. For instance … we could assume—' Kanitz was trembling, he mustn't say too little or too much now!—'we could assume that if an item like this is officially valued at a hundred and ninety thousand crowns … then we can assume that … that … that in a sale at auction you could expect to get at least a hundred and fifty thousand, yes, at least that! You could count on getting that in any event.'

"'How much, did you say?'

"The blood was suddenly throbbing and droning in Kanitz's ears. She had turned to him with a surprisingly decided air, asking her question like someone controlling anger only with difficulty. Had she seen through his mendacious game? Shouldn't I raise the sum quickly, he wondered, raise it by another fifty thousand? But a voice inside him was saying—go on, try it! And he staked everything on a single card. Although his pulse was beating like a drum in his temples, he said, in a down-to-earth manner, 'Yes, I'd expect it to make that amount at least. I think you could definitely expect to get a hundred and fifty thousand crowns.'

"But at that moment his heart missed a beat, and his still drumming pulse briefly failed him entirely. For the unsuspecting woman beside him said, in genuine amazement, 'As much as *that*? Do you really think it would make as much as *that*?'

"It took Kanitz some time to recover his composure. He had to force himself to breathe regularly before he could reply, in a tone of matter-of-fact conviction, 'Yes, dear lady, I can as good as vouch for it that you would at least get *that* sum.'"

Dr Condor interrupted himself again. At first I thought he was stopping only to light a cigar. But I realised that he was suddenly nervous. He took off his pince-nez, put them on again, stroked back his sparse hair as if it were in his way, and looked at me. It was a long, restless, enquiring look. Then he leant abruptly back in his chair.

"Lieutenant Hofmiller, perhaps I have already confided too much to you—more, anyway, than I originally meant to say. But I hope you won't misunderstand me. If I have told you frankly the story of the trick that Kekesfalva used to hoodwink that wholly unsuspecting young woman at the time, it was not to set you against him. The poor old man at whose table we dined this evening, sick at heart and distraught as we saw him, the man who has entrusted his child to my care and would give the last penny of his fortune to know that the poor girl could be cured, is no longer the man who thought up that shady stratagem, and it's a long time since he was. Now of all times, when he really needs help in his desperation, it seems to me important for you to hear the truth from me, and not from the malicious gossip of others. Please remember one thing, then—Kekesfalva, or rather still Kanitz at the time, had *not* gone to the Kekesfalva property that day intending to cheat the unworldly Fräulein Dietzenhof into letting him have the estate at a knock-down price. He simply meant to do one of his little deals on the side, no more. The extraordinary chance that came his way took him by *surprise*, and he wouldn't have been the man he then was if he hadn't exploited it to the full. But as you will see, it didn't turn out quite like that.

"I don't want to go into it at too much length, I'd rather summarise the details. But I will tell you this—those hours were to be the most moving and disturbing of his life. Think about it—here's a man who has been only an ordinary sort of agent so far, an obscure fixer of this and that, and suddenly the chance of becoming rich overnight drops into his lap like a meteor falling from the sky. He could earn more within the next twenty-four hours than he had earned in twenty-four years of petty bargaining, devoting himself entirely to his work—and there was another, extraordinary temptation too. He didn't have to pursue, confine or drug his victim to make her go to her fate—on the contrary, the sacrifice went willingly to the slaughter, actually licked the hand already holding the knife. The one danger was that someone else might step in to stop him. So he couldn't let the heiress out of his power for a moment, couldn't give her time to think. He had to get her away from Kekesfalva before Petrovic the manager came back, and while he was taking all these precautions he must not for a moment let her know that he himself had an interest in buying the estate.

"His plan to take the besieged fortress of Kekesfalva by storm before the relieving forces arrived was audacious—and risky—on a Napoleonic scale. But fortune favours the bold, in this case a bold gambler. A circumstance of which Kanitz was entirely unaware had secretly smoothed the path ahead of him, the very cruel yet natural circumstance that the unfortunate heiress had already, during her first hours in the castle she had inherited, encountered so much humiliation and hostility that all she wanted was to get away from it as fast as she could! Mean-minded natures never show themselves more resentful than when they see someone raised, as if on angel's wings, above their own dreary station in life. The servile will forgive a prince the most extravagant display of wealth sooner than tolerate the slightest presumption from someone of their own background. The domestic staff at Kekesfalva could not suppress their wrath

172

now that this north German woman—at whom, as they very well remembered, the irate Princess would often throw her brush and comb while she was doing the old lady's hair—was suddenly to become the owner of the Kekesfalva estate and thus their mistress. When news of the heiress's imminent arrival came, Petrovic boarded the train to Vienna so as to avoid welcoming her to the house. His wife, a vulgar woman who had once been a kitchen maid in the castle, greeted her with the words, 'Well, I reckon you won't want to be mingling with the likes of us, we won't be fine enough for you.' The manservant had slammed her suitcase down on the ground outside the door, leaving her to drag it indoors herself, while the steward's wife didn't lift a finger to help her. No refreshments had been prepared for her, no one took any notice of her, and at night she could hear from her window clearly audible conversations about a certain fortune-hunter who was nothing but a fraud.

"The unfortunate weak-willed heiress could tell from this reception that she would never have a moment's peace here. That was her sole reason, although Kanitz did not know it, for agreeing with alacrity when he suggested setting out that very day for Vienna, where he said he knew someone who was sure to buy the property. This grave, helpful and knowledgeable man with his melancholy eyes seemed to her like a messenger sent from heaven, and she asked no more questions. She gratefully gave him all the documents, listening with her calm blue gaze as he advised her on the investment of the proceeds of the sale. She must put it only into something absolutely safe, he said, such as gilt-edged bonds, government securities. And she must not entrust the slightest part of her fortune to any private person, it must all go into the bank, and a qualified notary should be appointed to manage it. There was no point whatsoever in dragging her lawyer into it now—what was legal business all about, if not making something straightforward look complicated? Of course, he kept earnestly interjecting, of course it was possible that she might get a higher price in three years' time, or five years' time. But think of all the expense incurred in the interim, and the law courts and the civil servants! And seeing once again, from the fear that came back into her eyes, how terrified this peace-loving woman was of courts of law and official business, he repeated the burden of his song over and over again, always winding it up with the final chord that said—quickly, get it done quickly! At four in the afternoon, when Petrovic came back, they were already in perfect agreement and on the express train to Vienna. All this had happened at such lightning speed that Fräulein Dietzenhof hadn't even had an opportunity to ask the name of the strange gentleman to whom she was entrusting the sale of her entire inheritance.

"They travelled first-class—it was the first time that Kekesfalva had ever sat on the red velvet upholstery of a first-class carriage—and in the same way, when they reached Vienna he booked her into a good hotel in Kärntnerstrasse, and took a room there himself. Now two things were incumbent on Kanitz—first, he had to get his usual accomplice in sharp practice, Dr Gollinger the lawyer, to draw up a bill of sale that very evening, so that his great coup could be given legally watertight form next day, but secondly, he dared not leave his victim alone for a minute either. So he resorted to what, in all honesty, I have to admit was a stroke of genius. He suggested that Fräulein Dietzenhof might like to spend her free evening at the Opera House, where a touring company was performing that evening in a production that had attracted a lot of attention, while he tried to get hold of the gentleman who, he knew, was looking for a large country estate. Touched by such thoughtfulness, Fräulein Dietzenhof happily agreed; he left her safely at the Opera House, where she would be occupied for the next four hours, and Kanitz himself took a horse-drawn cab—again, the first time in his life that he had hired one of those expensive vehicles—and hurried off to see his disreputable friend Dr Gollinger. However, Gollinger was not at home. Kanitz ran him to earth in a wine bar, promised him two thousand crowns if he would draw up the sales contract complete with all details that night, take the deed of sale to a notary and arrange for him to come at seven on the evening of the next day.

"Throwing money about for the first time in his life, Kanitz had kept the horse-drawn cab waiting outside the lawyer's house during his negotiations, and having given Gollinger his instructions, he now raced back to the Opera House as fast as the cab could go. He was lucky, and arrived just in time to meet Fräulein Dietzenhof, in transports of delight, in the foyer and escort her back to the hotel. Now he began a second sleepless night. The closer he came to getting what he wanted, the more nervously he feared that the deal, successfully as it had gone so far, might yet fall through. He got out of bed again and again to work out his tactics for the next day. He must hire another horse-drawn cab, keep it waiting everywhere, not let her go a step on foot just in case, by chance, she met her lawyer in the street. He must make sure she didn't read a newspaper—there might be something in it about the settlement of the Orosvár case, and then she might suspect that she was being cheated for the second time. In reality, however, all these fears and precautions proved superfluous, for the victim did not *want* to get away. She ran obediently after the bad shepherd like a lamb on a pink ribbon, and when our friend came down to the breakfast room of the hotel, worn out after a terrible night, there she was in the same dress—a dress she had made for herself—patiently waiting for him. And now began a strange merry-go-round, while our friend entirely unnecessarily dragged poor Fräulein Dietzenhof around in circles from morning to evening, warning her of all the imaginary problems that he had laboriously worked out during his sleepless night.

"I won't go into detail, but he dragged her to his lawyer's chambers, where he did a great deal of telephoning about other matters. Then he took her to a bank and asked for the manager, to get advice on the way she should invest the money from the sale, and opened an account for her; he took her on to two mortgage banks and an obscure real estate agent, as if he needed information from them. And she went along with it, she sat quietly and patiently in the waiting rooms of all these offices while he went about his pretended business inside. Twelve years of enslavement to the Princess had long ago accustomed her to waiting as the most natural thing in the world; it did not oppress or humiliate her, she just waited with her hands quietly folded, casting down her blue eyes when anyone passed by. She did as Kanitz told her, patient and obedient as a child. She signed forms at the bank without reading them, and wrote receipts for sums that she had not yet been paid so unthinkingly that Kanitz began to suffer from the unpleasant suspicion that this idiot might have been just as happy to get a hundred and forty thousand or even a mere hundred and thirty thousand crowns. She said yes when the bank manager advised her to invest in railway stock, she said yes when he also advised bank securities, and each time she looked anxiously at Kanitz. It was clear that all these business practices, these forms and signatures, even the sight of money itself naked and unashamed caused her great uneasiness, and all she wanted was to escape such incomprehensible affairs and sit quietly in a room, reading, knitting or playing the piano, instead of having her hopelessly impractical mind and anxious heart confronted with decision-making.

"But Kanitz tirelessly took her around on these errands of his own invention, partly because he really wanted to be sure, as he had promised, that the money from the sale was invested as securely as possibly, partly to keep her bemused. This went on from nine in the morning to five-thirty in the evening. By then they were both so exhausted that he suggested a little rest in a café. Everything essential had been done, he told her, the sale was as good as concluded, she would only have to sign the contract at the notary's office at seven o'clock and receive the money. Her face lit up at once.

"'Oh, then I could leave first thing in the morning?' The two cornflower-blue eyes were smiling radiantly at him.

"'Why, of course,' Kanitz reassured her. 'In an hour's time you'll be free as air, with no more worries about money and property. Your investments are perfectly secure, and will bring you six thousand crowns a year. You can live anywhere in the world, wherever you like.'

"And out of civility, he asked where she was thinking of going. Her face, so bright a moment ago, clouded over again.

"'I thought it would be best to go to my relations in Westphalia at first. I think there's a train going by way of Cologne tomorrow morning.'

"Kanitz immediately showed great enthusiasm. He told the head waiter to bring the railway timetable, looked through it and worked out all the connections. The express from Vienna through Frankfurt to Cologne, then change trains in Osnabrück. The most convenient train, he said, would be the nine-twenty express in the morning. By evening, that would get her to Frankfurt, where he advised her to spend the night so as not to tire herself too much. In his nervous enthusiasm he leafed on, and found an advertisement for a Protestant hostel where she could stay. She needn't worry about buying her ticket, he said, he would do that, and he would be there without fail in the morning to take her to the station. Such discussion passed the time more quickly than he had expected, and at last he could look at his watch and say, 'But now we must be off to the notary's office.'

"In just under an hour it was all over. In just under an hour our friend had cheated the heiress out of three-quarters of her fortune. When his accomplice Gollinger saw the name of Kekesfalva Castle and then the low sale price, he winked, unnoticed by Fräulein Dietzenhof, and gave his old companion in underhand dealings an admiring glance. Put it into words, and this friendly admiration said something like, 'Good work, old fellow! Quick off the mark, eh?' The notary too looked through his glasses at Fräulein Dietzenhof with interest; like everyone else, he had read about the Princess's disputed estate in the papers, and as a lawyer he thought there was something not at all right about the haste with which Kekesfalva was being sold on. Poor woman, he thought, you've fallen into the wrong hands. But it is not a notary's business to warn either buyer or seller about a sale. He has to stamp the deed, get it registered, and see that the fees are paid. So the good man, who had seen many dubious deals done before and sealed them with the imperial eagle of Austria, just bowed his head, folded up the document, and civilly asked Fräulein Dietzenhof to be the first to sign.

"The shy creature took fright. Undecidedly, she looked at her mentor Kanitz, and only when he had encouraged her with a nod did she go up to the table and write 'Annette Beate Maria Dietzenhof' in her neat, clear, upright German hand. Our friend followed her. Now it was all done, the deed signed and stamped, the price of the transaction in the notary's hands, and the bank account into which the cheque was to be paid next day was given. With that one stroke of his pen, Leopold Kanitz had doubled or tripled his fortune. From now on, he alone was lord and master of Kekesfalva.

"The notary carefully blotted the still wet ink of the signatures, then they all three shook his hand, and went down the stairs, Fräulein Dietzenhof first, followed by Kanitz with bated breath, and after him Dr Gollinger. It annoyed Kanitz very much that the latter kept tapping his accomplice's ribs from behind with his stick, and murmuring in his drink-sodden voice (in tones that only Kanitz could hear), '*Scoundrellus maximus, scoundrellus maximus!*' Nor was Kanitz happy that Dr Gollinger took his leave at the door with an ironically deep bow, because that left him alone with his victim, and he didn't like it.

"My dear Lieutenant Hofmiller, you must try to understand this unexpected change of mood. I won't turn emotional and say that our friend's conscience had suddenly pricked him. Since the signing of the agreement, however, the material situation of the two parties to it had changed considerably with that one stroke of his pen. You must remember that for the whole of those two days, Kanitz as buyer had been at odds with that poor girl as seller. She had been the enemy whom he must outwit strategically; she must be trapped and forced to capitulate. But now those financial-cum-military manoeuvres were over. Napoleon Kanitz had won hands down, and so the poor, quiet young woman walking with him down Walfischgasse side by side like two shadows, was no longer an opponent. And strange as it

179

sounds, nothing troubled our friend more in that moment of his swift victory than the fact that his victim had made it too easy for him. If you are going to do another human being wrong, for some mysterious reason it does the perpetrator of the injustice good to find out, or to imagine, that his victim has acted badly or unfairly in some detail or other. It salves his conscience to impute at least some small part of the blame to the person who has been deceived. But Kanitz could not accuse his victim of anything, not the least little thing; she had delivered herself up to him with her hands bound, looking at him all the time with unsuspecting gratitude in her cornflower-blue eyes. What could he say to her, now that he had done the deed? Congratulate her on the sale, meaning on her loss? He was feeling more and more uncomfortable. I'll see her to the hotel, he thought quickly, and that will be an end of it.

However, the victim beside him was also visibly uneasy. Her own demeanour was different, was thoughtfully hesitant. Although Kanitz had bowed his head, this change did not escape him. He sensed, from her faltering footsteps (he dared not look at her face), that she was busily thinking something over. Anxiety overcame him. At last, he said to himself, she's realised that I am the buyer myself. Now she'll probably fling accusations at me, she's probably already regretting her stupid haste, and maybe she'll run straight off to her lawyer tomorrow after all.

"But then—they had gone together all the way down Walfischgasse in silence, shadow beside shadow—then at last she plucked up courage, cleared her throat, and began. 'Forgive me … but as I am leaving first thing in the morning, I would very much like to settle everything … Above all I want to thank you for taking so much trouble and … and … and ask you to tell me at once … tell me how much I owe you for all you have done. It's taken up so much of your time, managing everything for me and … because I'm leaving early tomorrow … I'd very much like to have everything in order first.'

"Our friend's feet faltered, and his heart missed a beat. This was too much! He had not been prepared for it. He was overcome by the painful feeling you have if you hit a dog in anger, and the beaten animal comes crawling to you on his belly, looks at you with pleading eyes and licks your cruel hand.

"'No, no,' he protested, dismayed. 'You owe me nothing, nothing at all.' And at the same time he felt sweat breaking out of every pore. He thought he was ready for anything, he had learnt, years ago, to calculate every reaction in advance, and now something entirely new had happened to him. In his hard years working as an agent he had had doors slammed in his face, he had known people who wouldn't return his greeting, and there were some streets in the district where he operated that he preferred to avoid. But for someone he had tricked to thank him for it too—that had never happened before. And he felt ashamed in front of this first human being who trusted him in spite of everything, in spite of all he had done. Against his own will, he felt an urge to apologise.

"'No,' he stammered, 'for God's sake no … you don't owe me anything, I won't accept anything. I only hope I've done right, I hope I've acted as you would have wished … perhaps it would have been better to wait, indeed I'm afraid you could … you could have got rather more then … but you wanted to sell quickly, and I think that's better for you. By God, yes, I do believe that's better for you.'

"He was getting his breath back, and at that moment he spoke with genuine honesty.

181

"'Someone like you who knows nothing about business does well to leave it alone. Someone like that should … should be content with less so long as it's secure … Don't,' he added, swallowing hard, 'don't, I most earnestly beg you, don't let people lead you astray by saying that you made a poor sale, or sold too cheap. After every sale people of a certain kind are sure to come along later, talking grandly and saying they would have paid more, they'd have paid much more … but when it came to it they wouldn't have paid cash, they'd all have lumbered you with bills of exchange or stocks and shares or promissory notes … that's not right for you, really not, I swear it, I swear to you as I stand here before you, that bank is a first-class establishment and your money is safe. You'll get it paid regularly to the day and the hour … I swear you will. This way is better for you.'

"Meanwhile they had reached the hotel. Kanitz hesitated. I ought at least to ask her out, he thought, ask her to supper, or maybe to go to a theatre. But she was already putting out her hands to him.

"'I think I ought not to impose on you any longer … it's been troubling me all day to think of your giving up so much time to me. You've devoted yourself exclusively to my affairs for two days, and I really do feel no one could have done it more whole-heartedly. Once again I … I do thank you most sincerely. No one … ' and here she blushed a little, 'no one has ever been so kind and helpful to me before … I wouldn't have believed I could possibly be freed from my situation so quickly, that it could all be done so well and made so easy for me … I thank you very, *very* much indeed.'

"Kanitz took her hand, and could not help looking at her as he did so. Some of her usual anxious manner had been dispelled by her warmth of feeling. Her usually pale and frightened face suddenly showed glowing animation. She looked almost childlike with her speaking blue eyes and that little smile of gratitude. Kanitz sought for words in vain. But she was already wishing him goodnight and walking away, slender, light and sure of foot; her bearing had changed, it was the bearing of someone freed from a burden. Unsure of himself, Kanitz watched her go. He was still feeling: 'There's something else I wanted to say to her.' But the clerk at the reception desk had already given her the key to her room, and the pageboy took her to the lift. It was over.

"So that was how the sacrificial lamb parted from the slaughterer. But Kanitz stood there dazed for some minutes, as if it was his own head that he had struck with the hatchet, and stared at the deserted hotel foyer. Finally he let the crowd streaming along in the street outside carry him away, although he had no idea where he was going. No one had ever looked at him like that before, with such friendly gratitude. He involuntarily heard that 'Thank you very, *very* much!' ringing in his ears, spoken by the woman he had robbed and deceived! He kept stopping to wipe the sweat from his brow. And suddenly, outside the big glassware shop in Kärntnerstrasse, it so happened that as he was staggering mindlessly past the facade as if half asleep, he caught sight of his own reflection in one of the mirrors on display. He stared at himself as you might look at the photograph of a criminal in the newspaper, trying to work out just which of the man's features give away his criminality, the jutting chin, the cruel set of the lips, the hard eyes? He stared at himself, and seeing his own eyes behind his glasses he suddenly recollected the pair of eyes she had shown him just now. It would be good to have eyes like that, he thought, shaken badly, not red-rimmed, greedy, nervous eyes like mine. It would be good to have blue, shining eyes, full of ardent trust (my mother sometimes looked like that on a Friday evening, he remembered). Yes, it would be good to be that sort of person—better to let yourself be deceived than carry out the deception, better to be a decent human being with nothing on your conscience. No one else has God's blessing. All my clever tricks, he thought, haven't made me happy. I am still a restless, unhappy man. And so Leopold Kanitz went on down the street, a stranger to himself, and he had never felt more wretched than today, the day of his greatest triumph.

"At last he sat down in a café, thinking he was hungry, and ordered something. But every morsel nauseated him. I'll sell Kekesfalva, he thought as he brooded, I'll sell it again straight away. What would I do with a country estate? I'm no farmer. Do I want to live alone in a house with eighteen rooms, at odds with a rascal like Petrovic? It was a nonsensical idea. I should have bought it in the name of a mortgage bank, not in my own name … because suppose she does find out in the end that I was the buyer? And I don't want to make money out of selling it! If she agrees I'll give it back to her, taking twenty per cent or just ten per cent profit on the resale, she can have it back any time if she regrets the deal.

"This thought was a relief to his mind. I'll write to her tomorrow—or wait, I can suggest it to her myself early tomorrow, before she leaves. Yes, that was the right thing to do—offer her the option of buying it back of his own accord. Now he thought he could sleep easily. But in spite of the two poor nights he had already spent, Kanitz slept badly and little for a third night running. He still had the intonation of her *very*, of that 'Thank you very, *very* much!' in his ears, spoken in a strange north German accent, but so vibrant with true feeling that the excitement of it tingled in his nerves. No deal he had done in twenty-five years had given our friend so much cause for concern as this one—the greatest, most successful, most unscrupulous operation he had ever carried out.

"At seven-thirty in the morning Kanitz was already out and about. He knew that the express by way of Passau left at nine-twenty, and he wanted to buy something in a hurry—some chocolate, or a whole big gift box of chocolates. He needed to make some gesture of appreciation, and maybe he also secretly longed to hear that 'Thank you very, *very* much!'—an expression so new to him—spoken again in her fascinatingly foreign way. He bought a big box of chocolates, the most expensive and exquisite he could find, and even that did not seem to him good enough as a farewell present. So he also bought flowers in the next shop, a large bouquet of deep red blooms. His right and left hands thus laden, he went back to the hotel and asked the clerk at reception to have both taken straight up to Fräulein Dietzenhof's room. However, the clerk—ennobling him rather too soon, in the Viennese manner, replied, 'I'm so sorry, Herr von Kanitz, but the lady is already in the breakfast room.'

"Kanitz thought about it for a moment. Yesterday's parting had moved him so much that he was afraid another meeting might spoil that beautiful memory. But then he made up his mind to see her all the same, and with the box of chocolates in one hand and the flowers in the other he went into the breakfast room.

"She was sitting with her back to him. Even without seeing her face, he sensed something touching about the quiet, unassuming way this slender creature sat alone at her table, and against his will it affected him. Diffidently, he went up to the table and quickly put down the box of chocolates and the flowers. 'Something for your journey.'

"She gave a start, and blushed deeply. It was the first time that anyone had ever given her flowers—or almost the first time, because a member of the Princess's fortune-hunting family had once sent her a few spindly roses, hoping to make an ally of her, but the furious old lady, in a towering rage, had ordered her to send them back at once. And here came someone bringing her beautiful flowers, and no one could forbid her to accept them this time.

"'Oh no,' she stammered, 'how can they be for me? They are much … much too beautiful for me.'

"But she looked up with gratitude. Whether it was the reflection of the flowers, or the blood rising to her cheeks, a rosy glow spread over the embarrassment in her face. At that moment, old maid as she seemed likely to be, she was almost beautiful.

"'Won't you sit down?' she asked in her confusion, and Kanitz awkwardly sat down opposite her.

"'So you're really going away?' he asked, and there was an involuntary note of genuine regret in his voice.

"'Yes,' she said, bowing her head. There was no joy in her 'Yes', but no grief either. No hope and no disappointment. It was spoken quietly, with no particular tone of anything but resignation.

"In his embarrassment, and out of a wish to be useful to her in some way, Kanitz asked whether she had telegraphed ahead to announce her arrival. No, oh no, her family would only take fright—they hadn't received a telegram for years. But he presumed they were close relations, Kanitz enquired further. Close relations? … No, not at all close. A kind of niece, her late stepsister's daughter. She didn't know the niece's husband at all.

They had a little place in the country where they kept bees, and they had both written in a very friendly way, she said, telling her she could have a room there and stay as long as she liked.

"'But what will you do in that remote little place?' asked Kanitz.

"'I don't really know,' she replied, with her eyes cast down.

"Our friend was beginning to feel much moved. There was something so lost and abandoned about this poor creature, and such indifference in her acceptance of whatever was going to happen to her, that it reminded him of himself, of his own irregular, footloose way of life. He felt his own aimlessness in hers.

"'But there's no sense in that,' he said almost with vehemence. 'Living with distant relations is never a good idea. And you don't have to bury yourself in a little place like that any more.'

"She was looking at him with mingled gratitude and sadness. 'I know,' she sighed. 'I'm a little afraid of it myself. But what else am I to do?'

"She spoke tonelessly, and then raised her blue eyes to him as if hoping for advice of some kind. (It would be good to have eyes like that, Kanitz had told himself yesterday.) And suddenly, just how it happened he didn't know, he felt an idea, a wish make its way to his lips.

"'Then why not stay here instead?' he said. And still involuntarily, he added quietly, 'Stay here with me.'

"She stared at him in alarm. Only now did he realise that he had spoken entirely on the spur of the moment. He had not, as usual, weighed up his words, calculated their effect and thought them over before they slipped out. He had suddenly voiced a wish that he had not even admitted to himself, a wish that he didn't understand, but out it had come, vibrating with strong emotion. Only her violent blushing told him just what

187

he had said, and he was immediately afraid that she could have misunderstood him. She was probably thinking he meant—stay here as my lover. And he added hastily, to disabuse her of any such insulting idea, 'I mean—as my wife.'

"She abruptly sat bolt upright. Her mouth was working, whether in a sob or to say something angry he didn't know. Then she suddenly jumped up and ran out of the room.

"That was the worst moment in our friend's life. Only now did he understand his own folly. He had belittled, insulted and humiliated a truly good person, the only person who trusted him, because how could he, already an ageing man, a Jew, shabby, not physically attractive, a fixer who spent his time going about doing deals, how could he offer himself to a woman whose nature was so fine and delicate? Instinctively, he told himself she had every reason to run away in horror. Well, he thought grimly, it serves me right. She's seen me for what I am at last, she's shown me the contempt I deserve. That's better than to have her thank me for cheating her. Kanitz did not feel in the least offended by her sudden flight. At that moment, on the contrary—and he told me this himself—he was positively *glad* of it. He felt he had received due punishment, and it was only justice if from now on she thought of him with the same contempt that he felt for himself.

"But then she appeared in the doorway again; her eyes were moist, and she was in a state of great turmoil. Her shoulders were shaking. She came towards the table, and she had to clutch the back of the chair with both hands before she sat down again. Then she said softly, without looking up, 'Forgive me … please forgive me for behaving so badly … for jumping up like that. But I was so startled … how could you ask such a question? You don't even know me … you don't know me at all.'

"Kanitz was in too much consternation to find a word. He just saw, to his astonishment, that she was not angry but simply afraid. She was as alarmed by his sudden, senseless proposal as he was himself. Neither had the courage to speak to the other, neither had the courage even to look at the other. But she did not leave Vienna that morning. They spent all day together, from morning to evening. Three days later he proposed again, and two months after that they were married."

Dr Condor paused. "Well, let's have a last glass of wine—I've nearly finished my story. But let me just say this—it's rumoured in these parts that our friend cunningly wormed his way into the heiress's affections and trapped her with a proposal of marriage to get hold of the estate. I repeat, however, that's not true. As you now know, Kanitz already *had* the estate in his hands. There was no *need* for him to marry her, and not a trace of calculation in his courtship. Petty little agent that he was, he would never have found the courage to pay court to that refined, blue-eyed young woman out of cunning, Instead, he was overcome against his will by a feeling that was honourable and, wonderful to relate, remained honourable.

"For that ridiculous courtship was the prelude to a remarkably happy marriage. If opposites complement each other, the outcome is perfect harmony, and what may seem extremely surprising often turns out to be perfectly natural. It is true that the first reaction of this couple, when they so suddenly came together, was for each to be afraid of the other. Kanitz suspected that someone would tell her stories about discreditable deals he had done, and then she would turn away from him with scorn

189

at the last moment. He put extraordinary energy into covering up his past. He gave up all his shady practices, got rid of the promissory notes he held at a loss, and kept his distance from all his old associates. He found an influential man to stand sponsor when he had himself baptised, and spent a good sum of money on permission to have the aristocratic-sounding title 'von Kekesfalva' added to the name of Kanitz. After that, as usual in such cases, the original surname soon disappeared from his visiting cards without trace. But until the wedding day he lived in fear that today, tomorrow, the day after tomorrow she would withdraw her trust from him again in horror.

"In her turn, used as she was to twelve years of being accused by that dragon her old mistress of uselessness, stupidity, ill will and lack of intelligence, her spirit utterly broken by the woman's infernal tyranny, she expected her new master to shout at her all the time, mock her, abuse her shortcomings and neglect her. She was resigned to all that in advance, and was awaiting enslavement as her inevitable fate. But lo and behold, she could do no wrong; the man to whom she had entrusted her life thanked her for it every day, and always treated her with the utmost respect. The young woman was astonished, and could hardly understand so much affection. She had already begun fading away, but now she gradually blossomed. She looked pretty and developed soft curves, but it was still a year or two before she ventured to believe that she, always previously ignored, downtrodden and oppressed, could be loved like any other woman. However, the greatest joy for them both came with the birth of their child.

"In those years Kekesfalva returned to his business activities with new energy. He was no longer just an agent, he worked with purpose. He modernised the sugar factory, held shares in the rolling mill in the new suburb of Vienna Neustadt, and brought off a brilliant transaction in the liquor cartel that had everyone talking at the time. The fact that he grew rich, really rich this time, did not alter the couple's quiet, thrifty way of life. As if they did not want to remind people of themselves too much, they seldom invited guests, and the house that you now know was much simpler and more rustic at the time—and indeed it was so much happier, too, than it is today!

"Then his first time of trial began. His wife had been suffering internal pains for some time, she lost her appetite and grew thin, and she felt constantly tired and exhausted, but for fear of causing her busily occupied husband anxiety about her insignificant self she gritted her teeth when an attack came on, and said nothing about her pain. By the time it was impossible to conceal it any longer, it was too late. She was taken to Vienna by ambulance for an operation on her supposed stomach ulcer, which in fact was cancer. This was when I came to know Kekesfalva, and I have never seen a man suffer more savage and cruel despair. He could not, absolutely would not grasp the fact that medical science could not save his wife now, and he thought that we doctors did not do more—could not do more—out of mere apathy, indifference, and lack of skill on our part. He offered the Professor at the University Hospital fifty thousand, a hundred thousand crowns to cure her. On the day of the operation he was still summoning the leading authorities from Budapest, Munich and Berlin by telegraph, just to find one who would say that she might not have to go under the knife. And I shall never forget the madness in his eyes when she died during the operation—as was only to be expected, for there was no hope of saving her—and he screamed at us that we were all murderers.

"That was his road to Damascus. From that day on something had changed in the ascetic businessman. A god whom he had worshipped from childhood—money—had let him down. Now only one being on earth really mattered to him—his child. He engaged governesses and servants, had the house converted, no luxury was enough for him, a man who had once been so thrifty. He took his daughter at the age of nine, the age of ten, to Nice, to Paris, to Vienna, spoilt her and made much of her in the most ludicrous way, and whereas he used to put his whole mind to making money he now threw it around lavishly. Perhaps you weren't so wrong when you described him as aristocratic and distinguished, because for years now an unusual indifference to profit and loss has had him in its grip. He learnt to despise money when all his millions couldn't buy his wife back.

"It's getting late, so I won't tell you in detail about his adoration of his child; After all, it was understandable, for the little girl grew to be enchanting, a truly elfin creature in those years, slender, light-footed, with a bright, friendly smile for everyone in her grey eyes. She had inherited her mother's shy and gentle nature, her father's keen intellect. She blossomed, she was clear-minded and lovable, and wonderfully natural in her manner, as only children are who have never known the harsh, hostile side of life. And only if you understand the spell she cast on her father, who had never dared to hope that such a merry, friendly being could spring from his own dark and melancholy blood, can you really assess his desperation when the second disaster happened. He could not, would not grasp the fact—and indeed, he still can't—that his daughter, of all children, was to remain afflicted and crippled. I really shrink from telling you all the foolish things he did in his wild desperation. He drives all the doctors in the world to despair with his insistence, he tries, as it were, to force us to cure her at once by naming sums beyond all reason. I'll say no more about his telephone calls to me every other day for no reason at all except to give vent to his headlong impatience, but recently a colleague told me in confidence that the old man sits among the students in the University Library every week, clumsily copying out all the difficult technical terms from the encyclopaedia, and then he goes through medical textbooks in the confused hope that he himself might discover something that we doctors have overlooked or forgotten. I've had it reported to me by other people—you may smile, but this lunacy allows us to guess at the strength of his passion—that he has promised both the synagogue and the pastor of the local church large sums as donations, not being sure himself which God he should turn to—the God of his fathers whom he abandoned, or his new God, and tormented by the terrible fear that he has spoilt his chances with one or the other of them he has sworn to worship both.

"However, I'm sure you can see that I'm not telling you these details, verging as they do on the ridiculous, out of a liking for gossip. I just want you to understand what someone who *listens* to him means to that afflicted, desperate, annihilated man, someone who makes him feel that he understands his pain, or at least *wants* to understand it. I know how difficult he makes it with his obstinacy, his egocentric obsession, as if nothing in this world, which is full to the brim with unhappiness anyway, exists but his own and his child's misfortune. But now of all times he needs a friend who won't let him down, now that his utter helplessness is beginning to make him ill himself, and you are *really*—I mean it, Lieutenant, really—doing a good deed by taking a little of your youth, your vitality, your easy manner into that tragic house. That is the only reason, my one concern in case others might lead you astray, why I have perhaps told you more about his private life than I can really answer for. But I think I can count on you to keep everything I have told you strictly private between the two of us.'

"Of course," I said automatically. Those were the first words to pass my lips during his entire account. I was feeling numbed—not just by the surprising revelations that turned my ideas of Kekesfalva inside out like a glove; at the same time I was also dismayed by my own short-sighted folly. Had I still been going through the world with such a superficial view of it in my twenty-fifth year? As a daily guest in that house for weeks, and bemused by my own sense of sympathy, had I never ventured, out of some stupid notion of discretion, to ask either about Edith's disorder itself or about her mother, who was obviously sorely missed in that household? Had I never asked where that strange man Kekesfalva's wealth came from? How could I have missed seeing that those hooded, almond-shaped, melancholy eyes were not the eyes of a Hungarian aristocrat, but of a member of the Jewish race, made keener and at the same time weary by a thousand years of tragic struggle? How had I failed to see that very different elements mingled in Edith, how had I not recognised that something in that house must be under the spell of past events? Like lightning, a whole series of details now belatedly occurred to me—the coldness with which our colonel had once responded to Kekesfalva's greeting when they met, a mere two fingers half lifted to his cap? Or how my comrades at the table in the café had spoken of him as "that old Manichaean"? It was like having a curtain suddenly drawn back in a dark room, when the sun shines in your eyes so suddenly that they see a crimson blur, and your senses reel in that excess of unbearable radiance.

As if he had guessed what was going on in my mind, Condor leant towards me. Very much the doctor now, he laid his small, soft hand reassuringly on mine.

"Of course you weren't to know about that, Lieutenant Hofmiller, how could you? You've grown up in a self-enclosed, secluded world, and what's more you are at that happy age when you haven't yet learnt to regard anything unusual with initial suspicion. Believe me when I say, as an older man, that there is nothing to feel ashamed of in being deceived from time to time in your life. Indeed, it's a mercy not to have developed the sharp, diagnostic eye that suspects ulterior motives, and to begin by approaching everyone and everything with goodwill. Otherwise you would never have been able to help that old man and his poor sick child so much! No, don't wonder at yourself and above all don't feel ashamed—your good instincts led you to do exactly the right thing!"

He tossed the butt of his cigar into a corner, stretched, and pushed his chair back. "And now, I think, it's time I was on my way."

I stood up too when he did, although I still felt rather unsteady on my legs. For something strange was happening to me. I was extremely agitated, and indeed my perception was more alert than usual after hearing so much that was surprising, but at the same time I had a dull, sinking feeling in some part of myself. I clearly remembered that in the middle of his story I had wanted to ask Condor something, but I had not had the presence of mind to interrupt him. Yes, there was some detail that I wanted to ask at a particular point, and now that I had the opportunity to put questions I couldn't remember what it was. It must have been swept away by my emotions as I listened. In vain I groped my way back through the intricate course of

Condor's narrative—it was like feeling a very distinct pain in some part of the body without being able to pinpoint its exact location. As we walked out of the now half-empty wine bar, I was concentrating entirely on my efforts to remember.

We stepped outside the door, and Condor looked up. "Aha," he said, with a certain satisfaction, "I thought so all along. That moonlight was too bright for my liking. There's a storm about to break, and a violent one. We'd better hurry up."

He was right. The air among the sleeping houses was very close and sultry; but dark clouds, heavy with rain, were chasing over the sky from the east, from time to time partly covering the now dull, yellowish moon. Half of the firmament overhead was already entirely dark, its black, compact, metallic mass moving on like a giant tortoise, with flashes of distant lightning darting over it now and then, and at each lighting bolt something growled almost reluctantly in the background, like an animal provoked.

"It'll break in half-an-hour's time," was Condor's diagnosis. "I for one shall get to the station in the dry, but you'd better turn back, Lieutenant, or you'll be drenched to the skin."

But I vaguely knew that I still had something to ask him, although I couldn't say what it was; my memory of it was submerged in sombre black like the moon overhead in the storm clouds. I still felt that indistinct idea throbbing in my brain, like a persistent and restless pain.

"No, I'll risk it," I replied.

"Then let's hurry! The faster we walk the better—my legs are stiff from sitting so long."

His legs were stiff—that was the reminder I needed! Bright light immediately flooded my mind. All at once I knew what I had wanted to ask him earlier, what I *had* to ask him. It was my mission, or rather the mission that Kekesfalva had given me. All this time my unconscious mind had probably been brooding on his question—could Edith recover from her paralysis or not? And now I must ask it. So as we walked along the deserted streets I began, rather tentatively.

"Forgive me, doctor ... of course everything you told me was very interesting ... I mean very important to me ... But I'm sure you will understand that there's something else I want to ask you, something that has been troubling me for a long time and ... and well, you're her doctor. You know her case better than anyone else ... I'm a layman, I have no real idea about it ... and I would very much like to know what you really think of it. I mean, is Edith's paralysis just a passing phase, or is it incurable?"

Condor looked up sharply, with a single abrupt movement. His pince-nez were glittering, and I instinctively shrank from his keen gaze. It went through me like a knife. Did he somehow suspect that Kekesfalva had put me up to asking? Had he worked out what had happened? But then he lowered his head again, and without interrupting his swift pace, in fact even quickening it, he growled, "Of course! I ought to have been prepared for this. That's what it always comes down to. Curable or incurable, black or white. As if it were so simple! Even 'healthy' and 'sick' are two words that a good doctor can't really use with a clear conscience, because where does sickness begin and where does health end? As for 'curable' and 'incurable' ... well, of course those two expressions are extremely common, and medical practice can't do without them. But you will never get me to say that something is incurable. Never! I know that the cleverest man of the last century, Nietzsche, came up with the terrible maxim that a doctor should never

197

attempt to treat the incurable, but that is probably the most misleading of all the paradoxical and dangerous precepts that he left us to unravel. Precisely the opposite is true—the incurable, above all, are the patients whom a doctor ought to treat. What's more, it's in his treatment of the incurable that a doctor shows what he is really worth. It's a dereliction of duty for him to accept the term 'incurable' from the start. He's surrendering before the battle has even begun. Of course I know that it is simpler, a useful shorthand, to say that certain cases are downright 'incurable', turning away with an expression of resignation after pocketing your fee for the consultation—yes, it's very comfortable and lucrative to concentrate entirely on the cases that are known to be curable, where you can look up the therapy on page such-and-such of a medical manual. I'll leave that to the quacks who enjoy it. Personally, I consider it as pitiful an achievement as for a poet just to want to repeat what's been well said already, instead of trying to find words for what is still unsaid, or indeed is beyond normal verbal expression. Or for a philosopher to explain, for the ninety-ninth time, some recognised truth known for years, rather than looking for ways to express what isn't known or is unknowable. 'Incurable' is only a relative term, not absolute; incurable cases in medicine, a field where progress is always being made, occur only in the present moment, in the context of our own time, of what we know so far—I mean within our limited, opinionated worm's-eye view. But our own view is not all that matters. In a hundred cases where we see no possibility of a cure today—even though our knowledge is making huge strides—one may be discovered tomorrow or the next day, discovered or devised. So kindly take note"—he said this angrily, as if I had offended him—"as I see it, there are no incurable illnesses. On principle I will never give up hope for a patient, and no one will ever get me to say a case is incurable. The most I would ever say, even in the most desperate cases, is that an illness cannot *yet* be cured—cannot be cured, I mean, by medicine in its present state."

Condor was striding along so vigorously that I had difficulty in keeping up with him. But suddenly he slowed down.

"Perhaps I'm putting this in too complex and abstract a way. These things are hard to explain between a drink in the bar and the railway station. But maybe an example will illustrate what I mean better—incidentally, it is a very personal and a very painful example. Twenty-two years ago I was a young medical student, about the age you are today, and I had just started my second year. Then my father, until then a strong, perfectly healthy and tirelessly active man whom I loved and honoured enormously, fell ill. The doctors diagnosed diabetes. You probably know that diabetes is one of the most cruel and insidious diseases that a man can contract. For no apparent reason the organism stops processing nourishment, it no longer conveys fat and sugar to the body, and the victim in effect starves—it's a living death. I will spare you the details; they wrecked three years of my own youth.

"Now, listen—at the time medical science had no cure at all for diabetes. Patients were put on a strict diet, every gram was weighed, every sip of liquid measured, but the doctors knew—and of course as a medical student I knew too—that they were only postponing the inevitable end, that those two or three years meant terrible decline, starvation in the middle of a world full of food and drink. You can imagine how I, as a student and a future doctor, went from one authority to another at the time, how I studied the textbooks and specialist works. But wherever I went the reply, spoken or written, was that the disease was incurable—a word that I will not tolerate today. And I have hated that word ever since, because I had to stand by and watch the man I loved more than any other on earth die miserably, like a dumb animal, and there was nothing I could do about it. He died, in fact, three months before I qualified.

"And now, pay attention—a few days ago we members of the Medical Society heard a lecture by one of our leading biochemists, who told us that in America and the laboratories of several other countries, experiments have gone a long way towards finding a glandular extract to treat diabetes. He said it was certain that the disease would be defeated within a decade. Well, you can imagine how moved I was by the thought that at the time of my father's illness a few hundred grams of that substance might have kept the man I loved more than anyone in the world from the torment of his death, or we could at least have *hoped* to save and cure him. You must understand how the verdict 'incurable' embittered me at the time—I had dreamt day and night that some treatment for it could, should be found, that someone would succeed in finding it, maybe I myself. At the time when I was at university, we students were expressly warned in a printed leaflet against syphilis, which was described as incurable. And now it can be cured. So Nietzsche, Schumann and Schubert and who knows how many more of its tragic victims did not die of an 'incurable' illness, they died of an illness that was *not yet curable* at the time. They died prematurely in both senses, if you like to put it that way. And look at all the new, unhoped-for, fantastic developments we doctors hear about daily—developments that were unthinkable yesterday! So every time I am faced with a case that has made others turn away, shrugging their shoulders, I feel anger in my heart because I do not yet know the treatment for it that may come tomorrow or the next day, something still unknown—and I also feel hope—perhaps you will find it, I tell myself, perhaps someone will find it just in time for this patient, at the very last moment. Everything is possible, even the impossible—because where in our present state of knowledge we find ourselves facing barred doors, another door has often unexpectedly opened behind us. Where our methods fail, we must just try to find a new method, and where medical science won't help us there's always the possibility of a miracle—and yes, genuine miracles do still happen today in medicine. Miracles in the glare of bright electric light, in defiance of all logic and experience, and sometimes you can even prod them into happening. Do you think I'd be pestering that girl and letting her pester me if I didn't hope for a considerable improvement in her in the end? Hers is a difficult case, I admit, full of setbacks. For years I've been unable to make as much progress as I would like. And yet, and yet, I am not giving her up."

I had been listening intently. All he said was perfectly clear to me. But I must unconsciously have absorbed the old man's insistence and anxiety. I wanted to hear more, something more precise, more definite. So I asked, "Then you think that you have already made progress—I mean *some* progress in her improvement?"

Dr Condor did not reply. My remark seemed to have annoyed him. He marched on faster and more firmly on his short legs.

"How can you say I've made some progress with her? Have you seen any? And what do you know about it anyway? You've known the girl only for a few weeks, and I've been treating her for five years."

Suddenly he stopped. "And just so that you know, once and for all—I have made no essential improvement at all, nothing definitive, and that's what matters! I've tried this and that with her like any quack, pointless, useless! So far I have achieved nothing."

His vehemence alarmed me. Obviously I had wounded his sense of medical pride. I tried to make my peace.

"But Herr von Kekesfalva told me how refreshing Edith found the hydroelectric baths, and he said that especially since the inject—"

Dr Condor stopped dead and interrupted my half-finished word.

"Nonsense! Stuff and nonsense! Don't let the old fool mislead you! Do you really think hydroelectric baths and such stuff can reverse paraplegia like hers? Don't you know the medical tricks we play? When we don't know what to do ourselves, we play for time, we keep patients occupied with chatter and little activities so that they won't notice how baffled we are. Luckily for us, an invalid's own nature is usually our ally. Of course she feels better! Any kind of treatment, eating lemons or drinking milk, cold-water treatment or hot-water treatment, will bring about an initial change in the organism and provide a stimulus that the ever-optimistic patient takes for improvement. That kind of auto-suggestion is our best assistant; it even helps the biggest fools among us doctors. But there's a snag—as soon as the charm of novelty has worn off, reaction will set in, and then you have to switch your approach in a hurry, pretend there's a new treatment, and so we doctors manipulate our approach in really severe cases until perhaps the real, right method of treatment is found. No, no compliments, I know very well how little of what I would like to do for Edith has been done. Everything I've tried so far—don't fool yourself—all that electrical stuff and massage and so on has failed to get her on her legs again in the literal sense of the phrase."

Condor was criticising himself so fiercely that I felt I ought to defend him against his own conscience. I said, diffidently, "But ... but I've seen for myself that she can walk with the aid of those devices ... the things that stretch her legs ... "

However, Condor was not speaking any more, he positively shouted in my face now, in such a loud and angry voice that two people out walking late in the otherwise deserted street turned to look at us curiously.

"A fraud, I tell you, all a fraud! Devices to help me, not her! They're just to keep her occupied, don't you see? The child doesn't need them, I needed them because the Kekesfalvas were getting impatient. I couldn't stand up to the old man's urgings any more, I *had* to give him some confidence to keep him fighting. What could I do but lumber the impatient child with those heavy weights, as you might put a restraining device on a persistent offender? They were entirely unnecessary ... well, maybe they strengthen her sinews slightly. There was nothing else I could do ... I have to gain time. But I'm not at all ashamed of these tricks and devices. You've seen for yourself how successful they are—Edith persuades herself that she's felt better since being fitted with them, her father says triumphantly that I helped him, they're all enthusiasm for those wonderful, miracle-working devices, and you yourself ask me questions as if I knew the answers to anything!"

Interrupting himself, he took off his hat so that he could pass his hand over his damp forehead. Then he gave me a malicious sidelong glance.

203

"I'm afraid you don't like that very much. It doesn't fit your idea of the doctor as a healer who always tells the truth. In your youthful idealism you didn't see medical morality as quite like this, and now I can tell that you are ... brought down to earth, or even repelled by such practices! I'm sorry, but medicine has nothing to do with morality. In itself every disease is an act of anarchy, a rebellion against nature, and that's why we may legitimately use any means of combating it, *any* means. No, don't bother with feeling sorry for the sick—the invalid regards himself as outside the law, he upsets the natural order of things, and as with any rebellion we must act ruthlessly to restore order—we must use any weapon that comes to hand, because mankind as a whole and human beings as individuals will never be cured by kindness and the truth alone. If a deception will help the sick then it's not a pitiful pretence any more, but the best of medicine, and as long as I can't cure a case in fact, I must see how I can help the patient to endure it. And that's no easy matter, Lieutenant, thinking up new ideas for five years, particularly when you're not especially enthusiastic about your own skills. So never mind the compliments!"

A small, sturdy man, he faced me looking so indignant that I felt as if he would attack me physically if I ventured to demur. At that moment a bolt of blue lightning flashed from the sky like a jagged vein, and the deep sound of thunder growled and rumbled after it. Condor suddenly laughed.

"There, you see—Heaven itself gives us an angry answer. Well, my poor fellow—you've had a lot to put up with today, illusion after illusion cut away with the surgeon's scalpel. First the one about the Magyar nobleman, then the one about the caring, infallible doctor and helper. But you must realise how the old fool's paeans of praise irritate me! All that sentimentality goes against the grain, especially in Edith's case, because my slow progress rankles with me, and so does the thought that I've found nothing conclusive in her case and can't think of anything to do about it."

He walked on a little way in silence. Then he turned to me and spoke more warmly.

"I wouldn't like you to think I've given her up, as we so delicately put it. Far from it, I am particularly determined to do all I can for her, even if takes another year, another five years. And odd coincidences do happen—on the very evening after the lecture I mentioned to you, I was reading a Parisian medical journal and found the account of a case of paralysis, a very curious case. A man of forty who had been bedridden for two whole years, unable to move any of his limbs, and in four months Professor Viennot's therapy has got him to the point where he can happily climb five flights of stairs again. Think of it—a cure like that in four months, in a very similar case, whereas I've spent five years here getting nowhere. I was bowled over when I read that. Of course the aetiology of the case and the method of treatment weren't quite clear to me. Professor Viennot seems to have combined a whole series of treatments in a curious way: irradiation with sunlight in Cannes, some kind of mechanical device and a certain set of gymnastic exercises. The brevity of the case history as reported gives me no idea, of course, of whether and how far any part of his method might be practicable in our case. But I wrote straight to Professor Viennot to find out more, and it was purely for that reason that I subjected Edith to such a thorough examination again today—you need the opportunity to draw comparisons. So you see that I'm not lowering the flag, not by any means. On the contrary, I'm grasping at any straw. Perhaps there may really be a chance in this new treatment—I say *perhaps*, I say no more, and anyway I've talked far too much already. So that's enough of talking shop for me today!"

At this moment we were approaching the station building, and our conversation must soon come to an end, so I pressed him once more. "In that case, then, your opinion is that … "

But at that the short, stout little man suddenly stopped dead.

"I don't have any opinion," he snapped at me. "And there's no *in that case* about it! What do you all want me to do? I don't have a phone line to Almighty God. I haven't said anything. Absolutely nothing definite. I have no opinion, I don't believe or think or promise anything at all. And anyway I've talked far too much, so that's an end to it! Thank you for your company. You'd better turn back at once, or your coat will be drenched!"

And without shaking hands, visibly ruffled (I had no idea why), he walked away on his short legs and, as it struck me, his rather flat feet to the station.

Condor had been right. The thunderstorm that we had felt coming for some time was unmistakably close now. Thick clouds crowded the sky almost audibly; they looked like heavy black crates crashing together above the restlessly tossing crowns of the trees, and the scene was sometimes brightly lit up by a zigzag streak of lightning. The moist air, violently shaken from time to time by gusts of wind, carried the smell of burning on it. The town itself looked different, and as I quickly walked back even the streets did not seem the same as they had been a few minutes earlier, when they still lay with bated breath in the pale moonlight. Now shop signs were rattling and banging, as if woken in alarm by a bad dream, doors slammed, the cowls of chimney pots creaked, lights came on in many houses as figures in white nightshirts got up to see what was going on, and carefully closed their windows against the coming storm. The few late passers by hurried from one street corner to the next as if blown on a wind of fear, the large main square, where there were usually a few people out and about even at night, was entirely deserted, and the illuminated town-hall clock gaped at the unaccustomed void with a foolish, white gaze. But thanks to Condor's advice, I would be home before the storm really broke. Only two more streets, then through the garden in front of the barracks, and I would be in my own room, where I could think over all the surprising information that I had learnt in the last few hours.

The little garden outside our barracks lay in total darkness; the air was dense and heavy under the tossing foliage, sometimes a brief gust of wind hissed through the leaves like a snake, and then the sound died down into an even more eerie silence. I walked faster and faster. I had almost reached the entrance when a figure came out from behind a tree, emerging from the shadows. My steps faltered for a moment, but I did not stop—it was probably only one of the whores who used to look for custom among the soldiers here. But to my annoyance I realised that a stranger's footsteps were following me, and I turned, intending to confront the impudent creature so shamelessly pestering me and send her packing. A flash of lightning cut through the darkness at that very moment, and in the sudden bright light I saw, to my horror, an old man, shaky on his feet, breathing heavily as he followed me, his bald head bare, his round, gold-rimmed glasses sparkling—Kekesfalva!

In my first astonishment I couldn't believe my eyes. Kekesfalva in the little park outside our barracks—it was impossible. Only three hours earlier, when Condor and I took our leave, I'd left him in his house looking tired to death. Was I hallucinating, or had the old man lost his wits? Had he got up in the middle of a feverish fit, and was he now wandering around like a sleepwalker in his thin coat, without even an overcoat and hat? But there was no mistaking it, here he was. I'd have known the depressed, bowed, anxious way he walked among thousands.

"For Heaven's sake, Herr von Kekesfalva!" I cried. "How do you come to be here? Didn't you go to bed after all?"

"No ... or rather I couldn't sleep ... I wanted to ... "

"You must go home now, quickly! You can see that the storm will break in earnest any moment now. Don't you have the car here?"

"Over there ... waiting for me to the left of the barracks."

"Thank goodness! Then off you go—if your chauffeur drives fast he'll get you home in the dry. Come along, Herr von Kekesfalva." And as he hesitated, I took his arm to lead him away. However, he shook himself free.

"In a moment, in a moment ... I'll be off home in a moment, Lieutenant Hofmiller ... but ... but first tell me what he said!"

"Who?" My question and my astonishment were both genuine. Around us the wind was blowing more and more strongly, the trees groaned and bowed down under it as if to uproot themselves, any moment now torrential rain could begin to fall, and naturally I had only one idea in mind, how to get the old man home. Obviously his wits were wandering! But he stammered, almost indignantly, "Dr Condor, of course ... you walked back into town with him ... "

Only now did I understand. Of course this encounter in the dark was no accident. The old man had been waiting impatiently here in the little park just outside the barracks, wanting to know the answer for certain. He had been lying in wait for me at the entrance, where I couldn't escape him. He must have been pacing up and down in terrible anxiety for two or three hours, poorly concealed in the shadows of this run-down little town park where maidservants waited at night to meet their lovers. He had probably assumed that I would only be going the short distance to the railway station with Condor, and then I would return to the barracks straight away. Guessing nothing of that, I had kept him waiting for the two or three hours that I had spent sitting in the wine bar with the doctor, and the sick old man had waited as he used to lie in wait for his debtors—tough, patient, unyielding. There was something about his fanatical persistence that both irritated and moved me.

"Everything's fine," I reassured him. "I have every confidence that it will all turn out well. I'll tell you more tomorrow afternoon, I'll tell you every word we said. But now you must get back to the car. You can see that there's no time to lose."

"Yes, yes, I'm coming." Reluctantly, he let me lead him away. I managed to get him to go ten or twenty paces, and then I felt his limp weight hanging more heavily on my arm.

"Just a moment," he stammered. "Just a moment on the bench there. I can't … I can't go on."

And indeed the old man was swaying back and forth as if drunk. It took me all my strength to drag him over to the bench through the dark, while the thunder rumbled as it came closer and closer. The waiting had undoubtedly exhausted him, and no wonder. He must have stood on weary legs at his post for three hours, impatiently on watch for me, and only now that he had succeeded in getting hold of me did the strain show. Exhausted, as if felled by a heavy blow, he leant on the bench put there as a place where the poor could sit. Workmen also ate their midday snack on this bench, pensioners and pregnant women sat on it in the afternoons, and the whores used it at night when they were looking out for soldiers. Now old Kekesfalva, a man who was richer than anyone else in this town, sat there still waiting, waiting, waiting. And I knew what he was waiting for. I guessed at once that I would never induce the obstinate old man to move from this bench (and how awkward if one of my comrades happened to see me in this strange intimacy!) unless I could raise his spirits first. I had to reassure him before he would move. Once again I was overcome by pity, once again I felt that hot surge of emotion. It always made me powerless, sapping my own will. I leant closer to him and began talking.

The wind roared, whistled and howled around us, but the old man never noticed. For him, the sky, the clouds, the rain did not exist, there was nothing on earth but his child and the hope of curing her. How could I have brought myself to tell him, shaking with agitation and weakness as he was, the bleak facts of the matter—how could I have said that Condor was by no means sure of the best course to take? He needed something to cling to, just as a moment ago, near collapse, he had clung to my arm as I helped him along. So I hastily resorted to the few comforting words that I had been able to extract with such difficulty from Condor. I told him that Condor had heard of a new course of treatment, one that Professor Viennot had tried out in Paris with great success. At once I heard rustling and sensed movement in the dark; Kekesfalva, who had just been leaning back, limp and exhausted, was moving closer as if to warm himself against me. I ought not to have promised him anything else now, but my pity led me to say more than I could answer for. Yes, indeed, I encouragingly told him again and again, this treatment had been very successful, it had achieved surprising

210

results within three or four months, and probably—well, almost certainly—it would not fail with Edith. A certain pleasure in my own exaggeration came over me as I took in the miraculous effect of my reassurances. He kept avidly asking me, "Do you really think so?" or, "Did he really say that? Did he say it himself?" And in my impatience and weakness I fervently assured him that it was so, that was indeed what Condor had said. The weight of the old man as he leant on me became less. I felt his certainty growing as I talked, and for the first and last time in my life I guessed, in that hour, something of the intoxicating pleasure of creativity.

I don't know now, and never will, exactly what I promised Kekesfalva as he sat on the bench meant for the poor. For as he greedily drank in my words, his happiness as he listened egged me on to say more and more. We both ignored the blue lightning flashing around us, and the increasingly insistent growl of the thunder. We sat close together, talking and listening, listening and talking, and I assured him again and again, honestly believing it, "Yes, she'll soon get better, soon, she will certainly get better," just to hear his stammered, "Ah!" and, "Thank God!" and to sympathise with his intoxicated and intoxicating frenzy. I don't know how long we might have sat like that, but suddenly the final fierce gust of wind came that always precedes a heavy storm, clearing the way for it. Trees bowed low, their timber creaking and cracking. Chestnuts rained down on us like shots, and a huge cloud of dust blew around us.

"Home, you must go home," I said, and he did not resist. My comforting words had strengthened and healed him. He no longer staggered as he had just now; confused, but fast now, he hurried with me to his waiting car. The chauffeur helped him in. Only then did my mind feel easy. I knew he was safe.

I had comforted him. Now he would be able to sleep at last, poor broken old man, deeply, quietly, happily.

But in the brief moment when I was going to spread the rug over his feet, so that he would not catch cold, something appalling happened. He grasped my hands by the wrists, both of them, and before I could prevent him he raised them to his mouth and kissed them, right and left, right again and left again.

"I'll see you tomorrow … tomorrow," he stammered, and the car drove off as if blown away by the now icy wind. I stood there rooted to the spot. But the first heavy drops were falling, drumming, pelting down, echoing like hailstones on my cap, and I ran the last four or five dozen steps to the barracks through the torrent. Just as I reached the gate, dripping wet, a lightning bolt illuminated the stormy night, and after it a crash of thunder as if it were tearing the whole sky down. The lightning must have struck quite close, because the earth shook and windowpanes clinked. But although my eyes were dazzled by the garish light, I was not as shocked as I had been a moment before, when the old man had snatched up and kissed my hands in his passionate gratitude.

After such strong emotion I slept well and soundly. Only next morning did my first waking sensations show me how deeply I had been affected by both the sultry weather before the thunderstorm and the electric tension of my conversations that night. I felt numb. I surfaced from what seemed like unfathomable depths, stared first at my familiar room in the barracks as if it were a strange place, and then made vain efforts to remember when and how I had fallen into such an abyss of slumber. But

I had no time to think it all out properly. My other, military memory, which seemed to function separately from the personal kind, told me at once that we were going on special exercises today. Signals were already being given down below, horses were stamping audibly, from my batman's urgent reminders I realised that it was high time I got down there myself. I flung on the uniform laid out ready for me, lit a cigarette, ran downstairs to the yard, and off I went with the whole squadron drawn up ready.

As part of a column of mounted men you don't function like your normal self; you can neither think clearly nor daydream through the sound of a hundred hoof beats. We were riding at a brisk trot, and I felt nothing except that our group was on its way in loose formation out into the finest summer day you can imagine. The sky was washed clean of rain to the last little cloud and wisp of mist, the sun was strong, yet without any sultry heat, and all the contours of the landscape stood out clearly. Looking far into the distance, you saw every house, every tree, every field as real and clear as if you held it in your hand. The very existence of every bunch of flowers standing in a window, every curl of smoke rising from a roof, seemed to be heightened by the strong, clear, glassy colours; I hardly recognised the uninteresting road along which we trotted week after week at the same tempo to the same destination—its leafy canopy rising above our heads was so much richer and greener than usual. I felt wonderfully light and easy as I sat in the saddle, all the uncomfortable, dark, problematic notions that had been oppressing my nervous system for the last few days and weeks were gone. I seldom performed my military duties better than on that radiant summer morning. Everything went well and naturally, everything was as it should be and rejoiced my heart: the sky and the meadows, the pleasant warmth of the horses as they reacted obediently to every pressure of the rider's thighs and every pull on the reins, even to my voice when I gave orders.

A strong sense of physical wellbeing, like every intoxicant, has something about it that inhibits thought; intense enjoyment of the present moment makes you forget the past. So as I went my usual way to the castle after those refreshing hours in the saddle, I was thinking only vaguely of my nocturnal encounter with Kekesfalva; I was merely happy in my own lightness of heart and the joy of other people, because when you are happy you think of everyone else as happy too.

Sure enough, I had hardly reached the familiar gate of the little castle before I heard the voice of the usually carefully impersonal manservant welcoming me with a particularly cheerful note in it. "May I take you up to the tower, Lieutenant Hofmiller, sir? The young ladies are already waiting for you up there."

But why were his hands fidgeting so impatiently, why was he beaming at me so warmly? Why was he already hurrying so busily ahead? What's up with him, I couldn't help wondering as I started to climb the spiral staircase to the terrace, what's the matter with good old Josef today? He seems to be burning with impatience to get me up there as quickly as possible. What's come over the good fellow?

However, it was good to feel happy, good to climb the winding stairs with my strong young legs on this beautiful June day, seeing the summer landscape stretching out to infinity as I glimpsed it from the narrow windows in the walls of the tower, looking now north, now south, now east and then west. Finally, when I had only ten or twelve more steps to go to reach the terrace, something unexpected made me stop. To my surprise, I suddenly heard the faint music of a dance tune as I went on up the dark stairwell. The melody was played by violins, with cellos adding the lower notes, and sparkling, intertwining coloratura voices sang. I marvelled. Where did this music come from, close and yet far away as it sounded, ghostly yet also earthly, a popular song from an operetta sounding as if it came down from the sky? Was there an ensemble playing in the garden of an inn somewhere nearby, so that the wind was carrying every delicate phrase of the intricate melody up here? Next moment I realised that this airy orchestral sound came from nothing more than an ordinary gramophone on the terrace. How stupid of me, I thought, I sense magic everywhere today and expect miracles. A whole orchestra could hardly be installed on the terrace at the top of such a narrow tower! But after only a few more steps I felt uncertain again. No doubt about it, a gramophone was playing up there—and yet the singing voices were too free, too real to come out of the little box whirring away. Those were the live voices of girls, rising in childishly cheerful exuberance. I stopped and listened more intently. The soprano with the lower register was Ilona's voice, beautiful, full, voluptuous, as soft as her arms, but whose was the other voice singing with her? I didn't know it. Edith must have invited a friend to visit, some cheerful young girl with a sparkling voice, and I was very curious to set eyes on the songbird who had so unexpectedly settled on our tower.

My surprise was all the greater when, stepping out onto the terrace, I realised that only the two girls were there, Edith and Ilona, no one else, and it was Edith laughing and trilling in a voice entirely new to me—free, light, silvery in its elation. I was amazed; this sudden change seemed to me somehow unnatural. Only a healthy, self-confident woman would sing of her happiness so exuberantly. On the other hand, that poor sick child couldn't have been cured unless a genuine miracle had happened overnight. What, I marvelled, has delighted her, what has intoxicated her so much that this blessed certainty suddenly breaks from her throat and her soul? My first feeling is hard to explain—it was really discomfort, as if I had taken the girls by surprise naked, for either the sick girl had been hiding her true nature from me until now, or else—but why and how?—she had suddenly become a new woman?

But to my surprise, the two girls seemed to feel no confusion at all when they saw me. "Here you are!" cried Edith, and then, turning to Ilona, "Quick, do turn the gramophone record off!" And she was already waving to me.

"At last, at last—I've been waiting for you all this time. So quick—tell us all about it, tell us everything ... Papa muddled everything up so badly that I was left quite confused ... you know what he's like, when he's excited he can never tell you anything properly. Guess what, he came in to see me last night when that terrible storm was keeping me awake. I was so cold, there was a draught from the window, and I didn't have the strength to get over there and close it. I kept wishing someone would wake up and think of closing my window, and suddenly I heard footsteps coming closer and closer. I felt frightened at first—after all, it was two or three in the morning, and in my surprise I didn't recognise Papa, he looked so different. And he came straight in to see me, and then there was no stopping him ... you should have seen him, he was laughing and sobbing both at once ... can you imagine, Papa laughing out loud in such high spirits, dancing from foot to foot like a great big boy? Of course, when he began talking, I was so amazed, I just couldn't believe it ... I thought—either Papa has been dreaming, or I'm dreaming myself. However, then Ilona came in, and we were all talking and laughing until morning. But now, what about this new treatment to cure me?"

I tried not to give way to my utter consternation. It was like attempting to keep your footing when a strong wave flings itself against you and leaves you staggering. That one, last little phrase had explained everything to me in a flash. I alone was responsible for the unsuspecting girl's new, happy mood, I had implanted this ill-founded certainty in her mind. Kekesfalva must have told her what Condor had told me. But what, exactly, *had* Condor told me? And what had I said myself in passing it on? After all, Condor had expressed himself with the utmost caution, and what must I have added, a prey to my own foolish pity, to light up the whole household and make the desperate feel rejuvenated and the sick healthy again? What must I have said? …

"What is it … why do you hesitate like that?" Edith pressed me. "You know how much every word matters to me. So what did Condor tell you?"

"What did he tell me?" I repeated, playing for time. "Well … you know how it is. The outlook's very good … Dr Condor hopes for excellent results in the course of time and … and he intends, if I'm not mistaken, to try a new course of treatment, he's finding out about it. Apparently it's a very effective cure if … if I understood him correctly. Of course I'm no judge of these things myself, but at least you can rely upon it that if he … I think, I really do think he will make everything all right in the end."

But either she didn't notice how evasive I was being, or her impatience was ready to sweep away all obstacles. "I always knew it—I knew we'd get nowhere going on as we were. I know myself better than anyone … remember how I told you what nonsense it all is, the massaging and the hydroelectric treatment and the devices to stretch my legs? It all takes far too much time, how can anyone wait so long? … There, look, I took those things off my legs this morning without asking him … you can't imagine what a relief it was. I could move much more easily at once … I think it was only those horrible heavy weights that handicapped me. No, it has to be attacked quite differently, I've felt that for a long time. But … but now quick, tell me, tell me about this French professor's methods! Will I have to go to him there in France? Can't it be done here? I do so hate being in a sanatorium, I really can't stand it! And I don't like being with sick people! I have enough of that for myself … so what about it? Come on, do tell! Most important of all, how long will it take? Does it really work so fast? Four months, Papa says, the professor cured his patient within four months, and now the man can climb up and down stairs, and move and everything … that's … that would be amazing! Oh, don't sit there saying nothing like that, tell us about it again! When is he going to begin, and how long will the whole thing take?"

Slow this down, I told myself, don't let this wild delusion run away with her as if it were all sure and certain. I very cautiously tried to damp down her exhilaration.

"A definite period of time … well, of course no doctor can give assurances about that from the start. I don't think anyone can say for certain … and of course Dr Condor was speaking about the method only in general terms. He did say it seems to produce excellent results, but whether it's really reliable … I mean, one can only judge these things from case to case. At least, we'll have to wait until he—"

But her passionate enthusiasm had already outrun my tentative resistance. "Oh, come along, you don't know Dr Condor!

No one ever gets anything out of him for certain. He's so terribly over-cautious. But once he promises something, even if he sounds half-hearted about it, it's bound to happen. He can be relied on, and you don't know how much I need all this to be over, or at least to be certain that it *will* be over … patience, people are always telling me to have patience! But I need to know how long I must be patient. If someone said it will take another six months, it will take a year—very well, I'd say, I accept that, and I'd do anything I was told to do … but thank God the end's in sight! You've no idea how happy I've felt since yesterday. I feel as if I'd only just begun to live. First thing this morning we drove into the town—that surprises you, doesn't it?—but now I know that I'm over the worst I don't mind what people say and think, or whether they look at me and pity me … I want to go driving every day now, just to prove to myself that there's going to be an end to all this patient waiting at last. And tomorrow, Sunday—you do have Sunday off, don't you?— we have a wonderful plan. Papa has promised me we'll go out to the stud farm. I haven't been there for ages, not for four or five years … I didn't like to go out on the road. But tomorrow we're going to drive there, and of course you must come too. You'll be amazed when you find out the surprise Ilona and I have planned. Or … "—and she turned to Ilona, laughing— "or shall I give away the great secret now?"

"Yes, go along," laughed Ilona. "No more secrets!"

"Then listen, dear friend—Papa wanted us to go in the car. But it goes too fast, and it's so boring. I remembered Josef talking about the silly old Princess—you know, the one the castle used to belong to, she was a terrible old dragon—well, she always drove out in a coach and four, the big, brightly painted travelling carriage still standing in the coach house. She always

219

had the four horses harnessed up, even if she was only going to the railway station, to make sure everyone would know that she was the Princess. No one else for miles around ever drove in a coach like that! So think what fun to drive in state like the old Princess for once! The old coachman is still here ... oh, you won't know the old man, he retired when we bought the car. But you should have seen him when we said we'd like to drive out in the coach and four—he stalked around on his shaky legs and practically wept for joy because he was going to drive the coach again ... so it's all arranged, and we're leaving at eight in the morning. We'll have to get up early, and of course you must stay the night here. We'll give you a nice guest room down at the house, and Pista the chauffeur will fetch anything you need from the barracks—he's coming tomorrow, too, dressed like a footman, exactly the way it was in the old Princess's time! No, no protests, you *must* give us the pleasure of your company, you must, there's no getting out of it ... "

And on and on she went, like a whirring, tightly wound spring. I listened, numb and still bemused by this extraordinary transformation. Her voice was entirely different, the usually nervous inflection of her speech was light and fluent, and her familiar face might have been exchanged for another. Her sickly, sallow complexion had a fresher, healthier glow, and all her fidgety, staccato gestures were gone. I was facing a girl whose sparkling eyes and laughing, mobile mouth made her look slightly intoxicated. The warmth of her elation transferred itself to me, relaxing me, as any state of intoxication does. Perhaps it's true after all, I tried to persuade myself, or perhaps it *will* be true. Perhaps I haven't misled her, perhaps she will really get better quickly. After all, I told myself, I haven't told outright lies, or not too many of them—Condor really did read something

220

about an amazing new treatment, why shouldn't it work for this glowing, touchingly confident child, this sensitive creature who is so delighted and inspired by the mere breath of health? Why cast doubt on her high spirits when they light her up like this, why torment her with timid fears? Poor girl, she's tormented herself long enough. And as the enthusiasm aroused by an orator merely by his words also affects himself, giving him real power, so the confidence that my sympathetic exaggeration had brought into being in the first place increasingly took hold of me. When her father finally appeared he found us all in the most carefree mood; we were talking and making plans as if Edith were already better and perfectly healthy. When would she be able to learn to ride again, she asked, and would some of us in the regiment supervise her lessons and help her? And wasn't it time for her father to give the priest the money for the new church roof that he had promised? She laughed and amused herself with all these bold new projects, as if a certain cure was only to be expected, laughing and joking in such a carefree way that the last of my reservations were silenced. Only that evening, when I was alone in my room again, did a suppressed memory begin nagging at my mind—wasn't she going too far, promising herself all this? Oughtn't I to be sobering her dangerous confidence down? But I wouldn't let such thoughts trouble me. Why worry whether I had said too much or too little? Even if I had promised far more than in all honesty I should have done—well, that compassionate lie had made her happy, and to make someone happy can never be wrong or a crime.

The planned expedition began early in the morning with a little fanfare of merriment. When I woke up in my neat, clean guest room, with bright sunlight streaming in, the first thing I heard was the sound of laughing voices. I went over to the window, and saw all the household servants gathering in amazement around the old Princess's large travelling carriage, which must have been brought out of the coach house overnight. It was a magnificent antique, a real museum piece, built a hundred or perhaps a hundred and fifty years ago by the Viennese court coach-builder in Seilerstätte for an ancestor of the Orosvár family. The body of the coach, protected from the jolting of the massive wheels by elaborate springing, was painted in a rather naive style emulating old wall hangings, with pastoral scenes and allegories from classical mythology, and perhaps the once bright colours had faded. The interior of the carriage with its silk upholstery—we had a chance to appreciate it in detail during the drive—offered all kinds of ingenious comforts, like folding tables, little mirrors, and flasks of perfume. Not surprisingly, this gigantic toy from a past century had something unreal about it at first, like a fancy-dress party, but the pleasing result was that the household servants and other staff willingly exerted themselves to get the heavy vehicle launched down the country road. The mechanic from the sugar factory busily greased the wheels and tapped the metalwork to test that it was sound, while the four horses, adorned with bunches of flowers as if they were taking the carriage to a wedding, were put between the shafts, giving Jonak the old coachman a chance of proudly telling everyone what to do. Wearing his faded princely livery, and surprisingly spry on his gouty legs, he explained the tricks of his trade to the younger folk, who might be able to ride bicycles and drive a car if necessary, but not a coach and four. It was also Jonak who had told the cook last night how, when there were paper chases or similar amusements in the old days, the honour of the house required a lavish repast to be served in the most remote places, in woods and meadows, as neatly as if it were being eaten in the castle dining room. Under his supervision, the servants packed up damask tablecloths, napkins and cutlery in cases adorned with a crest to show that they contained the princely silverware. Only then did the cook, a white linen chef's toque above his beaming face, bring out the picnic food itself: roast chickens, ham and pies, freshly baked white bread, and whole batteries of bottles, each resting individually in a bed of straw so as to survive the jolts as the carriage went along the country road. A young fellow representing the cook went along with us to serve the picnic, and was given the place behind the carriage where, in the old days, the princely courier stood beside the footman on duty in his feathered hat.

Thanks to all this ceremony, there was something cheerfully theatrical about the arrangements, and as news of our strange expedition had spread quickly in the local countryside there was no lack of spectators. The farmers and their families from the neighbouring villages had come out in their colourful rustic Sunday best, while wrinkled old women and grey old men with their inevitable clay pipes came from the nearby almshouse. But most of all it was the bare-legged children from near and far who stared, amazed and enchanted, from the horses decked with flowers to the coachman holding the mysteriously intricate straps of the harness in his wrinkled but still sure hand. They were equally delighted with Pista, whom they usually knew in his blue chauffeur's uniform, but today he wore the old princely livery and held a shiny silver hunting horn in his hand, ready to give the signal for us to drive away. First, however, we had

to eat breakfast, and when we finally approached the festive
carriage we could not help noticing, with satisfaction, that we
ourselves presented a considerably less stately sight than the
grand coach and the neatly turned-out footmen. Kekesfalva
looked slightly comical when, in his usual coat and stiff-legged
as a black stork, he climbed into the carriage with its outdated
noble emblems. It would have been appropriate to see the girls
in rococo costume, their hair dusted with white power, black
beauty spots on their cheeks, holding coloured fans, and I myself
would probably have looked better in the white uniform of a
cavalry officer of Maria Theresia's time than in my modern
blue lancer's uniform. But even without historic costumes, it
made a fine show for the good people watching as at last we
settled into the large, heavy coach. Pista raised the hunting
horn, a clear note rang out as the assembled household staff
waved and cheered, the coachman skilfully cracked his whip
in the air with a sound like a shot. As the coach began to
move away, a violent jolt sent us tumbling against one another,
laughing, but then the coachman guided his four horses very
ably through the wrought-iron gate—it suddenly seemed to us
alarmingly narrow for the width of our coach—and we arrived
safely on the road.

It was hardly surprising that we attracted a great deal of attention as we bowled along, but the attention was remarkably
respectful. No one in the locality had seen the princely coach and
four for decades, and its unexpected reappearance seemed to
the farming families to portend some almost supernatural event.
Perhaps they thought we were going to court, or the Emperor
had come to visit these parts, or something else unimaginable
had happened, for hats were swept off everywhere we went as if
mown from their wearers' heads, and the barefoot children ran

along after us and wouldn't stop. If a vehicle coming the other way met us, a heavily laden hay wain or a country horse and trap, the driver would jump quickly down, take off his hat and hold his horses to let us by. We were the autocrats, the road was ours, the whole beautiful, luxuriant countryside with its fields of crops rippling in the wind was ours, the people and the animals were ours. It was like the old feudal times. Admittedly we didn't make fast progress in that massive vehicle, but that gave us plenty of opportunity to see and laugh at everything, and the two girls seized that opportunity. Novelty always enchants the young, and all these unusual features of the outing, our strange vehicle, the respect shown by the people at the unexpected sight we presented, and a hundred other little things heightened the girls' good humour until they were almost intoxicated by the fresh air and sunlight. Edith in particular, who hadn't really been out of the house for months, looked at the wonderful summer day with sparkling eyes, and seemed to be in a mood of boundless high spirits.

Our first stop was in a small village where the church bells were just ringing for Sunday service. The last latecomers could be seen making their way to the village along the narrow paths between the arable fields, but only the men's flat black silk hats and the women's brightly embroidered caps were visible above the tall sheaves. Coming from all points of the compass, this line of people moved like a dark caterpillar through the rippling gold of the corn still standing, and just as we turned into the main street (which was not particularly clean), greatly alarming a flock of cackling geese as they waddled away, the resonant echo of the bell stopped. Sunday matins was about to begin. Unexpectedly, it was Edith who insisted that we must all get out of the coach and join the congregation.

The simple country folk were greatly surprised to see such an extraordinary carriage stop in their unassuming marketplace, where the owner of the whole estate, known to them all by hearsay, got out and went into their little church to take part in matins with his whole family, which also seemed to include me. The sexton came running up, as if the former Leopold Kanitz were Prince Orosvár in person, and told us earnestly that the priest would delay the beginning of mass for us. Our path was lined by the congregation, their heads respectfully bowed, and a wave of sympathy ran through them when they saw Edith's infirmity as Josef and Ilona supported her and helped her into the church. Simple people are always moved to see that the rich, too, can suffer misfortune. There was a murmuring and whispering, and then some of the women thoughtfully brought cushions so that the frail girl could sit as comfortably as possible—of course in the front pew, which was quickly cleared for us. It was almost as if the priest were celebrating mass with special solemnity for our benefit. I was greatly touched by the moving simplicity of this little church—the clear singing of the women, the deeper, sometimes rough tones of the men, the children's naive voices all seemed to bear witness to a purer, more immediate faith than that of many more sophisticated church services, the kind that I knew from Sundays in St Stephen's cathedral or the Augustinian church at home in Vienna. Against my will, however, I was distracted from my own prayers when I happened to look at Edith, sitting next to me, and was startled to see the ardent fervour with which she was praying. I had never before seen any sign that she had been brought up to be devout, or was naturally pious, but now I saw her deep in prayer that was not, like most people's, a matter of habit. Her pale face was lowered as if she were walking into a strong wind, her hands held the front of the pew tightly, it was as if all her outward senses were turned on her inmost being, and as she automatically murmured the words of the service her entire bearing was that of a woman with her nerves strung up to a high point of tension, using her concentrated powers in the attempt to force something into being. Sometimes I felt the pew in front of us trembling, so fervently did the ardour of that ecstatic prayer transfer itself to the dark wood. I knew at once that she was turning to God to ask for some particular answer to her prayers, that there was something the sick, crippled girl wanted the Deity to provide, and it was not difficult to guess what it was.

Even when we had helped Edith back into the coach after the end of matins, she remained thoughtful for a long time, and did not say a word. She was no longer turning to look at everything with interest; it was as if that half-hour spent wrestling for her heart's desire had left her weary, exhausted. Naturally the rest of us said little. It was a quiet drive now, and the pace of the coach slowed down until we had nearly reached the stud farm just before midday.

Here, however, a special reception was waiting for us. The local young men, obviously told in advance about our visit, had chosen to ride the most high-spirited horses in the stud, and now came to meet us at a smart gallop in a kind of Arabian fantasia. It was a fine sight to see these young fellows whooping with delight, sunburnt in their open-necked shirts, and with long coloured ribbons dangling from their low-crowned hats. In white trousers of the kind worn by Argentinian cowboys, they raced up riding bareback, like a Bedouin horde intent on running us down. Our four coach horses were already pricking up their ears uneasily, and old Jonak had to rein them in sharply, bracing his legs on the coachman's box, as at a sudden whistle the wild band formed skilfully into a line and then escorted us to the stud manager's house like a cheerful cortège.

As a trained cavalryman I saw much there to interest me. The two girls, on the other hand, were shown the foals, and couldn't see enough of those skittishly inquisitive creatures, still not quite steady on their angular legs, and with mouths that didn't yet know what to do with the sugar lumps they were offered. While we were all so happily occupied, the kitchen lad, carefully supervised by Josef, had set out a fine picnic in the open air. Soon the wine proved so good and so strong that our cheerfulness, muted until now, became more and more exuberant. We were all talking away, feeling friendlier and more relaxed than ever, not the least cloud troubled the silky blue of the sky above us in those hours, nor did the sobering thought cross my mind that I had never before known the frail girl now laughing even more heartily and happily than the rest of us as anything but a desperate, disturbed invalid. And was the old gentleman patting and examining the horses with a veterinary surgeon's expertise, joking with the grooms and handing them tips, really the same man who, a couple of days ago, had been lying in wait for me by night like a sleepwalker, weighed down by a burden of crazed fear? Indeed, I hardly even knew myself, so light and easy did my limbs feel, as if all my joints had been oiled. After our picnic Edith was taken to the stud manager's wife's room to rest for a little while, and meanwhile I tried out a couple of the horses, racing across the paddocks with the grooms. I felt a hitherto unknown sense of freedom in letting the reins drop and giving the horses their heads. How good it would be to stay here, subject to no one, free as air in these open fields! My heart was a little heavy when, after galloping some way, I heard the call of the hunting horn in the distance, telling us it was time to set out for home.

To give us a change of scene, the experienced coachman Jonak had chosen a different route back. Another reason was probably that it led for some way through the cool shade of a little wood. And just as everything was turning out well on this successful day, a last surprise, and the best of all, awaited us—as we drove into a hamlet of about twenty cottages, the only road in this remote place proved to be barred by a dozen empty farm carts. Curiously enough, there seemed to be no one at all around to move them away so that our wide and heavy coach could pass; it was as if the ground had opened and swallowed up all the villagers. However, the reason for their unusual absence on a Sunday was soon explained when Jonak, handling his long whip with practised ease, cracked the lash in the air with a report very much like a pistol shot, for a few alarmed people came running. Any misunderstanding was soon happily cleared up—it turned out that the son of the richest farmer in the neighbourhood was getting married today to a poor relation of his, a girl from another hamlet, and the bridegroom's father, a rather stout man, red in the face in his wish to be attentive, came running out to welcome us from a barn cleared for dancing at the end of the village street barred by all those empty carts. Perhaps he thought that the owner of the Kekesfalva estate, that man of the world, had ordered up his coach and four on purpose to honour him and his son by coming to the wedding, or perhaps his vanity just led him to exploit the fact that we were driving by to enhance his reputation among the other villagers. At any rate, bowing low, he invited Herr von Kekesfalva and his guests to be kind enough to drink a glass of his own home-made Hungarian wine to the young couple's health, while the street was cleared for us. For our part, we were in much too good a mood to refuse this well-meant invitation. So Edith was carefully lifted out of the coach and we went in procession, as if celebrating a Roman triumph, down a broad path lined by the respectful villagers, whispering and marvelling, and so into the rustic dance hall.

The dance hall did indeed prove on closer inspection to be a barn cleared for the purpose, and a dais of loose planks standing on empty beer barrels had been erected. Members of the family sat around the bridal couple, enthroned at a long table standing on a low platform and covered with a coarse white linen cloth, with bottles and dishes of food standing on it. The usual local notables, the priest and the village policeman, were there as well. On the dais opposite sat the musicians, Gypsies of romantic appearance with moustaches, playing two fiddles, a double bass and a cimbalom, and the guests thronged the stamped earth of the dancing floor, while the children, who couldn't get into the crowded barn, watched cheerfully, some from the doorway, some perched on the rafters in the roof, dangling their legs.

Some of the less important family members were asked to move from the table of honour to make room for us, and amazement at the friendliness of their fine visitors was plain to see on the guests' faces as we mingled easily with the ordinary country folk. The bridegroom's father, swaying with his excitement, fetched a large jug of wine with his own hands, filled glasses, and raised his voice: "Herr von Kekesfalva's very good health!" The enthusiastic echo of this cry rang out into the village street. Then he brought along his son and the son's new wife, a shy girl with rather broad hips who made a touching picture in her colourful wedding dress, crowned with a wreath of white myrtle. Flushed with excitement, she curtseyed clumsily to Kekesfalva and respectfully kissed Edith's hand. Edith looked very much moved. The sight of a wedding usually affects young girls deeply because it makes them feel a mysterious solidarity with their own sex. Blushing, Edith drew the girl to her, embraced her, and as a sudden thought occurred to her she took a ring from her finger—a narrow, old-fashioned ring of no great value—and gave it to the bride, who was overwhelmed by this unexpected present. She glanced anxiously at her father-in-law, wondering if she ought to accept such a splendid gift, and as soon as he nodded proudly to her she burst into tears of happiness. A great wave of gratitude surged towards us as the simple folk, unused to any luxury, crowded up from all sides; it was clear from their glances that they would have liked to show us some special attention, but no one dared say a word to such distinguished gentlefolk. The old farmer's wife, tears in her eyes, was stumbling as if tipsy from one guest to another, dazed by the honour shown to her son at his wedding, while the bridegroom, quite bewildered, looked in turn from his wife to us and down at his heavy, well-polished boots.

At this point Kekesfalva did the best thing possible by putting an end to what was becoming an embarrassing display of respect. He shook hands warmly with the bridegroom's father, the young bridegroom himself, and some of the more notable guests, and asked them not to let us disturb their wonderful party. Let the young people go on dancing to their hearts' content, he asked, nothing could give us greater pleasure than for them to continue enjoying themselves. At the same time he beckoned over the leader of the musical ensemble, who had been waiting in front of the dais with his fiddle tucked under his right arm, frozen, as it were, while making a respectful bow, gave him a banknote and indicated that he should start playing again. It must have been a note of some high denomination, because the man straightened up as if he had received an electric shock, hurried back to his dais, looked at the other musicians, and next moment the four of them began playing as only Hungarian Gypsies can. The first notes on the cimbalom swept away any self-consciousness. Couples formed instantly, the dancing went on apace, wilder and more exuberant than before—unconsciously, all the young men and girls felt they wanted to show us how real Hungarians can dance. All at once the dance hall, respectfully silent a moment ago, was transformed into a heated whirlpool of swaying, leaping, stamping bodies, the glasses on the table clinked at every new bar of music, and the enthusiastic young people danced their hearts out.

Edith looked at the dancing, her eyes very bright. Suddenly I felt her hand on my arm. "You must dance too," she told me. Fortunately the bride hadn't yet been drawn back into the swirling crowd, but was still staring, dazed, at the ring on her finger. When I bowed to her she blushed at first at this great, almost excessive honour, but was willing to let me lead her into the dance. Our example encouraged the bridegroom. Prompted by a nudge from his father, he asked Ilona to dance, and now the player of the cimbalom was hammering away on his instrument like a man possessed, while the leader of the ensemble, daemonic with his black moustache, played his fiddle with brio. I doubt whether such bacchanalian dancing was ever seen in the hamlet, before or since, as on that wedding day.

But the cornucopia of surprises wasn't empty yet. Attracted to us by the handsome present of that ring to the bride, one of those old Gypsy women who are sure to be found at such festivities made her way up to the table and offered, volubly, to read Edith's palm for her. Edith was clearly in some difficulty. On the one hand she was genuinely curious, on the other she was ashamed to give way to such mumbo-jumbo in front of so many spectators. I quickly intervened, gently persuading Herr von Kekesfalva and the rest of our party to move away from the table raised on its platform so that no one could overhear the woman's mysterious prophecies, and anyone interested had no option but to watch from a distance, smiling, as the old Gypsy knelt down, with much incomprehensible muttering, took Edith's hand and studied it. Everyone in Hungary knows the old trick practised by such women, who give their customers only good tidings so as to profit by the news. But to my surprise Edith seemed strangely agitated by everything the bent old woman said in her hoarse, rapid whisper; I saw her nostrils begin to quiver in the way that always indicated strong emotion in her. Bending lower and lower, she listened, sometimes glancing around to see whether anyone could overhear. Then she beckoned her father over, whispered something to him in imperious tones, and he, as usual doing what she wanted, put his hand into his breast pocket and brought out several banknotes, which he gave to the old woman. The sum must have been enormous by the standards of this village, for the greedy old woman fell on her knees, kissed the hem of Edith's skirt, and stroked her lame feet faster and faster, murmuring strange invocations. Then she suddenly jumped up as if afraid that someone might take all that money away from her.

"Let's leave now," I quickly whispered to Herr von Kekesfalva, noticing how pale Edith had turned. I found Pista, and he and Ilona half-led, half-supported the girl, who was swaying on her crutches, to the coach. At once the music faltered; none of these good people could let us go without waving and calling goodbye. The musicians came up to the coach and played a final flourish, the whole village shouted and cheered, and old Jonak had some trouble in controlling his horses, which were not used to such a loud noise.

I was a little uneasy about Edith as I sat opposite her in the carriage. She was still trembling all over, and some violent emotion seemed to be preying on her mind. All at once a sudden sob burst from her throat—but it was a sob of joy. She laughed and cried at the same time. I felt sure that the cunning Gypsy woman had foretold a swift cure for her, and perhaps more besides.

However, even as she sobbed Edith protested impatiently, "Oh, leave me alone, leave me alone." Even shaken as she was, she seemed to be feeling some entirely new and remarkable pleasure. "Leave me alone, leave me alone," she kept repeating. "Yes, I know the old woman was out to deceive me, but why can't I be silly just once in a while? Why not let myself be well and truly deceived?"

It was already late in the evening when we drove in through the castle gate. All the others urged me to stay to supper, but I did not want to. I felt that quite enough, if not too much, had happened. I had been perfectly happy all that long, golden summer's day; anything more, anything extra could only detract from that. I preferred to go home now down the familiar avenue, my mind soothed by the summer air and the aftermath of the glowing day. I didn't want to wish for more, just to remember the day with gratitude and think it all over. So I said my goodbyes early. The stars were shining, and I felt as if they were looking down kindly on me. The breeze blew softly over the fields as light drained away, leaving them dark, and I felt as if it were singing. I was overcome by that pure delight you feel when everything seems good and happy, the world and the people in it, when you could embrace every tree and stroke its bark as if it were the skin of someone you love—when you feel like going into every strange house, sitting down with its unknown inhabitants, and confiding all your feelings to them; when your own chest is too narrow to contain your deep emotions, and you want to share them, let them pour extravagantly out—when you want to give away some of this excess of feeling, to squander it!

When at last I reached the barracks, my batman was waiting outside the door of my room. For the first time (everything today I felt as if for the first time) I noticed what a good-hearted, round, apple-cheeked face this rustic Ruthenian boy had. I must do something to give him pleasure, I thought. Better give him a little money to buy a couple of glasses of beer for himself and his girl. He can go out this evening, and tomorrow, and all week! I was already searching for a silver coin in my pocket. Then he stood to attention and announced, hands smartly down beside the seam of his trousers, "Telegram came for you, Lieutenant Hofmiller, sir."

A telegram? I immediately had an uncomfortable sensation. Who in the world would want to send me a telegram? Only bad news could seek me out at such speed. I quickly went over to the table. There lay the piece of paper, a sealed rectangle. Reluctantly, I tore it open. There were only a dozen or so words saying, with concise clarity: "Visiting Kekesfalva tomorrow. Must speak to you urgently first. Expect you at five, Tyrolean Wine Bar. Condor."

I had already once known a state of reeling intoxication switch within a single moment to crystal-clear sobriety. That had been last year, at the goodbye party of a comrade who was marrying the daughter of a very rich north Bohemian manufacturer, and was giving us a lavish evening's entertainment first. Our good friend was certainly not mean about it—he had whole batteries of bottles brought in, heavy, dark-red claret followed by so much champagne that, depending on our temperament, some of us waxed voluble and others turned sentimental. We hugged each other, we laughed, we ran riot, kicked up a lot of noise and sang heartily. We drank toasts again and again, tipping strong cognac and liqueurs down our throats, we puffed away at pipes and cigars until the overheated bar was enveloped in a kind of blue mist, and so in the end none of us noticed that the sky was growing lighter outside the dull windowpanes. It must have been about three or four in the morning, and most of us couldn't even sit up straight any more. Lolling over the table, we just looked up with blurred, glazed eyes when a new toast was announced, and if anyone had to go out for a moment he tottered and staggered or stumbled to the door like a full sack. None of us could speak or think clearly.

Then, suddenly, the door was flung open, the Colonel strode in (I shall have more to say about our colonel later), and as only a few of us even noticed or recognised him in all the racket we were making, he marched up to the table and struck its dirty top with his fist, making the plates and glasses clink. Then, in his harshest, most cutting voice, he ordered, "Quiet!"

And instantly, all at once, it was quiet. Even those who had dozed off blinked, and were wide awake. The Colonel briefly informed us that a surprise inspection by the divisional commander was to be expected that morning. He supposed, he said, that he could count on everything to go impeccably, and he hoped no one would bring shame on the regiment. And now a strange thing happened—all at once every one of us was in full possession of his wits. As if someone had flung open a window, the fumes of alcohol dispersed, our blurred faces changed, responding to the call of duty, everyone pulled himself together, and two minutes later the table, that scene of wild indulgence, was abandoned. We were all wide awake, our minds clear, and we all knew what we had to do. The men were roused, the orderlies got busy, everything was swiftly groomed and polished down to the last pommel on the last saddle, and a few hours later the much-feared inspection took place and went without a hitch.

In just the same way, as soon as I had opened that telegram my dreamy, gentle mood was gone like a shot. Within a second I knew what I had refused to understand for hours and hours on end—all that happy enthusiasm had been nothing but intoxication induced by a lie, and in my weakness, my fatal pity, I was guilty of a deception, or had made myself party to it. I guessed at once that Dr Condor was coming to call me to account for myself. Now I had to pay the price for my own cheerful mood of the last two days—and the exuberant high spirits of the others.

With the punctuality of impatience, and as a result quarter-of-an-hour early, I was standing outside the wine bar at the time he had fixed, and exactly at that time Condor drove up from the station in a carriage and pair. He came straight over to me without further formalities.

"Good to see you here on time. I knew I could rely on you. I think we'd better sit in the same little nook as before. We don't want anyone overhearing what we have to discuss."

I could tell that his former almost listless bearing had changed. He marched ahead of me into the inn in a manner that was both energetic and self-controlled, and asked the waitress who came hurrying up for, "A litre of wine—the same as we were drinking the day before yesterday. And then leave us alone; I'll call if I need you."

We sat down. Even before the waitress had put our wine down on the table, he began.

"Well, let's keep this short. I have to hurry, or out at Kekesfalva they'll suspect us of hatching Heaven knows what conspiracies. I had a hard job preventing the chauffeur from coming to town to drive me straight out there—he was intent on spiriting me away at any price. But now let's plunge *in medias res*, so that I can put you in the picture.

"Very well—first thing the day before yesterday I received a telegram. 'Please, dear friend, come as quickly as possible. Expecting you with all imaginable impatience. Most grateful, have every confidence in you. Yours, Kekesfalva.' I didn't like the sound of those superlatives. Why so impatient all of a sudden? I examined Edith only a couple of days ago. And why that telegraphic assurance of his confidence and his special gratitude? Well, I assumed there wasn't really any great urgency, I put the telegram with other correspondence. After all, the old man indulges in such exaggerations quite often. But what came yesterday morning put a different complexion on it—I had an endlessly long letter from Edith, a crazy, ecstatic letter, sent express, saying she had always known that I was the only person on earth who could save her, she couldn't tell me how

238

happy she was to think we had reached this stage at last. She was writing, she said, only to assure me that I could rely absolutely on her, she would certainly undertake to do everything I told her, however hard it was. But she wanted to begin the new course of treatment soon, at once, she was burning with impatience. And she repeated that I could expect anything of her, just so long as I began soon. And so on and so forth.

"However, with that remark about new treatment light dawned on me. I realised at once that someone must have been talking either to the old man or his daughter about the method tried by Professor Viennot. Such stories don't come out of thin air. And that someone, of course, had to be you, Lieutenant Hofmiller."

I must have made an instinctive movement, for he immediately went on in the same vein.

"No, no discussion of that point, please! I have not made the slightest reference to Professor Viennot's method in talking to anyone else. It's your doing alone if they believe at Kekesfalva that everything can now be put right within a few months, as easily as wiping dust away with a cloth. So as I said, let's spare ourselves any recriminations; we both talked indiscreetly, I to you, and then you at great length to the others. I should have spoken more cautiously to you—after all, the treatment of the sick is not your profession, so how would you know that invalids and their families do not use the same vocabulary as normal folk, that to their ears every 'perhaps' instantly becomes a 'certainly'? Hope has to be administered to them only in carefully measured droplets, or optimism will go to their heads and run away with them.

"But we'll agree that what's done is done. Let us draw a line under the subject of responsibility. I didn't ask you here to read you a lecture. However, now that you have meddled in my business, I feel in duty bound to explain the state of affairs to you—that's why I wanted you to come here."

At this point Condor raised his voice for the first time and looked straight at me. But there was no severity in his gaze. On the contrary—I felt that he was sorry for me. His voice now became milder.

"I know, my dear Lieutenant Hofmiller, that what I have to tell you now will touch a very painful spot. But as I have indicated, this is no time for soft sentimentality. I told you that on reading that report in the medical journal I wrote straight to Professor Viennot, asking for more information—I think that is all I said to you. Well, his reply came yesterday, by the same post as Edith's emotional screed. At first sight what he said sounds positive. Viennot has indeed had remarkable success with that patient of his, and several others. But unfortunately—and here's the rub—his method cannot be used in our case. Those he cured had disorders of the spinal cord resulting from tubercular infections—I'll spare you the medical details—where the motor nerves can be restored to their full function by changing the place on which pressure is exerted. In Edith's case her central nervous system is affected, so that Professor Viennot's procedures—lying motionless in a kind of metal corset, irradiation with sun-rays at the same time, his particular system of exercises—are ruled out from the start. In our case, I am very, very sorry to say, his methods are impracticable. Making the poor child endure all these elaborate procedures would probably mean tormenting her unnecessarily. Well—it was my duty to tell you that. Now you know the true state of affairs, and you can see how thoughtlessly you captivated the poor girl with the hope of being able to dance and run about again in a few months' time. No one would ever have heard such a foolish claim from me. However, now that you have promised over-hastily to bring the moon and the stars down from the sky for the Kekesfalvas, they will believe you and no one else, and rightly so. After all, it was you who reassured them."

I felt my fingers stiffen. Subconsciously I had been expecting all this ever since the moment when I saw the telegram lying on the table, and yet as Condor explained the situation with implacable objectivity I felt as if I had been hit on the head with a blunt hatchet. I instinctively went on the defensive. I didn't want to shoulder the whole responsibility myself. But what I finally managed to say sounded like the stammering of a schoolboy caught out doing wrong.

"But how did I … I mean, I only acted for the best. If I told Kekesfalva anything it was only out of … out of … "

"I know, I know," Condor interrupted me. "And of course he wormed it out of you, made you tell him, his desperate insistence can wear down anyone's defences. Yes, I know, I know you did it only out of pity, that's to say you weakened with the best and most creditable of intentions. But—I think I have warned you already—pity is a double-edged weapon. If you don't know how to handle it you had better not touch it, and above all you must steel your heart against it. Pity, like morphine, does the sick good only at first. It is a means of helping them to feel better, but if you don't get the dose right and know where to stop it becomes a murderous poison. The first few injections do the patient good, they are soothing, they relieve pain. But the organism, body and mind alike, has a fatal and mysterious ability to adjust, and just as the nerves crave more and more morphine, the mind wants more and more pity, more in the end than anyone can give. In both contingencies, there is a point when the inevitable moment comes where you have to say 'No', never mind whether patients hate you more for that final refusal than if you had never helped them at all. My dear Lieutenant, pity must be kept well under control, or it will do more harm than any amount of indifference—we doctors know that, judges know it, bailiffs and pawnbrokers know it. If they were all to give way to pity the world would grind to a halt—it's a dangerous thing, pity, a dangerous thing! You can see for yourself what your weakness has done in this case."

"Yes … but one can't … one can't simply leave another human being in despair … after all, there was nothing wrong with my trying to—"

But Condor suddenly spoke forcefully "Oh yes, there was— there was a great deal wrong with it! Responsibility, damn it, think of the responsibility of fooling someone else with your pity! A grown man should stop to think how far he plans to go when he meddles with something—not play about with other people's feelings! Admittedly you played with the feelings of those good folk for the kindest and most compassionate reasons, but in this world it makes no difference whether you hit hard or hesitantly, it all depends what you ultimately do, it depends on the final result. Pity—yes, that's all very well. But there are two kinds of pity. One, the weak-minded, sentimental sort is really just the heart's impatience to rid itself as quickly as possible of the painful experience of being moved by another person's suffering. It is a not a case of real sympathy, of feeling *with* the sufferer, but a way of defending yourself against the sufferer's pain. The other kind, the only one that counts, is unsentimental but creative. It knows its own mind, and is determined to stand by the sufferer, patiently suffering too to the last of its strength and even beyond. Only when you go all the way to the end, the bitter end, only when you have that patience, can you really help people. Only if you are ready to sacrifice yourself, only then!"

There was a note of bitterness in his voice. Involuntarily, I remembered what Kekesfalva had told me—that Condor had married a blind woman whom he couldn't cure more or less as a penance, and instead of being grateful she nagged him. But now he was placing his hand warmly, almost affectionately, on my arm.

"Well, I don't mean to be harsh. Your feelings got the better of you—it can happen to anyone. But now to business. After all, I didn't ask you here to discuss psychology with you; we have practical matters on hand. Naturally it's necessary for us to act in concert—we can't have you going behind my back and interfering with my intentions a second time. So listen. I am afraid I have to conclude from that letter of Edith's that our friends have fallen hopelessly prey to the delusion that all her complex disorders can be wiped away as if with a sponge, by means of that course of treatment which, as we know, will not do her any good. Although that folly has gone dangerously deep, there's no option but to operate on it at once, cut it right out—and the sooner the better for all concerned. Of course it will be an unpleasant shock. The truth is always bitter medicine, but a delusion like that can't be allowed to go further. You may take it from me that I shall attack it as gently as possible.

"And now to you. Of course the most comfortable thing for me would be to lay all the blame on you, to say you misunderstood me, you were exaggerating, or imagining things. I won't do that; I'd rather take it all on myself. Only, and I will tell you this to your face, I can't leave you out of the business entirely. You know that old man and his dogged persistence. If I were to explain to him a hundred times, and show him Professor

Viennot's letter, he would still be protesting, 'But you promised Lieutenant Hofmiller … and Lieutenant Hofmiller said … ' He would be citing you the whole time to pretend to himself, and me, that in spite of everything there was still some kind of hope. Without you to back me up I'll never convince him. Illusions can't be shaken off as easily as you shake the quicksilver down in a thermometer. Once you have one of those disorders so cruelly called incurable, you clutch at any straw for hope, see it as a solid plank and then make it a whole house. But such castles in the air are very bad for the sick, and it is my duty as a doctor to demolish them as quickly as I can before high hopes take up residence there. We must strike hard, without losing any time."

Condor stopped. He was obviously waiting for me to agree. But I dared not meet his gaze; images of yesterday, driven by my thudding heartbeat, were racing past my mind's eye. Our cheerful drive through the summer countryside, the sick girl's face glowing with sun and happiness. The way she petted the little foals and sat enthroned like a queen at the wedding party, the way the old man's tears kept running down into his laughing, trembling mouth. To think of destroying all that with a single blow! To turn a girl so wonderfully transformed, plucked out of her despair, back into what she had been before, to thrust her away into all the hells of impatience with a word! No, I knew I could never put my hand to that task. So I said, hesitantly, "But wouldn't it be better to … " and then my voice faltered again before his searching gaze.

"Better to do what?" he asked sharply.

"I was only wondering whether … whether it wouldn't be better to wait before making that revelation … at least for a few days, because … because yesterday I had the impression that her heart was already so set on that treatment … I mean *really* set on it ... and that now she would have what you called the ... the psychological strength ... I mean that she'd be able to draw on herself to do much more if ... if she was only left believing for a while that this new course of treatment, which she expects to do so much, would cure her in the end. You ... you didn't see, you ... you can't imagine the effect just hearing about it had on her. I really did get the impression that she was able to move much better at once ... and I wonder whether that shouldn't be allowed to take full effect. Of course," I said, my voice failing because I could tell that Condor was looking up at me in surprise, "of course I don't really understand these things ... "

Condor was still looking at me. Then he growled, "Well, who'd have thought it? Saul among the prophets! You seem to have acquired a thorough grounding in these subjects—you even remembered the part about the psychological powers! And your clinical observations into the bargain—without knowing it I seem to have picked up an assistant and adviser! As it happens," he went on, thoughtfully scratching his head with his nervous hand, "what you say is not so stupid—forgive me, I mean, of course, medically stupid. It's strange, really strange—when I read that ecstatic letter from Edith I wondered myself, for a minute, whether now that you had persuaded her a cure was coming her way in seven-league boots, that passionate belief of hers should not be exploited ... Not bad thinking at all, colleague! It would be child's play to stage the whole thing—I'd send her off to a spa in the Engadine valley in Switzerland where a friend of mine is a doctor, we'd leave her in the happy belief that she was having the new treatment whereas it would really still be the old one. At first the effect probably *would* be excellent, and we would get floods of enthusiastic, grateful letters.

The illusion, the change of air, the change of scene, her strong investment of energy, all that would indeed help enormously and reinforce the deception. After all, two weeks in the Engadine valley would probably be very stimulating even to you and me. But my dear Lieutenant Hofmiller, as a doctor I have to think not only of the beginning of a treatment but also of its progress, and above all of the final outcome. I have to take into account the setback that would inevitably—yes, inevitably—come as the result of such wildly exaggerated hopes. I'm a chess player, even in my medical profession, I play a patient game, I must not turn into a gambler, least of all when someone else has put down the stake and must pay."

"But … but you yourself think there could be a considerable improvement … "

"Certainly—at first we would get a good way forward. Women always react astonishingly well to feelings and illusions. All the same, think of the situation in a few months' time when what we call her psychological forces are exhausted, the will she has wound up to such a high pitch is used up, her passion spent, and still after weeks and weeks of tiring effort there is no cure, not the complete cure on which she now counts as a certainty. Please think of the catastrophic effect of that on a sensitive creature already consumed with impatience! We are not talking about a small improvement in this case, we are talking about something fundamental, of changing from the slow but sure method of patience to the bold and dangerous course of impatience! How is she ever to trust me again, or any other doctor or any other human being, if she sees that she has been deliberately deceived? Better the truth, then, cruel as it may seem; in medicine the knife is always the more merciful approach. We must not put this off! I could not be responsible, with a clear conscience, for such an underhand act. Think about it yourself! Would you have the courage to do that, in my place?"

"Yes," I replied without thinking, and instantly took fright at my quick reply. "I mean ... " I added cautiously, "I wouldn't confess the whole thing to her until she has at least made *some* progress ... forgive me, doctor, it sounds rather presumptuous of me, but you haven't had a chance of seeing how much she needs something to help her, as I have recently ... and yes, she must be told the truth ... but only when she can bear it, not now, doctor, I beg you ... not now, not at once."

I hesitated, confused by the curiosity and astonishment in his eyes.

"Then when?" he asked. "And above all, who's going to take the risk? An explanation will be necessary sometime, and disappointment will be a hundred times more dangerous then, indeed life-endangering. Would you really accept that responsibility?"

"Yes," I said firmly (I think only the fear that otherwise I must go out to Kekesfalva with him at once gave me that sudden determination). "I'll take the responsibility entirely on myself. I know for certain that it will help Edith enormously just now to be left for a while hoping for a full, final recovery. And then if it turns out necessary to explain that we ... that I may have promised too much, I'll admit it frankly, and I am sure she will understand everything."

Condor was looking at me with a fixed stare. "Good heavens," he finally murmured, "you expect a lot of yourself. And the odd thing about it is that you infect the rest of us with your belief in God's goodness—first our friends out there, and now, I'm afraid, it's affecting me too. Well, if you're really ready to take the restoration of Edith's mental equilibrium upon yourself should there be a crisis, then ... then of course the whole

247

thing takes on a different complexion. Then perhaps we really might risk waiting a few days for her nerves to calm down … but when you give such pledges there's no going back, Lieutenant. It's my duty to warn you solemnly of that. We doctors are bound to point out all the possible dangers of any operation to those most closely concerned—and to promise a girl who's been paralysed for so long that she will soon be entirely better is an operation to be undertaken as seriously as if you were performing it with a scalpel. So think hard about what you're taking on yourself—it calls for enormous strength to restore the confidence of someone you have once deceived. I don't like a lack of clarity. Before I abandon my original intention of telling the Kekesfalvas at once, and honestly, that Viennot's method is impracticable in this case, and we must unfortunately ask them to show yet more patience, I have to know whether I can rely on you. Can I count on you absolutely not to let me down?"

"Absolutely!"

"Well and good, then." Condor pushed his glass away from him abruptly. Neither of us had drunk a drop of the wine. "Or rather, I should say let's hope it turns out well and good, because I'm not entirely happy about this procrastination. I'll tell you here and now just how far I will go, and that's not a step beyond the truth. I will suggest treatment at Engadine, but I will explain that the Viennot method has not been proven, and I will expressly emphasise that neither of them must expect miracles. If they cloud their minds with pointless hopes all the same, trusting you as they do, it will be up to you—I have your word—up to you to come clean in good time. It may be a bold venture on my part to trust you rather than my medical conscience—well, I will take that upon myself. After all, we both mean well by that poor sick girl." Condor rose to his feet.

"As I said, I'm counting on you. If there should be some crisis arising from her disappointment, it's to be hoped that your impatience will do more than my patience. So we will leave the poor child a few weeks of confidence! And if in that time we really do see some improvement in her, then it will be you and not I who helped her. There, that's agreed. It's high time to go; I'm expected out at the house."

We left the inn. His carriage was standing ready for him outside. When he had climbed up, my lip trembled for a moment as if to call him back. But the horses were already setting off. The carriage, and with it something that could not be changed now, was set in motion.

Three hours later, I found a note on my table in the barracks, hastily written and brought by the Kekesfalvas' chauffeur.

Come as early as you can tomorrow. There's so much to tell you. Dr Condor has just been here. We're going away in ten days' time. I'm so excited!
    Edith.

Odd for me to pick up that book on that particular night. I didn't read much as a general rule, and the rickety bookshelf in my room in the barracks held only the six or eight military volumes of regimental rules and the army drill book—the alpha and omega of knowledge for us—along with some two dozen classic works that, without ever opening them, I had brought with me from military academy to every garrison where I was posted— perhaps just to give some look of containing personal possessions to the bleak, unfamiliar rooms where I was obliged to live. A few other books also lay around, poorly printed and badly bound volumes with half the pages still uncut, and I had come by these books in a curious way. Sometimes a hunchbacked little hawker with deep-set, strangely melancholy eyes would come into our café, pressing his wares on us: notepaper, pencils and cheap, somewhat risqué books for which he hoped to find a market in our masculine, military circles: the amorous adventures of Casanova, the *Decameron*, the memoirs of a diva, or amusing tales of garrison life. Out of pity for him—and there I go, pity again!—and also, perhaps, in self-defence against his importunate sales talk, I had acquired three or four of these smutty, badly printed volumes, and then left them casually in my bookcase.

That evening, however, when I was both tired and over-wrought, unable to sleep but also unable to think straight, and looking for reading matter to distract my mind and make me drowsy, I picked up the *Tales of a Thousand and One Nights*, hoping that those naive, vivid stories, which I vaguely remembered from childhood, would have the right narcotic effect on me. I lay down and began to read, in that state of near-somnolence when you feel almost too weary to turn the page, and if you come upon a couple of pages that happen to be still uncut you skip them for the sake of convenience. I read the opening story about Scheherazade and the Sultan with only part of my attention, then found myself reading on and on. And suddenly I was wide awake. I had come to the strange story of the young man who meets a lame old cripple on the road, and at that word "lame" I felt a sharp pang. Like a branding iron, the sudden association touched a nerve in me. In the story, the cripple calls out desperately to the youth, complaining that he can't walk and asking if the young man will let him sit on his shoulders and carry him for a while. The young man is sorry for him—sorry, you fool, I wondered, why feel sorry for him? But sure enough, he helpfully bends down and takes the old man on his shoulders.

However, the apparently helpless old man is a djinn, a wicked magician, and as soon as he is on the young man's shoulders he suddenly winds his bare, hairy legs firmly around his benefactor's throat and cannot be thrown off. Mercilessly, he rides the helpful, sympathetic lad as if he were a horse, whipping him on without mercy or consideration, allowing him no rest. And the unfortunate youth has to carry him wherever he wants to go; he has no will of his own left. He is the slave of the evil enchanter, the steed that carries him, and although his knees are trembling and his lips dry, it is his fate to go on and on, the victim of his own pity, carrying the wicked, cunning old man on his back.

I stopped reading. My heart was thudding as if it would burst. For even as I read, I suddenly *saw* that strange, sly old man as if in a vision, at first lying on the ground and opening his tearful eyes to beg the sympathetic young man for help, and then I saw him riding on his victim's back. The djinn had sparse white hair and wore gold-rimmed glasses. With the sudden lightning intuition that, in the normal way, can mingle and associate images and faces only in dreams, I had instinctively given the old man in the story Kekesfalva's features, and suddenly I myself had become the djinn's unhappy victim, whipped on and on. I even felt such physical pressure around my throat that my breath faltered. The book fell from my hands, I lay where I was, cold as ice, hearing my heart thud against my ribs as if they were made of hard wood. The grim huntsman chased me on and on in my sleep, going I didn't know where. When I woke in the morning with my hair damp, I was as exhausted as if I had just been on a long journey.

Riding out with my comrades in the morning did me no good, although I carried out my military duties watchfully and meticulously. My usual walk up to the castle in the afternoon did nothing to cheer me either—I still felt that sinister weight on my shoulders. Shaken as I was, I already realised that the responsibility now mine was not only new to me but impossibly difficult. On that night in front of the barracks when I had held out to the old man the prospect of a cure for his child in the near future, my exaggeration had been only a kindly meant white lie, uttered involuntarily and indeed reluctantly, not yet a conscious deception, not deliberately fraudulent. From now on, however, now that I knew no swift recovery was in fact to be expected, I had let myself in for cold, calculating, long-term dissembling. I must tell lies with an expression that gave nothing away, I must perjure myself like a hardened criminal who cleverly thinks out every detail of his crime in advance, weeks and months before committing it, as well as his defence against charges of guilt. For the first time I began to understand that you do not bring trouble on yourself so much through wickedness or brutality as—almost always—through sheer weakness.

Everything went just as I had feared at the Kekesfalvas' villa. As soon as I stepped out on the terrace at the top of the tower I was enthusiastically welcomed. I had brought a few flowers, on purpose to divert attention from myself at first. But after Edith's sudden cry of, "My goodness, why are you bringing me flowers? I'm not a prima donna!" I had to sit down beside the impatient girl, and she began to talk and talk, never stopping. She told her tale with a certain almost hallucinatory note in her voice. Dr Condor—"Oh, that extraordinary, that wonderful man!"—had given her new courage, she said. In ten days' time they were going to a Swiss sanatorium in the Engadine valley—why delay another day, now that things were finally going to happen fast? She had always known that her malady had been attacked in the wrong way so far, that all those hydroelectric treatments and massage and the stupid devices on her legs would never make her better on their own. Oh God, and it was high time for this, too, because twice, she said—adding that she had never told me this before—twice she had tried to put an end to her own life, but both times in vain. No one could live like this for ever, she said, never really alone for a single hour, always depending on others for everything she did and every move she made, with eyes always spying on her, always under supervision, and at the same time so oppressed by feeling that she was only a burden on everyone else, a nightmare, something not to be borne. Yes, it was time, high time, but I'd soon see what fast progress she made now that her disorder was going to be treated in the right way. What was the use of all those silly little improvements that never made her better in the end? If you weren't perfectly healthy you weren't healthy at all. Oh, how wonderful it was to look forward to that feeling, how wonderful …

This went on and on, a headlong, sparkling, ecstatic outpouring of words. I felt like a doctor listening to someone in fevered delirium and at the same time distrustfully feeling the patient's racing pulse, that infallible metronome, because he knows that such feverish heat is the sure clinical evidence of mental disturbance. When high-spirited laughter broke like sea foam over the racing tide of her words, I shuddered, because I knew what she did not know—I knew that she was deceiving herself, I knew that we were deceiving her. When she stopped talking at last, I felt as if I were suddenly waking with a start in a night express train because the wheels had suddenly pulled up short. But she had only interrupted herself abruptly.

"So what do you say about that? Why do you just sit there looking so stupid—oh, I'm sorry, I mean so scared! Why don't you say anything? Aren't you pleased for me?"

253

I felt caught in a guilty act. Now or never I must strike the right, heartfelt note of enthusiasm. But I was only a novice liar, and a pitiful liar at that. I didn't yet understand the art of deliberate deception. So I made an effort to cobble a few words together.

"How can you say such a thing? I'm just so surprised … surely you can understand that. Back at home in Vienna we always say that any delightful surprise leaves us speechless … and of course I'm very, very pleased for you."

Even I felt repelled by the cold, artificial sound of my own words. She must have sensed my misgivings at once, for suddenly her attitude changed. A touch of the sullen temper of someone abruptly shaken out of a dream dimmed her delight; the eyes that had just been sparking with enthusiasm were suddenly hard, the line between her brows deepened.

"Well, I haven't noticed you taking it as such a delightful surprise yourself!"

I realised how badly I had injured her feelings, and tried to soothe her. "But my dear child … "

That touched her on the raw. "Don't call me 'child'! You can't be so very much older than me! I suppose I can be allowed to wonder why you weren't very surprised, and most of all not very … very *interested* in all this. Come to think of it, surely you must be pleased? After all, this place will be shut up for a couple of months now, so you'll have more free time to sit about in the café with your comrades, playing taroc. You'll be free of the boring duties of a Good Samaritan! Oh yes, I can well believe you're glad of that. You have a nice time ahead!"

She spoke so forcefully that she hit my guilty conscience hard. I must certainly have given myself away. To distract her mind—for I knew by now how dangerous her petulance at such moments could be—I tried to strike a light, humorous note.

"A nice time—oh, is that how you imagine it? A nice time for cavalrymen—what, in July, August and September? That's when they really let the slave-drivers loose on us, didn't you know? First it's preparations for manoeuvres, then we're off to who knows where, maybe Bosnia or Galicia, then the manoeuvres themselves, and all those big parades! Officers all flustered, men feeling driven, military exercises to the nth degree from morning to night! They lead us a merry dance right up to the end of September."

"The end of September?" Suddenly she was thoughtful. "But then," she finally said, "then when will you be coming?"

I didn't understand. Really I did not understand what she meant. I asked, naively, "Coming where?"

Her brows arched again. "Don't keep asking such silly questions! Coming to see us! To see me."

"What, you mean in the spa in the Engadine valley?"

"Where else? Did you think I meant Tripsdrill amusement park or something?"

Only now did I understand her. When I had just spent my last seven crowns on the flowers I had brought her, when every trip to Vienna was a kind of luxury, even though as military men we could travel half price, the idea that I could afford a trip to the Engadine valley had really been too absurd even to occur to me.

"My word, now I really do see how you civilians imagine a soldier's life!" I said with a genuine laugh. "Going to the café, playing billiards, walking on the promenade, then putting on civilian clothes when we feel like it and just taking off for a couple of weeks. A quick little pleasure trip, nothing easier! Tip your cap to the Colonel, say, 'Cheers, Colonel, tell you what, I don't fancy playing a game of soldiers any more, so expect me when you see me!' A nice idea you have of the treadmill of the military life! Do you know that if one of us wants a single hour extra off, he has to buckle his belt well on, click his heels smartly when he reports to put his request, kowtow respectfully? All that fuss just for a single hour more of leave! And for a whole day, well, you need an aunt to die at the very least, or some other family funeral. I wouldn't like to see my colonel's face if I asked him, however humbly, for a week's leave to go to Switzerland in the middle of manoeuvres, just because I liked the idea! You might hear him utter a few expletives not to be found in any dictionary for family consumption! No, my dear Fräulein Edith, I'm afraid you think it's a little too easy."

"Oh, come along, anything's easy if you really want to do it! Don't act as if you were indispensable! I'm sure someone else could take charge of your Ruthenian rustics while you were away. Anyway, Papa can fix extra leave for you in no time at all. He knows a dozen people in the War Ministry, and if the word comes from on high you'll get what you ask for. And it won't hurt you to see more of the world for once than your riding school and parade ground. So no excuses—it's all settled. Papa will see to it."

It was stupid of me, but that dismissive tone annoyed me. After all, they spend your first few years in the army drilling a certain notion of your rank in society into you, and I felt it was condescending for a young, inexperienced girl like Edith to speak of doing as she liked with the generals of the War Ministry—godlike beings to us young officers—as if they were her father's employees. But I kept the light-hearted tone going, irritated as I felt.

"Yes, that's all very well—Switzerland, leave, the Engadine valley—oh, not bad at all. Excellent if it drops into my lap just as you imagine, with no need for me to bow and scrape and ask permission. But your father would also have to ask the top brass in the War Ministry to come up with a special stipend allowing Lieutenant Hofmiller to travel!"

Now she was the one to be taken aback. She sensed some cryptic reference that she didn't understand in my words. Her brows came down over her impatient eyes, her frown was deeper than ever.

"So do see reason, my dear child … sorry, I mean let's talk reasonably, Fräulein Edith. It really isn't as simple as you imagine. Tell me, have you stopped to think what a trip like that costs?"

"Oh, *that's* what you're talking about?" she said, not at all abashed. "Surely it can't be that much! A few hundred crowns at the most. That can't make such a difference."

But here I couldn't control my annoyance any longer, for she had hit my most sensitive point. I think I have already said how much I disliked being one of those officers in our regiment who had not a penny of their own, and having to depend on my pay and my aunt's small allowance went against the grain with me in military circles when other men spoke lightly of money in front of me, as if it grew on trees. This was *my* sore point, this was where *I* was lame, and had to rely on crutches of my own. That was the only reason why it annoyed me out of all proportion to hear this spoilt, wilful girl, even though she suffered infernal torments herself because of her disadvantages, unable to understand mine. Against my will, I spoke almost roughly.

"A few hundred crowns at the most? Oh, I suppose that's nothing. A little detail beneath an officer's notice! So naturally you think it's poor form for me to mention a little thing like that at all. Isn't that what you mean, poor form? Have you ever stopped to think what those like me have to live on? How we have to make do and mend?"

And as she was still looking at me with that frowning and, as I foolishly supposed, scornful expression, I was suddenly overcome by a need to show her the extent of my poverty. Just as she had hobbled across the room on her crutches on purpose to torment us, the able-bodied, to avenge herself on our good health by showing us that challenging sight, so I now felt a kind of angry pleasure in revealing my constrained, dependent circumstances to her.

"Do you have any idea of a lieutenant's pay?" I fired at her. "Have you ever stopped to think of that? Well, just for your information, two hundred crowns on the first of the month to last the full thirty or thirty-one days, and we're expected to live on that and keep up standards in line with our station in life. On that miserly sum a lieutenant has to pay his housekeeping expenses, bed and board, the tailor, the cobbler, and those little luxuries appropriate to his rank. Not to mention his plight if (God forbid) something happens to his horse. And if he manages his budget well enough to have a few coins left over, then he can splash out in that paradise the café, the place you're always teasing me about—ah, yes, if he's really saved hard he can buy himself all the delicacies this world has to offer in the shape of a cup of coffee frothed with milk."

I know today that it was stupid, indeed criminally stupid of me to let myself be provoked into expressing so much of my bitterness. How was a child of seventeen, spoilt and brought up in isolation from the real world, how was a lame girl always tied to her room to know anything about the value of money, and a soldier's pay, and the wonderful poverty in which we young officers lived? But the urge to revenge myself on someone for countless little humiliations, just for once, had somehow crept up on me, and I struck out blindly, mindlessly, without letting my own hand feel the force of the blow it inflicted.

As soon as I looked up, however, I knew how brutal I had been. With an invalid's quick perception, she had felt at once that she had unconsciously hit me in that most sensitive spot of mine. Irresistibly, a tinge of red crept into her face—I saw her try to defend herself against it, raising her hand as a shield. Obviously a particular thought had drawn the blood into her cheeks.

"And even so … and even so you buy me such expensive flowers?"

Now there was an awkward moment, and it lasted a long time. I was ashamed in front of her, and she in front of me. Each of us had unintentionally wounded the other, and now we were afraid to say anything else. All at once the warm wind in the branches of the trees could be heard, and the cackling chickens down below in the yard, and now and then, far away, the faint sound of a carriage or cart going along the road. Then she pulled herself together.

"And I'm stupid enough to go along with your nonsense! I'm *really* stupid, I'm quite cross with myself. Why should it bother you what a trip to Switzerland costs? If you come to see us of course you will be our guest. Do you think, if you're kind enough to visit us, that Papa would allow you to go to the expense of travelling? And I let you fool me … so not another word about it … no, not another word, I say!"

But this was a point on which I could not give way, for nothing was more intolerable to me, as I have said before, than the idea of being thought to sponge on other people.

"Yes, there will be another word! We don't want any misunderstandings. So to make it perfectly clear—I am not having anyone request leave from the regiment for me, and I am not going to ask for it myself. I don't like asking favours, or having exceptions made for me. I want to share with my comrades, like with like, I don't want anything extra or special treatment. I know you mean well, and I know your father means well. But many people just can't have all the good things in life served up to them on a platter … and let's not discuss it any more."

"So you don't want to come?"

"I didn't say I didn't want to come, I explained perfectly clearly why I can't."

"Not even if my father asks you to?"

"Not even then."

"And … not even if *I* ask you? If I ask you with all my heart, in a spirit of friendship?"

"Please don't. There's no point in it."

She bowed her head. But I had already seen the ominous quivering and working of her mouth that always heralded one of her moods of dangerous petulance. This poor spoilt child, whose slightest wish was the command of all in the house, had just had a new experience; she had encountered resistance. Someone had said no to her, and it left her bitter. She snatched up my flowers from the table and flung them angrily over the balustrade.

"Good!" she said, between her teeth. "Now at least I know what to think of your friendship. Just as well to have tested it and found out! You hide behind excuses simply in case some of your friends might talk in the café! Just because you're afraid to get a bad mark in the regimental report, you spoil your friends' pleasure! Very well, I won't ask you any more. You don't want to come and see us, and that's that! Good!"

I felt her anger hadn't died away entirely yet, because she repeated that "Good!" several more times, with a certain harsh obstinacy, at the same time bracing both her hands hard on the arms of her chair to raise herself in it, as if about to lunge forward in attack. Suddenly she turned sharply to me.

"Very well, that's the end of that. Our humble request is refused. You won't come and see us, you don't want to come and see us. It doesn't suit you. Good! We'll survive. After all, we used to get along perfectly well without you … but there's something I'd like to know—will you answer me honestly?"

"Of course I will."

"I mean really honestly—on your word of honour! Give me your word of honour."

"If you absolutely insist—on my word of honour."

"Good. Good." She kept repeating that hard, cutting "Good", as if using it like a knife to strip something away. "Good. Don't worry, I'm not going to request the pleasure of your distinguished company again. I just want to know one thing—and you've given me your word. Just this one thing. Well—so it doesn't suit you to come and visit us because you feel awkward about it, because it would embarrass you … or for reasons of some other kind, why should I care what they are? Good … good. That's settled. But now, tell me clearly and honestly—why do you come here to visit us at all?"

I had been prepared for any other question, but not this one. In my astonishment, and playing for time, I stammered a preparatory, "Why … why, that's simple! You didn't need to ask my word of honour … "

"Oh … simple, is it? Good. All the better. Go on, then."

There was no getting out of it now. It seemed to me easiest to tell the truth, but I realised that I must choose my words very carefully. So I embarked on my reply as naturally as I could.

"Oh, dear Fräulein Edith … don't go looking for any mysterious motives of mine! You know me well enough, after all, to know me as a man who doesn't think much about himself. I promise you, I never thought of examining the reasons why I seek out this person and that, why I like some people more than others. Upon my word—all I can say, and whether it's clever or stupid I don't know, is that I keep coming to see you because I like it here, I feel a hundred times better here than anywhere else. I think you imagine the life of a cavalry officer like something out of an operetta, always bright and merry, a kind of permanent carnival. Well, from the inside it's not all fun, and even our much-vaunted comradely spirit is sometimes not so straightforward. Where you get a few dozen harnessed to the same carriage, there's always one who's pulling harder than his neighbour, and when it comes to promotion and lists of ranking you can easily tread on someone else's toes. You have to watch every word you say, you're never quite sure of not arousing the ire of your superiors, in fact there's always the chance of a storm brewing. We're on military service—which means *serving*, and servants are dependent. Then again, a barracks and a table at the inn are not like a proper home, no one needs you there, no one really minds about you. Yes, I know we sometimes strike up good, faithful friendships among comrades, but ultimately that never provides a real sense of security. But if I come here to visit you, I leave such anxieties behind at the same time as I take off my sword, and if I talk so cheerfully to all of you here then … "

"Well … then what?" She snapped that quite impatiently.

"Then ... well, perhaps you'll feel I'm being impertinent for saying this so honestly ... then I persuade myself that you like to see me, I belong in your company, I feel a hundred times more at home here than anywhere else. Whenever I look at you like this, I have the feeling that ... "

Something instinctively stopped me short. But she immediately said firmly, "Well, what is it about me?"

"I have the feeling that here is someone to whom I'm not so useless as I am to my comrades in the regiment ... of course, I know I'm nothing much, sometimes I'm astonished that all of you here didn't get tired of me long ago. Often ... you don't know how often I've been afraid that I've been boring you for ages. But then I always think of you yourself, sitting here in this huge, empty house, and how you could be glad of someone coming to see you. And—do you understand?—that always gives me courage ... whenever I see you here on top of your tower, or in your room, I persuade myself it's a good thing I came, so that you didn't have to sit all day on your own. Can't you understand that?"

Here something that I hadn't expected happened. Her grey eyes glazed over. It was as if something in what I said had turned them to stone. Meanwhile, her fingers began to fidget restlessly, rising and falling on the arms of her chair, drumming first faintly and then harder on the wood. There was a slight, wry twist to her mouth. She suddenly said abruptly, "Oh yes, I understand. I entirely understand what you mean ... I think ... yes, I think that you really have told the truth now. You put it very, very politely and with a great deal of circumlocution. But I understood you perfectly. I understood exactly what you meant. You come, you say, because I'm so lonely—meaning in plain language that I'm stuck in this chair. That's the only reason

263

why you come out here every day, to act the Good Samaritan to a poor sick child—I expect that's how everyone speaks of me when I'm not within earshot. I know, I know. You come out of pity, yes, oh yes, I believe you—why bother to deny it? You're what they call a good person, you like to hear my father say so. 'Good people' like you feel sorry for every beaten dog and mangy cat—why not feel sorry for a cripple too?"

And suddenly a convulsion ran through her cramped body.

"Well, thank you very much! I can do without the kind of friendship that's only because I'm crippled … Oh, don't look so upset! Of course you're sorry the truth slipped out, you wish you hadn't admitted that you come only because you're so sorry for me, like that new maid the other day, only she meant it and said so straight out. But as a good person you put it much more tactfully, with more delicate feeling. You beat about the bush because I'm so lonely here all day long. It's only out of pity, I've felt that for a long time, you only come here out of pity, and you'd like to be admired for your kind self-sacrifice—but I'm sorry, I don't want anyone sacrificing himself for me! I can't stand it, not from anyone, least of all you … I forbid you to pity me, do you hear, I forbid you! Do you think I really depend on having you sit here with your 'sympathetic' looks and your tactful conversation? No, thank God, I don't need any of you … I can manage on my own, I can see this through for myself. And if one day I can't, then I know how to be rid of you all … here!" She suddenly flung her hand out to me, palm upwards. "Do you see that scar? I've tried it once already, but I was clumsy, the scissors were blunt and didn't cut the vein. So stupid—they came in time to bandage me up, or I'd be rid of you all and your despicable pity. I'll do it properly next time, you can be sure of that. Don't think I'm handed over to you defenceless, because

I'm not! I'd sooner die than have people pitying me. There!"
And she suddenly laughed out loud, a sharp, edgy laugh, rough
as a saw. "There, you see that's something my dear father forgot
when he had this tower converted for me … just so that I could
have a nice view, he thought. Sunlight, plenty of sunlight and
fresh air, that's what the doctor ordered. But this terrace will
come in very useful some day, that didn't occur to any of them,
not my father, not the doctor or the architect … look down
there!" She had suddenly braced herself and, with an abrupt
jerk, forced her swaying body towards the balustrade, clutching
it grimly with both hands. "It's four or five storeys down from
up here, and hard stone when you reach the bottom … that
will do. And thank God I have enough strength in my muscles
to haul myself over this balustrade. Walking with crutches
develops your arm muscles. One good effort and I'll be rid of
your wretched pity once and for all, and you'll all be glad, my
father and Ilona and you, because I'm a nightmare weighing
you all down. It's quite easy, you see … I just have to lean over
a little way and then … "

I had jumped up in great alarm when she leant dangerously
far over the balustrade, her eyes flashing, and I quickly took
her arm. But as if fire had touched her skin, she flinched,
screaming at me.

"Go away! How dare you touch me … go away! I have a right
to do what I want! Get away! Let go of me at once!"

And when I did not obey, but tried to force her away from
the balustrade, she suddenly swung her upper body round and
hit me hard in the chest. As she struck me, she lost her hold
and with it her balance. Her knees gave way entirely, as if a
scythe had cut through them, and she collapsed. She instinctively tried to grab hold of the table as she fell, and brought

265

the whole thing down. As I tried to catch her at the last minute in her ungainly fall, I heard the vase clinking as it broke, cups and plates smashed, spoons rattled to the ground and so, with a clang, the big bronze bell. It rolled along the terrace with its clapper still striking.

Meanwhile the crippled girl lay where she had fallen in a miserable little heap on the ground, helpless, shaking convulsively in her anger and sobbing with bitterness and shame. I tried to raise her light body, but she resisted, and shouted at me, "Go away … away … away, you horrible, beastly man!"

And so saying she flung out her arms, trying again and again to get up without my help. Whenever I came close, hoping to assist her, her body distorted in resistance, and she shouted, in her wild, defenceless rage, "Go away … don't touch me … get out of here!" I had never known anything so appalling.

At that moment there was a faint humming sound behind us. It was the lift coming up. Evidently the clang of the falling bell had alerted the manservant who always waited ready down below. He hurried up in alarm, discreetly casting his eyes down at once, easily raised her twitching body without looking at me—he must be used to helping her up—and carried the sobbing girl over to the lift shaft. Next moment the lift was on its quiet way down again. I was left alone with the toppled table, the smashed teacups, everything scattered in confusion as if a bolt of lightning had struck out of a clear blue sky, wrecking everything around with its force.

I don't know how long I stood like that on the terrace, surrounded by broken plates and teacups, utterly baffled by Edith's elemental outburst. I had no idea what to make of it. What had I said that was so foolish? How had I aroused her inexplicable fury? But behind my back I heard the familiar sound, like a steady breeze blowing, of the lift on its way back up. Once again the manservant Josef appeared, with a curious look of grief on his always well-shaven face. I thought he had simply come to clear up, and felt awkwardly that I was in his way standing there beside the wreck of the tea table. However, he came a little closer to me, eyes still cast down, picking up a napkin from the ground at the same time.

"Forgive me, Lieutenant Hofmiller," he said in his discreetly lowered voice—he was an Austrian servant of the old school, and always spoke as if he were bowing at the same time. "May I mop you up a little, sir?"

Only now, following his busy fingers, did I see that my uniform tunic and Pejacsevich trousers were very wet. As I bent down to try to help Edith when she collapsed, a teacup swept off the table must have emptied its contents over me, for the servant was carefully rubbing around the wet places with the napkin. As he knelt to attend to me, I looked down on his grey hair with its neat parting. I couldn't throw off the suspicion that the old man was kneeling down like that so that I would not see how upset he was.

"No, it's no good," he said apologetically at last, without looking up. "It will be best if I send the chauffeur to the barracks to fetch you a change of clothes, sir. You can't go back like that, Lieutenant. But depend on it, sir, it will all be dry in an hour's time, and I'll iron your trousers nicely."

He spoke almost with the matter-of-fact expertise of a valet. But a sympathetic and rather distressed note in his voice gave him away. And when I said that would not be necessary, and could he telephone for a cab instead, because I wanted to go straight back anyway, he unexpectedly cleared his throat and raised his kindly, rather tired eyes pleadingly.

"Please, Lieutenant Hofmiller, sir, won't you stay a little longer? It would be terrible if you were to leave now, sir. I know Fräulein Edith would be dreadfully upset if you didn't wait for a little while, Lieutenant Hofmiller, sir. Fräulein Ilona is with her now and … and has put her to bed. But Fräulein Ilona asked me to say that she will be with you very soon. Please, sir, won't you wait for her?"

Against my will, I was shaken. How they all loved the invalid! Every one of them treated her tenderly and made excuses for her! I felt an irresistible urge to say something kind to this good old man who, dismayed by his own venturing to plead with me, was very busy putting my tunic to rights again, and I clapped him lightly on the shoulder.

"Never mind that, Josef, it will be none the worse, it's sure to dry off quickly in the sun. I should hope your tea here isn't strong enough to leave a lasting stain. So never mind fussing over me, Josef, pick the tea things up instead, and I'll wait for Fräulein Ilona."

"Oh, how good of you to wait, sir!" He breathed a sigh of relief. "And Herr von Kekesfalva will soon be back, I know he will be glad to see you, sir. He specially asked me to say … "

But here I heard light footsteps coming up the stairs. It was Ilona. She too, like Josef a moment ago, kept her eyes cast down as she came towards me.

"Edith asks if you would come down to her bedroom for a moment. Just for a moment! She says I'm to tell you that she would be very glad of that."

We went down the spiral staircase together, saying not a word when we reached the house, crossed the reception room and

268

the room next to it, and came to the long corridor obviously leading to the bedrooms. Sometimes our shoulders touched by chance in this narrow, dark passage, and that may also have been because I felt so agitated and uneasy as I walked along. Ilona stopped at the second door leading off the corridor and whispered earnestly to me.

"You must be kind to her now. I don't know what happened up on the terrace, but I do know those sudden outbursts of hers. We all do. You mustn't take offence, though, really you mustn't. None of us here can imagine what it must be like, lying around helpless from morning to evening. She's bound to feel the nervous tension building up, and then it will break out sometime whether she wants or not, whether or not she even knows what she's doing. Only believe me, no one feels worse about it afterwards than Edith herself. We have to be twice as kind to her, just because she is so ashamed afterwards and torments herself."

I didn't reply, and there was no need. Ilona must have noticed how shaken I was anyway. Now she knocked cautiously at the door, and as soon as an answer came from the other side of it, a shy, soft "Come in", she warned me quickly, "Don't stay too long. Just for a moment."

The door opened without a sound, and I went in. At first glance all I could see in the large room, its windows darkened on the garden side by orange curtains drawn over them, was a reddish twilight. Only then could I make out the rectangular shape of a bed in the background. Diffidently, Edith's familiar voice spoke.

"Please sit down on the stool. I won't keep you more than a moment."

I went closer. Her small face was pale on the pillows under the shadow of her hair. A brightly coloured bedspread with a pattern of embroidered flowers came almost up to her slender, childish

269

throat. With a certain timidity, Edith waited for me to sit down. Only then did she raise her shy voice again.

"Forgive me for asking you to visit me in here, but I felt quite dizzy … I ought not to have sat out in the strong sunlight so long, it always confuses my mind. I really think I wasn't quite in my senses when I … but … but you'll forget all about it, won't you? You won't bear me a grudge for losing my temper so stupidly?"

There was so much anxious pleading in her voice that I was quick to interrupt her. "Why, what are you thinking of? … It was all my fault … I ought not to have kept you sitting out in all that heat."

"So you really, really won't … won't think too badly of me? Really not?"

"Of course not—not a bit."

"And you'll come to see us again … the same as ever?"

"Exactly the same. But on one condition, though."

She looked uneasy. "What condition?"

"That you'll trust me a little more, and not keep wondering whether you've hurt my feelings or injured me in some way! Who thinks of such nonsense among friends? If only you knew how different you look when you let yourself feel really happy, and how happy that makes all of us—your father, and Ilona, and me and everyone in the house! I wish you could have seen yourself on our outing the day before yesterday, when you were so cheerful, and the rest of us with you—I was thinking about that all evening."

"You were thinking of me all evening?" She looked at me a little uncertainly. "Really?"

"All evening. Oh, what a day that was! I'll never forget it. Wonderful, the whole drive, wonderful!"

"Yes," she repeated dreamily. "It was wonderful … won-der-ful … first driving through the fields, then the little foals, and the party in the village … all of it wonderful from beginning to end! Oh, I ought to go out like that more often! Perhaps it was really just all that stupid sitting at home, that silly habit of shutting myself away that got on my nerves so much. But you're right, I'm always too distrustful … or rather I have been since the accident. Before that, oh, my God, I can't remember ever feeling afraid of anyone … it's only since I've been so terribly unsure of myself … I always think that everyone's looking at my crutches and pitying me. I know how silly that is, silly childish pride, and it can make me horrible to myself … I know there's bound to be an effect, it will wear my nerves down. But how can I *not* be distrustful when it goes on for ever and ever? Oh, if only it could all be over at last, and then I wouldn't be so cross, so bad-tempered and angry!"

"But it *will* soon be over. You must just have courage a little longer, a little more courage and patience."

She raised herself slightly in her bed. "Do you think … do you honestly think this new treatment will work? You know, the day before yesterday when Papa came in to tell me, I was quite sure it would myself … but last night, I don't know why, I suddenly felt afraid that the doctor was wrong and had told me something that wasn't true, because I … because I remembered something. I used to trust Dr Condor like God himself once. But it's always the same … at first a doctor observes his patient, but in the long run the patient starts observing the doctor, and yesterday—I haven't said this to anyone but you—while he was examining me yesterday I sometimes felt that … oh, I don't know how to explain it … well, as if he was just putting on an act. He seemed to me so uncertain, so evasive, not as open and kind as usual. I don't know why, but I felt as if he was ashamed in front of me for some reason. Of course I was terribly glad to hear that he's sending me straight to Switzerland ... and yet somehow, in secret—mind, I'm not telling anyone else this ... I kept feeling that pointless fear ... oh, don't tell him, whatever you do!—the fear that there was something the matter with that new course of treatment ... as if he was just trying to pretend to me. Or perhaps to reassure Papa ... well, you see, I just can't shake that distrust off. But how can I help it? How can I not be suspicious of myself and everyone, after I've been told so often it will soon be over, and then it all goes on again so slowly, so dreadfully slowly. I can't, I really can't bear this eternal waiting much longer!"

In her agitation she was sitting up. Her hands began to shake. I quickly leant closer to her.

"No, don't ... don't excite yourself again! Remember what you promised me just now ... "

"Yes, you're right! It's no good tormenting myself, I'm only taking it out on other people. And it's not their fault! I'm enough of a burden on them already ... but no, I didn't want to talk about that, I really didn't ... I just wanted to thank you for not being cross with me for the silly way I got over-excited ... and for always being so good to me, when I don't deserve it ... and to think I said to you, of all people ... but no, we're not going to talk about that any more, are we?"

"No, never again. Trust me. And now you must have a good rest."

I got to my feet and was going to offer her my hand. Smiling up at me from her cushions, half still anxious, half reassured, she was a touching sight—a child still, a child on the point of going to sleep. All was well; the atmosphere had cleared like the sky after a thunderstorm. I went up to her in an easy, natural way, feeling almost cheerful. But she sat up suddenly, abruptly.

"For goodness' sake … whatever happened to your uniform?"

She had noticed the large damp patch on my tunic. Guiltily, she must have remembered that only the cups swept off the table as she fell could have caused that little accident. Her eyes immediately disappeared under hooded lids; her hand, already stretched out, shrank back in alarm. Because she took the silly little incident so seriously, I felt impelled to soothe her, and took refuge in a jocular tone of voice.

"Oh, that's nothing to worry about," I said, adding playfully. "A naughty little girl spilt something over me."

There was still distress in her eyes. But she gratefully reacted to my tone of voice, answering in the same vein.

"And did you punish the naughty little girl?"

"No," I said, still keeping the game going. "There was no need. She's a good girl again now."

"And you're really not cross with her any more?"

"Not a bit! You should have heard how prettily she said sorry!"

"Then you won't hold it against her?"

"No, indeed, it's all forgiven and forgotten. Mind you, she must go on being good, of course, and do everything she's told!"

"And what must she do, then?"

"Always be patient, always be good-tempered and cheerful. Not sit in the sun too long, go for plenty of drives, and do exactly as the doctor tells her. But now she must get some sleep—no more talking and thinking! Good night."

I gave her my hand. She looked captivatingly pretty lying there and smiling at me, her eyes sparkling. She laid five slender fingers, warm and relaxed, in my hand.

I turned to go, my heart eased. I was already turning the door handle when I heard a little chime of laughter behind me.

"Is she a good little girl now, then?"

"As good as gold. Top marks! But now go to sleep, go to sleep and don't think of anything unpleasant."

I already had the door half open when I heard that laughter behind me once more, childish, mischievous. And the voice came from the pillows again.

"Have you forgotten what a good little girl gets before she goes to sleep?"

"What does she get?"

"A good little girl always gets a goodnight kiss."

Somehow I was not entirely comfortable with that idea. There was an odd note in her voice, and I didn't like it. Her eyes had been too feverishly bright a little while ago. But I didn't want to provoke her, touchy as she could be.

"Yes, of course," I said, apparently casually. "I almost forgot."

I took the few steps back to her bed, and sensed, from the sudden silence, that she was holding her breath. Her eyes were fixed on me now, moving when I did, while her head lay motionless on the pillows. Her hands and finger were still; only those eyes followed my every movement and never left me.

Quick, I thought with increasing discomfort, quick, and I bent down swiftly and brushed her forehead with my lips, lightly, fleetingly. I deliberately hardly touched her hair, and felt only, at close quarters, the confusing scent of her skin.

But then both her hands, lying obviously in readiness on the bedspread, suddenly came up. Before I could turn my head away they clasped my temples firmly, and carried my mouth down from her forehead to her lips. She pressed her own mouth to it, sucking at my lips with such greedy heat that our teeth touched,

274

and her breasts rose and fell rapidly, urgently reaching up to my body as it bent over her. Never in my life had I received such a wild, fierce, desperately thirsty kiss as that crippled child gave me.

But even that was not enough. With frenzied force, she held me close to her until her breath failed her. Then she loosened her grip, her hands, agitated, moved away from my temples, and her fingers ran through my hair. But still she would not let go of me, except just for a moment, to lean back as if enchanted and stare into my eyes. Then she clutched me close again, aimlessly, hotly kissing my cheeks, my forehead, my eyes and my lips with fierce and at the same time helpless avidity. At each kiss she groaned and stammered, "Idiot ... idiot ... oh, you idiot ... " and gasped more and more heatedly, "You ... you ... you ... " Her assault on me was greedier and greedier, more and more passionate. Ever more fiercely, ever more convulsively she held and kissed me. Then a sudden convulsive spasm ran through her. She let go of me, her head fell back on her pillows, and only her eyes flashed at me in triumph.

Then she whispered, hastily turning away from me, both exhausted and ashamed, "Go away now, you idiot ... go away!"

I walked ... no, I staggered out. The last of my strength left me once I was in the dark corridor. My senses were spinning; I felt dizzy and had to support myself on the wall. So that was it! That was the secret of her restlessness—a secret revealed far too late in the day. It accounted for her aggressive attitude to me, which I had never before been able to explain. My horror was boundless. I felt like someone who, bending over a flower and thinking no harm, is attacked by an adder. If the sensitive child had struck me, called names, spat at me—well, the frail state of her nerves meant one had to be prepared for unpredictable behaviour at any time, and none of that would have astonished me as much as this one thing—the fact that she, disabled, sick, could love and wish to be loved. To think that this child, this half-being, this imperfectly formed, helpless creature had the *audacity*—I can't call it anything else—to love and desire with the conscious, sensuous love of a real woman! I had thought of everything else, but not that a girl mutilated by fate, without the strength to drag her own body about, could dream of someone as a lover, as *her* lover, that she so entirely misunderstood me when I came to see her again and again, solely out of pity. But next moment I realised with new horror that nothing was so much to blame as my own passionate pity if this girl, lonely and shut away from the world, expected the only man who visited her out of sympathy in her dungeon day after day, deluded by his own pity, to show her another and more tender feeling. Idiot that I indeed was, hopelessly simple-minded in my total inability to guess as much, I had seen her only as a suffering cripple, a child and not a woman. Not for a minute had it crossed my mind, even for a fleeting second, that under the covers over her was a breathing, feeling body waiting, the body of a woman who felt desire and wished to be desired in return, like other women. At the age of twenty-five I had never entertained any idea that women who were sick, disabled, immature, old, outcast, marked out from other women by fate would *dare* to love. A young, inexperienced man facing real life nearly always forms his ideas of the world on the model of what he has heard and read, and inevitably dreams of his own experience in terms of other people's images and examples. And in the books and plays I knew, or at the cinema (where everything is two-dimensional and simplified), it was exclusively young, attractive people who desired each other, and so I had supposed—hence also my general timidity with women—that you must be particularly good-looking and specially favoured by Fate to arouse a woman's interest. That was why I could be so free and easy in the company of those two girls, because anything erotic in our relationship seemed to be ruled out from the first, and I never suspected that they could see more in me than a nice boy, a good friend. Even if I sometimes felt attracted to Ilona's pretty, sensuous looks, I had never thought of Edith as a member of the opposite sex, and certainly not the shadow of an idea had crossed my mind that her poor body contained the same organs and her soul felt the same desire as the bodies of other women. Only at that moment did I faintly begin to understand (and this is something that most writers never mention) that the outcasts, the ugly, the faded and afflicted, the social misfits desire with a much more passionate and dangerous longing than those who are happy and healthy, that they love with a dark, fanatical, black love, and no passion on earth is felt more greedily and desperately than by those of God's stepchildren who have no hope, but feel that their earthly existence can be justified only by loving and being loved. In my ignorance and inexperience, I had never ventured to guess at that terrible secret—a lust for life cries out in panic most fiercely of all from the lowest, grim depths of despair. Only now did that realisation strike me like a red-hot knife.

Idiot! Now I understood why she came out with that particular word in the midst of her turbulent emotions, while she clung to me pressing her half-developed breasts close to my chest. Idiot—yes, she was right to call me an idiot! It must have been

277

obvious to everyone else from the first—her father and Ilona, Josef and the rest of the domestic staff. They must all of them have suspected that she nurtured loving, indeed passionate feelings—perhaps they suspected it with horror, probably with dark foreboding. Everyone but me, fooled as I was by my own pity, playing the part of good, kind, sometimes clumsy friend, joking all the time, never noticing how my incomprehensible failure to understand was tormenting her ardent feelings. Just as in a bad farce the unfortunate hero is at the centre of an intrigue, every member of the audience has known for ages what a fix he is in, and only he, the idiot, goes on acting in deadly earnest, never understanding what a tangled web he is caught up in (while everyone else has seen every twist and turn in the web from the first)—so all of them in the house must have seen me groping around in a silly game of emotional blind man's buff, until the blindfold was suddenly snatched awry from my eyes. But in the same way as a single light flaring up is enough to illuminate a dozen objects in a room at the same time, I now, in retrospect—too late, too late!—recognised, to my shame, the meaning of many little incidents over all these weeks. Only now did I see why she was so angry whenever I cheerfully called her "child"—she didn't want to appear a child to me, but a woman, to be desired as a lover. Only now did I see why her lips often quivered restlessly when her lameness obviously distressed me, why she hated my pity so bitterly—obviously her feminine instinct recognised that pity is far too lukewarm a feeling, an emotion to be felt between brother and sister, a poor imitation of real love. How the unhappy girl must have waited for some word, some sign that I understood—and it never, never came! How she must have suffered, listening to me chattering on inconsequentially, while she was racked by impatience, waiting with a trembling

278

heart, waiting for the first tender gesture, or at least waiting for me to understand, at long last, how passionate her feelings were. I had not said anything, I had not done anything, and yet I hadn't stayed away, thus both strengthening her feelings by my daily attendance and distressing her by my lack of perception—how understandable it was, then, that her nerves finally failed her and she fixed on me as her prey!

The realisation of all this now flooded into me, illustrated by a hundred images, while I leant against the wall in the dark corridor, breathless and with my legs feeling almost as weak as hers. I twice tried to stagger further, and only at the third attempt did I get as far as the door leading out of the corridor. From here, I thought quickly, I can get into the salon, and then through the door on the left of it into the hall, where I could pick up my sword and cap. So I must get across the salon and then leave, get away from here before the manservant appears. Down the steps and away, well away! Escape from this house before anyone sees me, I thought, and subjects me to an interrogation. I must get out of here without seeing her father, or Ilona, or Josef—they all of them left me, like a fool, to entangle myself further and further in this web! I must get away!

But it was too late! Ilona was waiting in the salon, and had obviously heard me coming. As soon as she caught sight of me the expression on her face changed.

"Jesus and Mary, what's the matter? You're so pale ... Has ... has anything else happened to Edith?"

"No, nothing," I just managed to stammer, and was about to go on. "I think she's asleep. Excuse me—I have to go home."

But there must have been something alarming in my brusque manner, because Ilona firmly took my arm and guided me—no, pushed me, into an armchair.

279

"Here, sit down for a minute first. You must pull yourself together … and your hair, what on earth do you think it looks like, all untidy … No, stay where you are"—for I was about to get to my feet—"I'll get you a cognac."

She went over to the sideboard and filled a glass. I knocked it straight back. Ilona was looking at me in concern as I put the glass down with a shaking hand (never in my life had I felt so weak, so exhausted), and she sat down with me and waited in silence, sometimes cautiously casting me an anxious sidelong glance, as if she were watching an invalid. At last she asked, "Did Edith … say anything? I mean, anything about you personally?"

I sensed, from her sympathetic tone of voice, that she guessed it all. And I was too weak to deny it. I just murmured quietly, "Yes."

She didn't move. She didn't reply. I noticed only that she was suddenly breathing faster. Cautiously, she leant closer to me.

"And this … this was really the first time you realised?"

"How could such a thing occur to me … such nonsense! Such madness! How can she think that … why pick on me? Why me?"

Ilona sighed. "Oh God—and she always thought you kept coming here for her sake … she thought that was why you visited us. I … I never believed that, because you were so … so unselfconscious, and so full of a different kind of warm feeling. I was afraid from the first that you were only sorry for her. But how could I warn the poor child, how could I be cruel enough to talk her out of a delusion that made her happy? For weeks she's been living only for the idea that you … And then, when she kept asking me and asking me whether I thought that you really liked her, I couldn't be unkind … I had to soothe her and make her feel better."

I couldn't restrain myself any longer. "Well, now it's quite the opposite. You must talk her out of it, you really must talk her out of it. It's nothing but delusion on her part, a fever, a childish fancy … the usual crush adolescent girls get on a uniform, and if another military man turns up tomorrow she'll transfer her crush to him. You must explain that to her … you must set the record straight at once. After all, it's pure chance that I happen to be here, that I was the one who came to this house and not another man, a better man, one of my comrades. Such things wear off quickly at her age … "

But Ilona shook her head. "No, my dear friend, don't deceive yourself. It's serious with Edith, deadly serious, and getting more dangerous every day … no, dear friend, I can't suddenly make something so difficult easy for you. Oh, if you only knew what it's like in this house! She rings her bell three or four times in the night, wakes up the rest of us without a thought, and when we hurry to her bedside terrified that something has happened to her there she is, sitting up in bed distraught, staring into space and always asking us the same question. 'Don't you think he really may like me a little, just a very little? I mean, I'm not so ugly.' And then she demands a mirror, but she tosses it away again at once, and next moment she realises that she's deluding herself—only for it all to begin again a couple of hours later. In her desperation she asks her father, and Josef, and the maidservants. Yesterday she even summoned that Gypsy woman from the outing the day before—you'll remember her—asked her to come and see her again in secret, and got her to predict the same future for her as before. She's written letters to you five times, long letters, and then torn them up again. She thinks and talks of nothing else from morning to evening, from early to late. Sometimes she wants me to go

281

to see you and find out if you like her just a little or whether … whether she's a nuisance to you, because you never say anything, you avoid speaking out. She wants me to go and see you at once, to catch up with you on your way home, and the chauffeur has to get ready and fetch the car. Three times, four, five times she'll tell me exactly what I must say to you, how to put my question. And at the last moment, when I'm standing ready in the front hall, her bell rings again, I have to go back to her in my hat and coat and swear to her on my mother's life never to make the slightest allusion to what she said. Oh, how would you know what goes on? It's all over for you once you close the front door behind you. But the moment you've gone she's repeating every word you said to her, asking what I think, and whether I believe that … And if I tell her, 'Well, you can see how much he likes you,' she screams at me, 'You're lying! That's not true! He didn't say a kind word to me today.' But at the same time she wants to hear what I think all over again, I have to repeat it three times over and assure her that … And then there's her old father. He's been very upset since all this began, yet he loves and idolises you like his own child. You should see him when he's been sitting beside her bed, tired out, for hours on end, petting and soothing her until she finally falls asleep. And then he himself paces restlessly up and down all night, up and down in his room … And you—you really didn't notice anything at all?"

"No!" In my desperation it came out as a loud cry. "No, I swear, nothing at all, not the least little thing! Do you think I'd have kept on coming here, do you think I could have sat talking to you all, playing chess and dominoes, playing gramophone records, if I'd guessed? But how can she have deluded herself to the point where she thinks that I … that I of all people …

how can she expect me to go along with such nonsense, such childishness? ... No, no, no!"

The idea of being loved against my will was so terrible that I was about to jump up, but Ilona firmly took my wrist.

"Hush! I beg you, dear friend, don't get so worked up, and above all keep your voice down! She has a way of hearing things through walls. And please, for Heaven's sake, be fair to her. The poor girl took it as a good sign that the news came from you, you were the one who told her father about this new cure. He went straight to see her and wake her up in the middle of the night. Can't you imagine how the two of them sobbed and thanked God that their terrible trials were over? And they're both convinced that once Edith is better, a young woman like other young women, you'd ... well, I don't need to spell it out to you. That's why you *can't* upset the poor child now, not when she needs strong nerves to face the new cure. We have to be very, very careful and never let her guess—God forbid!—that the idea of it is so ... so *dreadful* to you."

But my desperation had made me ruthless. "No, no, no!" I insisted, bringing my hand down on the arm of the chair. "No, I *can't* ... I *won't* have her loving me, not like that ... And I can't go on acting now as if I didn't notice anything, I can't sit here at my ease saying sweet nothings ... I can't! You don't know what happened ... what happened in there, and ... oh, she misunderstands me entirely. I only felt sorry for her. It was only pity, that's all, no more."

Ilona did not reply, but looked straight ahead of her. Then she sighed.

"Yes, I was afraid of that all along. All this time I've had a feeling that ... but my God, what's going to happen now? How can she be told?"

283

We sat there in silence. Everything had been said. We both knew that there was no way out of it, none. Suddenly Ilona sat up very straight, with an intent, listening expression on her face, and almost at the same time I heard the crunch of the car drawing up on the gravel outside. It must be Kekesfalva. Ilona quickly got to her feet.

"You'd better not see him now … you're too upset to talk to him calmly. Wait a moment, I'll get you your cap and sword. Your best way is to go out into the park through the back door. I'll think of some reason why you can't stay this evening."

She quickly fetched my things. Luckily Josef had hurried out to the car, so I was able to get past the outbuildings of the house unnoticed. Once I was in the park, the fear of having to answer questions quickened my pace. It was the second time I had fled from that fateful house surreptitiously, like a thief in the night.

So far, as a young and inexperienced man, I had always thought that the longings of unrequited love were the worst possible affliction of the heart. On that day, however, I began to divine that there is another and perhaps much worse torment than feeling love and desire, and that is to be loved against your will, when you cannot defend yourself against the passion thrust upon you. It is worse to see someone beside herself, burning with the flames of desire, and stand by powerless, unable to find the strength to snatch her from the fire. If you are unhappily in love yourself you may sometimes be able to tame your passion, because you are the author of your own unhappiness, not just its creature. If a lover can't control his passion then at least his suffering is his own fault. But there is nothing someone who is loved but does not love in return can do about it, since it is beyond his own power to determine the extent and limits of that love, and no willpower of his own can keep someone else from loving him. Perhaps only a man can feel the full hopelessness of such a relationship, because only a man will feel not just pain, but also somehow guilty about his rejection of it. When a woman is defending herself against unwanted passion, deep in her heart she is only obeying the law of the relationship between the sexes; an initial rejection of all advances is, so to speak, every woman's primeval instinct, and even if she rejects the most burning desire no one can call her inhuman. However, it is disastrous when Fate readjusts the scales, and a woman has overcome her natural reticence to the point where she confesses her passion to a man, offering him her love without any certainty that it will be returned—and he, the object of her passion, remains cold and unresponsive! In fact that's a tangle that can never be resolved, for to refuse a woman what she wants means injuring her pride and her sense of modesty. A man turning down a woman's desire for him is wounding all that is finest in her. However gently he tries to withdraw, whatever courteously evasive words he finds, it is no good. The offer of mere friendship insults a woman who has shown how vulnerable she is—all rejection on his part looks like cruelty, and if her love for him is unrequited he always feels guilty through no fault of his own. This is a terrible bond, and it cannot be undone—you thought you were free, you belong to yourself and owe no one anything, and suddenly you are hunted and cornered, the prey of someone else's unwanted desire. Deeply wounded, you know that someone—a woman, a stranger!—is waiting for you, thinking of you, longing and pining for you! She wants you, she cries out for you with every fibre of her being, with her body and her blood. She wants your hands, your hair, your lips, your body. She wants your night and your day, your emotions, your sexual desire and all your thoughts and dreams. She wants to share everything with you, take everything from you and suck it in, breathe it into her. Day and night, whether you are sleeping or waking, there is someone somewhere in the world now, wakeful, burning with passion as she waits for you, someone watching you and dreaming of you. You don't want to think of her although she is always thinking of you, but that's no use, and trying to run away is no use either, because you are no longer just yourself but a part of her. A stranger is suddenly carrying you about with her, like a mirror on the move—or no, not a mirror, which reflects only your image, willingly offered to it, whereas the stranger who loves you has already absorbed you into her bloodstream. She always has you in her, she takes you with her wherever you may run. You are always the captive of someone else, somewhere else, no longer yourself, never free, unconstrained and guiltless, always hunted, always under an obligation, you always feel her thinking of you. It is like a steadily burning conflagration. With hatred and horror, you have to endure the longing of this stranger who suffers for lack of you, and I know now that to be loved against his will is the most senseless yet inescapable misfortune that a man can suffer, the worst of all tortures. However innocent he is, it makes him feel guilty.

Not in my most fleeting daydreams had I ever imagined that a woman might love me so fiercely. Of course I had often heard comrades boasting of how this or that girl was "running after them", perhaps I had even laughed cheerfully with the others at the indiscreet tales told of such immodest advances, because at the time I didn't yet know that every form love takes, even the most ridiculous and absurd, involves the life of another human being, and even indifference leaves you running up a debt to love. But what you have only heard and read easily passes you by, and the heart can learn the essential reality of feeling only from personal experience. I had to discover for myself the painful dilemma of having someone else's passionate love on my conscience before I could feel sympathy for both parties—one forcing itself on the other's notice, the second forcefully defending itself against the overwhelming emotion of the first. But what an unimaginable excess of responsibility I bore in this case! For if it takes a cruel and almost brutal heart to disappoint a woman's affections, how much more terrible was the "No", the "I don't want to", that I must say to that impetuous child! I had to injure someone already injured, inflict an even deeper wound on someone already painfully wounded, snatch away the last crutch of hope from a girl whose inner resources were not strong. I knew that if I fled from the love of this child who had inspired only pity in me, I would be endangering and perhaps destroying her. I was aware at once, with cruel clarity, how monstrously guilty I would be if, although I could not accept her love, I did not at least make some pretence of responding to it.

But I had no choice. Even before I consciously understood the danger, my body had put up its own defences to her abrupt embrace. Our instincts are always wiser than our waking thoughts, and in that first second of horror when I tore myself away from the love she was forcing on me, I already felt a dark premonition of what was to come. I knew I would never have the saintly strength to love the crippled girl as she loved me, probably not even enough pity simply to *bear* her passion. It racked my nerves.

I already guessed, in that first reaction of flight, that there was no way out for me, no middle course that I could take. One or other of us must be made unhappy by this ridiculous love of hers, and perhaps it would be both.

How I got back to the town that evening I shall never be sure. All I know is that I walked very fast, and only one idea repeated itself with every heartbeat—get away, get away! Away from that house, from that dilemma, run for it, take flight, disappear! Never set foot in the villa again, never see those people again, never see anyone at all again! Hide, make myself invisible, refuse any more obligations, never get involved in anything again! I know I tried thinking plans out further—leave the army, get money somewhere or other, and then go out into the world, far, far away, so far that her crazy longing couldn't reach me. But all that was a daydream rather than clear thought; one word kept hammering in my temples—away, away, get away!

Later, my dusty shoes and the rips torn in my trousers by thistles showed me that I must have run straight across country, through meadows and fields and across roads. At any rate, by the time I finally found myself back on the main road the sun was already sinking behind the rooftops. I started with surprise like a sleepwalker when someone unexpectedly clapped me on the shoulder from behind.

"Hello, Toni, so there you are! And high time too. We've been looking for you high and low, we were just about to telephone them up at that castle of yours."

I saw that I was surrounded by four of my comrades, including Ferencz, Jozsi and Captain Count Steinhübel.

"But never mind that now! Guess what, Balinkay suddenly dropped in, back from Holland or America or God knows where. Anyway, he's invited all the officers and gentlemen volunteers of the regiment to dinner this evening. The Colonel's coming, and the Major, and it'll be quite a spread—this evening at the Red Lion, eight-thirty. A good thing we found you—the Colonel wouldn't have liked you to be missing. You know how highly he thinks of Balinkay! When he turns up we all have to stand to attention."

"Who did you say has turned up?"

"Why, Balinkay, of course! Don't look so blank! Surely you know about Balinkay?"

Balinkay? Balinkay? All my thoughts were still in wild confusion, and I had to search my mind like a lumber room for some recollection of the name. Ah yes, it was *that* Balinkay—the man who'd once been the black sheep of the regiment. Long before I was posted to this garrison he had served here as second lieutenant and then first lieutenant. He had the reputation of being the best horseman and the most congenial companion in the regiment, and also a confirmed gambler and ladykiller. But something embarrassing had happened, I'd never asked exactly what. Anyway, within twenty-four hours he'd resigned his commission and gone off to travel the world. All kinds of strange stories went around about him. In the end he'd retrieved his fortunes by marrying a rich Dutchwoman he'd met at Shepheard's Hotel in Cairo, a widow worth millions, owner of a shipping line with a fleet of seventeen vessels, as well as large plantations in Java and Borneo. Since then, though he was seldom seen, he'd been regarded as our regiment's patron saint.

Colonel Bubencic must have helped this Balinkay out of some appalling fix back in the past, because Balinkay's loyalty to him and the regiment was nothing short of touching. Whenever he was in Austria he came over here especially to visit the garrison, and he would throw his money about so freely that it was the talk of the town for weeks. He seemed to feel a need to wear his old uniform just for an evening, be one of the lads with his comrades again. When he was sitting at the officers' regular table, easy-going and relaxed, you felt that he was a hundred times more at home in that smoky, badly whitewashed room in the Red Lion than in his grand feudal palace on an Amsterdam canal; the men of the regiment were, and always would be, his children, his brothers, his real family. Every year he donated prizes for our steeplechase, two or three crates of liqueurs and champagne regularly arrived at Christmas, and every New Year the Colonel could count for certain on a generous cheque to be paid into the bank for the mess funds. Anyone in lancers' uniform, with our facings on the collar, knew that if he was ever in trouble he could rely on Balinkay—a letter to him, and his problems would be over.

At any other time I would have been genuinely pleased to have the chance of meeting this legendary figure. But just now, in my present dismay, the thought of amusement, loud noise, toasts and speeches seemed to me the most unbearable thing on earth. So I tried to get out of it as quickly as possible, saying that I didn't feel too well. But with a hearty "Nonsense! No excuses today!" Ferencz had taken my arm, and against my will I had to give way. I listened to him, my mind still elsewhere, as he led me on, telling me about the people Balinkay had already helped out of trouble, saying that he had found his, Ferencz's, brother-in-law a job at once, and wondering aloud whether we might not make our fortunes faster by boarding a ship and going off to his properties in the East Indies. From time to time our lanky, grizzled friend Jozsi added a sharper note to tone down Ferencz's enthusiasm. Would the Colonel so happily welcome his blue-eyed boy back, he mocked, if Balinkay hadn't hooked his nice fat Dutch trout? She was said to be twelve years his senior, and: "If you're going to sell yourself," laughed Count Steinhübel, "you should at least make sure the price is right."

In retrospect, it seems to me strange now that, even bemused as I was, every word of that conversation stuck in my memory. But when your waking mind is numbed you can feel nervous irritation at the same time, and even when we entered the big room in the Red Lion, thanks to the hypnotic effect of military discipline I was reasonably well able to do the work assigned to me. And there was plenty of it. Our entire stock of streamers, banners and emblems, usually brought out only for the regimental ball, was found, a couple of orderlies hammered noisily and vigorously at the walls, next door Steinhübel was drilling the bugler on when and how to blow his call. Jozsi, who had the neatest handwriting, was told to write out the menu, in which all the dishes were given humorous names with double meanings, and I was to draw up the seating plan. Now and then an inn servant was already arranging chairs and tables neatly, the waiters brought in clinking batteries of bottles of wine and champagne that Balinkay had brought from Sacher's in Vienna in his car. Curiously enough, all this activity did me good, because the noise drowned out the dull thudding in my temples and the questions in my mind.

Finally, at eight, all was ready. Now we just had to go back to barracks, tidy ourselves and change for dinner. My batman Kusma had been given his orders. My coat and patent-leather boots were ready. I quickly dipped my face in cold water and glanced at the time—ten minutes to go. Our colonel was a stickler for punctuality. So I quickly got dressed, throwing my dusty shoes into a corner.

But just as I'm standing in front of the mirror in my underwear to comb my hair, there is a knock at the door. "Tell them I'm not available," I order my batman. He scuttles obediently off, and there is a moment's whispering outside my room. Then Kusma comes back, holding a letter.

A letter for me? Standing there in shirt and underpants, I take the rectangular blue envelope. It is thick and heavy, almost a small parcel, and at once I know I am holding fire in my hand. I don't even have to look at the handwriting to see who is writing to me.

Later, later, a quick instinct tells me. Don't read it, don't read it now! But against my will I have already opened the envelope, and I am reading and reading the letter. It rustles more and more in my shaking hand.

It was a sixteen-page letter written fast in an agitated hand, a letter such as you write and receive only once in a lifetime, with sentences flowing inexorably on, like blood from an open wound, unparagraphed, without any punctuation to speak of, word overtaking, then outrunning, then tumbling over word. Even now, many years later, I see every line, every letter before me, even now I could recite the contents of that letter from beginning to end by heart at any hour of the day or night, I read it so often. Months and months after that day, I was still carrying the folded blue papers around in my pocket, taking them out again and again, at home, in the barracks, in dugouts and by campfires during the war, and only when the enemy had attacked our division on both flanks and were retreating to Volhynia did I destroy it, fearing that this confession of one ecstatic moment might fall into the hands of strangers. *I have written to you six times already*, it began

and then I always tore the letter up, because I didn't want to give myself away, not that. I held out as long as I could. I have struggled with myself for weeks and weeks, hiding my feelings from you. Every time you came to see us, so friendly, guessing nothing, I ordered my hands to keep still, my eyes to seem indifferent, so as not to trouble you, and I've often been harsh and haughty on purpose, however much my heart was yearning for you—I tried everything in a human being's power, and even more. But then that happened today, and I swear it came over me against my will. It attacked behind my back. I can't understand now how it could have happened—afterwards I would have liked to hit myself, chastise myself, I was so dreadfully ashamed. Because I know, I do know what a mad delusion it would be to force myself on you. A lame creature, a cripple has no right to love—how could I, crushed and afflicted as I am, be anything but a burden to you, when I even disgust myself, I hate myself? I know that someone like me has no right to love anyone, and certainly none at all to be loved. She ought to crawl away into a corner and die, not upset other people's lives with her presence—yes, I do know that, I know it, and it is killing me to know it. I should never have dared to make advances to you, but who but you made me feel sure that I wouldn't be the pitiful freak I am now for much longer? That I would be able to move and walk about like other people, like all the millions of people who don't even know what a blessing every step they take by themselves is, what a wonderful thing. I firmly made up my mind to say nothing until it was all real, until I was a woman like any other and perhaps—perhaps!!!!—worthy of you, beloved. But my impatience, my longing to be well again was so mad that in that second when you

293

bent over me I actually believed, I honestly believed, I truly but foolishly believed I was that other girl, the new, healthy girl! I'd wanted it
and dreamt of it for so long, and now you were close to me—and for
a moment I forgot my horrible legs, I saw only you, I felt like the girl I
would want to be for you. Can you understand that even in the middle
of the day you can dream for a moment, if you always dream the same
dream, day and night, year after year? Believe me, my dear one, only the
nonsensical delusion that I was already free of my disability confused
me, only that impatience not to be an outcast and a cripple any more
let my heart carry me away so crazily. Please understand—I had been
longing for you so very much and for such a long time.

But now you know what you ought never to have known until I was
really better again, and you also know for whose sake I want to be cured,
for just one person on earth—for you, only for you! Forgive me, my very
dearly beloved, for this love, and I will ask you just one thing—don't be
afraid, do not feel horror of me! Don't think that because I once made
advances I will ever trouble you again, or that frail and repellent to myself
as I am, I will try to cling to you. No, I swear it—you will never hear
anything like that from me again, I won't show you my feelings. I will
just wait, wait patiently for God to take pity on me and make me better.
So please, I beg you, don't be afraid of my love, dearest, remember that
you felt more pity for me than anyone else, think how terribly helpless
I am, fixed to my chair, unable to take a step on my own, powerless to
follow you or hurry to meet you. Remember, please remember, that I am
a prisoner who must wait in her dungeon, wait patiently or impatiently
until you come and give me an hour of your time, until you let me see
you, hear your voice, feel that you are there in the same room—be aware
of your presence, the first and only happiness that has been granted to
me for years. Think of that, think how I lie and lie waiting day and
night, and every hour stretches out to such length, I can hardly bear the
strain. And then you come, and I can't jump up like anyone else, I can't

run to meet you, I can't touch and hold you. I have to sit and tame my feelings, dam it all up and keep quiet, I have to guard every word I say, every glance, every note in my voice just so that you couldn't think I am being bold enough to love you. But believe me, beloved, even that happy torture has always meant happiness to me, and I praised myself and liked myself better every time I managed to control myself and you went away, guessing nothing, free and easy in your mind, knowing nothing about my love. The pain was all mine—the pain of knowing how hopelessly in love with you I was.

But now it has happened. And now, my dear one, now that I can't deny what I feel for you any more, now I do beg you don't be cruel to me. Even the poorest, most pitiful creature has its pride, and I couldn't bear it if you despised me because I couldn't silence my heart. I am not asking you to return my love—no, by God who I hope will cure and save me, I would not dare to be so bold. Not even in dreams do I dare to hope that you could love me as I am today—you know I don't want any sacrifice or any pity from you. I want nothing except for you to tolerate my waiting in silence until at last the time has come! I know that even that is a great deal to ask of you. But is it really too much to give another human being the small, pitiful happiness that you would willingly give to any dog—the happiness of being able to look up at its master with a silent gaze from time to time? Must the dog be rejected at once, whipped away with scorn? It is only this one thing, I do assure you, just this one thing that I couldn't bear—if, pitiful as I am, I repelled you because I gave myself away. If you were to punish me even beyond the punishment of my own shame and despair, then there would be only one way for me to go—and you know what that is, because I showed you.

Don't be afraid—that isn't a threat! I don't want to alarm you, extort pity from you instead of your love—pity, the one thing your heart has yet given me. I want you to feel entirely carefree—I do not, for God's sake, want to unload my own burden on you, weigh you down with guilt when you are guilty of nothing—I only want this one thing, for you to forgive what happened and forget it entirely, forget what I said, forget what I let slip. Please just give me that reassurance, that one poor little certainty! Tell me at once—a single word will do—that I am not repellent to you, that you will come and see us again as if nothing had happened. You cannot guess how dreadful I feel at the thought of losing you. Since the door closed behind you I have been tormented by the fear, I don't know why but it is a mortal fear, that it was closing for the last time. You looked so pale at that moment, there was such fear in your eyes when I let go of you that I suddenly felt icy cold in the midst of my burning heat. And I know—Josef has told me—that you went straight out of the house. All of a sudden you were gone, with your sword and your cap. He looked for you in vain, in my boudoir and everywhere, so I know that you fled from me as if I were the plague or some other dreadful infection. But no, my dearest, I am not blaming you, I understand you entirely! I of all people, afraid of myself when I see those heavy things on my feet, I know how horrible, moody, tormenting, impossible I have become in my impatience. I of all people can understand why you would be afraid of me—oh, I can understand it only too well if people run from me, shudder to think of such a monster near them. And yet I beg you to forgive me, because there is no day or night without you, only despair. Just a note—send me a quick note, or a blank sheet of paper, a flower, any kind of sign! Just something to show me that you are not rejecting me entirely, I have not become a horror to you. Remember that I shall be gone in a few days' time, gone for months—so in ten days' time your troubles are over. And if mine then begin again a thousand times over, don't think of that, think of yourself, just as I am always thinking of you. Another week and you are released—so come to see us just once more, and first send me a word, give me a sign! I can't think, can't breathe, can't feel until I know that you have forgiven me. I will not, cannot go on living if you refuse me the right to love you.

I read and read. I kept going back to begin again at the beginning. My hands were shaking, the thudding in my temples grew louder and louder, so horrified, so shaken was I to find that I was loved with such desperation.

"Good heavens, look at you, still loafing about in your underwear while everyone's waiting impatiently. The whole lot of them are sitting down, keen to start dinner, including Balinkay, the Colonel's due to arrive any moment now, and you know what a fuss the old boy kicks up if one of us is late. Ferdl sent me off specially to see if anything had happened to you, and here you are reading sweet nothings from some girl, I suppose. Come along, get a move on, and look lively or we'll both be for it!"

This is Ferencz, bursting into my room. I don't even notice him until he brings his heavy paw down on my shoulder in fraternal fashion. At first I can't take in any of what he's saying. The Colonel? Ferdl sent Ferencz over? Balinkay? Oh yes, now I remember, Balinkay's convivial evening! I swiftly snatch up my trousers and coat, and with the speed I learnt at military academy fling them on automatically, without really being aware what I'm doing. Ferencz gives me an odd look.

"What the devil's wrong with you? You're not yourself. Not bad news from somewhere, I hope?"

I'm quick to dismiss this idea. "No, nothing like that. I'm coming." And in a trice we're on the stairs, but then I suddenly turn back.

"Oh, for God's sake, what is it now?" Ferencz shouts after me, exasperated. But I am only picking up the letter that I left lying on the table, and I tuck it away in my breast pocket. We do indeed get to the big dining room of the Red Lion at the last minute. The whole company has gathered at the long table, which is shaped like a horseshoe, but no one quite likes to start laughing and joking until the senior officers are seated. We are like schoolboys when the bell has just rung and their teacher is expected to appear at any moment.

And the orderlies are already opening the door for the staff officers, who come in with spurs clinking. We all rise from our chairs and stand briefly to attention. The Colonel sits down to Balinkay's right, the highest-ranking major to his left, and at once the table becomes animated, plates clink, spoons clatter, everyone is eating and drinking, they're all talking at once, deep in lively conversation. Only I sit among my cheerful comrades almost as if I weren't there at all, putting my hand to my tunic over the place where something thuds and hammers like a second heart. Whenever I do so I feel the letter rustling through the soft, yielding fabric as if a fire were being fanned; yes, there it is, moving close to my breast like something alive, and while the others talk and feast at their leisure, all I can do is think of that letter, and the desperate distress of the girl who wrote it.

The waiter serves me, but I leave the food untouched. I am deep in thought, dazed, it's like being asleep with my eyes open. I vaguely hear words around me, to right and left, without understanding them. My comrades might as well be speaking a foreign language. I look ahead of me, I see faces beside me, moustaches, eyes, noses, lips, uniforms, but all dull and muted, like items on display seen through a shop window. I am here yet not here, fixed where I sit yet with my mind elsewhere. Soundlessly, I am murmuring phrases from the letter in my mind, and sometimes, when I can't remember how it goes on, or I get confused, my hand itches to reach for my breast pocket, just as we surreptitiously used to read forbidden books during tactics lessons at military academy.

Then a knife strikes a glass energetically, and there is sudden silence, as if the sharp steel cut through the noise. The Colonel has risen to his feet and is embarking on a speech. He leans both hands on the table to steady himself as he speaks, and his sturdy body moves back and forth rhythmically as if he were on horseback. He opens by barking out the word "Comrades!" with the letter r rolled like a drum beating for the attack, and then launches into his well-prepared address to us. I listen hard, but my mind refuses to take it in. I hear only a few phrases, emphatically spoken and with further rolling of the r-sound: " ... honour of the arrrmy ... the spirit of the Austrrrian cavalrrry ... loyalty to the rrregiment." But in between I hear the ghostly whisper of other words, soft, pleading, loving, as if they came from another world. The letter is speaking to me at the same time: "My very dearly beloved ... don't be afraid ... I will not, cannot go on living if you refuse me the right to love you ... " Then the Colonel's rolling r intrudes again: " ... he has not forgotten his comrrrades while far away ... nor his Austrrrian fatherland ... " The other voice comes in again like a sob, a muffled cry: "Tell me at once ... a single word will do ... that I am not repellent to you ... "

Then there is a crashing like an artillery salvo. "Hip, hip, hooray!" They are all on their feet as if in obedience to the raising aloft of the Colonel's glass, and there's a prearranged cry of "Three cheers for Balinkay!" We all clink glasses and drink the health of Balinkay, who is waiting for the torrent of cheering to die down before replying in relaxed, easy and humorous tones—he'll say only a few words, he assures us, nothing too taxing, he'd just like to say that in spite of everything and everyone he never feels as happy anywhere in the world as among his old comrades. And he ends with a toast. "Here's to the regiment! Long live His Majesty our gracious commander-in-chief the Emperor!" Steinhübel signals to the bugler to play another bugle call, and everyone sings the national anthem in chorus, followed as always by the song familiar to all regiments of the Austrian army. You simply insert your own regiment's name at the appropriate spot.

We are the Austrian army of great renown and fame,
We're lancers of the cavalry, the —th it is our name.

Then Balinkay walks up and down the table, glass in hand, drinking a separate toast with every one of us. Suddenly, feeling my neighbour nudge me hard, I meet a pair of bright grey eyes. "Hello there, friend!" Bemused, I return his nod, and only when Balinkay stops at the next man along do I realise that I forgot to clink glasses with him. But it has all disappeared again into a multicoloured fog, through which I see faces and uniforms merging in a curious blur. Good heavens—what's that blue mist in front of my eyes all of a sudden? Have the others already begun smoking, is that why I feel it's so hot and stuffy in here? Quick, I must drink something. I gulp down the contents of one, two, three glasses without even knowing what is in them. I just have to rid my throat of that foul, bitter taste. And I must smoke a cigarette quickly myself. But when my hand goes to my pocket for my cigarette case, I feel the faint rustle of the letter again, and I snatch my hand back. Once again, through the cheerful noise, I hear only the sobbing, pleading words: "I do know, what a mad delusion it would be to force myself on you … "

But then a fork is tapped on a glass once more, requesting silence. This time it is Major Wondraczek, who never misses a chance to air his poetic talents in humorous verse and comic song. We all know when Wondraczek gets to his feet, propping his imposing paunch against the table with a roguish, meaning leer on his face, that the risqué part of the evening's festivities is inevitably about to begin.

And there he is in position, his pince-nez over his rather long-sighted eyes, and he unfolds a sheet of foolscap with much ceremony. It is the obligatory piece that he feels it his duty to deliver to enliven any party, and this time it sets out to embellish Balinkay's life story with a series of double entendres. Several of my neighbours dutifully laugh along with him at every allusion, whether out of politeness to a superior officer or because they are slightly tipsy themselves. Finally he concludes the whole performance, and shouts of "Bravo!" ring out from the assembled company.

But I am suddenly overcome by horror. The coarse laughter is like a claw tightening on my heart. How can they laugh like that when someone, somewhere, is crying out and suffering in unimaginable pain? How can they joke and tell dirty stories while another human being is in a state of desperation? I know that once Wondraczek has finished his comic turn the evening will lapse into horseplay. There will be singing, they'll sing the latest hilarious verses of the song about 'The Landlady on the River Lahn', they'll crack jokes and fall about with uproarious laughter. Suddenly I can't stand the sight of their well-meaning, cheerful faces. Didn't she ask me to send her a note, a single word? Why don't I go to the telephone and call Kekesfalva's house? I can't keep another human being waiting like that! I have to say something, I have to …

"*Bravo, bravissimo!*" Everyone is applauding, chair legs scrape the floor as they are pushed back and crash down again, the floor itself echoes with the sudden impact of forty or fifty cheerful and slightly befuddled men getting to their feet, and dust rises from the floorboards. The Major beams proudly, takes off his pince-nez and folds up the paper, nodding to the officers kindly and with a touch of vanity as they crowd around him with their congratulations. As for me, I seize my chance to leave the room at this moment of uproar without a word to anyone. Perhaps they won't notice. And if they do, I don't care, I can't bear that laughter any more, that self-satisfied merriment, as if they were all slapping themselves on their well-filled stomachs. I can't, I cannot stand it any more!

"Leaving already, sir?" asks the orderly on cloakroom duty in surprise. Oh, go to hell, I mutter silently to myself, pushing my way past him without a word. Now down the street, around the corner, up the stairs of the barracks to my floor, and I'll be alone!

The corridors are empty, somewhere a sentry is pacing up and down, water runs from a tap, a boot falls to the floor. But a soft, strange sound comes from one of the men's dormitories, where lights have been put out according to the rules. Instinctively, I prick up my ears—a couple of the Ruthenians are singing or humming a melancholy song quietly in unison. After undoing the brass buttons of the brightly coloured uniforms so foreign to them and taking them off at night, when they are nothing but naked men who used to lie in the straw at home, they sing these melancholy ditties before going to sleep, remembering their homes, the fields, perhaps girls they had liked. Usually I take no notice of this humming and singing because I don't understand the words, but this time their sadness inspires a sense of fraternity in me. I would like to sit down with one of them and talk to him, although he wouldn't really understand what I was saying—yet it was possible that all the same he would give me a sympathetic look from his mild, cow-like eyes, understanding me better than the merrymakers around the horseshoe-shaped table of the Red Lion. Oh, to have someone to help me out of the hopeless tangle I'm in!

On tiptoe so as not to wake my batman Kusma, asleep in the room outside mine and snorting heavily, I steal into my room, throw down my cap in the dark, and take off my sword and collar, which has felt as if it were choking me for some time. Then I put on the light and go over to the table—at long last I will re-read that letter at my leisure, the first deeply moving letter that a woman had ever written the man I was then, so young and uncertain of myself.

But next moment I shrink back with alarm. There on the table *is* the letter—how is that possible? In the circle of lamplight, there lies the letter that I thought I had put safely in my breast pocket—yes, there it is, rectangular blue envelope, the now familiar handwriting.

For a moment my senses reel. Am I drunk? Am I dreaming with my eyes open? Have I lost my mind? Only just now, taking off my tunic, I heard the rustle of the letter in my breast pocket. Am I so distracted that I put it down here and forgot about it a minute later? I put my hand in that pocket. No—anything else really *was* impossible—there it still is. So now I understand what's going on. Only now am I really wide awake. The letter on the table must be another, a second letter that arrived later, and my good batman Kusma carefully put it there for me next to the Thermos flask, so that I would see it as soon as I came home.

Another letter! A second letter within two hours! My throat instantly tightens with foreboding. I suppose it will go on like

303

this every day now, every day and every night, letter after letter, one after the other. If I write to her she will write back; if I don't answer her she will demand an answer. She'll always be wanting something from me, every day, every day! She will send me messages and telephone me, she will lie in wait for me, listen for my every footstep, will want to know when I go out and when I come back, who I am with and what I am saying and doing. I can see already that I'm lost—they will never let me go again—oh, the djinn, the djinn, the old man and the cripple! I'll never be free again, that desperate, needy girl will never let me go, not until one of us is destroyed, she or I, by this senseless, unhappy passion.

Don't read it, I tell myself. Certainly don't read it tonight. Don't let yourself in for anything else! You're not strong enough to stand up to that pushing and pulling, it will tear you apart. Better just destroy the letter, or send it back unopened! Whatever you do, don't let the fact that some perfect stranger loves you weigh on your mind, your awareness, your conscience! To the devil with the Kekesfalvas! I didn't know them before, and I don't want to know them any longer. But then a thought suddenly shakes me—suppose she has done some kind of harm to herself because I didn't send an answer? Or perhaps she *will* do herself some harm. I can't leave a desperate human being entirely without an answer! Just don't feel guilty, I tell myself, don't feel guilty! So I tear the envelope open. Thank God, this one is only a short letter. A single page, ten lines or so, and no signature.

Destroy my earlier letter at once! I was crazy, I was out of my mind. None of what I wrote is true. And don't come and see us tomorrow! Please be sure not to come! I must punish myself for humiliating myself in front of you so miserably. So don't on any account come tomorrow, I don't want you to, I forbid you to. And no reply! On no account reply! Please let me rely on you to destroy my earlier letter, forget every word of it! And think no more of it.

Think no more of it—what a childish request, as if strained nerves will ever submit to being harnessed by the will! Think no more of it, while ideas are chasing around the small space between my temples like timid runaway horses, their hooves hammering painfully away at me. Think no more of it, when memory keeps feverishly confronting me with images, while my nerves are on edge, and all my senses tense with rejection and counter-rejection! Think no more of it while the sheet of notepaper still scorches my hand with its burning words, while I pick it up and put it down again, and compare the first and second letters until every word is branded on my mind! Think no more of it when I can think only of one thing—how to get away, how to defend myself? How to save myself from that avid longing, the excessive emotion that was so unwelcome to me?

Think no more of it—exactly what I want myself, and I put out the light, because light keeps all ideas too vivid and wakeful. I want to crawl away and hide in the dark. I tear off all my clothes to breathe more easily, I throw myself on the bed hoping to feel less. But my thoughts will not let me rest. They flutter around my tired mind in confusion, like bats in their ghostly flight, greedy as rats nibbling and making their way through my leaden weariness. The more quietly I lie, the more restless are my memories, conjuring up flickering images in the darkness. So I get up again and put the light on once more to banish the ghosts. But the first thing that the lamplight, maliciously, falls on is the pale blue rectangle of the letter, and over the chair hangs my tea-stained tunic, a reminder and a warning. Think no more of it—exactly what I want myself, but it can't be done by willpower. So I wander up and down the room, back and forth, flinging open cupboards and the drawers in the cupboards one by one until I find the little glass container with my sleeping pills in it, and I stagger back to bed. But there is no escape. Even in dreams the scrabbling rats of my dark thoughts are on the move, gnawing at the black dish of sleep, always the same thoughts, always the same, and when I wake up in the morning I feel as if vampires had gutted me and sucked my blood dry.

So reveille comes as a relief, and my military duties—a kinder and better form of captivity—do me good. It is good to mount my horse and trot on with the others, to have to pay attention and concentrate the whole time. I have to obey and I have to command. For the hours of military exercises, perhaps four hours in all, I can escape, I can ride away from myself.

At first all goes well. Luckily there is a great deal to do today: preparation for the large-scale manoeuvres, a closing parade with every squadron drawn up in line to ride past the commanding officer, every horse's head and every sword point perfectly aligned. Such spectacular parades call for hard work, you have to begin all over again ten or twenty times, keep your eye on every single lancer, and the whole exercise demands such close attention from every one of us officers that I have no choice but to keep my mind entirely on what I am doing and forget everything else—thank God!

But when we stop for ten minutes' break to give the horses a breathing space, my roving eye happens to wander to the horizon. Against the steely blue of the sky, the fields with their sheaves and reapers stretch far and wide around us; the line of the horizon is straight—except, beyond a wood, for the curious outline of a tower like a toothpick seen in silhouette. That, I think with a moment's shock, is her tower with the terrace on it—I cannot help that idea returning, I cannot help staring and remembering—it's eight in the morning, she will have been awake for some time and thinking of me. Perhaps her father is going to her bedside and talking about me, or perhaps she is sending for Ilona or Josef to ask whether a letter has come, the letter she longs for (oh, I should have written after all!)—or perhaps she has already gone up to the tower and is staring this way from there, clinging to the balustrade, staring in my direction just as I am now staring in hers. And as soon as I remember that there is someone there wanting so much to see me, I feel that familiar tugging sensation, pity clawing at my own heart. Now the exercise is resuming, commands shouted on all sides, the various groups coming together and moving apart in their predetermined formations, while I myself am shouting "Wheel left!" and "Wheel right!" in the general turmoil. I am in the thick of it, but my mind is elsewhere. At the deepest, most individual level of my consciousness I am thinking of nothing but the one thing that I don't want to think of, that I ought not to think of.

"Good God above, what the devil d'you think you're doing? Back! Get apart, you rabble, disengage!" It's Colonel Bubencic speaking, red as a turkey cock in the face, galloping up and shouting across the entire parade ground. And with good reason. Someone must have given the wrong command, because two lines of men who were supposed to swerve as they passed each other, one of them mine, have ridden head to head at full tilt and are now dangerously intermingled. In the confusion a couple

307

of horses shy and bolt, others rear up, one of the lancers has fallen from his mount and is under the horses' hooves, the ranks of men are in uproar. We hear the clink of weapons, horses whinnying, stamping and thunderous noise as if we were in the middle of a real battle. Only gradually do the officers who come galloping up manage to separate the shouting tangle of men. At a call on the bugle the squadrons, now back together, get into close formation again to present a united front. But now an ominous silence descends. Everyone knows that someone will be called to account. The horses, still foaming at the mouth after their near collision, and perhaps infected by their riders' own nervousness, are restless, pulling at the reins, so that the whole line of helmets sways slightly, like a steel telegraph wire stretched taut in the wind. The Colonel now rides forward into this tense silence. Even the way he sits in the saddle, feet braced in the stirrups, slapping his riding crop against his boots, makes it clear that a storm is brewing. A light pull on his reins, and his horse stands still. Then a couple of words, like the sound of a chopper falling, carry sharply over the whole parade ground. "Lieutenant Hofmiller!"

Only now do I realise how this happened. I was the man who gave the wrong command. My thoughts must have been straying. I was thinking once again of the terrible business that had upset me so much. I alone am to blame. The responsibility is all mine. A slight pressure of the thighs, and my gelding trots past my comrades, who look away in embarrassment as I approach the Colonel. He is waiting motionless some thirty feet in front of the line of men. I stop at the prescribed distance from him. By now even the faintest clinking and chinking of the men's equipment has died away. A final, soundless, truly deadly silence sets in, like the silence at an execution before the firing squad is given the command. Everyone, even the least of the Ruthenian farmers' boys back there, knows what lies ahead for me.

I would rather not remember what happens next. At least the Colonel deliberately lowers his dry, cutting voice, so that the men can't hear the names he is calling me, but sometimes a good round curse—"Bloody fool!" or "Sheer damn idiocy!"—rises in the silence. And the way he is snorting, red as a lobster in the face, accompanying his staccato remarks with a slap of the crop against his boot, tells all of them, right to the back row, that I am being hauled over the coals like a schoolboy, or worse. I sense a hundred curious and perhaps amused glances on my back, while the choleric Colonel tips a load of verbal manure over me. None of us, in months and months, has suffered such a storm of abuse as I do on this fine June day with swallows flying unwittingly overhead against that steely blue sky.

My hands tremble on the reins with impatience and anger. I would like to strike my horse smartly on his hindquarters and gallop off and away. But in obedience to the regulations I sit there impassively, my face frozen, and I have to wait patiently while Bubencic concludes by saying that he is not letting such a pathetic incompetent muck up the entire exercise. I'll be hearing more from him tomorrow, he says, and he doesn't want to see my face again today. Then, swift and sharp as a kick, he snaps, "Dismiss!" slapping his own boot with his riding crop one last time.

However, I have to put my hand obediently to my helmet before I can turn and ride back to the front line. None of my comrades will look me in the face, they all cast their eyes down under the shadow of their helmets in embarrassment. They are all ashamed for me, or at least that is how I feel. Luckily I don't have to ride the gauntlet between them all the way; a word of command cuts it short. Another bugle call, and the exercise begins again, the front breaks up and resolves into separate lines. Ferencz takes advantage of this moment—why are the least intelligent also the kindest?—to bring his horse up to mine as if by chance and whisper, "Don't take it to heart! Could happen to anyone."

He means well, but it's more than I can take. "Mind your own business!" I snap at him, turning away. At that moment I have felt, in my own person for the first time, how pity can wound you with its clumsy efforts. For the first time—and too late.

Chuck it in! I'll chuck it all in, I think as we ride back to the town. I'll get away from here, away, I'll go somewhere else, I'll find some place where no one knows me, where I'll be free of everyone and everything! I just want to get away, away—subconsciously that word becomes part of the rhythm of my trot. Back at the barracks I throw the reins to one of the lancers and leave the yard. I'm not going to eat in the officers' mess today, I don't want to be the butt of mockery, still less an object of pity.

But I don't really know where to go. I have no plan and no destination in mind—I feel I can't live in either of my two worlds, the Kekesfalva estate outside town and the barracks here. But I must get away, get away, my hammering pulse tells me, away, away. I feel the word thudding in my temples. I have to get out of here, go somewhere, anywhere away from this damn barracks, away from the town! Down the unattractive main street once more and then just go on and on.

But suddenly someone calls a cheerful "Afternoon!" behind me. Instinctively I stare at the speaker. Who's greeting me as if he knew me—this tall man in civilian clothes, breeches, grey coat, plaid cap? Never seen him before—at least, I don't remember him. This stranger is standing beside a motor car, and two mechanics in blue overalls are busy hammering away at it. And now, obviously not noticing my confusion, he is coming towards me. It's Balinkay, whom I have seen before only in his uniform.

"Exhaust wheezing again," he laughs, pointing to the car. "Happens whenever I take her for a spin. I guess it'll be a good twenty years before anyone can really rely on chugging along the road in these contraptions. Horses were simpler; at least you knew where you were with a horse."

I feel a strong, instinctive liking for this stranger. His movements are so free and easy, and he has the warm, bright eyes of a man who takes life as it comes. And as soon as I hear his unexpected greeting, an idea flashes into my mind—you could confide in him, I tell myself. Within a fraction of a second, at the speed with which the brain works at moments of great tension, I have associated a whole chain of other ideas with this first one. He is in civilian clothes, he's his own master. He's been through something similar to my plight himself. He helped Ferencz's brother-in-law, they say he helps anyone who asks him, why wouldn't he help me? Before I've even taken a deep breath, this whole swiftly forming chain of thought has coalesced into an abrupt decision. I pluck up my courage and go closer to Balinkay.

"Excuse me," I say, amazed at my own audacity, "but could you spare me five minutes?"

He looks a little startled, but then his teeth flash in a smile. "With pleasure, my dear Hoff ... Hoff? ... "

"Hofmiller," I say.

311

"Entirely at your disposal. Where would we be if a man had no time for a comrade? Like to go into the restaurant, or shall we go up to my room?"

"Up to your room, if it's all the same to you, and I really want only five minutes. I don't mean to delay you"

"Take as long as you like. It's going to be another half-an-hour before they get that clatterbox on the road again. Only you won't think my room very comfortable. The landlord always wants to give me a grand first-floor room, but call it sentimental if you like, I prefer to stay where I once did in the old days. And when I was there … but never mind that."

We go upstairs. It is true, his room is a very modest one for such a rich man. Single bed, no wardrobe, no armchair, just two rickety wicker chairs between the window and the bed. Balinkay takes out his gold cigarette case, offers me a cigarette and eases my way by saying at once, "Well, my dear Hofmiller, what can I do for you?"

No havering, I tell myself, and I come out with it at once.

"I'd like to ask your advice, Balinkay. I want to resign my commission and get out of Austria. Do you happen to know of any openings for me?"

Balinkay suddenly looks serious. His features set into a graver expression, and he tosses his cigarette away.

"Nonsense—a young fellow like you? What's got into your head?"

But I suddenly feel determined. The decision that I hadn't even yet made ten minutes ago is strong and hard as steel.

"My dear Balinkay," I say, in the firm tone that precludes any further discussion, "would you be kind enough to allow me to forgo explanation? Every man knows what he wants to do and what he has to do. No one else, no outsider can understand

312

these things. Believe me, I have to draw a line under my life in the army."

Balinkay looks at me thoughtfully. He must have seen that I mean it.

"Look, I don't want to meddle with your affairs, but I assure you, Hofmiller, this isn't a good idea. You don't know what you're doing. I'd guess you're around twenty-five, twenty-six, you'll soon make the grade to first lieutenant. And that's quite an achievement. Here you have your military rank, you're someone. But the moment you branch out on your own, you're lower in the social scale than any ruffian, any grubby errand boy, because that sort don't go around weighed down with our prejudices. Believe you me, when one of us takes off his uniform there's not much of his old self left, and I do beg you, don't deceive yourself just because I happen to have hauled myself out of the mire again. That was pure chance, a one-in-a-thousand chance, and I hate to think what's become of others who didn't have the luck to get a helping hand from the good Lord."

His firm tone carries conviction. But I feel that I must not give way.

"I do know it means going down in the social scale," I tell him. "But I have to go away, there's nothing else for it. So please don't try changing my mind. I know I'm nothing out of the ordinary, and I can't say I've ever learnt much, but if you were kind enough to put in a good word for me somewhere I promise not to let you down. I know I wouldn't be the first. You found a job for Ferencz's brother-in-law, didn't you?"

"Oh, Jonas," says Balinkay dismissively, "but what was he to start with anyway? A little provincial civil servant, it's easy enough to help someone like that. Move him from one office stool to a slightly better one and he feels like God Almighty. It doesn't matter to him where he wears the seat of his trousers shiny, he was never used to anything better. But to find something for a man who once wore a star on his collar, well, that's another story. No, my dear Hofmiller, the best jobs are always taken already. If you want to start out again in civilian life you have to begin at the bottom, right down on the lowest rung of the ladder, where it doesn't exactly smell of roses."

"That doesn't make any difference."

I must have said those words with great vigour, because Balinkay looks at me first with curiosity, then with a strangely fixed glance that seems to come from far away. Finally he moves his chair closer to me and places his hand on my arm.

"Look, Hofmiller, I'm not responsible for you, and I'm not about to read you a lecture. But I've been through this kind of thing myself, and you may believe me when I tell you it *does* make a difference, a great difference, when you suddenly go from the top to the bottom, off your cavalry officer's horse and into humdrum everyday life … and I'm saying this to you as a man who once sat in this shabby little room from twelve noon until darkness fell, telling myself just the same as you—it won't make any difference. I'd resigned my commission around eleven-thirty, and I didn't want to sit in the officers' mess with the others or walk down the street in broad daylight in civilian clothes. So I took this room—now you know why I always want it again—and I waited here until it was dark so that no one could give a pitying glance on seeing me slink away in a shabby grey coat with a bowler hat on my head. I stood at that window, that very window, and I looked down once more at the others strolling around. There were my comrades, all in uniform, upright and free, each of them a little god, and each of them knew who he was and where he belonged. And I felt that I was nothing now

314

but a speck of dirt. It was as if I'd stripped off my skin along with my uniform. Of course you're thinking, nonsense—one coat is blue, another is black or grey, and who cares if you go walking with a sword beside you or an umbrella in your hand instead? But I can still feel the shock, I feel it to the marrow of my bones, of stealing out by night on my way to the station, and how two lancers passed me on the corner and neither of them saluted. And I remember humping my own case into a third-class carriage, where I sat among the sweaty farmers' wives and labourers—yes, I know all this is stupid, and unjust, and the military man's idea of his honour is only a delusion—but after eight years of service and four years of military academy it's in your blood. You feel maimed at first, or like someone with an oozing sore in the middle of his face. God keep you from going through that yourself! I wouldn't live that evening all over again for any money, the evening when I stole away from here, making a detour around every lamp post until I reached the station. And that was only the beginning."

"But Balinkay, that's just why I want to go somewhere else, somewhere far away, where none of these things exist and no one knows anything about me."

"That's exactly the way I talked, Hofmiller, exactly the way I thought! Get far away and the slate will be wiped clean, a *tabula rasa*! I'd sooner be blacking boots or washing dishes in America, I told myself, like the tales you read in the newspapers about self-made millionaires! But it takes a fair amount of money even to get to America, Hofmiller, and you don't yet know what it means for the likes of us to have to bow and scrape. As soon as a former officer of the lancers doesn't feel those stars on his collar any more, he can't even stand on his own two feet with any dignity, let alone talk the way he used to. You feel stupid and embarrassed even with your best friends, and when you have to ask for something your own pride keeps you quiet. Yes, my dear boy, I went through a lot I'd rather not remember back then—humiliations, a sense of disgrace. I've never told anyone that before."

He had got to his feet and was waving his arms vigorously about, as if his coat suddenly felt too tight for him. Suddenly he turned round.

"However, I don't mind talking about it now. Because today I'm not ashamed of it any more, and if my story's in time to show you your plan in less of a rosy light, well, that may do you some good."

He sat down again, moving closer to me.

"I expect you've been told the whole story of my wonderful catch, haven't you? How I met my wife in Shepheard's Hotel? I know it's the talk of all the regiments, they'd like to have it printed and published, a fine example of the heroic prowess of an Imperial Austrian military officer. Well, it wasn't as wonderful as all that, and only a part of the story is true. Yes, I really did meet her in Shepheard's Hotel. But only she and I know *how* I met her, she hasn't told anyone, and nor have I. And I'm telling you only so you'll understand that money doesn't grow on trees for our sort. So to cut a long story short, when I met her at Shepheard's Hotel I was working there—prepare for a shock!—as a room waiter—yes, my dear boy, I was an ordinary, humble waiter. Obviously I didn't take the job for fun, it was a case of sheer stupidity and a former military man's pitiful ignorance of the world. An Egyptian had been staying at the same run-down boarding house as me in Vienna, a fellow who made out that his brother-in-law was manager of the Royal Polo Club in Cairo, and he said if I gave him two hundred crowns as commission he could get me a job there as a trainer. They thought highly of polished manners and good names at the Polo Club, he said, and well, I'd always been a good polo player, and the salary he mentioned was excellent—in three years I'd have earned a tidy little sum and could start up in some good line of business on my own. What's more, Cairo is some way off, and you mix with a good class of people playing polo. I won't bore you by telling you how many doorbells I had to ring, how many embarrassed excuses I heard from people who used to call themselves my friends, but in the end I managed to scrape together the few hundred crowns I wanted for my crossing and my kit—you need riding clothes for a club like that, and evening dress. Even though I travelled steerage class, the voyage went remarkably quickly. But by the time I was in Cairo I had just seven piastres in my pocket, and when I ring the bell at the Royal Polo Club I find a black man gawping at me, saying he doesn't know anyone called Efdopulos, or his brother-in-law, no, they don't need any trainer, and in any case the Polo Club is about to close—by now you'll have realised that my Egyptian acquaintance was a rogue who had cheated me, fool that I was, out of my two hundred crowns. I hadn't had the sense to ask to see the letters and telegrams he claimed to have had. I can tell you, my dear Hofmiller, we're not up to such tricks, and it wasn't the first time I'd fallen for a tall story as I looked for employment. But this was a blow right in the solar plexus. For there I was, I didn't know a soul in Cairo, I had only those seven piastres. Not only was I in a real fix, life there cost a lot. I'll spare you the account of how I lived and what I ate over the first six days. I'm surprised, myself, that you can survive that sort of thing. And you see, another man in that position will go to

317

the consul and try to scrounge a passage home. But there's the snag—once we're used to the army it sticks in our throats. We can't sit around on benches in waiting rooms along with dockers and kitchen maids who have lost their jobs, we can't endure the look a petty consular clerk will give a man when he's deciphered the words 'Baron Balinkay' in a passport. We'd sooner go straight to the dogs—so just think what a stroke of luck it was for me when I heard by chance that they needed an assistant waiter at Shepheard's Hotel! And as I had evening dress, tails and all, and the tailcoat was even new (I'd lived on the proceeds of my riding gear for the first few days), and on the grounds that I could speak French, they hired me on probation. At first that seems all right. You stand there in your spotless white shirt front, you wait at table, you serve the food, you cut a good figure, but then again, as a humble room waiter you sleep with two others in a baking hot attic under the roof, sharing it with about seven million fleas and bedbugs, and in the morning the three of you have to wash one by one in the same tin bowl—not to mention the fact that to people like you and me a tip burns the hand like fire, and so on and so forth—well, never mind all that! I went through it, and it's enough for you to know that I survived.

"And then there was the business over my wife. She'd just been widowed, and she had come to Cairo with her sister and brother-in-law. This brother-in-law was the most objectionable character imaginable—broad, fat, flabby, loud-mouthed, and there was something about me that he didn't care for. Perhaps I was too elegant for his liking, perhaps I didn't bow humbly enough to Mynheer, and one day when I didn't serve him his breakfast at exactly the right time he shouted 'You stupid fool!' at me … well, something like that gets to you when you were

once an army officer—and it gave me such a jolt that before
I could stop to think what I was doing I flew off the handle. I
assure you, for two pins I'd have smashed my fist into his face.
Well—I stopped myself at the last minute because, you see, that
whole business of being a waiter had felt like a masquerade
anyway, and next moment—I don't know if you'll understand
this—I was taking an almost sadistic pleasure in thinking that I,
Baron Balinkay, now had to put up with this kind of thing. So
I just stood still, smiling at him slightly—but condescendingly,
you understand, looking down my nose, which made the man
go greenish white in the face with anger, sensing that somehow
I was his superior. Then I walked coolly out of the room, with
an ironically civil bow—he almost burst with rage. But my
wife—my future wife, I mean—was there, and she must have
noticed the bad feeling between the two of us, and somehow
she could tell—she told me so herself later—from the way I'd
flared up that never in my life had anyone allowed himself to
speak to me like that before. So she followed me out into the
corridor to say she was afraid her brother-in-law was rather
agitated, she hoped I wouldn't take it ill—and to tell you whole
truth, my dear Hofmiller, she even tried to slip a banknote into
my hand to put things right.

"When I refused it she must have sensed for a second time
that I wasn't quite the usual run of waiter. But that would
have been the end of the matter, because in those few weeks
I'd scraped enough money together to pay my passage home
without having to beg from the consul. I went to the consulate
only to get information. And then chance came to my aid,
that one-in-a-thousand chance. The consul just happened
to be walking through the anteroom to his office, and he
was none other than Elemér von Juhácz. God knows how

319

often I've sat talking to him at the Jockey Club. Well, so he welcomed me warmly and invited me to his club—and by another coincidence, so it was coincidence piled on coincidence, I tell you this just to show how many amazing coincidences must come together for someone like you or me to get himself up on dry land again—by another coincidence, my future wife was there. When Elemér introduced me as his friend Baron Balinkay, she went scarlet. She recognised me at once, of course, and now she felt terrible about trying to give me a tip. But I could tell at once what kind of woman she was, and she's a fine, right-minded woman, because she didn't try ignoring the subject, she said honestly and frankly what a mistake she'd made. After that everything happened very fast … that's another story, and not for telling here. But believe me, such coincidences don't happen every day, and in spite of my money and in spite of my wife, for whom I thank God a thousand times every morning and every evening, I wouldn't like to go through those experiences of mine before I met her again."

I instinctively offered Balinkay my hand.

"Thank you very much for warning me. I have a better idea of what lies ahead now. But word of honour, I can't see any other way. Do you really not know of any employment I might find? They say your wife and you do a great deal of business."

Balinkay said nothing for a moment, and then he sighed sympathetically.

"Poor lad, you certainly seem to be in a bad way—don't worry, I won't put you through an interrogation. I can see enough for myself. Once you get to that stage, no amount of persuasion is any use. Well, a comrade has to lend a hand, and I don't suppose I need to say I won't be backward in that.

Just one thing, Hofmiller, I'm sure you have enough sense not to think I can simply snap my fingers and set you up in grand style in one of our companies. Such things don't happen in a good organisation, it only makes for bad feeling if one man suddenly gets preferential treatment. You'd have to start at the very bottom, maybe spend a few months on tedious clerical work in an office before you could be sent over to the plantations, or we could think up something else for you. But as I said, I'll start the wheels turning. We're leaving tomorrow, my wife and I, we'll spend a week or ten days strolling around Paris, then we'll be in Le Havre and Antwerp for a few days, looking into our agencies there. But we'll be back in around three weeks' time, and I'll write to you as soon as I'm home in Rotterdam. I won't forget, don't worry. You can rely on the word of a Balinkay."

"I know," I said, "and I really am most grateful."

But Balinkay must have picked up the slight note of disappointment in what I said. Indeed, he had probably suffered such setbacks himself, because experiencing that kind of thing develops your ear for these nuances.

"Or is that leaving it too late for you?"

"No," I said hesitantly. "Of course not, as soon as I know something's certain. But ... but well, it would be better if ... "

Balinkay thought for a moment. "Would you be free today, for instance? I mean because my wife is still in Vienna, and the business is hers, not mine, so it's for her to say."

"Oh yes ... of course I'm free," I said quickly. It had occurred to me that the Colonel didn't want to see my face again today.

"Excellent! Famous! Then you'd better come along with me in that clatterbox of mine. There'll be room for you next to the chauffeur. No spare space in the back, because I've said I'll take

321

my old friend Baron Lajos and his good lady with me. We'll be at the Hotel Bristol in Vienna at five, I'll have a word with my wife at once, and then you're up and running, she's never yet said no if I ask her a favour for a comrade of mine."

I shook his hand warmly, and we went downstairs. The mechanics had taken off their blue overalls, the car was ready, and two minutes later it was chugging along the road with us inside.

There is something heady and intoxicating about physical and mental speed alike. As soon as the car was out of the town streets and in open country I felt curiously relaxed. The chauffeur drove fast, trees and telegraph poles flew away behind us as if chopped down at an angle, as we passed through the villages house tottered against house, an unsteady picture, while white milestones loomed ahead and then retreated before you had time to read what they said. The strong wind blowing in our faces gave me some idea of the daring pace at which we were bowling along. But my astonishment at the speed with which my own life was racing on at the same time was even greater. I had taken so many decisions in these few hours! In the usual way, hazy ideas tinged with many shades of feeling hover between vague wishfulness, dawning intention and final performance, and it is even secretly pleasurable to begin by toying uncertainly with decisions before making up your mind to carry them through. This time, however, everything had happened at dreamlike speed, and as the villages and roads and trees and meadows retreated into the background, finally and never to return, as the car engine hammered away, everything that had made up my life until now was speeding into the distance: the barracks, my military career, my comrades, the Kekesfalvas, their castle, my room, the riding school, my entire apparently secure and well-regulated life. A single hour had changed my ideas of the world.

At five-thirty we drew up outside the Hotel Bristol, jolted about, covered with dust, yet wonderfully refreshed by the exhilarating drive.

"Hey, you can't come up and meet my wife like that!" laughed Balinkay, looking at me. "Anyone would think someone had tipped a sack of flour all over you. And maybe it would be better for me to have a word with her alone first—I can speak more freely then, and there'll be nothing for you to feel awkward about. I think you'd better go to the cloakroom, have a good wash, and then sit in the bar. I'll come back in a few minutes' time and tell you what she says. And don't worry, I'll make sure it goes the way you want."

Sure enough, he didn't keep me waiting long. Five minutes later he came back, laughing.

"There, what did I tell you? Everything's fine—that is, if it suits you. You can think it over as long as you like, and you can say no any time. My wife—she really is a clever woman—knew just the thing at once. You board a ship for the Dutch East Indies, mainly so that you can learn the local languages and have a good look around. You'll go as assistant to the purser, get a uniform, eat at the officers' table, travel about a bit when you get to the East Indies, and help with the clerical work. Then we'll find you a position either back here or over there, just as you like, my wife's promised that."

"Oh, thank you so—"

"No need to thank me. Perfectly natural for me to help you out. But once again, Hofmiller, don't do this without thinking.

As far as I'm concerned you're welcome to set off the day after tomorrow and report for duty—I'll send the director a telegram anyway, so that he'll know your name, but of course it would be a good idea for you to sleep on it. I'd say you were better off in the regiment, but *chacun à son goût*. As I said, if you want to join the ship you can do just that, and if you change your mind we won't complain. Well," he said, offering me his hand, "whichever way you decide, yes or no, I've enjoyed meeting you. So long!"

I looked at this man, sent to me by Fate, with strong emotion. With his wonderfully easy manner he had lightened the worst of my burden—asking for help, hesitating, the torment of making up my mind. And now there was nothing left for me to do but observe the one little formality of resigning my commission. Then I would be free and delivered from my troubles.

The chancery registration form, a folio sheet measured to the precise millimetre specified for its particular format, was perhaps the most essential requisite of the pre-war Austrian civil service and military administration. Every petition, every official document, every report had to be made out on this form, neatly trimmed to size. Its unique format clearly marked the line between official and private papers, and some day, perhaps, the millions and millions of registration forms filed away in the chancery offices will give an idea of the entire social history of the Habsburg monarchy. No communication was considered correct unless it was entered on this white rectangle, and so the first thing for me to do was to buy two such forms in the nearest tobacconist's, along with a "lazy man's guide"—the lined sheet to place under the form so that you were sure to write neatly—and the proper size of envelope. Then I would go over to a café, for all business, whether serious or frivolous, is transacted in cafés in Vienna. In twenty minutes' time, around six o'clock, I could have my resignation written out, and then I would be my own master and mine alone.

I remember every detail of the way in which I filled out that form with uncanny clarity—after all, this was the most important decision of my life so far. I remember the small, round marble-topped table in a window corner of the café on the Ringstrasse, I remember the briefcase on which I placed the sheet of paper, then using a knife to help me fold it exactly down the middle so that the line of the fold would be faultless. I can still see the rather watery blue-black ink before me in photographic detail, and I remember the little shake I gave myself as I set to work to give the first character I wrote the right rounded, attractive curve. For I wanted to carry out this, my last military duty, particularly correctly. As the wording of the form was predetermined, I could emphasise the solemnity of my resignation only by taking special care to write well and neatly.

But as I was writing out the first lines, I fell into a curiously dreamy state of mind. I stopped writing, and began thinking what would happen tomorrow, when my form reached the regimental offices. Probably the first reaction would be a baffled look on the face of the duty sergeant, and then surprised whispering among the clerks—you don't hear of a lieutenant simply resigning his commission every day. Then the form would be passed on from office to office until it reached the Colonel himself. I suddenly saw him before me to the life, jamming his pince-nez over his long-sighted eyes, startled by the first words and then, in his usual choleric way, banging his fist down on

325

the table—that forthright officer is only too used, I thought, to seeing his subalterns happily wagging their tails the day after he has bawled them out when he says something jovial to show that the storm has passed over. But this time, I thought, he will see that he's come up against someone as obstinate as he is, none other than young Lieutenant Hofmiller, who's not putting up with that sort of thing. And when it comes out later that Hofmiller has resigned his commission twenty or forty heads will suddenly look up in surprise. All my comrades, each in his own way, will be thinking—what a fine fellow Hofmiller is! He's not taking rough treatment. This may turn out pretty awkward for Colonel Bubencic, they'll think. As far as we can remember no one in the regiment has left with more credit than Hofmiller, no one's behaved better in resigning his commission.

I am not ashamed to admit that while I indulged in this daydream, I began feeling very pleased with myself. Vanity is always one of the strongest motives for our actions, and weak natures are particularly inclined to succumb to the temptation of doing something that will make them appear strong, brave and determined. For the first time I had a chance to show my comrades that I was a real man, a man who respected himself! I wrote out the prescribed twenty lines of formal resignation faster and faster and, as I thought, in an ever more energetic hand. What had begun as an irritating formality became a personal pleasure.

Now for the signature, and then it would be done. A glance at the time—it was six-thirty. I must call the waiter over and pay. Then I would walk along the Ringstrasse in my uniform once again, for the last time, and catch the night train home. Tomorrow I would hand in that form, everything would be signed, sealed and decided, and my new life would begin.

326

So I took the sheet of paper, folded it first lengthwise and then across, to stow the fateful document away carefully in my breast pocket. At that moment something unexpected happened.

This was the unexpected thing—in the split second as I put away the rather large envelope in my breast pocket with a sense of certainty, self-confidence, even happiness—you always feel glad when a task is completed—I felt something rustling in there already, leaving no room for my envelope. What's in there? I wondered, instinctively feeling for it. But my fingers were already shrinking away, as if even before I myself remembered they knew what I had forgotten, what was already in my breast pocket. It was Edith's letter, both her letters sent to me yesterday, the first and the second.

I can't precisely describe the emotion that overcame me at this abrupt reminder. I think it was not so much alarm as a kind of shame. For at that moment a mist of self-delusion cleared from my eyes. In a flash I saw that all I had done and thought in the last few hours had been entirely unreal—my resentment of my disgrace during exercises, the pride I felt in heroically resigning my commission. But I was not resigning because the Colonel had torn me off a strip (after all, he did that to someone every week). In reality I was running away from the Kekesfalvas, from my fraudulent practices, my responsibility. I was running away because I couldn't bear to be loved against my will. Like someone severely ill who forgets his real, mortal suffering when he has an ordinary toothache, I had forgotten what really drove me mad, made me a coward and sent me running away, or at least I was trying to forget it. I had transferred my reason for wanting to get away, instead, to my minor and ultimately unimportant mishap. But now I saw that I was not making a heroic farewell gesture because my honour was wounded. I was taking to cowardly, pitiful flight.

However, something once done weighs heavily, and now that I had written my formal resignation I didn't want to change my mind. Damn it all, I said angrily to myself, what's it to me if she is waiting and weeping out there? They've given me enough trouble and caused me enough confusion. What's it to me if a stranger loves me? With her millions, she'll find someone else, and if she doesn't it's not my fault. Isn't it enough for me to be throwing up my career and leaving the army? What business of mine are her hysterics and whether she gets better or not? I'm not a doctor …

But as the word 'doctor' came into my mind my thoughts stopped short, like a machine rotating at high speed suddenly braking at a signal. The word 'doctor' had reminded me of Condor. And it's *his* business, I told myself at once. He's paid to cure the sick. She's his patient, not mine. Let him pick up the pieces! I'd better go straight to him and tell him I'm getting right out of this muddle.

I look at the time. A quarter to seven, and the express train doesn't leave until after ten. So I have plenty of time, I don't need to explain much, just that I want nothing more to do with it. But where does he live? Did he never tell me, or have I forgotten? Well, as a general practitioner he must be in the telephone book, so I hurry off to the telephone booth and leaf through its pages. Be … Bi … Bu … Ca … Co … there were several Condors: Condor, Anton, businessman … Condor, Dr Emmerich, general practitioner, Vienna Eight, 97 Florianigasse, no other doctors on the whole page—that must be him. I repeat the address to myself two or three times as I run, I don't have a pencil on me, I've forgotten everything in my desperate haste—I call the address out to the nearest horse-drawn cab, and while it carries me quickly and smoothly on its rubber tyres I am making my plan. I shall be brief but firm. No acting as if I hadn't made up my mind. I certainly won't let him suspect that I'm leaving because of the Kekesfalvas, I must present my departure as a fait accompli. It all began months ago, I shall say, but only today have I heard of the excellent position open to me in the Netherlands. If he asks a lot of questions all the same, I must simply decline to answer them. After all, *he* didn't tell *me* everything. I must stop thinking of other people all the time.

The cab stops. Has the driver lost his way, or did I give the wrong address in my haste? Can Condor really live in such a shabby place? He must be earning pots of money from the Kekesfalvas alone, and no eminent doctor lives in a tumbledown place like this. But no, he does live here, there's his plate up in the hall of the apartment building. "Dr Emmerich Condor, second courtyard, third floor, consulting hours two to four." Two to four, and now it's nearly seven. Still, he'll surely see me. I quickly pay off the cab and cross the poorly paved yard. What a wretched staircase this is, a spiral staircase with its steps worn down, the paint on the walls peeling, graffiti all over them, a smell of plain cooking, of WCs with the doors not properly closed. Women in dirty dressing gowns are talking in the corridors, looking suspiciously at this cavalry officer whose spurs clink as he passes them rather awkwardly in the dim light.

At last I reach the third floor, another long corridor, doors to the right and left and one in the middle. I am about to put my hand in my pocket to find a match and strike it, so that

I can see me the right number on the door, when a rather untidily clad maidservant comes out of the left-hand door carrying an empty jug. She is probably going to buy beer to go with her master and mistress's supper. I ask whether Dr Condor lives here.

"Yes, does," she says, in a Bohemian accent, "but is not at home, is gone to Meidling, says to mistress will be back soon for supper. You come in and wait."

Before I have time to think that over, she is leading me in.

"Can put things there." She points to an old softwood wardrobe, about the only piece of furniture in this dark little front hall. Then she opens the door to the waiting room, which looks a little better furnished; at least there are four or five chairs round a table, and the wall on the left is lined with books.

"Can sit there," she said, pointing with some condescension to one of the chairs. I understand her meaning. Condor's practice must be for the poor; rich patients are not received like this. What a strange man, I think again, what a very strange man. He could make a fortune out of Kekesfalva alone if he wanted.

Well, I wait. It turns into the usual nerve-racking session in a doctor's waiting room, when without really wanting to read anything you leaf through the well-thumbed magazines, long out of date, trying to fool your own uneasiness with a show of busy occupation. You keep standing up, sitting down again, looking at the clock ticking in the corner, its pendulum slowly swaying. Twelve minutes past seven, fourteen minutes past seven, a quarter past seven, sixteen minutes past seven, and you stare as if hypnotised at the handle of the door to the consulting room. Finally—it is twenty-past seven—I can't keep still any longer. I have changed chairs twice already, so I get to my feet and go over to the window. There's an old man down in the yard, limping as he oils the wheels of his handcart—a delivery man of some kind, obviously. On the other side of a kitchen window with a light in it a woman is ironing, another woman is bathing her small child in what I think is a tub. Somewhere or other—I can't identify the floor for certain, but it must be just above or just below me—someone is practising scales, always the same scales over and over again. I look at the clock once more, twenty-five-past seven, half-past seven. Why doesn't he come home? I can't and won't wait any longer! I feel that waiting is making me uncertain of myself, leaving me feeling awkward.

At last—I breathe a sigh of relief—I hear the click of a door closing in the next room. I immediately sit down. I must go carefully now, keep quite cool in front of him, I tell myself. Speak lightly, say I am only dropping in to say goodbye, and ask him casually to go out to see the Kekesfalvas soon and, if they should wonder what has happened to me, explain that I had to leave the army and go to the Netherlands. Oh, damn it all, for God's sake why does he still keep me waiting? I clearly hear a chair being pushed back next door. Has that stupid servant girl forgotten to tell him I'm here?

I am about to go out and remind the servant of my presence. But all at once I stop. For whoever is moving about in the next room, it can't be Condor. I know his footsteps very well. I know exactly—from the night when I accompanied him back into town—how he walks in his squeaking shoes, heavily, awkwardly, short of leg and short of breath. Whoever is next door, however, pacing up and down the whole time, has a very different step, more hesitant, more uncertain, a shuffling tread. I don't know why those unfamiliar footsteps upset me so much, why I listen to them so intently. But it is as if someone next door is listening with my own uneasiness and uncertainty. Suddenly I hear a very faint sound at the waiting-room door, as if someone were pressing down the handle, or just fiddling with it in, and sure enough it moves. The thin strip of brass moves visibly in the dim light, and the door opens just a crack, a narrow, dark crack. Perhaps it is only a draught of air, only the wind, I tell myself, because no one normally opens doors so surreptitiously, no one but a thief breaking in by night. But no, the crack is growing wider. The person on the other side of the door must be pushing it very cautiously, and now I see a human shape in the dark. Fixed to the spot, I stare. Then a woman's voice just beyond the opening door asks tentatively, "Is ... is there anyone in here?"

My answer dries up in my throat. I know at once that only the blind can speak like that and ask such questions. Only the blind walk with that shuffling gait and feel their way so quietly, only they speak so tentatively. And at that moment a memory surfaces in my mind. Didn't Kekesfalva tell me that Condor had married a blind woman? This must be his wife, it can only be his wife standing beyond the opening door asking that question and unable to see me. I stare intently at her shadowy form in the dim light, and finally I make out a thin woman in a full-skirted house dress, with grey and rather untidy hair. Good heavens, this woman, devoid of any charm or beauty, is his wife. How terrible to feel her staring at me with such dead eyes, and to know that she can't see me, while at the same time I feel, from the way her head comes forward as if she is listening, how hard all her senses are trying to make out the stranger whom she cannot see in this room. The strain of it distorts her large, heavy-lipped mouth more unattractively than ever.

I am deprived of words for a second, Then I stand up and bow—I bow although of course bowing to a blind woman is pointless—and I stammer, "I … I'm waiting to see the doctor."

She has opened the door fully now. Her left hand is still clutching the handle as if she needed some kind of support in the dark room. Then she moves cautiously forward, her brows rise above her sightless eyes, and a different, harsh voice sharply addresses me.

"You're outside consulting hours. When my husband comes home he needs to eat and rest before he does anything else. Can't you come back tomorrow?"

Her face works with every word she speaks. Obviously she can hardly control herself. A hysteric, I think at once. I mustn't irritate her. So I murmur—stupidly, bowing as if to empty air again—"I'm so sorry, ma'am … of course I wouldn't dream of consulting the doctor on medical matters so late. I just want to give him some news … it's about one of his patients."

"His patients! His patients all the time!" Her voice changes from bitter to tearful. "Someone came for him at one-thirty last night, he was off on his rounds at seven in the morning, and he hasn't been home since consulting hours were over. He'll fall ill himself if he doesn't get any rest! But never mind that now. You're not within consulting hours, I told you. They end at four. Write down what you want to tell him, or if it's urgent you'd better go to another doctor. There are plenty of doctors in the city, four on every street corner."

She gropes her way closer to me, and I guiltily retreat from her angry face, in which the whites of her wide-open eyes suddenly look very bright.

"Go away, I said. Go away! Let him eat and sleep like other people! Why do you all keep clinging to him? In the night, first thing in the morning, all day long—his patients all the time, he's suppose to work his fingers to the bone for all of them, and charge nothing! Because you all feel he's weak you cling to him and no one else. Oh, how thoughtless you are! Nothing on your minds but your own illnesses, your own troubles, that's all any of you know about! But I won't have it, I won't allow it. Go away, I told you, go away at once! Leave him alone for a change, let him have just one hour to himself in the evening!"

She has made her way to the table. Some kind of instinct must have told her roughly where I am standing, for her eyes are staring straight at me as if they could see me. There is so much genuine and yet sick desperation in her anger that I instinctively feel ashamed of myself.

"Yes, of course, ma'am," I say apologetically. "I entirely understand that the doctor needs his rest … I won't trouble you any longer. Please just allow me to leave a word, or perhaps telephone him in half-an-hour's time."

But, "No!" she cries desperately. "No! No! No telephoning! The telephone is ringing all day long, they all want something from him, they're all full of questions and complaints! As soon as he's put a morsel of food in his mouth he has to jump up and answer it! Come back tomorrow during consulting hours, I said, it can't be as urgent as all that. He must be left in peace for once. Go away … go away, I said!"

And the blind woman, hesitantly, groping her way, makes for me with her fists clenched. This is terrible. I feel that her outstretched hands will seize me any moment now. However, just then the front door clicks in the hall outside, and then latches shut again. This must be Condor. She listens, gives a start, and her features change at once. She begins trembling

334

all over, her hands, clenched into fists just now, suddenly open in an imploring gesture.

"Don't keep him now," she whispers. "Don't tell him anything. He must be tired, he's been out and about all day … please have some consideration! Don't you feel any sym—"

But at that moment the door opens, and Condor comes into the room.

He must have taken in the situation at first glance. But for a second he lost his composure.

"Ah, you've been keeping Lieutenant Hofmiller company," he said in the jovial manner behind which, as I had noticed before, he liked to conceal tension. "How good of you, Klara."

As he spoke, he went over to the blind woman and affectionately stroked her untidy grey hair. At his touch her entire expression changed. The anxiety that had just been distorting her large, heavy-lipped mouth disappeared at that one loving caress, and with a helplessly diffident, almost girlish smile she turned to him as soon as she sensed that he was close. Her rather angular brow looked pure and bright in the reflected light. After such a violent outburst of feeling, there was something indescribable about this expression of personal reassurance and security. She seemed to have forgotten my presence entirely in the happiness of knowing that he was so close. Her hand, as if magnetically attracted, went out to him through the empty air, and as soon as her tentatively searching fingers touched his coat she began stroking his arm again and again. Understanding that she wanted to be as close to him as possible, he went to her, and she leant against him like a woman entirely exhausted sinking into rest. Smiling, he put his arm around her shoulders and repeated, without looking at me, "How kind of you, Klara." It was as if his voice itself caressed her.

"I'm sorry," she began apologetically, "but I had to explain to this gentleman that you ought to have your supper first, you must be terribly hungry. Out and about all day, and people telephoning you a dozen or fifteen times in between whiles … I'm sorry, I did tell this gentleman he had better come back in the morning, but … "

"But this time, my dear," he laughed, caressing her hair again (I realised that he did that so that the laughter in his voice would not hurt her feelings), "this time you were wrong to put him off. Fortunately this gentleman, Lieutenant Hofmiller, is not a patient but a friend, and he promised long ago to visit me when he was in Vienna. His only time off is in the evening, because he has his military duties by day. Now we just have to settle the main question—do you have something nice we can give him for supper too?"

Once again that anxious, tense look came into her face, and I realised, from her immediate alarm, that she wanted to be alone with him after he had been out all day.

"Oh no, thank you very much all the same," I hastily declined the invitation. "I have to leave very soon. I mustn't miss the night train. I really only wanted to bring messages from out in the country, and I can do that in just a couple of minutes."

"Is everything all right there?" Condor asked, looking me keenly in the eye. Somehow or other he must have guessed that something was *not* all right, because he added quickly, "Listen, my dear friend, my wife always knows how I'm feeling better than I do myself, and it's a fact that I'm very hungry. I doubt if I'll be much use to anyone until I've had something to eat and smoked a cigar. So if it's all right, Klara, you and I will go and have our supper quietly now, and ask the Lieutenant to wait just a little while. I'll find him a book to pass the time, or he could rest—I think you must have had a very strenuous day," he said, turning to me. "When I get to my cigar I'll come back and join you, in my slippers and dressing gown if you have no objection."

"And I really will stay only ten minutes, ma'am," I said. "After that I'll have to hurry off to the station to catch the train."

This remark made her face brighten again. She turned to me in an almost friendly manner.

"What a pity you won't eat with us, Lieutenant. But I hope you will come to supper some other time."

Her hand came out to me, a very delicate, slender, already rather lined and faded hand. And I watched, with genuine respect, as Condor steered his blind wife carefully through the doorway, neatly making sure she did not brush past anything to right or left, as if he were holding something unimaginably fragile and precious.

The door stayed open for two or three minutes, and I heard the slightly dragging footsteps move away. Then Condor came back again with a different expression on his face, the keen, watchful expression that I knew was his at moments of stress. He must have understood that I had not come to his home unannounced without some urgent reason.

"I'll be back with you in twenty minutes, and then we can discuss it quickly. I think you ought to lie down on the sofa meanwhile, or stretch out in this easy chair. I don't like the look of you, my dear fellow, you appear to be exhausted. And we must both be fresh and able to concentrate."

Then, quickly changing his tone of voice, he called so that he could be heard a couple of rooms away, "Back directly, dear Klara, I was just giving the Lieutenant a book to keep him occupied while he waits."

Condor's trained eye had not been wrong. Only now that he mentioned it did I notice how terribly tired I was, after a disturbed night and a day full of stress and strain. Taking his advice—I already felt inclined to do whatever he wanted—I lay back in the easy chair of his consulting room, my head on the cushions, my hands lying on the softly upholstered arms. Outside, twilight must have fallen during my tedious wait; I could hardly make out anything in the room except from the silvery glints of the medical instruments in the tall glass-fronted cabinet, and night was now like a dome covering the corner at the back of the room where the easy chair in which I was resting stood. I involuntarily closed my eyes, and at once saw, as if in a magic lantern slide, the blind woman's face in that unforgettable change from alarm to sudden happiness as soon as Condor's hand touched her and his arm went around her. What a wonderful doctor, I thought, if only you could help me too, and I felt, confusedly, that there was something else I wanted to think out further, about someone else who had looked just as restless and distressed and alarmed, there was someone in particular I wanted to think of, and I had come here for that purpose. But I couldn't do it any more.

Suddenly a hand touched my shoulder. Condor, moving very quietly, must have come into the almost entirely dark room. Or perhaps I really had dropped off to sleep. I tried to get up, but he gently pressed my shoulders back again firmly.

"Stay where you are, and I'll sit down with you. It's better to talk in the dark. I'll ask you just one thing, let us talk quietly. Very quietly. You know how the blind sometimes develop magical powers of hearing, and with them a mysterious instinct for guessing right. Well"—and his hand moved from my shoulder down my sleeve to my own hand as if hypnotically—"well, tell me what it is, don't feel shy. I saw at once that there was something wrong with you."

How strange—at that moment a memory came back to me. I had had a friend at cadet school, Erwin was his name, a delicate, blond, almost girlish boy. I think that without admitting it to myself I was a little in love with him. We almost never talked to each other during the day, or if we did it was on unimportant subjects; we were probably both ashamed of our secret feelings, which we had never mentioned to each other. Only at night in the dormitory, after lights out, did we sometimes pluck up the courage to lean on our elbows next to each other in our beds, talking under cover of darkness, while everyone else was asleep, telling each other our childish thoughts and ideas, then always avoiding one another again next day, with the same awkwardness. It was years and years since I had remembered those whispered confessions that had been the secret happiness of my boyhood years. But now, as I lay stretched out in the easy chair, with the darkness around me, I entirely forgot my intention of pretending to Condor. Without meaning to, I was perfectly honest. Just as I used to tell my friend at cadet school about my little setbacks and wild, large-scale dreams, I now told Condor—and there was the secret pleasure of confession in my account—about Edith's sudden outburst, my horror, my anxiety and dismay. I told him everything in that silent darkness, where nothing stirred except the lenses of his pince-nez that glinted faintly from time to time when he moved his head.

Then there was silence, and after it a curious sound. Condor had obviously been pressing his fingers together and snapping the joints.

"So that was it," he said quietly, sadly. "And fool that I was, I overlooked a thing like that. It's always the same—you don't see the invalid behind the malady. For all our accuracy in examination and diagnosis of symptoms, we can miss the essence of what is going on in a human being. That's to say, I did feel something different about the girl; you'll remember that I asked the old man, directly after examining her, whether anyone else had been treating her—and that sudden, heated desire to get better quickly, quickly, did make me wonder. Yes, I wondered whether someone else was involved, and I was right. But idiot that I was, I thought only of some quack or hypnotist. I suspected that some kind of mumbo-jumbo might have turned her head. The one thing that didn't occur to me was the simplest, most logical of explanations. Falling in love is practically an organic phenomenon in girls of that age. How infuriating that it had to happen just now, and so forcefully—oh God, that poor, poor child!"

He had got to his feet. I heard his short steps pacing up and down, and the sigh he gave.

"Terrible, and it has to happen just when we've arranged the trip to Switzerland. And no God can turn back the clock now, because she's suggested to herself that she must be cured for your sake and not her own. The reaction will be appalling when it comes. Now that she hopes for so much, wants so much, no minor improvement will satisfy her, no mere sign of progress. My God, we've taken on a heavy responsibility!"

I felt sudden resistance. I didn't like the way he was dragging me into it. After all, I had come here to shake off the whole entanglement. So I interrupted him firmly.

"I entirely agree. There's no foreseeing the consequences. It's time there was an end to this crazy delusion. You must intervene, act firmly. You must tell her … "

"Tell her what?"

"Well … that this idea of being in love is just childish nonsense. You must talk her out of it."

"Talk her out of it? Talk her out of what? Talk a woman out of her ardent passion? Tell her she ought not to feel what she does feel? Tell her not to fall in love when she *is* in love? That would be the worst, most stupid thing anyone could do. Have you ever heard of logic winning the day in conflict with passion? Ever heard of anyone telling a fever not to be feverish, or a fire not to burn? Yes, what a fine, a truly humane idea it would be to tell a sick, lame girl to her face, 'Don't for God's sake think that you, too, may be allowed to love! For you of all people it's presumptuous to show any emotions or expect any in return—you're a cripple, so you have to keep quiet. Naughty girl, you must stand in the corner! Resign yourself, give up!' That's what you obviously want me to tell the poor girl. Do please think what the wonderful result would be."

"But you're the one who must … "

"Why me? It was you who expressly took all the responsibility on yourself. Why me now, all of a sudden?"

"I can't admit to her myself that … "

"Nor should you! Nor ought you to! First send her crazy, then suddenly demand reason! That's all we need! Of course you

341

can't say or do the least thing to make the poor child guess that her feelings embarrass you—that would be like hitting someone on the head with a hatchet!"

"But … " I said, my voice failing me, "but after all, someone must make it clear to her that … "

"Make what clear to her? Be good enough to express yourself more precisely!"

"I mean … that … that it's absurd, out of the question … so that she doesn't … when I … when I … "

I stopped. Condor was silent too. He was obviously waiting. Then he suddenly took two firm steps to the door and reached for the light switch. The flood of bright light, sharp and pitiless, forced me to close my eyes instinctively. Three electric bulbs flared into glaring light, and all at once the room was bright as day.

"Well," said Condor forcefully, "I see it's a bad idea to make you too comfortable, Lieutenant Hofmiller. It's easy to hide behind darkness, but when certain subjects are under discussion it is better to look someone in the eye. So let's have no more of this havering, Lieutenant Hofmiller—there's something wrong here. You won't persuade me that you came only to show me that letter. There's something more behind it. I can tell that you have something definite in mind. Either you had better tell me honestly what it is, or I must thank you for calling and suggest that you leave."

His pince-nez flashed keenly at me. I was afraid of their circular reflection, and looked down.

"Your silence is not very impressive, Lieutenant Hofmiller. It doesn't exactly suggest a clear conscience. But I am beginning to form some idea of what you're playing at. No beating about the bush, please—is it your intention, after receiving that letter—or the other one—to put a sudden end to what you call your friendship with her?"

He waited. I did not look up. His voice took on the insistent tone of an interrogator.

"Do you know what would happen if you ran for it now? Now that you've turned the poor girl's head with your wonderful pity?"

I did not reply.

"Well, then I'll allow myself to tell you how I'd describe such a course of action myself—wriggling out of it like that would be pitiful cowardice … Oh, come on, don't draw yourself up with that military hauteur! We can leave the officer and his code of honour out of this! There's more at issue here than such nonsense. This is about a living, feeling human being, a young and valuable one at that, and one for whose well-being I am responsible. In such circumstances I feel no inclination at all to keep a civil tongue in my head. At least let me free you of any illusions. With that end in view, I will tell you clearly what you'd be taking on your conscience. Running away at such a critical moment—please don't close your ears to this!—would be a crime against an innocent being, and I am afraid it would be more—it would be murder!"

The small, sturdy man had come close to me, fists clenched like a boxer. Perhaps I ought to have thought him ridiculous in his soft dressing gown and down-at-heel slippers, but his honest fury was overpowering as he shouted at me again, "Murder! Murder! Murder! Yes, and you know it yourself. Or do you think that proud, sensitive creature will *get over* revealing her heart to a man for the first time if that honourable man's answer is to run away in panic as if he'd seen the Devil? May I suggest a little more imagination on your part? Didn't you read the letter, or doesn't your heart see anything? Even a normal healthy woman would find such rejection hard to bear. Such a blow would destroy the balance of her mind for years! And this girl, who is held together only by her senseless hope of a cure, the hope *you* gave her—this broken, betrayed human being—do you think she would get over such a thing? If the shock of it didn't finish her off she would do it herself! Yes, she would do it herself—someone in despair cannot endure a humiliation like that. I am convinced she would not survive such brutality, Lieutenant, and you know it as well as I do. And *because* you know it, your running away would not only be weakness and cowardice, it would be base, premeditated murder."

I instinctively retreated from him even further. The moment he spoke the word "murder", I had seen it all in a flash, as if in a vision—the balustrade of the terrace on top of the tower, and how she had clutched it with both hands! How I had to take hold of her and snatch her back at the last minute! I knew that Condor was not exaggerating. She would do exactly that, throw herself over—in my mind's eye I saw the paving stones far below, I saw everything at that moment as if it were just happening, as if it had already happened, and there was a roaring in my ears as if I myself were plunging down those four or five storeys to the bottom of the tower.

But Condor still persisted. "Well, don't deny it! Show some courage for once. It's your professional duty."

"But doctor ... what am I to do? I can't force myself to ... oh, I can't say what I don't mean! How can I seem to go along with her crazy delusion? ... " And I lost control of myself. "No, I can't bear it, I can't bear it! I can't and won't bear it!"

I must have been shouting, because I felt the iron grip of Condor's fingers on my arm.

"Hush, for God's sake!" He quickly went to the light switch and turned it off again. Now only the lamp on the desk was casting a dim cone of light from under its yellow shade.

"Oh, God help us—I have to talk to you as if you were one of my patients. Now then—sit down quietly on this chair, where even more difficult subjects have been broached."

He moved closer to me.

"So no more going off the deep end, and take it slowly and calmly, will you? Let's take this one thing at a time. First—you moan 'I can't bear it!' But that doesn't tell me enough. I have to know *what* you can't bear. Why are you so horrified to think that the poor child has fallen passionately in love with you?"

I took a deep breath, preparing to answer, but Condor quickly intervened.

"Don't be too hasty! And most important of all, don't feel ashamed. In principle I can understand that your first reaction would be alarm when you hear such a passionate declaration. Only an idiot is pleased to think of himself as a ladykiller, only a fool is puffed up with pride at such an idea. A decent man is more likely to feel dismayed when he discovers that a woman has lost her heart to him, and he can't return her feelings. I understand all that. But as you are so extraordinarily, so very extraordinarily upset, I have to wonder—is there some special feature of this case, I mean in the particular circumstances … "

"What circumstances?"

"Well … the fact that Edith … I find it hard to put these things into words … I mean does her … her physical disability perhaps make you feel a certain reluctance … give you a physiological distaste for her?"

"No, no … nothing like that," I protested forcefully. After all, it was her very helplessness, her defencelessness, that had so irresistibly attracted me, and if I had now and then felt something strangely close to a lover's tenderness it was only because her suffering, her physical disability and isolation, had shaken me so much. "No, never!" I repeated with almost bitter conviction. "How can you think such a thing?"

"Good. That does to some extent reassure me. A doctor often has opportunities to observe that kind of psychological inhibition in those who appear the most normal of human beings. To be sure, I've never been able to understand men in whom the smallest flaw in a woman's appearance engenders that idiosyncratic state of mind, but there are countless men who do feel that when, out of all the millions upon millions of cells that make up a human body, the smallest detail, say of pigmentation, is not quite right, it immediately rules out any possibility of an erotic relationship. And unfortunately it is always impossible to overcome such revulsion; that's the case with all instincts. So I am doubly glad that you are not one of those men, and it is not because she is lame that you shrink from her. However, then I can only assume that ... may I speak plainly?"

"By all means."

"If you took fright not because of the fact of her disability itself but because of the consequences ... I mean, if it was not so much that you feared that poor child's love for you as that you were secretly afraid other people might learn of it and mock it ... then in my view your extreme distress is nothing but a kind of fear—forgive me—of looking ridiculous in front of other people. In front of your military comrades."

I felt as if Condor had driven a sharp, thin needle into my heart. For what he described was what I had felt, unconsciously, for a long time, only I had not dared to think of it. From the very first day I had shrunk from the idea that my comrades might

mock my strange relationship with the lame girl—mock it with
the basically kindly but soul-destroying teasing typical of their
kind for any of us 'caught' in the company of an oddity or a less
than elegant woman. For that reason alone, I had instinctively
erected a double barrier between the two worlds in my life, the
world of the regiment and the one where I mingled with the
Kekesfalvas. Condor's assumption was correct—as soon as I
was aware of Edith's passionate love my principal feeling had
been of shame in front of others: her father, Ilona, Josef the
old servant, my comrades. I had felt ashamed of that fatal pity
of mine even to myself.

But now I felt Condor's hand stroking my knee, as if
magnetically.

"You mustn't feel ashamed. If anyone understands how you
can be afraid of people as soon as something is out of tune with
their well-regulated ideas, then I do. You have seen my wife. No
one could understand why I married her, and everything that is
not on the straight and narrow line of what we call normality
makes them first curious, then malicious. My medical colleagues
whispered that I had botched her treatment, and married her
only out of fear of the consequences—my friends, or so-called
friends, spread the rumour that she was rich, or was expecting
a large legacy. My mother, my own mother refused to meet her
for two years. She had had another match in mind for me, the
daughter of a professor—he was the most famous specialist in
internal medicine at the university—and if I had married the
girl I would have been a lecturer three weeks later, then a professor myself, and I'd have lived in clover all my life. But I knew
that it would destroy the woman I did marry if I let her down.
All she believed in was me, and if I had taken that belief from
her she would have been unable to go on living. And I will tell

you frankly, I have never regretted my choice. For believe me, doctors of all people seldom have a perfectly clear conscience. We know how little we can really do to help, we know that as individuals we can do nothing to mitigate the immeasurable extent of daily suffering. We scoop out only a thimbleful, a few drops from that unfathomable ocean, and those we think cured one day show the symptoms of another malady the next. We always have a sense of having been too remiss, too negligent, and then there are the real mistakes we make, the wrong conclusions we inevitably reach—and it is always good to know that you have helped at least *one* human being, there is *one* person whose trust you have not disappointed, you have done *one* thing well. After all, we need to know whether we have just made our way through life in dull stupidity or whether we have lived for some purpose. Believe me"—and I felt his warm and almost affectionate presence close to me again—"it is worth taking on a difficult task if that means making life easier for someone else."

The deeply felt emotion in his voice touched me. All of a sudden I felt a slight burning sensation inside me, that familiar pressure as if my heart were expanding. I felt the memory of that unhappy child's desperate loneliness awakening my pity again. And now, I knew, that torrent of feeling would well up in me again, and there was nothing I could do about it. But no, I told myself, don't give way! Don't let yourself be dragged into all that again! I looked up with determination.

"Doctor—everyone knows the limits of his own strength, at least to some degree. So I must warn you, please don't count on me! It's up to you, not me, to help Edith now. I've already gone much further than I meant to in the first place, and I'll tell you honestly, I'm nowhere near as good or as self-sacrificing as you think. I'm at the end of my tether! I can't bear to be adored and idolised any more, to act as if I wanted that or would put up with it. It's better for you to understand the situation now than be disappointed later. I give you my word of honour as a military man that I am warning you honestly if I now repeat— don't count on me, don't overestimate me!"

I must have spoken very firmly, because Condor looked at me, rather taken aback.

"That sounds almost as if you had come to some definite decision." He suddenly got to his feet. "The whole truth, please, and not just half of it. Have you already done anything … anything irrevocable?"

I stood up too.

"Yes," I said, taking my petition to resign my commission out of my pocket. "Here. Please read that for yourself."

Casting me an uneasy glance, Condor hesitantly took the sheet of paper before going over to the little circle of lamplight. He read it slowly and in silence. Then he folded the paper up again and said very calmly, in a matter-of-fact tone suggesting that he was stating the obvious, "I take it that, after what I told you just now, you are fully aware of the consequences? We have established the fact that if you run away the effect on the child will be tantamount to murder. Murder or suicide. It is therefore, I assume, perfectly clear to you that this document represents not just a request to resign your commission, but a … a sentence of death on that poor child."

I made no reply.

"I have asked you a question, Lieutenant Hofmiller! And I repeat it—are you aware of the consequences? Will you take the full responsibility for this on your conscience?"

I still said nothing. He came closer, holding the folded sheet of paper, and handed it back to me.

"Thank you. I want nothing more to do with the matter. Here—take it!"

But my arm was paralysed. I didn't have the strength to raise it. And I did not have the courage to meet Condor's probing gaze.

"Then you do not … do not intend to proceed with this death sentence?"

I turned away and clasped my hands behind my back. He understood.

"May I tear it up, then?"

"Yes," I said. "Please do that."

He went back to the desk. Without looking at him, I heard a sharp sound as the paper tore once, twice, three times, and then I heard the torn scraps fall, rustling, into the waste-paper basket. In a curious way, I felt light at heart. Once again—for the second time on this fateful day—a decision had been made for me. I didn't have to make it myself now. It had happened of its own accord.

Condor came towards me and gently made me sit down in the easy chair again.

"Well … I think we have just averted a great, a very great misfortune! And now to business! At least I'm glad of this opportunity to have come to know you better—no, don't protest. I am not overestimating you, I don't consider you the wonderful, good man whom Kekesfalva praises to the skies, I think of you as my partner, and a highly unreliable one because of the uncertainty of your feelings and the impatience of your heart. Glad as I am to have prevented your senseless escapade, I don't like the way you make up your mind and then change it again so quickly. People so subject to fluctuating moods ought not to be given serious responsibilities. You're about the last person I'd turn to for anything requiring stamina and steadfastness.

"So listen, please! I'm not asking you for much—only for what is absolutely necessary. We have induced Edith to begin a new course of treatment—or rather, she thinks it's new. For your sake she has said she's prepared to go away for months, and as you know we leave in a week's time. Very well. I need your help during that week, and I will relieve your mind at once by repeating, only during that one week! All I'm asking you is to promise not to do anything abrupt and unexpected during that single week, and above all not to do or say anything to show how unwelcome the poor child's love is to you. That's all I want from you now—and I think it is the least I can ask—a week of self-control in the interests of saving another human being's life."

"Yes ... but then what?"

"We won't think of that just now. When I have to operate on a tumour I can't spend for ever wondering if it will recur in a few months' time. When I'm called in to help, the one thing I can do is to give that help without hesitating. In any case it's the only right thing because it is the only humane thing to do. The rest is in the hands of chance, or as those more devout than I would say, in the hands of God. We can't do everything in a few months! Perhaps her condition really will improve more quickly than I thought, perhaps her passion will die down when there's distance between you—I can't consider all contingencies in advance, and you certainly shouldn't try! Concentrate all your powers on not letting her see, within this crucial time, that her love is ... is so abhorrent to you. Keep telling yourself—a week, six or seven more days, and I am saving a human being, I will not injure or offend her, disturb or discourage her. A week in which you are determined to act like a man—do you think that's too much for you?"

"No," I said spontaneously. And I added even more firmly, "Of course I can do it, of course!" Now that I knew there was a term set to my task I felt a new strength.

I heard Condor breathe a sigh of relief.

"Thank God. Thank God! Now I can tell you how afraid I was. Believe me, Edith really wouldn't have got over it if you had simply run away in response to her confession of love in that letter. These next few days in particular are crucial. We'll see how at all develops later. For now let us leave the poor child a little happiness—a week of unsuspecting happiness. You can guarantee to manage that single week, can't you?"

Instead of speaking, I gave him my hand.

"Then I think everything is all right again, and we can rejoin my wife with our minds at ease."

But he did not get to his feet. I sensed a little hesitation in him.

"Just one more thing," he added quietly. "We doctors always have to think of the unforeseen; we must be prepared for anything to happen. Should there be some kind of development—I don't have anything definite in mind, but should your resolve fail you, and should distrust of you then plunge Edith into a crisis, you must let me know at once. On no account must anything irrevocable be done during this short but dangerous phase. If you don't feel up to your task, or you inadvertently give yourself away within that one week, then don't be ashamed—for God's sake don't be ashamed to tell me so! I've seen enough naked bodies and damaged souls in my time. You can visit me or telephone me at any time of day or night, and I shall be ready to come to your aid, because I know what's at stake. And now," he said, and I heard the chair beside mine creak, which told me that Condor was rising to his feet, "now we had better go over to the living room. We've talked for quite a long time, and my wife easily gets anxious. Even after years I have to be on my guard against putting a strain on her nerves. Someone once wounded by Fate remains vulnerable for ever."

He took the couple of steps to the light switch again, and the electric bulbs came on. When he turned to me, his face looked different. Perhaps it was just the bright light that showed its contours so sharply, because I noticed the deep lines on his forehead for the first time, and I saw from his whole bearing how tired, how truly exhausted the man was. He always has to think of other people, I reflected. And suddenly my wish to take flight from the first real setback I had known seemed to me pitiful, and I looked at him with deep gratitude.

He seemed to notice that, and smiled.

"How good," he said, clapping my shoulder, "that you came to see me and we were able to discuss all this. Suppose you had simply gone away without stopping to think. The memory of it would have weighed on you all your life, because you can run away from everything else, but not yourself. And now let's join my wife. Come along, my dear friend."

I was moved to hear him call me his friend at that moment. He knew how weak and cowardly I had been, and yet he did not despise me. With that one word he was giving me confidence again, as an older man speaking to a younger one, a man of experience to an uncertain beginner. I followed him, feeling light at heart and with my mind at rest.

We went through the waiting room, and Condor opened the door to the room beyond it. His wife was sitting at the dining table, which had not yet been cleared, doing some knitting.

Nothing about her busy activity would have led anyone to think that it was a blind woman's hands so skilfully and confidently clicking the needles, with a little basket containing wool and scissors ready to hand. Her head was bent, and only when she raised the empty pupils of her eyes to us, and the lamplight was reflected in them, did you realise that she was indeed blind.

"Well, Klara, have we kept our promise?" said Condor affectionately as he went over to her, speaking in the soft, gentle voice that he always used to her. "It didn't take long, did it? And I wish you knew how glad I am that Lieutenant Hofmiller came to see me! I should tell you—but sit down for a moment, my dear friend," he said to me, "I should tell you that he is in the garrison stationed in the town close to the Kekesfalvas' house. You'll remember my little patient."

"Oh yes, the poor lame girl, of course!"

"And now Lieutenant Hofmiller has brought me news from them without any need for me to go there specially myself. He visits them almost every day to amuse the poor girl a little and keep her company."

The blind woman turned her head in the direction where she assumed I must be sitting, and for the first time I saw a soft expression smoothing out her harsh features.

"How kind of you, Lieutenant! I can imagine how much good that must do her." And her hand as it lay on the table instinctively moved closer to me.

"Yes, and he's kind to me as well," Condor went on. "Otherwise, considering the state of her nerves, I'd have to go out there much more often to cheer her up. It takes a weight off my mind to know that in this last week before she goes to convalesce in Switzerland, Lieutenant Hofmiller will keep an eye on her. She doesn't always give other people an easy time, but he's really wonderful with the poor girl, and I know he won't let me down. I can rely on him more than I do on any medical assistant or colleague."

I realised at once that by pledging me to keep my promise in front of this other helpless woman, Condor was binding me to it yet more firmly, but I willingly undertook to give that pledge.

"Of course you can rely on me, doctor. I'll be sure to go out there every day this week, and I'd phone with the news if anything should happen, however slight. However," I said, looking at him over the blind woman's head with a wealth of meaning, "however, I'm sure there won't be anything of that kind, there'll be no difficulties. I'm as good as certain of it."

"And so am I," he assured me, with a little smile. We understood one another entirely. But then I saw his wife's mouth begin to work nervously. You could tell that she had something on her mind.

"I haven't apologised to you yet, Lieutenant. I'm afraid I was a little … a little brusque to you just now. But that silly girl the maid didn't tell me anyone had called, I had no idea who was in the waiting room, and Emmerich has never mentioned you to me before. So I thought it was some stranger intruding on his time, and he's always so tired when he gets home."

"You were perfectly right, ma'am, and indeed you should have spoken to me more sternly. I'm afraid—forgive me for speaking frankly—I'm afraid your husband gives too much of himself to his patients."

"Everything!" she interrupted me forcefully, moving her chair closer in her emotion. "I can tell you, he gives them everything—his time, his peace of mind, his money. He forgets to eat and sleep for thinking of his patients. Everyone exploits him, and blind as I am there's nothing I can do to help, I can't take any of the burden off his shoulders. All day long I keep thinking—I'm sure he hasn't had anything to eat yet, he'll be on the train or in a tram again, and then they'll wake him up in the middle of the night. He has time for everyone but himself—and my God, who thanks him for that? No one! No one!"

"Really no one?" he said playfully, smiling down at the agitated woman.

"Well, of course I do!" she said, blushing. "But there's no way that I can help him! I'm always quite sick with anxiety by the time he gets home from work. Oh, I wish you could bring a little influence to bear on him! He could do with someone to make him rest a bit. We can't help everyone in the world!"

"No, but we must try," he said, looking at me as he spoke. "That's what we're here for. That and nothing else." I felt the full force of his warning. But I could hold his gaze now that I knew I had made up my mind.

I got to my feet. At that moment I had made a vow. As soon as the blind woman heard my chair scraping on the floor she raised her eyes.

"Must you really go already?" she asked with genuine regret. "What a pity, what a pity! But you will call on us again, won't you?"

I was feeling very odd. What is it about me, I asked myself, that makes everyone trust me, makes this blind woman seem to look up at me with a radiant expression, makes this man, not much more than a stranger to me, put his arm around my shoulders in such a friendly fashion? As I went down the stairs I could no longer understand what had driven me here an hour ago. Why had I really wanted to run away? Because a poor, disabled girl was in love with me? Because someone

wanted to help herself by clinging to me? Helping someone
else was wonderful, the only thing truly worthwhile. And that
realisation now made me do something of my own free will
that only yesterday had seemed to me an intolerable sacrifice—
I felt grateful for the overwhelming, burning love of another
human being.

A week! Now that Condor had set a time limit to my task, I
felt certain of myself again. Only one hour still filled me with
alarm, or rather, only that first moment in that hour when I
must meet Edith again for the first time since she had confessed her love. I knew it would be impossible for us to be entirely unselfconscious after such heartfelt intimacies—her first
glance after that burning kiss she had given me was bound to
ask—have you forgiven me? And perhaps the more dangerous
question—will you put up with my love, will you return it? I had
a very clear idea that her first blushing glance, her concealed
and yet inevitable impatience, might be the most perilous and
at the same time the crucial moment. A single clumsy word,
an insincere gesture, and the secret I must not tell would be
cruelly given away. That would lead me to adopt the brusque
and wounding manner against which Condor had so urgently
warned me. But once that moment was over I would be safe,
and I might also have saved her.

However, as soon as I entered the Kekesfalva house next day
I realised that the same fears had made Edith perceptive, and
she had made sure that we did not meet on our own. Even
from the front hall I heard the chatter of female voices. At a
time when guests never usually disturbed our meeting she had

invited acquaintances to visit her, protection to help her through the first difficult moment.

Even before I entered the salon Ilona—either on Edith's instructions or on her own initiative—came to meet me with an unusually impetuous welcome, took me in and introduced me to the local chief district officer's wife and daughter, the latter a pale-faced, freckled, sharp-tongued girl, of whom I knew nothing except that Edith didn't like her. So the awkwardness of our first sight of each other was, so to speak, glossed over while Ilona was getting me to sit down at the table. We drank tea and talked. I made assiduous conversation to the pert, freckled provincial girl, while Edith talked to her mother. This division of labour, deliberate and not a matter of chance, meant that our unspoken self-consciousness was diverted into different channels, and we had got over that first critical moment. I could avoid looking at Edith, although I could feel her glance sometimes resting uneasily on me. And even when the two ladies had finally risen to say goodbye, clever Ilona swiftly and neatly ensured that the situation would go smoothly.

"I'll just show these ladies out, and meanwhile perhaps you two could begin a game of chess. I have a few preparations to make for our trip to Switzerland, but I'll be back with you in an hour's time."

I could now ask Edith, "Would you care for a game of chess?" and as the other three left the room she replied, lowering her eyes, "Yes, that would be delightful."

She kept her gaze on her lap as I set up the board and, with much ceremony to gain time, put the chessmen in place. To decide who would make the first attacking and the first defensive moves, we generally followed the usual chess custom whereby you hold one white and one black piece behind your back, hidden in your closed fists. But the choice, demanding a spoken "Right" or "Left", would still mean that we must speak to each other directly, and by common consent we both avoided even that. I just set up the pieces without further comment. We didn't want to talk, we wanted to confine our thoughts to that board of sixty-four squares, look only at the chessmen, not even at the other player's fingers moving. And so we played chess, pretending to be as absorbed in our tactics as the most experienced grandmasters, who forget all else around them and concentrate their attention exclusively on the game.

But soon the game itself showed that we were deceiving ourselves. In our third match Edith's chess-playing skill failed her. She made wrong moves, and I could tell from the nervous fidgeting of her fingers that she couldn't preserve this improbable silence much longer. In the middle of the game she pushed the board away.

"Oh, that's enough! Give me a cigarette!"

I took one out of the chased silver box and carefully struck a match for her. As the light flared up, I could not avoid meeting her eyes. They were staring, unmoving, turned neither on me or in any other particular direction, as if frozen in icy anger. They had a strange, fixed look, but her raised eyebrows were arched tremulously above them. I recognised the storm signals that always heralded one of her nervous outbursts.

"No!" I cried, genuinely alarmed. "Please don't!"

However, she flung herself back in her chair. I saw the trembling pass into her whole body, while her fingers dug deeper and deeper into the upholstered chair arms.

"Don't, don't!" I begged her again. I couldn't think of anything to say but that one imploring word. However, the tears she had been holding back were already breaking through. It was not loud, wild sobbing but, even more terrible, a quiet, deeply distressing flood of tears with her mouth kept grimly closed. She was ashamed of her tears herself, and yet it was beyond her power to control them.

"Oh, don't—I do beg you, don't!" I said, and leaning closer I placed my hand on her arm to soothe her. At once a tremor like an electric shock ran through her shoulders and then right through her convulsed body.

Suddenly the trembling stopped. She was still again, unmoving. It was as if her whole body were waiting, were listening, trying to work out what that touch of mine meant. Was it affection, or love, or just sympathy? The way she waited with bated breath was terrifying; as she sat there, her entire motionless body was straining to understand. I could not pluck up the courage to remove my hand now that it had so abruptly calmed her rising storm of tears. But nor could I find the strength to force my fingers to make the tender gesture that Edith's body, her burning skin—I could feel it—yearned for so much. I left my hand where it was, as if it were not a part of me, and I felt as if all her blood, warm and pulsating, were running towards that one place on her arm.

My hand stayed there for I don't know how long, because time stood as still during those minutes as the air in the room. But then I felt a slight effort as she tensed her muscles. Turning her eyes away from me, she gently moved my hand off her arm with her own right hand, and further towards her. Slowly, she drew it closer to her heart, and then, tentatively and tenderly, her left hand joined it. Now they were both holding my own large, heavy, bare masculine hand firmly and gently, and very, very softly they began cautiously caressing it. At first her delicate fingers merely wandered around the motionless but acquiescent palm of my hand as if with curiosity, gliding over the skin like the gentlest breath of air. Then I felt her light, childlike caresses venturing to move tentatively from my wrist to my fingertips, tracing the shape of my fingers on the inside and the outside, the outside and the inside again; I felt her stop briefly as if in shock when she reached my fingernails and felt those too, then tracing the veins back and down to my wrist again, and once more up and down—it was a tender exploration, never bold enough to take my hand really firmly, press and hold it. These playful caresses were like warm water washing around me, both respectful and childish, amazed and ashamed. And yet I felt that her loving nature was taking possession of me entirely in caressing that one small part of myself. Involuntarily her head had sunk back further in her chair, as if to enjoy touching me all the more; she lay there like a woman asleep and dreaming, eyes closed, lips softly open, and her face was both bright and calm, while her slender fingers kept stroking my hand from wrist to fingertips with ever renewed delight. There was nothing greedy in that ardent touch, only a sense of amazed bliss to be granted fleeting possession of some part of my body at last, showing me how immeasurably she loved me. I have never since, even in the arms of the most passionate of women, felt such deep emotion as in that tender, almost dreamlike game.

I don't know how long this went on. Such experiences are outside ordinary time, and that shy stroking and caressing aroused some kind of intoxicating, beguiling and hypnotic feeling that moved and shook me more than her earlier fierce, burning kiss. I still could not find the strength to withdraw my hand—"I cannot go on living if you refuse me the right to love you," I remembered her saying—and in a hazy, dreamy state of mind I was enjoying that constant caress moving over my skin and into my tingling nerves. I let her go on, I was powerless, defenceless, yet at the same time ashamed to be loved so much when I felt nothing in return but a timid confusion, a frisson of embarrassment.

In the end, however, I could not bear to go on sitting there without moving—I was not tired of the caresses, of the warm wandering of her delicate fingers, the light, shy touch of them; I was ill at ease because my own hand lay there so unresponsive, as if it did not belong to me, and the woman caressing it were not part of my life. I knew, as you hear bells ringing in church towers when you are drowsy, that I must respond to the caress in some way—either by rejecting or returning it. But I did not feel strong enough to do either. I only knew that I must put an end to this dangerous game, and so I cautiously made myself move. Slowly, very, very slowly, I began withdrawing my hand from her light clasp—imperceptibly, I hoped. But sensitive as she was, she noticed the onset of this withdrawal at once, even before I did. Suddenly, as if in alarm, she let go of my hand. Her fingers dropped away, limp, and suddenly the tingling warmth was gone from my skin. Rather clumsily, I retrieved my hand once she had let go of it—for at the same time her face had darkened, and once again that childishly sulky look was hovering at the corners of her mouth.

"Don't, don't!" I whispered. I still couldn't think of anything else to say. "Ilona will be back soon." And when I saw that at these empty, meaningless words she just began to tremble more violently than ever, that sudden warm surge of pity came over me again. I bent down to her and dropped a fleeting kiss on her forehead.

Her eyes, however, stared back at me, stern, grey and cold, as if they were seeing through me, as if they could guess my thoughts. I had not deceived her quick, sensitive perception. She had seen that I was rejecting her tender affection by withdrawing my hand, and she knew that my hasty kiss had not been an expression of real love, only of pity and awkwardness.

That was my mistake during these days, my unforgivable, irreparable mistake—hard as I tried I could not summon up all the patience I needed, the ultimate ability to dissemble. My resolve not to let her guess, from any word or gesture of mine, that her love was unwelcome to me was useless. Again and again I recalled Condor's warning of the danger and the responsibility I would bear if I injured someone so vulnerable. Let her love you, he had said repeatedly, conceal your feelings, keep up the pretence just for that one week to spare her pride. Don't let her guess that you are deceiving her—deceiving her twice over by assuring her cheerfully that she will soon be well again, while at the same time you are trembling with fear and shame. Pretend to be unselfconscious, entirely at your ease, I kept reminding myself, try to put warmth into your voice, tenderness and affection into your hands.

But there is always something fiery, dangerous and mysterious in the air between a woman who has once shown a man her feelings for him and the man himself. Those who love have an uncanny perception of what makes the beloved truly happy, and as it is the essence of love to wish for boundless ardour, anything measured and temperate is alien and indeed intolerable to it. Love detects rejection in every inhibition of the beloved, every evidence of restraint, it suspects unwillingness in any reluctance to make an unconditional commitment, and it is right. There must obviously have been something awkward, confused and clumsy in my attitude at the time, a touch of falsity in my voice, for none of my efforts could withstand her watchful waiting for some sign from me. I could not manage it, I could not convince her, and she suspected, with increasing uneasiness, that I was not giving her the real and only thing she wanted from me, my love in return for hers. Sometimes, in the middle of a conversation—and just when I was trying my hardest to make her believe in the warmth of my feelings—she would suddenly raise her grey eyes, and then I had to lower my own eyelids. I felt as if she were probing my heart, exploring its depths.

Three days passed like this, and they were a torment for both of us. I constantly sensed that silent, avid waiting in her glances, in her silence. Then—I think it was on the fourth day—she adopted a curious attitude of hostility. At first I did not understand it. I had arrived at my usual time in the afternoon, bringing flowers. She accepted them without really looking at them and casually put them aside, showing by this deliberate indifference that I could not expect to buy my freedom with gifts. After an almost scornful, "Oh, why do you bring me such lovely flowers?" she immediately retreated behind a barrier of ostentatious and inimical silence again. I tried casual small talk. But she answered only "Oh yes?" or "Fancy that" or "Very strange", while making it abundantly clear that my conversation didn't interest her in the least. She intentionally, in the interests of outward show, emphasised her indifference; she toyed with a book, opened it, put it down again, fidgeted with all kinds of objects, once or twice made a great show of yawning, and then, in the middle of a story I was telling her, called for the servant and asked whether he had packed her chinchilla-fur coat. When he assured her that he had, she turned back to me with a chilly, "Oh, do please go on." It was only too easy to guess the unspoken corollary to that remark—"but I'm not at all interested in anything you say."

Finally I felt my powers falter. I glanced at the door more and more often, hoping for someone to come in, Ilona or Kekesfalva, and release me from my desperate chatter. But those glances did not escape her notice either. With a note of hidden contempt she asked, apparently full of concern for me, "Are you looking for something? Is there anything you want?" I am ashamed to say that all I could think of was to reply with a stupid, "No, nothing at all." It would probably have been more sensible of me to take up her challenge openly and ask, "What exactly do you want me to do? Why are you plaguing me? I can leave if you'd rather." But I had told Condor that I would avoid saying anything brusque or challenging, so instead of throwing off the burden of her hostile silence I foolishly let the conversation drag on for two hours, feeling as if I were walking on hot and silent sandy ground, until finally Kekesfalva appeared, looking diffident as he always did these days, and asked, perhaps with even more awkwardness than I was feeling, "Shall we go in to dinner?"

And then there we were sitting around the table, with Edith opposite me. She didn't look up once, she said not a word to anyone. All three of us were aware of her dogged and aggressively offensive silence. I tried all the harder to lighten the atmosphere. I talked about our colonel, who like a habitual drunk regularly suffered from a disorder at a given time of year, in his case in June and July when he became more and more obsessed with the forthcoming manoeuvres, turning more pernickety and agitated the closer the date for them came. Although I felt as though my collar was strangling me, I padded this stupid story out by embroidering it with many silly details. However, only the others laughed; they too were obviously forcing themselves to cover up for Edith's embarrassing silence. She was now yawning ostentatiously for the third time during dinner. Keep talking, I told myself, and so I said that we were being worked to death these days, no one knew whether he was coming or going. Even though two lancers fell off their horses with sunstroke yesterday, I added, that crazy slave-driver our colonel made more demands on us every day. We could never predict when we'd be allowed to get out of the saddle; he had the most pointless exercise carried out twenty to thirty times running. I'd managed to get away just in time to come here today, I said, but whether I'd be able to arrive punctually tomorrow was known only to the Lord God and the Colonel, who considered himself God's representative on earth anyway.

That was an innocent enough remark; surely no one could be offended and take it amiss. I had turned to Kekesfalva as I uttered it, speaking in a cheerful, light-hearted tone, and without looking at Edith at all, for I had had quite enough of the way she sat staring into empty air. However, there was a sudden clinking sound. She had thrown down the knife she had been playing with right across her plate, and as we looked up, our attention caught, she let fly.

"Well, if it's so difficult for you, you'd better stay in your barracks or go to that café of yours tomorrow. I dare say we shall be able to bear it."

That took our breath away, and we all stared at her. It was as if someone had fired a bullet through the window.

"But Edith … " protested Kekesfalva helplessly.

However, she threw herself back in her chair and said in petulant tones, "I for one feel sorry for anyone worked so hard! Why shouldn't Lieutenant Hofmiller have a day off duty for once? I'd be glad to think of him enjoying some leisure."

Kekesfalva and Ilona looked at each other in dismay. They both realised at once that her pent-up feelings were attacking me for no good reason. From the anxious way they turned to me, I guessed that they feared I would reply in kind to this incivility, and for their sake I took pains to pull myself together.

"I think you may be right, Edith," I said, as warmly as my thudding heart would allow. "I'm not very good company for anyone just now, not when I'm worn down like this. I've felt myself that you were bored all afternoon today! You shouldn't have a tedious fellow like me descending on you. But how long before I can come and see you here again? Pretty soon the house will be empty and you'll all be away. I can hardly imagine it—we can be together again for only four days in all, or strictly speaking three and a half days, before you … "

Opposite me at the table, Edith uttered a short, sharp laugh, with a sound like fabric tearing.

"Huh! Three and a half days! Very funny. He's worked out to the nearest half a day when he'll finally be rid of us again! I expect he's marked off the day of our departure on his calendar as a red-letter day. Careful, though, it's easy to get your sums wrong. Huh! Three and a half days, three and a half, a half, a half … "

She was laughing more and more hysterically, at the same time darting us hard, glittering glances, but she trembled as she laughed. You'd have thought some malignant fever had hold of her, although she shook as if with mirth. I could tell that she would have liked to jump up, which would indeed have been the most natural and normal thing for a young woman in such a state of agitation to do, but with her helpless legs she couldn't move from her chair. Held there in her anger as if spellbound, she had something about her of the vicious but tragic defencelessness of a caged animal.

"I'll go and find Josef," Ilona whispered to her. She herself, used as she was to guessing in advance every movement that Edith was about to make, had turned very pale. Edith's father immediately went to her side. But his fears proved groundless; when Josef came in, Edith allowed him and Kekesfalva to help her away without a word of farewell or apology. Our dismay had obviously made her aware of the hysterical fit she had thrown.

I was left alone with Ilona, feeling like someone who has fallen out of an aircraft and, dazed with alarm, staggers to his feet not quite sure what has happened.

"You must try to understand," Ilona whispered to me hastily. "She can't sleep at night just now. The idea of the trip to Switzerland gets her so worked up, and ... oh, you don't know ... "

"Yes, I do know, Ilona, I know all about it," I said. "That's why I'll be coming back tomorrow."

Keep going, I told myself firmly as I walked back to town, badly upset by the scene Edith had made. See it through at any price. You promised Condor, you gave your word of honour. Don't let her nervous, edgy moods deter you. Remember, all that hostility is just the despair of a girl who loves you, and you owe her a debt because your heart does not respond. See it through to the end—there are only three and a half days to go, three more days and you'll have done it! Then you can relax, be easy in your mind for weeks, for months! So be patient now, patient—only this last short time to go, these last three and a half days, three days!

Condor's instincts had been right. We take fright only at what can't be measured or understood—everything with a term set to it, however, everything definite is just a test of the lengths to which our endurance will go. Three days—I can do that, I felt, and the idea gave me confidence. Next morning I was impeccably correct in carrying out my military duties, which is saying something when we had to be on the parade ground an hour earlier than usual that day, carrying out manoeuvres at a speed that sent sweat running down the backs of our necks. To my own surprise, I even earned an involuntary, "Well done!" from our hard-bitten colonel. His fury today was reserved for Count Steinhübel, on whose head the storm duly broke. Enthusiastic connoisseur of horses that Steinhübel was, he had bought a new, high-stepping chestnut only a couple of days ago, a young, purebred, restive animal. Unfortunately, Steinhübel was so sure of his horsemanship that he had incautiously failed to try the horse out in advance. In the middle of the Colonel's pep talk the ill-omened chestnut, taking fright at the shadow of a bird, had reared up, and during an assault exercise he simply shied and bolted. If Steinhübel hadn't in fact been such a good horseman, the whole front line would have seen him thrown over his horse's head, and only after a positively acrobatic struggle did he get the terrified animal back under control. However, the Colonel had nothing to say in praise of that considerable achievement. Once and for all, he growled, he didn't want any circus tricks on the parade ground; if the Count didn't know anything about horses he might at least attend the riding school and avoid acquitting himself so poorly in front of the men another time.

Steinhübel greatly resented these slurs on his horsemanship. Even riding back to barracks, and then as we ate lunch, he kept explaining again and again how unjust the Colonel had been. His new mount was too high-spirited, that was all; we'd see what a fine horse the chestnut was once he, Steinhübel, had finished breaking him in. But the more the irate Steinhübel worked himself into a fury, the more our comrades teased him. He'd let himself be conned into buying that horse, they joked, which infuriated him more than ever. The debate waxed ever more vehement.

During this stormy discussion, one of the orderlies comes up behind me. "Someone on the telephone for you, Lieutenant Hofmiller, sir."

I jump up with dark forebodings. Over these last few weeks telephone calls, telegrams and letters have brought me nothing but bad news and ensuing distress. What does she want now? I wonder. I expect she's sorry she gave me this afternoon off. Well, if she's regretting it, then everything is going smoothly.

But anyway, I close the soundproofed door of the telephone kiosk behind me, as if that would cut off any contact between my military and private worlds.

It's Ilona's voice that I hear. "I just wanted to say," she says down the phone (sounding rather awkward, it seems to me), "I just wanted to say it would be better if you didn't come to see us today. Edith isn't feeling very well … "

"Nothing serious, I hope?" I interrupt her.

"No, no … I just think we'd better let her rest today, and then … " Here she hesitates for quite a long time. "And then … well, a day or so here or there makes no difference, not now. We must … we have to put off the trip to Switzerland."

"Put it off?" There must have been horror in my voice, because she quickly adds, "Yes … but we hope only for a few days. And anyway we can talk this over tomorrow, or the next day ... perhaps I'll telephone you meantime. Anyway, I just wanted to let you know ... better not tomorrow and ... and warm regards, and we'll see you soon!"

"Yes, but ... " I stammer into the receiver. However, there is no answer. I listen for a few more seconds, still no answer. She has hung up. Odd—why was she in such a hurry to end the call? It was as if she were afraid of being asked more questions. That must mean something ... and why put off the trip? It was all arranged down to the very day. A week hence, Condor said. A week, I have prepared my mind well for that, and now am I to ... no, impossible, this is impossible. I can't stand this constant chopping and changing ... I have my own nerves to think of. I must get some rest sometime, after all.

Is it really so hot in this telephone kiosk? I fling the sound-proofed door open as if I were stifling, and make my way back to my place. Apparently no one has thought anything of my absence. The others are still enjoying their needling of Steinhübel, and beside my empty chair, waiting patiently for me, is the orderly with the platter of meat. I automatically help myself to two or three slices, just to get rid of the orderly, but I do not pick up my knife and fork. There is a pounding in my temples as if a little hammer were busy chiselling the words "Put off" mercilessly into the bone of my skull. "Put off! The trip has been put off!" There must be some reason. Something must certainly have happened. Has she been taken seriously ill? Did I offend her? Why does she suddenly prefer not to go away? Condor promised me I wouldn't have to hold out for more than a week, and I've already struggled through five days of it ... but I can't go on any longer ... I just can't!

371

"Hey, where are your wits wandering, Toni? Don't you fancy a good plain roast? That's what comes of your fine dining at the castle, they spoil you there! I'm always saying, it's not good enough for him here these days!"

Ferencz again with his well-meant jovial laugh, that way he has of suggesting that I'm sponging on the grand folk at the castle.

"Oh, for God's sake spare me your silly jokes!" I snap at him. All my pent-up fury must have been in my voice, because the two ensigns opposite stare at me in surprise. Ferencz puts his knife and fork down.

"Don't you take that tone with me," he says menacingly. "I suppose a man may be allowed his little witticisms! If you can eat better elsewhere, fair enough, that's your business. But at our table here in this mess I'll allow myself to point out that you're turning up your nose at our midday meal."

Our neighbours at table look at the two of us with interest. The clatter of forks on plates is suddenly subdued. Even the Major narrows his eyes and gives us a sharp look. I can see it's time to make up for my flash of temper.

"And I suppose you'll admit, Ferencz," I reply, forcing a smile, "that I can have a headache once in a while and feel, well, not too good."

"Oh, sorry, Toni," says Ferencz at once. "How was I to know? Yes, sure enough, you *have* been looking out of sorts. These last few days it did strike me that you were under the weather. Well, don't worry, you'll soon pull through!"

The little incident has been smoothed over. But my anger is still feverishly working away inside me. What are they up to there at the castle? Back and forth, chopping and changing, blowing hot and cold—I'm not going to be plagued like that! I said three days, three and a half days to go and not an hour more! So who cares if they've put off the trip to Switzerland or not? I'm not having my nerves torn to shreds any longer, I'm not letting my damned pity torment me. This will drive me out of my mind!

I have to exercise self-control not to show the anger that still has me in its grip. I feel like picking up the glasses and crushing them in my fingers, or banging the table with my fist—I must do something violent to relieve this tension. I can't go on sitting there helplessly, waiting and wondering whether they are going to start writing letters and telephoning again, whether they are putting off the trip to Switzerland or not. I can't take any more of this. I must do something.

My comrades are still deep in conversation opposite me. "And I tell you," our lean friend Jozsi is saying, still needling Steinhübel, "that horse-dealer Neutitscheiner diddled you. I know something about horses myself, and you'll never get the better of that frisky chestnut, no one will master him!"

"Really? I'd like to see if that's so," I suddenly interrupt their conversation. "I'd like to have a shot at mastering your chestnut. Tell you what, Steinhübel, any objection to my taking him out for an hour or two? I could try to finish breaking him in for you."

I don't know what put that idea into my head. But my need to take out my anger on someone or something, to relieve my feelings with violent action, is working so feverishly in me that it jumps at the first chance that comes to hand. Everyone looks at me in surprise.

"Best of luck!" laughs Count Steinhübel. "You'll be doing me a favour if you feel up to it. I got cramp in my fingers today, I had to pull the brute round so hard. Good idea for him to have someone fresh put him through his paces. Let's do it at once! Come on, quick march!"

Everyone jumps up in high spirits, looking forward to some fun. We go off to the stables to take the horse Caesar out—maybe Steinhübel was a little too hasty in giving his refractory mount the name of an invincible hero. Caesar seems to find it rather unsettling to have such a talkative company gathering around his box. He snorts and paws the ground and prances around in the confined space, he tugs at his halter, making the boards creak. Not without some difficulty, we manoeuvre the suspicious animal into the riding school.

In general I was only an average horseman, unable to come anywhere near matching that impassioned cavalry officer Steinhübel. Today, however, he could have found no one better than me to finish breaking in his horse, and the unruly Caesar could have had no more dangerous opponent. For this time anger steels my muscles; my savage desire to get the better of something, force the horse to submit to me, make it an almost sadistic pleasure to show this recalcitrant animal at least (for you can't strike at those who are out of reach!) that there were limits to my patience. It does the bold horse no good to race around like a rocket, kick out at the walls of the riding school, rear and buck in his attempts to throw me. I am putting my heart into the struggle, and I pull mercilessly at the snaffle as if to break all Caesar's teeth. I dig my heels into his ribs, and this rough treatment soon begins to calm him. His tough resistance provokes, entices and inspires me, and at the same time remarks of approval from the officers who were my audience—"Good God, he's showing him a thing or two!" and "Who'd have thought it of Hofmiller?"—spur me on to greater and greater self-confidence, while as always with physical achievement, that confidence affects my temper as well. After half-an-hour of struggle, showing the horse no mercy, I sit triumphant in the saddle, while the humiliated animal is grinding his teeth and steaming and dripping as if he has come out of a hot shower. His throat and bridle are flecked with white as he foams at the mouth, his ears droop obediently, and after another half-an-hour the refractory horse is as gentle and docile as you could wish. I don't have to exert the pressure of my thighs now, and could easily dismount to accept the congratulations of my comrades. But there is still too much pugnacity in me for that, and I am enjoying my heightened state of physical exertion so much that I ask Steinhübel's permission to take the horse over to the parade ground for an hour or so—at a trot, of course—so that the sweating animal can cool off.

"By all means," says Steinhübel, smiling at me. "I can see you'll bring him back to me safe and sound, and there'll be no more playing up from Caesar. Well done, Toni, my compliments!"

So to the loud applause of my comrades I trot out of the riding school, and keeping the exhausted horse on a short rein I take him through the town and into the meadows. The horse's pace is easy and relaxed now, and I feel at ease and relaxed myself. I have taken all my fury and bitterness out on the stubborn animal during that strenuous hour, Caesar trots on now like a lamb, all his fighting instinct gone, and I have to admit that Steinhübel is right, he's a fine, high-stepping animal. No one could hope for a better, smoother, livelier gallop, and gradually my original discontent is giving way to a pleasant and almost dreamlike sense of well-being. I ride him through the countryside for a good hour, and finally, at four-thirty, it seems time to go slowly home. Both Caesar and I have had enough for one day. I ride back at a comfortable jog trot down the familiar road back to the town, feeling a little drowsy myself. Then, behind me, I hear a car horn hoot, a sharp, loud sound. The frisky chestnut pricks up his ears and begins to tremble. But I sense the horse's nervousness in time, pull briefly on the reins, and use the pressure of my thighs to guide him away from the middle of the road and to the roadside under a tree, so that the car can pass unimpeded.

It must have a considerate driver, who understands my careful sideways movement in good time. Slowly the noise of the engine dies to a murmur as the car passes at a very slow speed. It is almost unnecessary for me to keep such a sharp eye on the trembling horse and tense my thighs against his sides in the imminent expectation of a leap sideways or backwards, for when the car has passed us the horse stands still. I have time to look up. But as I do, I see someone waving to me from the open car, and I recognise Condor's round bald head beside Kekesfalva's, which is egg-shaped and sparsely covered with white hair.

I don't know whether it is I or the horse trembling now. What does this mean? Condor here, and he didn't let me know? He must have been to see the Kekesfalvas; the old man was beside him in the car. But why didn't they stop for a word with me? Why did they both pass me as if we were strangers? And what brings Condor out here again? His consulting hours in Vienna are two to four—he would usually be there now. They must have summoned him for some particularly pressing reason, they must have telephoned him early this morning. Something must have happened, and it is certainly connected with Ilona's call to me, telling me they have to put off the trip to the Engadine valley and I had better not go out there today. Yes, something definitely must have happened, and it is being kept from me! Has she done herself some kind of harm after all? Yesterday evening there was something so determined about her, the sarcastic self-assurance that only someone who is hatching a dangerous and ill-intentioned plan can show. Yes, she must have harmed herself in some way! Ought I not to gallop straight off after the car? I might yet catch up with Condor at the station!

But perhaps, I remind myself, he isn't leaving yet. No, he won't go back to Vienna if something really terrible has happened, not without leaving a message for me. Perhaps I'll find a note from him at the barracks. He is a man, I know, who won't do anything without me, at odds with me. He won't let me down. Now to get back quickly! I am sure I shall find a word, a letter, a note for him in my room. I must hurry!

On reaching the barracks I stable the horse hastily and run up the side staircase, avoiding all idle chatter and congratulations. Sure enough, Kusma is waiting outside the door of my room, and I see from his anxious face and hunched shoulders that something is up. There is a gentleman in civilian clothes waiting in my room, he announces with some dismay, and he didn't like to turn the gentleman away because he was so very pressing. Kusma really has strict orders not to let anyone into my room, but Condor probably gave him a tip—hence Kusma's anxiety and uncertainty. That turns to surprise when, instead of bawling him out, I just murmur amiably, "That's all right," and make for the door. Thank God, Condor has come! He'll tell me everything.

When I quickly push the door open, a figure instantly moves as if materialising from the shadows at the far end of the darkened room; Kusma has let down the roller blinds because of the heat. I am about to hurry to welcome Condor when I see that it

377

isn't Condor after all. Someone else is waiting for me, the very last person I would have expected to see here. It is Kekesfalva; if the room were even darker I would still know him from his timid way of rising and bowing. And before he clears his throat as a prelude to addressing me I know in advance the humble, diffident voice in which he will speak.

"Forgive me, Lieutenant Hofmiller," he says, bowing, "for arriving unannounced. But Dr Condor has asked me to give you his warm regards and apologise for not asking the car to stop … it was high time to get to the station, he had to catch the Vienna express, because this evening … and … and so he asked me to tell you immediately how sorry he was … that's the only reason why I … I mean, why I ventured to come up to see you myself … "

He stands before me, head bent as if an invisible yoke were weighing his shoulders down. In the darkness his bony skull gleams through the sparse hair neatly parted over it. The entirely unnecessary servility of his bearing is beginning to incense me. A sense of discomfort tells me plainly—there's some definite purpose behind all this awkward beating about the bush. An old man with a weak heart doesn't climb three floors up just to deliver a civil message. And he could have done that equally well over the telephone, or it could have waited until tomorrow. Careful, I tell myself, Kekesfalva wants you to do something for him. He's already emerged from the darkness once before, he starts by seeming as humble as a beggar, and finally he forces his will on you like the djinn in your dream, half-strangling the man who takes pity on him. Don't let yourself in for it! Don't ask him any questions, don't try to find out what's going on, say goodbye and escort him downstairs as soon as you can!

But the man facing me is old, and his head is humbly bowed. I see his thin, white hair, and as if in a dream I remember my grandmother's white head as she sat knitting, telling me and my siblings fairy tales. One can't be uncivil enough to send a sick old man away. So I indicate—has experience taught me nothing?—the chair where he can sit.

"Too kind of you to go to all this trouble, Herr von Kekesfalva! It was really very good of you. Won't you sit down?"

Kekesfalva doesn't answer. He probably didn't hear me clearly. But at least he understood my gesture. Hesitantly, he sits down on the very edge of the chair I offered him. It suddenly occurs to me that he must have accepted the charity of strangers in just this intimidated way in his youth. And there he sits now, a millionaire, on the poor, shabby cane-seated chair in my room. He ceremoniously takes off his glasses, gets a handkerchief out of his pocket and begins cleaning both lenses to gain time. You'd like me to speak first, I think, you want me to ask questions, I even know what you want to be asked—is Edith really ill, and why is the trip to Switzerland being put off? But I am on my guard. If you have something to say to me, I think, you can start the ball rolling! I'm not going a step to meet you! No—I'm not to be lured into another trap, I've had enough of this damned pity, enough of people wanting more and more from me all the time! Let's have an end to all this sly obfuscation. If you want me to do something then tell me straight out, but don't hide behind this silly pretence of polishing your glasses! I'm not taking your bait any more, I've had enough of my pity!

As if he had heard the unspoken words behind my closed lips, the old man finally, with a look of resignation, puts his now spotlessly shiny glasses down in front of him. He obviously senses that I am not going to help him, and he will have to begin himself. Head still bowed, he begins to speak without turning his eyes to look at me. He speaks to the tabletop as if hoping for more pity from the hard, cracked wood than I shall give.

"I know, Lieutenant Hofmiller," he begins uneasily, "I know I have no right—I certainly have no right to take up your time. But what am I to do, what are we to do? I can't go on, we can none of us go on like this—God knows what's come over her, I can't talk to her any more, she won't listen to anyone … and yet I know she doesn't mean any harm, she's just … just unhappy, dreadfully unhappy … she does these things only out of despair, believe me, only out of despair."

I wait. What does he mean? *What* things does she do? What exactly? Come on, out with it! Don't keep havering like that, why don't you just tell me what's wrong?

But the old man stares blankly at the table. "And we'd talked it all over, the whole thing was prepared in advance. The sleeping car ordered, good rooms reserved for us, and yesterday afternoon she was still full of impatience to be off. She herself chose the books she wanted to take, she tried on her new clothes and the fur coat I'd ordered from Vienna, and now suddenly she took this idea into her head, I don't understand it. Yesterday evening after dinner—you remember how upset she was. Ilona doesn't understand it, no one understands what's suddenly come over her. But she says—she screams and shouts—that she's not going away, not for anything, no power on earth can induce her to go away. She's going to stay here, she says, she'll stay here even if the house burns down over her head. She won't go along with this pretence, she's not deceived, she tells us. The idea of this course of treatment is just to get her to go away, to be rid of her. But we're all wrong, she says, she is simply not going away, she is staying, staying, staying."

A cold shudder runs down my back. So that's what was behind yesterday's angry laughter. Has she noticed that I can't go on like this myself, and is she staging these scenes to make me promise to go to Switzerland too?

Don't agree to any such thing, I tell myself. Don't show that this upsets you. Don't let the old man know that the idea of her staying wears your nerves to shreds! So I intentionally pretend not to understand, and say very casually, "Oh, that will soon pass off! You know better than anyone how changeable her moods are. And Ilona telephoned me to say the trip was only being put off for a few days."

The old man sighs, and that sigh breaks out of him with a dull sound as if he were vomiting something up. You might have thought that the abrupt effort of sighing tears the last of his strength out of him.

"Oh God, if only that were true! But the terrible thing is, I think—we all think—that she will never want to go away again at all. I don't know … I don't understand it—but suddenly she doesn't seem to care about the new treatment and whether it will cure her or not. 'I'm not going to let this torture me any more,' she says 'I'm not letting anyone try ideas out on me, none of it makes any sense!' She says such things, says them in a way that makes the heart stand still. 'I won't be deceived any more,' she says, and then she screams and sobs, 'I can see through it all—all of it!'"

I think quickly. For God's sake, did she notice something? Have I given myself away? Has Condor done something incautious? Can she have deduced, from some careless remark, that this new Swiss course of treatment is not all she expects? Has her quick perception, her terribly distrustful perception, shown her that we are really sending her away to no good purpose? I approach the subject cautiously.

"I don't understand that … when your daughter has always had such complete faith in Dr Condor. If he has recommended this course of treatment so warmly … then no, I simply don't understand it."

"Yes, but that's just the point! That's the crazy part of it—she doesn't want to have the treatment any more, she doesn't *want* to be cured. What do you think she said? 'I'm not going away, not for anything, I'm sick and tired of all these lies! I'd rather be the cripple I am and stay here … I don't want to be cured any more, I don't want to be cured, there's no point in it now.'"

"No point in it?" I repeat, at a loss.

But the old man bows his head even lower. I don't see his eyes swimming with tears any more, and it is only from his sparse white hair that I can tell he has begun trembling violently. Then he murmurs, almost inaudibly, "'There's no point in getting better,' she said, sobbing, 'because he … he … '"

The old man takes a deep breath as you might before making an enormous effort. Then finally he comes out with it. "'Because he … he feels nothing but pity for me,' that's what she said."

When Kekesfalva says *he* I suddenly feel cold as ice. This is the first time he has alluded to his daughter's feelings in front of me. I noticed some time ago that he had obviously taken to avoiding me, and indeed hardly dared to look at me, whereas he used to show me such affectionate concern. But I knew it was shame keeping him away from me; it must have been dreadful for old Kekesfalva to see his daughter making advances to a man who didn't want them. Her secret confessions must have tormented him, he must have felt deeply ashamed of her unconcealed longings. We had both lost the ability to behave easily and naturally in each other's company. If you have something to hide, or something that you *must* hide, it is difficult to be frank and unselfconscious.

But now he has put it into words, and we are both stricken to the heart. After those revealing remarks we sit there, mute, avoiding each other's eyes. There is silence in the air above the table between us in the small room. Gradually that silence spreads, rising to the ceiling like a black gas, filling the whole room from above, from below, a void pressing in on us from all sides, and the old man's difficult breathing tells me how the silence is choking him. Another moment and the pressure will stifle us both—unless one of us breaks it, destroys that oppressive, murderous void with a word.

Suddenly, something happens. At first I notice only that he makes a movement, a curiously clumsy, awkward movement. Then I see the old man fall forward abruptly in a soft heap as the chair tumbles to the floor behind him with a clatter.

My first reaction is—it's a heart attack. A stroke or a heart attack; after all, Condor told me he has a weak heart. Horrified, I make haste to help him up. But next moment I realise that the old man didn't fall off the chair, he pushed himself off it. As I moved quickly to help him, I failed to notice it at first, but he sank from the chair to his knees on purpose and now, as I try to raise him, he moves closer to me, takes my hands and begs me, "You must help her ... you are the only one who can help her ... Condor says so too, only you, no one else! I beg you to show mercy ... it can't go on like this ... she'll do herself harm, this will kill her!"

Although my hands are shaking, I haul the kneeling man forcibly up again. But he clasps my hands as they help him up,

383

I feel his fingers press desperately like claws into my flesh—the djinn, the djinn of my dream strangling the man who pitied him. "Help her," he gasps. "For Heaven's sake help her … we can't leave the child in such a state … I swear this is a matter of life or death … you can't imagine what terrible things she says in her despair … she must do away with herself, she whispers, she sobs, so that you can be rid of her and at peace, we can all be rid of her at last … And she isn't just saying it, she means it in deadly earnest … She's already tried twice, once by cutting her wrists, the second time with sleeping tablets. When she really sets out to do something no one can make her change her mind, no one but you, only you can save her now. Only you, I swear, no one but you … "

"But of course, Herr von Kekesfalva … please calm yourself … of course I'll do everything in my power. If you like we can go back to your house at once, and I'll try talking to her, persuading her. I'll come with you at once. You decide what I must say to her, what I must do … "

At this point he suddenly let go of my arm and stared at me. "What you must do? Don't you really understand, or don't you *want* to understand? She has opened her heart to you, offered herself to you, and now she's mortally ashamed of it. She wrote to you, and you didn't reply, and now she is tormenting herself day and night thinking you want to send her away, get rid of her, because you despise her … she is out of her mind with the fear that you feel revulsion for her because she … because she … Don't you understand that being kept on tenterhooks like that will kill a proud, passionate girl like my child? Why don't you give her some confidence in herself? Why don't you say a word, why are you so cruel to her, so heartless? Why are you torturing that poor innocent child so horribly?"

"But I've done all I could to reassure her ... I told her—"

"You didn't tell her anything! Don't you see for yourself that you are sending her out of her mind with your visits and your silence, when she's waiting for just one thing ... the one word that every woman wants to hear from the man she loves ... she would never have dared to hope for anything while she was still so frail ... but now that she is sure to get better, now that she'll be perfectly healthy again in just a few weeks' time, why can't she hope for the same as any other young girl, why not? She has shown you, told you how impatiently she's waiting for a word from you ... she *can't* do more than she has already done ... she can't beg in front of you ... and you never say a word, you never say the only thing that can make her happy! Is the idea really so terrible to you? You would have everything a man can desire. I'm old and sick, I'll leave all I possess to you, the castle and the estate and the six or seven million I've made over forty years. It will all be yours ... you can have it tomorrow, any day, any hour, I don't want anything for myself any more ... all I want is for someone to care for my child when I'm gone. And I know you're a good man, a decent man, you will spare her, you will be good to her!"

His breath failed him. He sank back in the chair again, weak and defenceless. But my own strength was exhausted, too, and I dropped onto the other chair. So there we sat opposite each other exactly as we had sat before, exchanging neither words nor glances for I don't know how long. I felt only, from time to time, the way the table shook slightly from the strong tremors running through him. Then—after what seemed an eternity—I heard a sound like something hard dropping on a hard surface. His bowed forehead had sunk to the tabletop. I could tell how the old man was suffering, and I felt a great need to comfort him.

"Herr von Kekesfalva," I said, leaning over him. "Trust me … we'll think all this over, think it over at our leisure … I repeat I'm entirely at your disposal … I'll do everything in my power. But that … what you were suggesting just now … that's … that's *not* in my power, it's entirely impossible."

He shook faintly, like an animal already in a state of collapse receiving one last deadly blow. His lips, salivating slightly in his agitation, worked frantically, but I did not give him time to say anything.

"It's not possible, Herr von Kekesfalva, so please let's not discuss it any further. Think about it yourself! Who am I? Only a lieutenant living on his pay and a small monthly allowance—no one can build a life with such limited means, hardly enough for one person to live on, let alone two … "

He tried to interrupt me.

"Yes, I know what you're going to say, Herr von Kekesfalva—money isn't a consideration, you think, all that would be taken care of. And I know that you're rich and … and that I could have all that from you … But it's just because you're rich, and I'm nothing, a nobody … that very thing is what makes it impossible. Everyone would think I did it for the money, they'd think I … and believe me, there's Edith herself to think of, all her life she'd never shake off the suspicion that it was only because of the money that I married her in spite of … in spite of the special circumstances. Believe me, Herr von Kekesfalva, it's impossible. I honestly, genuinely think highly of your daughter and … and I like her … but you must understand what I'm telling you."

The old man did not move for some time. At first I thought he simply hadn't taken in what I was saying. But gradually a movement did run through his exhausted body. He laboriously raised his head and stared into the empty air. Then he took hold of the edge of the table with both hands, and I realised that he was trying to brace his weight on it, trying to stand up, but he couldn't do it at once. Twice, three times he could not summon up the strength. At last he managed to get to his feet, and stood there, still swaying with the effort, a dark figure in the dim light, his pupils staring like black glass. Then he said in a new and shockingly indifferent tone of voice, as if his own human voice had failed him, "Then … then it's all over."

It was dreadful to hear that voice and the terrible note of resignation in it. Still staring straight ahead, not looking down, his hand groped its way over the tabletop to his glasses. However, he did not put them on over those stony eyes—why would he want to see now, why would he want to live now?—but stuffed them clumsily into his pocket. Once again those blue-tinged fingers (Condor had seen their colour as a sign of death) wandered around the table until they finally found his crumpled black hat as well. Only then did he turn to go, murmuring without looking at me, "Please forgive me for troubling you."

He had jammed the hat on his head at a crooked angle; his feet would not obey him properly, and he was swaying and shuffling feebly. Like a sleepwalker, he staggered on towards the door. Then, as if suddenly remembering something, he took off his hat, bowed, and repeated, "Please forgive me for troubling you."

He actually bowed to me, poor defeated old man, and that gesture of courtesy in the midst of his distress was more than I could bear. Suddenly I could sense that warmth, the heat of the flowing current of sympathy rising in me and burning my eyes, and at the same time I felt myself weaken as I was overcome, yet again, by pity. I couldn't let the old man go like this, when he had come to offer me his child, whom he loved more than anything else on earth. I couldn't let him go into despair, go to his death. I couldn't tear the heart out of him. I must say something more, something comforting, reassuring, something to soften the blow. So I hurried after him.

"Herr von Kekesfalva, please don't misunderstand me … you can't go like this and then tell her … it would be terrible for her just now, and … and not entirely true."

I was getting increasingly upset, because I could see that the old man wasn't even listening to me. His despair made him into a pillar of salt as he stood rigid, a shadow in the shadows, the image of living death. My need to reassure him became more and more impassioned.

"It really wouldn't be quite true, Herr von Kekesfalva, I swear … and nothing would be worse for me than to think I had offended your daughter, I'd hurt Edith's feelings … or … or made her feel I didn't really like her. No one has warmer feelings for her, I assure you, no one can like her better than I do … it's really just her imagination that … that I'm indifferent to her … on the contrary, on the contrary … I only mean there'd be no sense if just now I were to … if I said anything today. What's most important is for her to spare herself … so that she really will get better!"

"But then … once she's cured? … "

He had suddenly turned to me. The pupils of his eyes, still dead and stony just now, seemed to flash in the darkness.

I took fright. I instinctively sensed the danger. If I promised anything now, then I was pledged to keep my promise. But at that moment it struck me that everything she hoped for was a delusion. She was not going to get better, or not at once, in any case. It could take years and years. We mustn't think too far ahead, Condor had said, as I reminded myself, we must comfort her and keep her calm now! So why not leave her a little hope, why not make her happy, at least for a short time?

And so I said, "Well, yes, when she is cured, then of course … then I would … then I would come to see you of my own accord."

He stared at me. A tremor ran though him as if some power inside him were imperceptibly giving him new strength.

"May I … may I tell her that?"

I sensed danger again. But I could not withstand his pleading look any longer. I replied firmly, "Yes, tell her that," and offered him my hand.

His eyes were sparkling as they filled with tears and brimmed over. Lazarus must have looked like that when he rose from the grave, bemused, to see the sky and the blessed light of day again. I felt his hand tremble more and more strongly in mine. Then he began lowering his head further and further. Just in time I remembered how he had bent before to kiss my hand, and this time I hastily snatched it back, repeating, "Yes, please do tell her. We don't want her feeling anxious. The most important thing of all is for her to get better soon, for her own sake, for us all!"

"Oh yes," he ecstatically repeated, "she must get better, get better soon. She'll be happy to go away now, oh, I'm sure of that. She'll be happy to go away at once and get better, because of you, for you … from the first I knew God had sent you to me … no, no, I can't thank you enough, may God reward you! I'll go now … no, stay where you are, don't go to any trouble, I'm leaving."

And with a very different bearing, with a light, springy step I had never seen in him before, he strode to the door, his black coat-tails flying. The door closed with a clear, almost cheerful click after him. I was left standing alone in the dark room, in some dismay, which is only natural when you have come to a decision without thinking it out properly in advance.

But only an hour later I was to become fully aware of what I had really promised in my weak-minded mood of pity. I was to understand the responsibility I had taken on myself when my batman, knocking timidly at the door, brought me a letter on blue notepaper, in the now familiar format.

We're leaving the day after tomorrow. I promised Papa. Forgive me for being so horrible these last few days, but I was so upset to think I was nothing but a nuisance to you. Now I know why I want to get better and who I must get better for, so I'm not afraid any longer. Do come as early as you can tomorrow. I'll be waiting for you more impatiently than ever before.

Forever yours, E

Forever—I felt a sudden shudder at the word that binds a man irrevocably, for all eternity. But there was no going back now. Once again my pity had got the better of my willpower. I had given myself away. I was not my own man any more.

Get a grip on yourself, I thought. That was the last thing they would extract from me, a half-promise that I would never have to keep. One more day, I told myself, two more days when you must put up with this senseless love of hers, and then they'll be going away and you can be yourself again. But the closer the afternoon came the more uncomfortable I felt, and the more the idea of meeting her confidently loving eyes with a lie in my heart troubled me. It was no use making myself talk easily to

my comrades. I felt only too clearly the hammering in my skull.
My nerves were on edge, my gums were suddenly dry as if a
stifled fire were smoking and smouldering inside me. On pure
impulse I ordered a cognac and tossed it back. It was no help;
my throat was still tight and dry. So I ordered another, and only
when I asked for the third did I realise what I was doing—this
was Dutch courage to keep me from being cowardly or sentimental when I went out to Kekesfalva. There was something in me
that I wanted to anaesthetise first, perhaps fear, perhaps shame,
perhaps a very good feeling and perhaps a very bad one. Yes, that
was it—that's why soldiers get a double ration of brandy before
they attack. I wanted to dull my wits and my understanding of
the dubious, perhaps dangerous situation into which I was walking. However, the only effect of those three cognacs was to make
my feet feel leaden and set off a buzzing sound inside my head,
like the high-pitched noise of a dentist's drill before it hits the
truly painful spot. It was not a confident, not a clear-headed and
least of all a cheerful man who went down the long avenue—or
did it seem to me so endless only today?—and then, hesitantly,
up to the house with his heart hammering.

But it all turned out to be easier than I expected. Another
and better kind of bemusement awaited me, a finer and purer
intoxication than I had sought in strong liquor. Vanity can be
beguiling, gratitude can go to your head, affection can inspire
delight. At the door good old Josef exclaimed happily, "Oh,
Lieutenant Hofmiller, sir!" as he swallowed, stepped from foot
to foot in his emotion, and now and then glanced surreptitiously at me as you might look up at the picture of a saint in
church. "Please go straight into the salon! Fräulein Edith has
been waiting for you, sir," he whispered in the excited tones of
a man ashamed of his enthusiasm.

I wondered, in astonishment, why does this stranger, this old manservant, look at me so ecstatically? Why does he seem so fond of me? Does it really make someone kind and happy to see kindness and sympathy in others? If so then Condor was right—if you help only one other human being you have made sense of your life, and it was truly rewarding to sacrifice yourself for others, to the full extent of your powers and even beyond. Then any sacrifice was worthwhile, even a lie if it made others happy was more important than the truth. Suddenly I felt my tread was sure and steady. A man who knows he brings joy with him walks in a new way.

But here was Ilona already coming to meet me, also radiant, her dark eyes embracing me as if with soft arms. She had never been so warm to me or pressed my hand so cordially before. "Thank you!" she said, with a note in her voice as if she were speaking through a warm, moist summer shower of rain. "I'm sure you have no idea yourself what you've done for the child. You have saved her, God knows you have saved her life. Come along, quick, I can't tell you how anxiously she is waiting for you."

Meanwhile the other door moved slightly. I had a feeling that someone had been standing on the other side of it, listening. The old man came in, his eyes no longer full of death and horror as they had been yesterday, but of a tender radiance. "How good of you to come. You'll be amazed to see the change in her. In all these years since her accident I've never seen her so happy and cheerful. It's a miracle, a genuine miracle! Oh, my God, to think what you've done for us, to think what you've done for us!"

He was overcome even as he spoke. He swallowed, and sobbed, and was ashamed of his emotion, which was gradually infecting me. For who could be cold in the face of such gratitude? I hope I have never been a vain man, one of those who admire or overestimate themselves, and to this day I do not consider myself either good or strong. But a warm surge of confidence, created by the wildly enthusiastic gratitude of the others, was irresistibly streaming into me. All my fear was carried away as if on a golden wind. Why shouldn't I let myself be loved with an easy mind, when it made others so happy? I was positively impatient to go into the room that I had left in such desperation the day before yesterday.

And there in her easy chair sat a girl whom I hardly recognised, she looked so bright and happy. She was wearing a pale-blue silk dress that made her seem even more girlish, more childlike, there were white flowers in her pale-red hair—were they myrtle?—and around her chair stood a colourful array of baskets of flowers (I wondered who had given them to her). She must have known for some time that I was in the house; no doubt, as she waited, she had heard the cheerful greetings and my approaching footsteps. But today there was none of that nervously probing, watchful expression in her eyes, the look that had recently been turned distrustfully on me from under her lowered lids when I came in. She was sitting relaxed and erect in her chair, and today I quite forgot that the rug on her lap concealed an infirmity, and the easy chair was really her dungeon, for I was so amazed by this new girlish creature. She seemed more childlike in her joy, but more womanly in her beauty. She noticed my surprise, and took it as a gift. The old tone of our carefree friendly conversations was struck as soon as she invited me in.

"At last, at last! Please do sit down beside me. And please don't say anything. I have something important to say to you first."

393

I sat down, feeling entirely at my ease. For how can anyone be confused and awkward after such a bright, friendly welcome?

"I just want you to listen to me for a minute, and you won't interrupt me, will you?" This time, I felt, she had thought out every word in advance. "I know all that you told my father. I know what you are going to do for me. And now, please believe what I say, word for word. I promise that I will never—never, do you hear?—ask why you did this, whether for my father's sake or really for mine. Whether it was just pity on your part or—no, please don't interrupt, I don't *want* to know, I'm not going to dwell on that any more, tormenting myself and everyone else. It's enough that you have brought me back to life, and now I shall go on living … that since yesterday I have only just *begun* to live. If I get better I shall have only one person to thank for it, you and no one else."

She hesitated briefly, and then went on. "And now I'll tell you what I myself will promise. I thought it all through last night. For the first time I thought about it all like a healthy person, not the way I did before when I was still uncertain, when I was so confused and impatient. It's wonderful—at last I know what it's like not to feel afraid, wonderful to be able to tell in advance, for the first time ever, what it's like to feel I'm normal, and I owe that ability to you. So I will do absolutely everything the doctors ask me to do, everything, to make a human being out of the unnatural thing I am now. I won't give in, I won't let my efforts flag now that I know what's a stake. I will work at it with every fibre of my body, every nerve, every drop of blood, and I think if you want something so very much you can make God let you have it. I'll do it all for you, I won't expect you to make any sacrifice. But if I don't succeed … please don't interrupt!—or if I don't succeed entirely, if I can't be *perfectly* healthy again, if I can't move about as well as other people, don't be afraid! I will bear it all by myself. I know that there are sacrifices one ought not to accept, least of all from the person one loves. So if that course of treatment fails, although I am hoping for so much from it—for everything!—then you will never hear from me again, never see me again. I promise I will never be a burden to you, I don't want anyone to take me on as a burden, certainly not you. There—that's all I wanted to say. Now, not another word! We have only a few hours together left over the next couple of days, and I would like to spend them happily."

She spoke in a different voice; you could call it the voice of an adult. And her eyes were different, not a child's restless eyes now, nor the weary, demanding eyes of an invalid. I felt that she loved me with a different love, not in her original playful manner, not with her later avidly tormented emotion. And I myself saw her now with other eyes, not with the old pity for her misfortune, I did not have to be anxious and cautious with her, I could be clear and forthright. For the first time I unexpectedly felt real tenderness for this delicate girl, radiant as she was with the anticipation of the happiness she dreamt of. Without being really aware of it, I moved close to her to take her hand, and this time it did not tremble at my touch. Her slender wrist lay still in my grasp, fitting into my hand, and I was happy to feel the little hammer of her pulse beating peacefully.

Then we talked at our leisure about her forthcoming journey and little everyday things, we discussed what had happened in the town and in the barracks. I no longer understood why I had been tormenting myself, when it was all so easy—you sat beside a girl and held her hand. I was not making a painful effort any more, I was not hiding my feelings, we were showing each other warmth. I did not resist these tender emotions any more, I accepted the knowledge of her feelings for me without shame, indeed with pure gratitude.

And then we went in to dinner. The silver candleholders shone in the candlelight, the flowers rose from their vases like coloured flames. The light of the crystal chandelier was reflected from mirror to mirror, the house around us was silent, like a darkly curving shell holding a bright pearl inside it. Sometimes I thought I heard the quiet breathing of the trees outside, and the warm wind wafting over the grasses, for fragrant air came in through the open windows. It was all lovelier and better than ever. The old man sat there like a priest, upright and solemn; I had never seen either Edith or Ilona look so young and happy, old Josef's shirt front had never been so white, nor had the smooth-skinned fruit glowed in such colours. We sat there and ate and drank, talked, and were glad of the new harmony among us. Laughter flew from one to the other as carefree as a bird chirping, playful waves of merriment ebbed and flowed. Only when Josef filled our glasses with champagne, and I was the first to raise mine to Edith, drinking, "To your very good health!" did everyone suddenly fall silent.

"Oh yes, to my health," she breathed, looking at me as trustingly as if my wish had power over life and death. "I so want to get it back—for you!"

"May God grant it!" Her father had risen. He could not control his tears; they moistened his glasses, and he took them off to clean them with much ceremony. I felt that his hands could hardly help moving to touch me, and I did not object. I too felt a need to show him gratitude. I went up to him and embraced him, and his beard brushed my face. When I moved away from him I saw that Edith was looking at me. Her lips were trembling slightly, and I guessed how much she longed for the same ardent touch. So I leant quickly down to her and kissed her on the mouth.

That sealed our betrothal. I had not kissed the girl who loved me after deliberate reflection, but on a purely emotional impulse. It had happened without my conscious will or knowledge, but I did not regret the small, pure sign of affection. For she did not raise her throbbing breast to me wildly, thrusting herself on me as she had before, and although she was glowing with happiness she did not cling to me. Her lips received mine with humility, as if the kiss were a great gift. None of the others said anything. And then I heard a timid sound from the corner of the room. At first it seemed to be an awkward clearing of someone's throat, but when we looked up I saw that Josef the manservant was sobbing quietly in the corner. He had put down the bottle he was holding and turned away; he didn't want us to notice his unseemly emotion, but each of us felt the warmth of his awkward tears in our own eyes. I suddenly felt Edith's hand in mine. "Let me hold it for a moment."

I didn't know what she meant to do. Then something cool and smooth was slipped onto my fourth finger. It was a ring. "To remind you of me when I am away," she said apologetically. I did not look at the ring, I just took her hand and kissed it.

I was God that evening. I had created the world, and behold, it was full of kindness and justice. I had created a human being with a brow that shone pure as the morning, and eyes reflecting the rainbow of happiness. I had spread a table with prosperity and plenty, I had caused the earth to yield its fruits, its wine and food. These wonderful witnesses to my abundance were heaped up before me like sacrificial offerings, they came in shining dishes and laden baskets, and the wine sparkled, the fruits tasted sweet and delicious. I had brought light into this room and into the hearts of the people in it. The light of the chandelier flashed like the sun in our glasses, the damask cloth was white as snow, and I felt proud. My companions loved the light that I radiated, and I took their love and felt intoxicated by it. They offered me wine, and I drank deeply. They offered me fruit and choice dishes, and I relished their gifts. They offered me reverence and gratitude, and I accepted their homage like the sacrificial offerings of food and drink.

I was God that evening. But I did not look down remotely from a raised throne on my words and deeds, I sat there, kind and affable among my creations, and I vaguely saw their faces through the silvery mist of the clouds surrounding me. On my left sat an old man; the bright light of my kindness had smoothed out the wrinkles on his furrowed brow and extinguished the shadows darkening his eyes. I had taken death from him, and he spoke in the voice of a man risen from the dead, grateful for the miracle made manifest in him. Beside me sat a girl who had been an invalid, fettered and oppressed and hopelessly entangled in her own confused thoughts. But now the light of returning health shone around her. I had raised her from the hell of fear to the heaven of love with the breath of my mouth, and her ring sparkled on my finger like the morning star. Opposite her sat another girl, and she too was smiling gratefully, for I had brought beauty to her face and the dark, fragrant wealth of hair around her pale brow. I had given them all gifts and raised them up by the miracle of my presence, they all had my light in their eyes, when they looked at one another the brightness of their gaze was my doing. When they talked to each other, I and only I was the subject of their discussion, and even when we fell silent I was in their thoughts. For I alone was at the centre of their happiness, I was its beginning and its origin. When they praised one another, they were praising me, and when they showed their love for each other they meant it for me as the creator of all love. And I sat among them, glad to see my works, and I saw that it was good to have been kind to my creations. I magnanimously drank in their love with the wine, and relished their happiness with the delicious food.

Yes, I was God that evening. I had calmed the troubled waters, I had cast darkness out of human hearts. But I had also taken away my own fear; my mind was at peace as it had never been before in all my days. Only when the evening grew late, and I rose from the table, did I feel slightly mournful. It was the eternal sadness of God on the seventh day, when his work was done, and I saw that mild sadness of mine reflected in the others' empty faces. For now came the moment of farewell. We had all been strangely moved, as if we knew that something unparalleled was now coming to its end, one of those rare hours of complete ease that, like clouds, do not return. For the first time I felt real regret at the thought of leaving Edith. Like a true lover, I postponed the moment of leaving the girl who loved me. How pleasant it would be, I thought, to sit beside her bed, stroking the delicate, tender hand in mine again and again, seeing the rosy smile of happiness light up her face. But it was late. So I just swiftly embraced her and kissed her mouth again. I felt her hold her breath, as if to keep the warmth of my own for ever. Then I went to the door, with her father accompanying me. One last look back, a greeting, and then I went, walking freely and confidently, as you walk away from a good deed well done.

I went the few steps into the front hall, where the servant was standing ready with my cap and sword. I only wish I had walked faster, I wish I had been less considerate of old Kekesfalva's feelings, for he still couldn't bear to see me go. Once again he embraced me, caressed my arm to show me yet again how grateful he was for what I had done for him. Now he could die in peace, he said, his child would be cured, everything was good now, and it was all because of me, all my doing. I felt it increasingly embarrassing to be caressed and flattered like that in front of the servant, who still stood waiting patiently with his head bowed. I had already shaken the old man's hand and said goodbye several times, but he always began again. And I, made foolish by my pity, stayed standing there. I could not find the strength to tear myself away, although a sombre voice inside me said firmly—this is enough, this is too much.

Suddenly I heard the sound of a disturbance of some kind through the door. I pricked up my ears. A quarrel must have begun in the next room; I clearly heard a vigorous argument in progress, and with horror I recognised the voices of Ilona and Edith. One seemed to want to do something, the other was trying to dissuade her. "Please, I beg you," I heard Ilona admonishing Edith, "please stay where you are." And more roughly came Edith's angry, "No, leave me alone, leave me alone!" I listened to them more and more uneasily, through the old man's chatter. What was going on behind the closed door? Why had the peace been disturbed, my peace, the divine peace of this day? What was Edith demanding so imperiously, what was Ilona trying to prevent? There—suddenly I heard that unpleasant sound, the click-click of the crutches. For God's sake, surely she wasn't going to come out here after me without Josef's help? But that hasty, wooden sound came again, click-click … click, right, left

... click-click ... right, left, right, left—instinctively I thought of her swaying body as she moved on the crutches. She must be close to the door now. Then there was a clatter and a thud as if some solid mass had flung itself against one half of the door. Next came the gasping sound of strenuous effort, and the handle of the door, heavily pressed down, clicked open.

A dreadful sight met my eyes. Edith was leaning against the doorpost, still exhausted by her efforts. She was clinging grimly to the post with her left hand in order to keep her balance, and she was clutching both crutches in her right hand. Ilona, visibly distraught, was behind her, obviously trying either to support her or hold her back by force. But Edith's eyes were flashing with impatience and anger. "Leave me alone, I told you!" she screamed, rejecting Ilona's unwanted assistance. "I don't need anyone to help me. I can do it by myself."

And then, before Kekesfalva or the manservant had grasped the situation, something incredible happened. The crippled girl bit her lip as if about to make a mighty effort, and looking at me with wide, burning eyes she pushed herself away from the doorpost that had been supporting her with a single movement, like a swimmer taking off from the beach, intending to walk towards me on her own, without her crutches. As she moved she swayed as if she were plunging into the emptiness of space, but she quickly flailed both hands in the air, the empty hand and the hand holding the crutches, to regain her equilibrium. She bit her lip again several times, put one foot forward and dragged the other after it, with staccato movements to right and left like the movements of a puppet running through her body. But she did it. She was walking! She was walking with her eyes wide open and turned on me, walking as if an invisible wire were pulling her along, he teeth pressed into her lip, her features spasmodically contorted. She was walking, swaying back and forth like a boat in stormy seas, but she was walking alone for the first time without her crutches, without other help—a miracle of sheer willpower must have brought her legs temporarily back to life. No doctor has ever been able to explain to me how the lame girl was able to reanimate her dead, weak, stiff legs that one and only time, and I cannot describe what it was like, for we were all staring at her as if turned to stone. Even Ilona forgot about following her to protect her. However, Edith took those few tottering steps as if impelled by a storm within her; it was not exactly walking, more like flying close to the ground, the unsteady, tentative flight of a bird with broken wings. But willpower, that daemonic force of the heart, kept her going on and on. Very close to me now, she was already reaching out her arms, which had been flapping, bird-like, to help her stay on her feet. She stretched them out longingly to me in the triumph of her achievement, and her tense features were already relaxing into an exultant smile of happiness. She had done it, she had worked the miracle—only two more steps, no, just one last step. I could almost feel the breath from her mouth as it broke into a smile, and then the terrible thing happened. The vigorous, ardent movement with which she was already spreading her arms in anticipation of the embrace she would have won made her lose her balance. Her knees gave way as if at the stroke of a scythe. She fell with a crash just in front of my feet on the hard tiles. And in my first horrified reaction I instinctively flinched away, instead of doing the most natural thing in the world and going to help her up.

But already, and almost simultaneously, Kekesfalva, Ilona and Josef had made haste to raise the groaning girl. I realised, still incapable of looking at Edith, that they were carrying her away by their combined efforts. I heard only the stifled sobs of her desperate anger, and the dragging footsteps of the others cautiously carrying their burden. At that second the mist of exaltation that had veiled my eyes all evening cleared. In that flash of enlightenment I saw everything with terrible clarity. I knew the poor girl would never get better. The miracle she had hoped my love would perform had not happened. I was not God any more, only a small, pitiful human being whose weakness did wicked damage, whose pity had disturbed and destroyed her. I was aware, terribly aware, of just what my duty was. Now or never was the time to keep faith with her, now or never I must help her, run after the others, sit beside her bed, reassure her, tell her untruthfully how wonderfully well she had walked, how she would soon be better! But I had no strength left in me for that desperate deception. I felt afraid, dreadfully afraid of her pleading and then greedily demanding eyes, afraid of the impatience of her wild heart, afraid of someone else's unhappiness when I could not assuage it. And without thinking what I was doing I snatched up my sword and cap. For the third and last time, I fled from that house like a criminal.

Oh, for air—I need a breath of fresh air! I am stifling. Is it such a sultry night here among the trees, or is it the effect of the wine, all the wine I've drunk? My tunic is sticking to my body, an unpleasant feeling, and I tear the collar open. I wish I could throw my coat away, it weighs down so heavily on my shoulders. Air, just a breath of fresh air! I feel heat and throbbing pressure, as if my blood were trying to break through my skin, and there is a hammering in my ears, click-click, click-click—is that still the horrible sound of those crutches, or is it the pulsing in my temples? Why am I running like this? I must try to think. What really happened? Think slowly, calmly, I tell myself, don't get stuck at that click-click, click-click sound. Well then—I got engaged to be married ... no, I was obliged to get engaged to be married ... I didn't want to, I never thought of doing such a thing ... and now I'm engaged to be married, now I've been caught ... But no, that's not true. After all, I told the old man it wouldn't be until she's better, and she'll never be better. So my promise counts only if ... no, it doesn't count at all! Nothing has happened, nothing at all has happened. Then why did I kiss her, why did I kiss her on the mouth? It's not as if I wanted to ... oh, pity, damn that pity! They kept setting traps for me, and now I'm caught. I actually got engaged, they were both there, her father and the other girl, and the servant ... and I don't want to, I don't want to ... what am I going to do now? Think calmly! Oh, that horrible, eternal click-click, that click-click ... it will always be hammering in my ears now, she'll always be hobbling after me on her crutches ... It's done, it can't be undone, I've let her down, they've let me down. I got engaged. I was obliged to get engaged.

What's that? Why are the trees reeling about? And the stars, it hurts to look at them whirring in the sky—there must be something the matter with my eyes. Such pressure in my head. This dreadful sultry heat! If I could just cool my forehead somewhere then I could think properly again. Or if I had something to drink to wash the muddy, bitter taste out of my throat. I've been this way so often—isn't there a spring of water beside the path ahead? No, I passed it some time ago, like an idiot I must have been running, that's why I get such a dreadful throbbing and hammering in my temples. Something to drink, and then maybe I could think again. At last, as I come to the first low-built houses, I see light in a window with curtains only half-drawn, the yellow light of an oil lamp. That's right—I remember now—there's a little inn just outside the town where the carters always stop in the morning to warm themselves with a glass of schnapps. I'll ask for water there, or something strong or bitter to get the slime out of my throat! Something to drink, anything! Without thinking, with the avidity of a man parched to death, I push the door open.

The stifling reek of evil-smelling tobacco meets me as I step into the dimly lit cavern. At the back is the bar where they sell spirits, in front is a table where some road-menders sit playing cards. A lancer is leaning against the bar with his back to me, joking with the landlady. He feels the draught as I come in, and as soon as he looks around his mouth drops open in alarm; he immediately pulls himself together and clicks his heels. What's he afraid of? Oh, he probably thinks I'm an officer come to inspect the place, and he should have been back in barracks long ago. The landlady also looks uneasy, and the workmen stop in the middle of their game. Something about me must attract their attention. Only now, too late, do I remember; this must be one of those inns frequented only by the rank and file. As an officer, I'm not even supposed to set foot in it. Instinctively I turn to go.

But the landlady is already hurrying up deferentially, asking what she can do for me. I feel that I ought to apologise for bursting in like this. I'm not very well, I say, can she get me a soda water and a glass of slivovitz? "Coming, sir, just coming," and she is already hurrying off again. I really just want to stand at the bar and toss both the water and the spirits straight down my throat, but all at once the oil lamp in the middle of the room begins to rock, the bottles on the shelf move silently up and down, the floorboards under my feet are suddenly soft, swinging and swaying and making me stagger. I must sit down, I tell myself, and with the last of my strength I totter over to the empty table. The soda water arrives, and I drink it in a single draught. Ah, cold and good—for a moment the taste of vomit in my mouth goes away. Now to toss back the strong slivovitz and then stand up. But I can't, I feel as if my feet were sunk in the floor, and my head is pounding with a dull throb. I order another slivovitz. Then I'll have a cigarette and get out of here!

I light my cigarette. I'll just stay sitting for a moment, my dazed head propped on both hands, and think, think, think it all out point by point. Right—so I got engaged ... I was obliged to get engaged ... but that doesn't count because ... no, no wriggling out of it, it does count, it does. I kissed her on the mouth, I did it of my own accord. But only to set her mind at rest, and because I knew she will never get better ... she fell full length like a block of wood, how *can* I marry someone like that, she's not a real woman, she's ... but they won't let me go, they'll never set me free ... the old man, the djinn, the djinn with the face of an honest citizen and the gold-rimmed glasses, the djinn clinging to me, holding my arm, he'll always drag me back to my pity, my damn sense of pity. Tomorrow the news will be all round the town, they'll put a notice in the paper, and then there's no going back ... Might it be better to prepare my mother and father at home for the news so that they don't hear it from someone else, even maybe from the newspaper? Should I explain why and how I got engaged, and say there's no hurry about it, I didn't really intend to do it, it was only out of pity I got embroiled in the whole thing? My pity, my damn pity! They certainly won't understand it in the regiment, not one of my comrades will understand. What was it

Steinhübel said about Balinkay? "If you're going to sell yourself you should at least make sure the price is right ... " Oh God, what will they say about this? Even I myself can't understand how I came to get engaged to that ... to that sickly creature. And imagine when Aunt Daisy finds out, Aunt Daisy is shrewd, it's no use pretending to her, she won't think much of this. It won't be any good spinning her tales about Hungarian nobility and castles, she'll look them straight up in the *Almanach de Gotha* and within two days she'll have found out that Kekesfalva used to be Lämmel Kanitz and Edith is half-Jewish, and as Aunt Daisy sees it nothing could be worse than bringing Jews into the family ... It will be all right with Mother, the money will impress her—six million or seven million, he said ... But I don't care about his money, I'm not really planning to marry her, not for all the money in the world ... I only said I would if she gets better, that's all ... but how am I going to explain that to them? All my comrades in the regiment have something against the old man, and they're damn particular about these things. The honour of the regiment, yes, I know, I know ... even Balinkay wasn't forgiven for his marriage. He sold himself, they said scornfully, sold himself to that old Dutch trout. And when the family see those crutches ... no, I'd rather not write home about that, no one needs to know about it yet, no one at all, I'm not having the entire officers' mess making fun of me! But how am I going to avoid them? Maybe I ought to go to the Netherlands and see Balinkay? That's it—I haven't said I'm turning down his job yet, I can go to Rotterdam any day, leaving Condor to cope with the situation here, after all, he's the one who and landed me in this mess, he and no one else. It's up to him to see how he can straighten things out, it's all his fault. Yes, I'd better go straight to him and explain it all ...

explain that I simply can't … It was dreadful to see her just collapse like a sack of oats … I *can't* marry a girl like that … That's it, I'll tell him I'm not going along with his plans … I must go to see Condor now, at once … Get me a cab! Where to? Florianigasse—what was the number again? Ninety-seven Florianigasse … and drive fast, you'll get a good tip but drive fast, whip up the horses … ah, here we are, I recognise the place, the run-down building where he lives, I know it again, the disgustingly dirty spiral staircase. What a good thing it's so steep—ha, ha, ha, she won't get up here on those crutches, I'll be safe there from that click-click … What? Is that slovenly maidservant at the door again? Does the slut spend her whole time standing at the door? "Is the doctor at home?" "No, but he soon coming." Bohemian fool! Well, let's sit down and wait in there. Always waiting for that fellow, he's never at home. Oh God, if only that blind woman doesn't come shuffling in again … I don't want her around just now, my nerves won't stand it. Always showing such consideration … Jesus and Mary, here she comes, I hear her steps next door … no, thank God, it can't be her, that tread is too firm, the blind woman doesn't walk like that. It must be someone else walking about and talking inside that room … but I do know the voice. What? How on earth … but that's … that's Aunt Daisy's voice, and yes, how is it possible? How does Aunt Bella come to be here too all of a sudden, and Mama, and my brother and my sister-in-law? Nonsense, this is impossible, I'm in Condor's waiting room in Florianigasse. My family don't know the place, how can they all have arranged to meet at Condor's apartment? But it *is* the family, I know that voice, Aunt Daisy's screech … for God's sake, where can I hide? The sounds next door are coming closer and closer … now the door opens … it opened of its own accord, both halves of it, and—oh, good heavens!—there they all are standing in a semicircle as if they were about to have a photograph taken. They're looking at me, Mama in her black taffeta dress with the white ruffles, the one she wore to Ferdinand's wedding, and there's Aunt Daisy in a dress with puff sleeves, her gold lorgnette raised to her sharp, haughty nose, that nasty pointed nose, I've hated it ever since I was four years old! My brother in tails—why is he wearing tails in the middle of the day? … and my sister-in-law Franzi with her fat, flabby face … oh, this is horrible, horrible! Look at them staring at me, and Aunt Bella smiling her sour smile, it's as if they were waiting for something … but they're all in a semicircle, it's like being at a formal audience, they're all waiting and waiting … what are they waiting for?

But, "Congratulations!" says my brother solemnly, walking out in front of the others with his top hat in his hand. I think he says it rather sarcastically, damn him, but "Congratulations, congratulations!" say the others, nodding and bowing to me.

How … how do they know already, and why are they all here together? Aunt Daisy doesn't get on with Ferdinand … and I haven't said a word to anyone!

"Many congratulations, well done, well done … seven million, that's a tidy sum, you've done well … seven million, there'll be plenty to spare for the whole family," they say, all talking at the same time and grinning.

"Well done, well done," says Aunt Bella, licking her lips. "Now my Franz can go on with his studies. A good match!"

"Said to be aristocratic, too," bleats my brother from under his top hat.

But Aunt Daisy's parrot-like screech interrupts him. "Well, we'll have a good look at this aristocratic background of hers!"

And now my mother is coming closer to me, whispering shyly, "Won't you introduce your fiancée to us?"

Introduce her … all I need is for everyone to see her crutches, and find out where my stupid pity has landed me … I should just about think not! And then—how can I introduce her to them, when we're in Condor's place in Florianigasse up on the third floor? That cripple could never manage the eighty steps up here! But why are they all turning around as if something were going on in the next room? Now I feel it myself … I feel the draught of air behind me … someone must have opened the door there. Is someone coming after all? Yes, I hear something coming … there's a groaning and a squealing from the stairs, and something is making its way … hauling and dragging itself and panting on the way up … click-click, click-click … for God's sake, she can't really be coming up? She won't put me to shame like that with her crutches … I'd like to crawl away from this malicious crowd and sink into the ground … but how terrible, it really is her, it can't be anyone else … click-click, click-click, I know the sound … click-click, click-click, closer and closer … she'll be here in a moment … I'd better lock the door. But here's my brother taking off his top hat, and he bows to the click-click sound behind him … who's he bowing to, and why so low? Then, suddenly, they all begin to laugh out loud, making the windowpanes ring.

"Oh well, oh well, so that's it! Ha ha ha, so that's what his seven million look like, here comes his famous seven million … and those crutches too as her dowry! Ha ha ha … "

I wake with a start. Where am I? I stare frantically around me. My God, I must have dropped off to sleep, I went to sleep in this wretched hovel. I look round in some alarm. Did anyone notice? The landlady is calmly polishing glasses, the lancer is still there but showing me only his broad, sturdy back. Perhaps no one saw me go to sleep. I can't have nodded off for more than a minute, two minutes at the most, because my cigarette end is still glowing in the ashtray. But that dream has drained all the warmth from my dazed mind; all at once I know, with icy clarity, what has happened. I must get out of this inn! I throw down some money on the table, go to the door, and at once the lancer stands to attention. I can still feel the strange looks the workmen give me as they look up from their cards, and I know that as soon as I close the door they will start gossiping about the eccentric officer who came in here wearing his uniform, I know that from this day on everyone will be laughing at me behind my back. Everyone, everyone, no one will show any pity to a man fooled by his own pity.

Where now? Not home, anyway! Not up to my empty room, alone with my dreadful thoughts! It would be a good idea to have another drink, something cold, strong, because once again my mouth tastes unpleasantly of gall. Perhaps it's my thoughts that I would like to vomit up—I must wash them away, burn them away, dull their edge. It is a dreadful feeling! I'll go into the town! And wonderful to relate, the café on the town-hall square is still open. Light shows between the drawn curtains over the windowpanes. I need something to drink now, something to drink!

I go in, and as soon as I am through the door I see they are still all together at our regular table, Ferencz, Jozsi, Count Steinhübel, the regimental doctor, all my friends. But why is Jozsi staring in such surprise, why does he surreptitiously nudge his neighbour, why are they all giving me such piercing glances? Why does their conversation suddenly stop dead? Just now they were still in the middle of a lively discussion, all talking at once so hard that I could hear them all the way to the door. Now, as soon as they set eyes on me, they all sit there in silence, looking embarrassed. Something must be going on.

Well, I can't turn back now that they have seen me. So I stroll over as casually as possible. I don't feel happy about this, I don't feel in the least like merriment or cheerful talk. And also, I sense some kind of tension in the air. Usually one of them will wave to me, or send a cheery, "Evening!" flying halfway across the room like a cannonball, but today they sit there like schoolboys caught in mischief of some kind. Feeling stupidly self-conscious I pull up a chair, saying, "May I join you?"

Jozsi gives me an odd look. "Well, what do *you* lot say?" he asks, nodding to the others. "Do we let him join us? Ever known him stand on such ceremony before? This is certainly old Hofmiller's day for ceremony!"

This sally must have been meant as some kind of joke on Jozsi's part, for the others grin or stifle suggestive laughter. Yes, there's something going on. Usually, when one of us turns up after midnight, they ask where he's been and why and lard their joking with heavy insinuations. Today no one turns to me, they all seem embarrassed. I must have intruded on their comfortable, lazy evening like a stone dropped into water. At last Jozsi leans back, half-closes his left eye like a marksman taking aim, and asks, "Well, are congratulations in order?"

"Congratulations? On what?" I am so surprised that for a moment I really have no idea what he is talking about.

"Why, the pharmacist—he's only just left—said something about the manservant up at the castle, how he telephoned him to say that you had ... had got engaged to ... to, well, let's say to the young lady up there."

Now they are all looking at me. Two, four, six, eight, ten, twelve eyes staring at me. I know that if I admit it there'll be uproar next minute, witticisms, jeers, mockery, ironic congratulations. No, I can't admit it. Impossible in front of my exuberant comrades, all of them ready to make fun of me!

"Nonsense," I snap, trying to get myself out of it. But that evasive denial isn't enough for them. My friend Ferencz, genuinely curious, slaps me on the back.

"Tell us, Toni, then I was right, was I—it isn't true?"

He means well, he's a good sort, but he shouldn't have made it so easy for me to say "No." Nausea seizes me in the face as I anticipate their jovial, mocking curiosity. I feel how absurd it would be to declare, here at this table, something that I can't explain even to myself. Without thinking properly, I reply angrily, "Not a bit of it."

Silence reigns for a moment. They look at one another, surprised and, I think, slightly disappointed. Obviously I've spoilt their fun. However, Ferencz props his elbows on the table and bellows proudly, triumphantly, "There, didn't I tell you so? I know Hofmiller inside out! Like I just told you, it's a lie, a lying tale invented by the pharmacist. I'll have something to say to that stupid pill-roller tomorrow, I'll tell him to leave us officers alone, he can go smearing other men's reputations! I'll tell him so to his face, might well knock him down into the bargain. Who does he think he is? Dragging a decent man's good name down into the gutter like that—that wagging tongue of his playing a dirty trick on one of us! But there you are—see, didn't I say so? Hofmiller would never do a thing like that! He's not selling off his good straight legs, not at any price!"

Then, turning to me, he claps me on the shoulder with his heavy hand in the friendliest way imaginable.

"Toni, I'm really glad it's not true! You'd have brought shame on yourself and all the rest of us, you'd have shamed the whole regiment."

"And to shame us all in *that* way!" Count Steinhübel joins in. "With the daughter of that old profiteer who ruined Uli Neuendorff with his dirty tricks. It's bad enough that such folk can get rich and buy castles and noble titles. Oh yes, I'm sure he'd like to hook one of us for his darling daughter! What a villain! He knows best why he avoids me in the street."

In the increasing uproar, Ferencz is getting more and more worked up. "That bastard the pharmacist—I've a good mind to go and ring the night bell at his shop and box his ears! If you ask me, it's outrageous! Just because you go visiting at the castle a few times, that's no reason to tell such dirty lies about you!"

At this point Baron Schönthaler, a lean and aristocratic greyhound of a man, joins in.

"D'you know, Hofmiller, I didn't like to say anything—*chacun à son goût* and all that. But if you really want to know, I didn't much care for it when I heard how you kept going up there. We officers ought to be careful when we do someone the honour of calling on him. I don't know much about the kind of business that fellow Kekesfalva did or does, nothing to do with me, and I don't go around poking my nose into other people's affairs. But we have to stand on our dignity a little—well, you see how easily talk starts going the rounds. We don't want to mix with persons we don't know. Our sort have to keep our hands clean, y'know—touch pitch and some of it will stick. I'm only glad you didn't get drawn further in."

They are all talking excitedly at the same time, abusing the old man, coming out with wild stories about him, they make fun of "his lovely daughter the cripple", again and again one turns to another to praise me for not getting better acquainted with "such riff-raff". And I sit there in silence, rigid, tortured by their unwelcome praise, I feel like shouting, "Keep your filthy mouths shut!" or, "I'm the villain! It's not the pharmacist, he told the truth, I didn't! He wasn't lying, I'm lying. It's me, I'm the cowardly, pitiful liar!" But I know it's too late—too late for everything! I can't change my mind now, I can't take back what I said. So I sit there staring ahead of me in silence, a cold cigarette between my grimly clenched teeth, and I am horribly aware that with my silence I have wickedly, murderously let that poor, innocent girl down. I wish I could sink into the ground! I wish I could destroy myself, dissolve into thin air! I don't know where to look, I don't know what to do with my hands. Their shaking might give me away. I cautiously clasp them, lacing my fingers together with painfully hard pressure, hoping that will help me to control my tension for a few moments.

But as my fingers link I feel something hard, some foreign body between them. My fingers instinctively explore it. It is the ring that Edith gave me an hour ago, blushing as she put it on my finger. The engagement ring that I willingly accepted! I no longer have the strength to take this sparkling evidence of my mendacity off my finger, so with the furtive gesture of a thief I quickly turn the stone towards the inside of my left-hand finger before giving my comrades my right hand as I say goodnight.

The town-hall square lay spectrally clear in the glacial white of the moonlight. The edges of every paving stone were clear-cut, every line pure and straight, pointing up to the rooftops. I felt the same icy clarity. My mind had never been clearer and less clouded than at that moment; I knew what I had done, and I knew what my duty was now. I had become engaged at ten in the evening, and three hours later I had cravenly denied my engagement. In front of seven witnesses—one captain, two first lieutenants, one regimental doctor, two first lieutenants and an ensign of my regiment, and with the engagement ring on my finger, I had gone behind the back of a girl who loved me passionately. I had compromised a suffering, helpless, unsuspecting human being. I had let my comrades abuse her father without a word of protest, I had let them unjustly call a man who told them the truth a liar. Tomorrow the whole regiment was sure to know my shame, and then it would all be over. The comrades who had just been clapping me in fraternal fashion on the shoulder would refuse to shake hands or exchange any greeting with me tomorrow. Once unmasked as a liar, I could no longer wear the sword of an officer, but nor could I go back to the others, the family I had betrayed and allowed to be slandered. Even Balinkay would have no more to do with me. Those three minutes of cowardice had destroyed my life; there was nothing for me now but my revolver.

Sitting at that table, I had already been well aware that this was the only way for me to redeem my honour. As I wandered down the street, all I thought about now was the precise method of carrying out my decision. All the thoughts in my head fell neatly into place, as if the white moonlight were shining on them through my cap, and I felt as indifferent as if I were taking a rifle apart as I divided up my time for the next two or three hours, the last hours of my life. I must do everything properly, I mustn't forget or overlook anything. First a letter to my parents, apologising for inevitably causing them pain. Then one to Ferencz, asking him in writing not to challenge the pharmacist to account for himself; my death would settle the matter. Then a third letter to the Colonel, requesting him to hush it all up as far as possible and saying that I would like my funeral to be in Vienna, no delegation from the regiment, no wreaths. A few words, perhaps, to Kekesfalva, simply asking him to assure Edith of my heartfelt affection, and hoping she would not think too badly of me. Then to put my affairs in order, with a list of any small debts to be paid, a note that my horse should be sold to cover anything outstanding. I had nothing to leave to anyone. My batman was to have my watch and my few clothes—oh, and I would like the ring and the gold cigarette case to be returned to Herr von Kekesfalva.

What else? Oh yes, I remind myself I must burn Edith's two letters, and indeed all the letters and photographs in my possession. I want to leave nothing of myself behind, no memory, no trace. I hope to attract as little attention as possible in my death, just as I have lived without ever causing much of a stir. All the same, it adds up to a good deal of work for two or three hours, because every letter must be neatly written, so that no one can think afterwards that I had acted in fear or confusion. Then would come the last and easiest part—to lie down in bed, cover my head well with two or three blankets and the heavy quilt on top of them, so that no one in the next room or the street outside hears the detonation when I fire the shot—that was what Captain Felber had done once. He shot himself at midnight, and no one heard a sound. They didn't find him with his skull shattered until morning. And then I must put the barrel of the gun against my temples under the bedclothes. My revolver is reliable; it so happens that I oiled the breechblock only yesterday. And I know I have a steady hand.

Never in my life, I must repeat, have I done anything more clearly, precisely and exactly than in making these arrangements for my death. By the time I reach the barracks after an hour of apparently aimless wandering, I have the list all worked out in my head, minute by minute. My steps have been steady all that time, my pulse regular, and with a touch of pride I notice how steady my hand is as I put the key into the keyhole of the little side door that we officers always used after midnight. I haven't missed the tiny opening by so much as a fraction of an inch. Now to cross the yard and climb the three flights of stairs. Then I will be alone, I can begin what I have to do and at the same time put an end to it all. But as I approach the shadow of the gateway across the moonlit quad, I see a figure moving. Damn it all, I think, one of my comrades coming back and getting in just before me. He'll want to say good evening and maybe have a long chat.

Next moment, however, I am irritated to recognise, from the broad shoulders, that it is Colonel Bubencic. Colonel Bubencic, who bawled me out only a few days ago. He seems to be waiting in the gateway on purpose. I know the old boy doesn't like his officers coming in late. But what the hell? That's no business of mine. Tomorrow I'll be reporting to a very different authority. So I walk on with grim determination, pretending not to have noticed him. However, he is already stepping out of the shadows. He growls sharply at me, "Lieutenant Hofmiller!"

I go up to him and stand to attention. He examines me keenly.

"I suppose it's the latest fashion for young gentlemen to wear their coats half-unbuttoned, is it? You think you can come in

418

after midnight like a sow dragging her teats along the ground? Next thing we know you'll be going about with your flies undone too. I won't have this sort of sloppiness. Even after midnight I expect my officers to be neatly dressed, understand?"

I obediently click my heels together. "Yes, sir."

He turns away with a contemptuous expression on his face, and without another word he marches over to the stairs. His broad back is a heavy outline seen against the moonlight. Suddenly I am infuriated to think that the last words I hear in my life are to be his reproof. To my own surprise, I do something entirely instinctive, as if my body were acting of its own accord—with a few quick steps I hurry after him. I know that what I am doing is pointless—why spend my last hour on earth trying to explain or justify myself to a bone-headed old boy like the Colonel? But I suppose all would-be suicides are illogical enough to succumb to vanity only ten minutes before they plan to lie with their faces distorted in death. What they want is to set the record straight before they leave this life, although they will never know any more about it. A suicide will shave himself (for whose benefit?) and put on clean underclothes (again, for whose benefit?) before firing a bullet into his brain. I remember once hearing of a woman who made up her face, went to the hairdresser to have her hair waved, and applied the most expensive Coty perfume before throwing herself off the top of a four-storey building. Only this vanity, for which there is no logical explanation, got my muscles moving, and now, as I hastily followed the Colonel, I did so, I must emphasise, not in the fear of death or out of sudden cowardice, but because of an absurd instinct to wipe the slate clean rather than disappear into the void with my reputation smirched, leaving confusion behind.

The Colonel must have heard my footsteps, because he turned abruptly, and his small piercing eyes stared at me in surprise from under his bushy brows. Obviously the sheer impropriety of a junior officer's venturing to follow him without permission was more than he could grasp. I stopped two steps away from him, raised my hand to my cap in a salute and said, calmly returning his menacing glare—my voice must have been as blank as the moonlight was pale—"With respect, sir, may I have a few words with you?"

Those bushy brows shot up in surprise. "What, now? At one-thirty in the morning?"

His expression was forbidding. He was probably about to make some angry retort or tell me to report to him in the morning. But there must have been something in my face that troubled him. For a moment or so those hard, keen eyes scrutinised me, and then he barked, "Here's a fine state of affairs! Still, just as you like. Come up to my room, and get a move on!"

Meek as a shadow, I followed the Colonel in the dim lamplight along passages and up stairways, places now sombre and empty, but redolent of the body odour of many men. Colonel Svetozar Bubencic was one hundred per cent a soldier of the old school, and the most feared among all our superior officers. Short-legged and bull-necked, he had a low forehead, and under those bushy brows a pair of sharp, deep-set eyes that had seldom been known to look at anyone with favour. His sturdy body and heavy, massive stature unmistakably betrayed his rustic origins (he came from the Banat area of the Balkans), but with that low, bovine forehead and iron skull he had slowly and

420

doggedly made his way up through the army to reach the rank of colonel. It was true that his lack of any cultural education, his rough tongue, his profanity and his unpolished manners had kept the Ministry posting him to a series of provincial garrisons for years, and it was tacitly agreed in high places that he would never rise to become a general. Unpolished and plain-spoken as he was, however, there was no one to match him in the barracks or on the parade ground. He knew every last paragraph of the army rules as well as any puritan Scot knows his Bible, and never regarded them as elastic precepts that could be adjusted for the sake of harmony; he saw them almost as religious commandments to be accepted without question by every soldier. He devoted himself to his military service as the faithful devote themselves to God, he did not indulge in amorous adventures, he neither smoked nor gambled, he had hardly ever been inside a theatre or a concert hall in his life, and like his supreme commander Emperor Franz Joseph he had never read anything but the army rules and *Danzer's Army Gazette*. Nothing on earth mattered to him outside the Imperial and Royal Austrian Army, and within the army the cavalry, within the cavalry only the lancers, and among the lancers only one regiment, his own. The whole point of his life was to ensure that everything in this regiment of his functioned more smoothly than in any other.

A man of limited vision is hard to tolerate when he has power at his disposal, and hardest of all to tolerate in the army. Since military service consists of a thousand meticulous precepts, most of them out of date and fossilised, rules that only a committed old soldier knows by heart and only a fool expects to be taken literally, no one in the barracks ever felt safe from an officer so fanatical in observing those sacred regulations. This stickler for exactitude was a sturdy figure on horseback, sat enthroned at table looking around with eyes sharp as needles, and terrorised the staff of the army canteens and offices. A cold wind of anxiety always preceded his advent, and when the regiment was drawn up for inspection and Bubencic slowly rode past on his thick-set chestnut gelding, his head slightly lowered like a bull about to charge, all movement in the ranks stopped dead, as if enemy artillery had come up and the guns were already unlimbering and taking aim. We all knew that the first inevitable salvo might be fired at any moment and could not be diverted, and no one could tell in advance if he might not be its target. Even the horses stood rooted to the spot and never twitched an ear, no one's spurs clinked, we hardly dared to breathe. Then the tyrant, visibly relishing the terror that he spread among us, rode along the line at his leisure, subjecting man after man to close inspection. Nothing escaped his accurate and beady eye. His iron gaze saw everything, a cap worn very slightly too low, a poorly polished button, every speck of rust on a sword, any negligence in grooming a horse, and as soon as he spotted the slightest contravention of the rules a storm of abuse broke. His Adam's apple bulged apoplectically like a tumour suddenly appearing beneath his tight uniform collar, his forehead beneath his cropped hair turned red, thick veins stood out on his temples. And then he let rip in his harsh voice, pouring buckets of filthy profanity down on the unwitting offender's head. Sometimes the vulgarity of his language was so embarrassing that we officers looked at the ground, feeling ashamed of him in front of the men.

The men themselves feared him like the Devil incarnate. He would have them on fatigues or in the cells for the least little thing, and sometimes he even drove his heavy fist into a man's face in his fury. We called the Colonel the Bullfrog because of the way his fat neck swelled almost to bursting point in anger. Once, when he was letting fly in a box in the stables, I myself saw a Ruthenian in the neighbouring box make the sign of the cross in the Russian way and utter a fervent prayer. Bubencic drove the poor fellows to the point of exhaustion, hitting out at them, making them repeat their rifle drill until their arms were nearly breaking, and forcing them to ride the most recalcitrant horses until the blood ran down their thighs. Oddly enough, however, his honest rustic victims preferred this tyrant, in their dull and intimidated way, to all the officers who took a less harsh line with the men, but preserved their personal distance. It was as if some kind of instinct in them said that this severity from a stubborn and bigoted man was decreed by divine providence, and it cheered the poor devils that we officers were no more immune than they were to his outbursts, for you immediately find it easier to take the worst punishment if you know that it may hit your neighbour just as hard. In some mysterious way, equal treatment compensates for violence. The men always liked telling the story of young Prince W, who was related to the imperial family, no less, and therefore thought that he could do as he liked. But Bubencic had him in the cells for two weeks like any huckster's son, and wouldn't relent, however many dignitaries phoned from Vienna to plead for leniency for Prince W. The noble delinquent was not spared a day of his detention—an act of defiance, incidentally, that cost Bubencic any further promotion.

Yet more remarkable was the fact that even we officers could not help feeling a certain liking for him. We too were impressed by the dogged honesty of his implacable nature, and above all by his unconditional solidarity with us as his comrades. Just as he would not have a speck of dust on a lancer's tunic or a splash of dirt on the saddle of the last man to pass by, he would not put up with injustice. He felt that any scandal in the regiment was a slur on his own honour. We were his protégés, and we knew very well that if anyone was in trouble his best course was to go straight to the Colonel, who would begin by bawling him out but then set to work to get him out of whatever mess he was in. When someone was waiting for promotion to come through, or if one of us was in financial difficulty and needed a loan from military funds to tide him over, the Colonel would go straight to the Ministry and put his mind to ensuring that everything went the way he wanted. However much he infuriated and tormented us, every one of us felt, in some remote corner of his heart, that in his own crude and bigoted way this rustic from the Banat showed more loyalty and honesty than any of the aristocratic officers in defending the spirit and tradition of the army, its invisible aura, which meant more to us impecunious junior officers than our pay.

Such was Colonel Svetozar Bubencic, chief slave-driver of our regiment, in whose wake I was now climbing the stairs, and later he was to call himself to account in the same upright and single-minded way as when he took us to task, with the same keen sense of honour. After General Potiorek's disastrous defeat in the Serbian campaign, when just forty-nine lancers out of a whole regiment that had set out in good order got safely back over the River Save, he was the last man left on the enemy bank, and seeing the panic-stricken rout of the retreat, which he considered as a terrible blot on the army's reputation, he did what very few generals and senior officers in the Great War did after a defeat—he took his heavy service revolver and put a bullet through his own head. He did not want to witness the downfall of Austria, which the terrible images of our regiment in flight seemed to portend to his dull mind.

The Colonel unlocked his door. We entered his room, which was plain and spartan, more like a student's lodgings. It contained an iron camp bed—he was not going to sleep in more comfort than Emperor Franz Joseph did in the Hofburg—two colour prints, the Emperor on the right, the Empress on the left, four or five cheaply framed souvenir photographs of the regiment drawn up for inspection, or regimental dinners, a couple of crossed swords and two Turkish pistols—that was all. No comfortable easy chair, no books, just four cane chairs round a hard, empty table.

Bubencic vigorously stroked his moustache once, twice, three times. We all knew that abrupt movement of his; it was the visible sign of dangerous impatience. Finally he growled briefly, without offering me a chair, "Well, make yourself comfortable. Now, no havering, out with it! Money problems, eh? Or trouble with women?"

It was difficult for me to speak standing up, and in addition I felt exposed to his impatient glance in the bright light. I just indicated briefly that no, it was not money problems.

"Trouble over a woman, then! Again! I don't know why you fellows can't let it alone! As if there weren't enough women to be had easily enough. Go on, then, and no beating about the bush—what's the nub of your problem?"

I said, as briefly as I could, that I had got engaged to Herr von Kekesfalva's daughter today, and then three hours later I had simply denied the fact. But I didn't want him to think, I said, that I was trying to excuse my own dishonourable conduct—far from it, I had come just to tell him as my commanding officer in private that, as an officer, I was fully aware of the conclusions I had to draw from my behaviour. I knew my duty, and I would do it.

Bubencic stared at me rather blankly.

"What's all this nonsense? Dishonourable conduct, drawing conclusions? Drawing conclusions from what, and why? This doesn't amount to much! So you got engaged to Kekesfalva's daughter? I saw her once—odd tastes you have, she's a sickly, crippled girl. And then you changed your mind? Nothing much to that either, plenty of men have changed their minds and no one thinks the worse of them for it. Or have you maybe? … " He came closer to me. "Been up to a little hanky-panky with her, have you, and now there's a little stranger on the way? That wouldn't look so good, I must say."

I was ashamed of myself, and getting annoyed as well. The casual, almost deliberately frivolous way in which he misunderstood it all was getting me down. I clicked my heels.

"With respect, sir, I would like to say that I was telling a downright lie when I said no, I was not engaged, in front of seven officers of this regiment at our regular table in the café. I lied to my comrades out of cowardice and embarrassment. Tomorrow Lieutenant Hawliczek is going to accuse the pharmacist who told him about it of making the story up, but the pharmacist told the truth. Tomorrow everyone in the town will already know that I told a lie at the officers' table, and I'm not worthy to be an officer myself."

Now he was staring at me in surprise. His slow mind had obviously begun working at last. His face gradually darkened.

"Where did you say this was?"

"At our regular table in the café."

"In front of your comrades, right? They all heard you?"

"With respect, yes, sir."

"And the pharmacist knows you said it?"

"He will tomorrow. Along with the whole town."

The Colonel tugged at his heavy moustache and twisted its ends as hard as if he were trying to tear it out. I could see that something was at work behind his low brow. He began pacing up and down in annoyance, his hands clasped behind his back, up and down he went once, twice, five times, ten times, twenty times. The floor shook slightly under his hard tread, and his spurs jingled faintly. Finally he stopped again in front of me.

"Well, what are you thinking of doing now, then?"

"There's only one way out—I'm sure you know that yourself, sir. I just came to say goodbye, and ask you, with respect, to make sure that—afterwards—everything is done quietly and as far as possible inconspicuously. I don't want to bring shame on the regiment."

"Nonsense," he muttered. "Bloody nonsense. An upstanding, healthy, decent young man like you, over a crippled girl! I dare say that old fox Kekesfalva tricked you, and then you couldn't see your way out of it. Well, what the devil are those folk at the castle to do with us? But as for your comrades, and if that rascally pharmacist knows about it ... yes, of course that's a difficult business!"

He began pacing up and down again, even more vigorously than before. Thinking seemed to put a considerable strain on him. Every time he turned and came back towards me his face was a shade darker, and the veins at his temples stood out like

427

fat black roots. At last he stopped pacing, with a determined expression on his face.

"Right, pay attention. This sort of thing has to be nipped in the bud, and fast. Once word gets around there's not much to be done about it. First, which of our officers was present last night?"

I listed the names. Bubencic took his notebook out of his breast pocket—the notorious little notebook bound in red leather that he produced like a weapon whenever he caught out one of the regiment in unseemly conduct. Once you were entered in that notebook you could wave goodbye to your next leave. In his rustic manner, the Colonel licked the tip of his pencil before scrawling name after name with his fleshy, broad-nailed fingers.

"Is that all?"

"Yes, sir."

"Sure you've mentioned every one of them?"

"With respect, quite sure, sir."

"Good." He put the notebook back in his breast pocket as if he were sheathing a sword, with the same sharp sound as his utterance of that final "Good".

"Right—that's that, then. I'll send for them tomorrow one by one, before any of them sets foot on the parade ground, and God have mercy on any man who dares to remember what you said once I'm through with him. I'll see about the pharmacist separately. I'll spin him some kind of yarn, depend upon it, I'll think something up. Maybe that you wanted to ask my permission before saying anything officially, or … or wait!" He suddenly came so close to me that I could smell his breath, and looked me in the eye with that probing gaze. "Tell me honestly, and I mean *really* honestly, had you been drinking beforehand … I mean before you committed this act of folly?"

I felt ashamed. "With respect, sir, I did have a few cognacs before I left, and when I was still out there at ... at dinner with the family I had a good deal to drink ... but ... "

I was expecting a furious outburst. Instead, he suddenly beamed broadly at me. Rubbing his hands together, he roared with laughter. He looked very pleased with himself.

"Famous, excellent, now I know what to do! That's the way to get us out of the mire and away scot free! Clear as day! I'll just tell 'em all you'd gone on the spree, been drinking like a fish, hadn't the faintest what you were saying, couldn't even hear straight and must have misunderstood whatever they asked you. Stands to reason. And I'll tell the pharmacist I tore you off a strip myself for staggering over to the café dead drunk like that. Right, that's point one dealt with."

I was feeling increasingly bitter. He entirely misunderstood me. I didn't like the way this well-meaning old bonehead was trying to get me out of the mess I was in. He might even think I'd come to him out of cowardice, wanting him to help me. For God's sake, why couldn't he understand the pitiful nature of what I'd done? I pulled myself together.

"With respect, Colonel Bubencic, sir, it doesn't make anything any better where I'm concerned. I know what I've done, I know I can never look a decent person in the face again. I don't want to live with all that on my conscience, and ... "

"Oh, hold your stupid tongue!" he snapped at me, and added more mildly, "Sorry, but let me think in peace and don't keep on chattering like that—I know best myself what I have to do, I don't need any lessons from a toffee-nosed young prig. You think this is all about you, eh? No, my lad, that was just point one. Now for point two—you must clear out of here first thing in the morning. I can't be doing with you any more. We have to let the grass grow over this kind of thing, so you can't stay here a day longer, or there'll be more stupid questions and idle talk, and that doesn't suit me. I won't have anyone in my regiment being asked prying questions, people looking askance at him. I won't stand for it. You're transferred to the reserve troops at Czaslau, starting tomorrow … I'll write out the order myself and give you a letter for the Lieutenant Colonel. What it says is none of your business. All you have to do is scarper, and leave the rest to me. Get your batman to help you pack this evening, and you're to leave the barracks so early tomorrow that not a man jack among the rest of 'em sees you. On parade at noon they'll be told you're posted elsewhere on urgent business, that should keep 'em all quiet. How you settle things later with the old man up at the castle and the girl is none of my business either. Concoct some tale of your own to get you out of that fix—all that bothers me is not having any fuss kicked up about it and no talk in the barracks. So that's all settled—come up here five-thirty in the morning, all ready, I'll give you the letter, and then off you go, quick march. Understand?"

I hesitated. This wasn't what I had come for. I didn't want to make my escape. Bubencic noticed my unwillingness, and repeated, almost like a threat, "Understand?"

"With respect, yes, Colonel Bubencic, sir," I replied in a cool military tone. In my mind I was telling myself—let the old fool say what he likes. I'll do what I have to do.

"Right—so that's it. First thing tomorrow morning, five-thirty."

I stood to attention. The Colonel came over to me.

"You of all people, getting involved in such idiotic stuff! I'm not glad to let them have you in Czaslau. Always liked you best of the young 'uns, myself."

I could tell that he was wondering whether to offer me his hand. The look in his eyes had softened.

"Anything else you need? If I can help at all, don't hesitate to ask, I'll be happy to do it. I wouldn't want anyone to think you were ostracised, nothing like that. Anything I can do, then?"

"No, Colonel Bubencic, sir, but thank you very much indeed."

"All the better, then. Well, God be with you. At five-thirty first thing tomorrow morning."

"With respect, yes, sir."

And now I look at him as you look at someone you are seeing for the last time. I know that this is the last person on earth to whom I will ever speak. Tomorrow only he will know the whole truth. I click my heels smartly as I stand to attention, straighten my shoulders and turn to leave.

But even with his slow mind, the Colonel must have noticed something about me. Something in my eyes or my bearing must have aroused his suspicions, for when my back is turned to him he barks out an order.

"Come here, Hofmiller!"

I turn around. Eyebrows raised, he looks me up and down with those piercing eyes, then he growls, in a tone that is both gruff and kindly, "I don't like the look of you, boy. There's something the matter with you. Strikes me you're trying to fool me, you're planning something stupid. But I'm not having you commit some folly over a wretched affair like this ... some folly with your revolver or the like. I'm not having it, do you understand me?"

"With respect, yes, sir."

"Never mind all that 'with respect'! You don't take me in ... I wasn't born yesterday." His voice softens. "Give me your hand."

I hold it out. He takes it firmly.

"And now," he adds, looking me sharply, "now, Hofmiller, give me your word of honour that you won't do anything stupid tonight! Give me your word of honour that you'll be here at five-thirty in the morning to start for Czaslau."

I can't hold his gaze.

"My word of honour, sir."

"Good. I was afraid you might do something on the spur of the moment. One never knows with you excitable young men. Always too quick off the mark with everything, including your revolvers … later you'll see sense for yourself. A man survives this kind of muddle. Just wait and see, Hofmiller, nothing terrible is going to come of this, nothing at all. I'm going to sort it all out, and you'll never do the same again. Right, now off you go. I'd have thought of it as a great loss."

Our decisions depend far more than we like to admit on the familiar criteria of our rank in life and our environment. A large part of the mind automatically accepts impressions and influences made on us long before, and if a man has been brought up from childhood in the drill of military discipline, the psychological effect of an order from a superior officer is compelling and cannot be ignored. Every military command has a power over him that is logically inexplicable, but cancels out his own will. Even if he is well aware of the pointlessness of what he is told to do, in the straitjacket of his uniform he does what he is told to do like a sleepwalker, without resisting and almost unconsciously.

I myself, having spent fifteen of my twenty-five years in training at military academy and then in barracks, stopped thinking and acting for myself as soon as I heard the Colonel's order. I wasn't thinking at all any more, I only followed orders. My brain knew nothing except that I had to report promptly at five-thirty in the morning, ready to set off, and before then I must make all my preparations flawlessly. So I woke my batman, told him briefly that as a result of urgent orders we were setting off for Czaslau in the morning, and with his assistance I packed my belongings one by one. We just finished in time, and on the stroke of five-thirty I was duly standing in the Colonel's room to sign the army forms. Unobserved, as he had specified, I left the barracks.

It's true that this hypnotic sapping of my willpower lasted only as long as I was still within the military sphere of influence, and until I had finished carrying out the Colonel's orders. My mind shed its paralysis with the first jolt of the engine that set the train moving, and I came back to myself with a start, like a man knocked flat by the blast from an explosion who stumbles up and discovers, to his amazement, that he is unhurt. My first astonishment was to find that I was still alive. My second was that I was sitting in a train puffing its way along the tracks, snatched from my normal daily life. And as soon I began to remember, it all came back to me at feverish speed. I had wanted to put an end to it all, and someone had taken the revolver out of my hand. The Colonel had said he would sort it all out. But he meant only, as I now reflected to my dismay, so far as the regiment and my alleged good reputation as an officer were concerned. My comrades could be standing in front of him in the barracks at this very moment, and of course they were swearing a solemn oath not to let a word slip about the incident. But no orders could keep them from thinking their own thoughts, and they would all know how cravenly I had run away. Perhaps Bubencic will talk the pharmacist round, I think now, but what about Edith, her father, the others? Who's going to tell them, who will explain it all to them? Seven in the morning, I tell myself, she'll be waking up, and her first thought will be for me. Perhaps she's already looking down at the parade ground from the terrace—that terrace, why do I shudder whenever I think of the balustrade?—looking through the telescope, perhaps she sees our regiment trotting there, and doesn't know, doesn't guess that one man is absent. But when afternoon comes she will begin waiting, and then I won't arrive, and no one will have said anything to her. I didn't write her even a line. She'll telephone, she'll be told that I have been transferred, and she won't understand, she will be unable to grasp it. Or even worse—she *will* understand, she'll understand immediately, and then … Suddenly I see Condor's warning expression behind the polished lenses of his pince-nez; I hear him again telling me that running away "would be a crime … it would be murder!" And another image is already superimposed on the first—Edith bracing herself to get out of her chair and fling herself against the balustrade of the terrace, the abyss below, the suicidal expression in her eyes.

I must do something, I must do something at once! I must send her a telegram from the station, use the telegraph wires to give her a message. I absolutely must keep her from doing anything rash in a moment of despair, anything final. No, wait; Condor had said that *I* was not to do anything sudden and irrevocable, and if anything went wrong I was to let him know at once. I promised him solemnly, and as a man of honour I must keep my promise. Thank God I have two hours to wait in Vienna. My connection doesn't leave until midday. Perhaps I can reach Condor in time. I *must* reach him.

As soon as the train gets into the station I leave my luggage with my batman, telling him to take it on to the North-West Station and wait for me there. Then I take a cab straight to Condor's apartment, praying (I am not usually a devout man)— God, let him be at home, let him be at home! He's the only man to whom I can explain, he's the only one who can understand me and help me.

But only the maidservant comes to the door with her casual, shuffling gait, a brightly coloured scarf that she evidently wears when doing housework tied around her head. No, the doctor's not at home. Can I wait for him? He won't be back before midday, she says. Does she know where he has gone? She doesn't; he goes from one patient to another. Could I perhaps speak to Frau Condor? She agrees to ask, shrugging her shoulders, and goes away.

I wait. The same room, the same waiting as before, and— thank God—the same quietly dragging footsteps now in the next room.

The door is opened hesitantly, uncertainly. Once again, it is as if a draught of air has opened it, only this time Frau Condor's voice greets me warmly.

"Is that you, Lieutenant Hofmiller?"

"Yes, ma'am," I say, bowing to the blind woman—the same pointless folly again!

"Oh, my husband will be so terribly sorry. I know how much he'll regret being out just now. But I hope you can wait. He'll be back at one o'clock at the latest."

"I'm afraid not—I can't wait. But ... but it's very important. Couldn't I telephone him, reach him at some patient's home?"

She sighs. "No, I'm afraid that won't be possible. I don't know just where he's gone, and then you see ... the people he prefers to treat can't afford telephones. But perhaps I myself could … "

She comes closer to me, a timid expression on her face. She wants to say something, but I can see that she is diffident about coming out with it. At last she tries.

"I … I can tell … I feel that it must be very urgent and … if there were any possibility then of course … of course I would tell you how to find him. But … but perhaps I could give him a message myself as soon as he comes in … I expect it's about that poor girl, the child you are always so good to. If you like I will be happy to … "

And now something odd happens; ridiculously, I cannot look the blind woman in the face. I have, I don't know why, a feeling that she already knows or has guessed everything. The idea makes me feel so ashamed that I can only stammer, "That's very, very kind of you, ma'am … but I don't want to put you to the trouble. If you'll allow me, I can tell him the essentials myself in writing. But you're sure, really sure that he will be home before two o'clock, aren't you? Because the train he'll need to catch leaves not long after two, and he must … I mean it's really, really necessary for him to go out there, please believe me. I promise you I'm not exaggerating."

"Why, of course I believe what you say. And don't worry. He will do whatever he can."

"And may I write to him?"

"Yes, do write to him … this way, please."

She goes ahead of me with the uncanny certainty of someone who, although blind, knows where everything is in this room. She must tidy his desk dozens of times a day, feeling around on it with her careful fingers, because she takes three or four sheets of paper out of the left-hand drawer with the sure touch of a sighted woman, and puts them perfectly straight on the blotting pad in front of me. "You will find pen and ink there." Once again she points to precisely the right place.

I write five pages without stopping once. I tell Condor he must go out there at once, *at once*—I underline it three times. I tell him everything, as briefly and as honestly as I can. I tell him that I did not stand firm; I denied my engagement in front of my comrades—only he, I tell him, knew from the first that my fear of what people might say, my pitiful fear of the talk and laughter of others, was to blame for my weakness. I do not conceal the fact that I wanted to take my own life, and the Colonel saved it against my will. But at that moment I had been thinking only of myself. Only now, I write, do I realise that I am making someone else, an innocent girl, suffer with me. He must go at once, I repeat, he will understand how urgent it is for him to go out there *at once*—again I underline the words—and tell them the truth, the whole truth. I don't want him to gloss anything over, I don't want him to present me as innocent, as any better than I am, and if she can forgive my weakness all the same, then our engagement will be more sacred to me than ever. Now, indeed, it is truly sacred to me, and if she will allow me I will leave the army and go to Switzerland with them. I will stay with her whether she is cured soon, or later, or never, only one thing in life matters to me, and that is to prove that I was not lying to her, only to others. I ask him to tell her all that honestly, the full truth, because only now do I know how deeply I am pledged to her, more than to anyone or anything else, more than to my comrades or the army. Only she could judge me, only she could forgive me. It was now up to her to decide whether she would, and I asked him—it really was a matter of life and death, I said—to drop everything else he had to do and go out there on the early afternoon train. He must, must be there at half-past four in the afternoon, no later, he must be there at the time when she would usually be expecting me. It was the last thing I would ever ask him. Would he help me this one last time, and *at once*—this time I underline the words four times—just this once he must go out there, or all would be lost.

When I put the pen down I realised immediately that I had finally, and for the first time, made up my mind. Only in writing that letter had I come to know what the right decision was. For the first time, too, I was grateful to Colonel Bubencic for saving my life. I knew that I was pledged to only one person, to her, the girl who loved me, from now on for the rest of my life.

At that moment I also noticed that the blind woman was still standing beside me, never moving. Once again I was overcome by the ridiculous notion that she had read every word of the letter and knew all about.

"Forgive my incivility," I said, jumping to my feet. "I'd entirely forgotten that … but … but it was so important to me to let your husband know at once … "

She was smiling at me.

"I don't mind standing for a while," she said. "Only your letter mattered. I am sure my husband will do whatever you are asking him … I felt at once—I know every tone of his voice—that he is fond of you, very fond. And don't worry," she said, her voice sounding still warmer. "Please don't worry. I am sure everything will turn out all right."

"God grant it may!" I said with genuine hope—isn't it said that the blind can see into the future?

438

I bent down and kissed her hand. When I looked up, I couldn't understand how this woman, with her grey hair, her bitter mouth and the sadness of her blind eyes, could have struck me at first sight as ugly. Her face was radiant with love and human sympathy. I felt as if those eyes that never reflected anything but darkness knew more about the reality of life than all the eyes that see the world shining in its full brightness.

I said goodbye feeling like someone recovering from illness. Suddenly it no longer seemed to me any sacrifice to have promised myself again, and for ever, to another woman who had suffered and was an outcast from normal life. Why love the healthy, confident, proud and happy? They don't need it. They take love as their rightful due, as the duty owed to them, they accept it indifferently and arrogantly. Other people's devotion is just another gift to them, a clasp to wear in the hair, a bangle for the wrist, not the whole meaning and happiness of their lives. Love can truly help only those not favoured by fate, the distressed and disadvantaged, those who are less than confident and not beautiful, the meek-minded. When love is given to them it makes up for what life has taken away. They alone know how to love and be loved in the right way, humbly and with gratitude.

My batman is waiting faithfully on the station concourse. "Come along," I say, smiling at him. All of a sudden I am curiously light at heart. I know, with a sense of relief that I have never felt before, that I have done the right thing at last. I have saved myself, I have saved another human being. I don't even regret my stupid cowardice last night now. On the contrary, I tell myself, this way is *better*. It's better that it turned out like this, that the people who trusted me now know I'm no hero, no saint, not a god graciously looking down from the clouds to raise a poor sick creature up to him. If I accept her love now I am no longer making a sacrifice. No, it is for me to ask forgiveness this time, for her to grant it. And that's the better way.

I have never felt so sure of myself before. Only once, fleetingly, did a shadow of fear cross my mind, and that was when a fat man rushed into the carriage in Lundenburg, gasping for breath, and dropped on the upholstered seat. "Thank God I caught it! If the train hadn't been six minutes late I'd have missed it."

I instinctively feel a pang of anxiety. Suppose Condor hadn't come home at midday? Or suppose he had arrived too late to catch the afternoon train? Then it would all have been in vain. Then she will wait and wait. At once the terrible image of the terrace flashes into my mind again—I see her hands clutching the balustrade as she stares down, already teetering on the brink of the abyss. For God's sake, she *must* hear how sorry I am for my betrayal in time, before she falls into despair, before, perhaps, the worst happens! I'd better send her a few words by telegraph at the next station we come to. Something to give her confidence, just in case Condor hasn't told her in time.

In Brünn, the next station, I jump out of the train and run to the station telegraph office. But what's going on? Outside the door a dense, dark, agitated crowd has gathered to read a message pinned up there. Using my elbows ruthlessly, I force my way through the throng to the little glazed door in the post office. Quick, a form, quick! What should I write? Not too much.

Edith von Kekesfalva, Kekesfalva. Warm good wishes, am halfway through my journey. Thinking of you. Posted in Czaslau on service, back soon. Condor will tell you the rest. Will write when I arrive.

Ever your Anton

I hand in the telegram. How slow the woman behind the counter is! Sender's name and address, formality after formality. And my train leaves again in two minutes' time. Once again I have to push my way through the crowd clustering around the notice. It is even larger now. I want to ask what's going on, but the whistle tells me my train is about to leave. I just have time to jump into the carriage. Thank God, that's all dealt with. Only now do I realise how tired I am after these two strenuous days and two sleepless nights. On arriving in Czaslau in the evening, I need all my strength to stagger one floor up to my hotel room. Then I fall into sleep as if I were falling into a chasm.

I think I must have gone to sleep the moment I lay down—it was like sinking with my senses numbed into a dark, deep torrent, far, far down into depths of unconsciousness that I had never known before. Only after that, much later, did I begin to dream. I don't remember the beginning of the dream, only that I was standing in a room again, I think in Condor's waiting room, and the terrible wooden sound that had been tapping in my temples for days began again, the rhythmic sound of crutches, that dreadful click-click, click-click. At first it came from far away, as if it were out in the street, then it came closer, click-click, click-click, and now it is very close, very loud, click-click,

click-click, and finally so dreadfully close that I wake from my dream with a start.

I stare open-eyed into the darkness of the strange room. But there it is again—a tapping sound, knuckles knocking on wood. No, I'm not dreaming now, someone is knocking, knocking on my door. I jump out of bed and quickly open it. The night porter is standing outside.

"You're wanted on the telephone, Lieutenant Hofmiller, sir."

I stare at him. I, wanted on the telephone? Where … where am I, anyway? A strange room, a strange bed … oh yes … I'm in … I'm in Czaslau. But I don't know a soul here, so who can be telephoning me in the middle of the night? Nonsense! It must be at least midnight. But the porter goes on pressing me. "Quick please, Lieutenant Hofmiller, sir, a long-distance call from Vienna, I didn't quite catch the name."

At once I am wide awake. From Vienna! It can only be Condor. He must want to tell me his news, say she has forgiven me. It's all right. I snap at the porter, "You hurry back down, say I'm coming at once."

The porter disappears, I hastily fling my coat on over my shirt, which is all that I am wearing, and go after him. The telephone is in the corner of the ground-floor office, the porter already has the receiver to his ear. Impatiently, I push him aside although he tells me, "The connection's been cut," and listen to the receiver myself.

Nothing. Nothing but a distant surging, humming sound … sssf, sssf, sssf, like metallic mosquito wings far away. "Hello, hello," I shout, and I wait and wait. No answer. Only that mocking, pointless humming. Am I shivering like this because I have nothing on but my shirt and my coat, or is it fear? Perhaps something has gone wrong. Or perhaps … I wait, I listen with the hot rubber ring of the receiver held tight to my ear. At last there is a clicking. I am on another line. I hear the voice of the switchboard operator.

"Do you have your connection?" the operator asks

"No!"

"But you were connected just now—a call from Vienna. One moment, please, I'll see what I can do."

More sounds on the line. A switching sound on the phone, a growling, crackling and gurgling. Then rushing, roaring noises, and as they gradually die away only the faint humming and surging on the wires again. Suddenly there's a voice, a harsh, growling bass.

"Prague HQ here. Is that the War Ministry?"

"No, no!" I shout desperately down the telephone. The voice mutters something else indistinct and goes away, is lost in the void. Only that stupid humming and surging again, and then a babble of distant, incomprehensible voices. At last the switchboard operator is back.

"I'm sorry, I've just been checking. The connection had to be broken—there was an urgent army call coming through. I'll let you know when the subscriber calls again. Please hang up meanwhile."

I hang up, exhausted, disappointed, embittered. What can be worse than to have caught a voice in the distance and then lose it again? My heart is hammering as if I have just climbed a huge mountain. What was it about? Only Condor can have been the caller. But why was he calling me now, at half-past midnight?

The night porter approaches courteously. "You can wait up in your room, sir. I'll run up as soon as the call comes through."

443

But I decline the offer. I don't want to miss the call again. I don't want to lose a minute. I must know what has happened. Because many kilometres away, I can already feel it, something must have happened. It can only have been Condor—or the people at Kekesfalva; only Condor can have given them the address of the hotel. It must have been important, must have been urgent, you don't rouse a man from his bed at midnight for anything else. All my nerves are on edge. I'm needed. Someone wants me to do something. Someone has something important to tell me, a matter of life and death. No, I can't go up to my room, I must stay at my post down here. I don't want to lose a minute.

So I sit down on the hard wooden chair that the night porter, rather surprised, gives me, and I wait, my bare legs hidden by my coat, my eyes glued to the telephone. I wait for quarter-of-an-hour, half-an-hour, trembling with uneasiness and perhaps with cold, wiping away the sweat that suddenly breaks out on my forehead with my shirtsleeve. At last—*rrrr! rrr!*—the telephone rings. I rush to it, snatch up the receiver. Now I shall find out what's happened!

But it is another stupid mistake, as the porter immediately points out to me. It wasn't the telephone ringing after all, only the hotel doorbell outside. The porter quickly unlocks the door to let in a couple out late. A captain strides through the open doorway with a girl, glances briefly in surprise at the odd character in the porter's lodge wearing an open-necked shirt, bare legs showing under an officer's coat. With a murmured goodnight he disappears up the dimly lit staircase with his girl.

Now I can't stand it any more. I turn the handle of the telephone and get the operator on the line. "Hasn't my call come through yet?"

"What call?"

"From Vienna … I think it was from Vienna. Over half-an-our ago."

"I'll just ask. Wait a few minutes, please."

Wait! Wait another few minutes! Minutes, minutes … a human eing can die in a second, someone's fate can be decided, a whole world can end in a second. Why am I kept waiting such criminally long time? This is torture, madness. The clock says alf-past one. I've been sitting here for an hour now, shivering nd freezing and waiting.

At last, at long last I hear the ringing tone again. I strain every ense to listen, but it is only the operator telling me, "I made nquiries. The call was cancelled."

Cancelled? What does that mean? Cancelled? "Just a moment," I ask the operator, but she has already hung up.

Cancelled? Why cancelled? Why do they call me in the middle f the night and then cancel the call? Something must have appened, something I don't know about, but I must know what t is. I can't get past the time and distance between me and the aller—this is sheer horror! Shall I telephone Condor myself? No, not now, not in the middle of the night. It would frighten is wife. It was probably too late for him as well, and he would refer to telephone me again in the morning.

I cannot describe that night. A succession of confused thoughts nd images chase through my mind, while I myself am both weary and wide awake, waiting all the time with every nerve tretched, listening to every footstep on the stairs and in the orridor, to every bell ringing and every clinking sound out in he street, listening to every movement, every noise, while at the ame time I am staggering with weariness, drained, exhausted, nd then at last I sleep, a sleep that is much too deep, goes on much too long, a sleep as timeless as death and unfathomable as the void.

When I wake up it is bright daylight in the room. A glance at the time shows me that it is ten-thirty. For God's sake—and I was supposed to report for duty immediately, on the Colonel's orders! Once again, before I can begin thinking about personal matters, military discipline automatically takes me over. I get into my uniform, dressing fast, and run downstairs. The porter tries to stop me. No, everything else can wait until later. First I must report for duty. I gave the Colonel my word of honour.

With my uniform belt correctly buckled, I enter the regimental office. But its only occupant is a small, red-haired non-commissioned officer, who looks at me in alarm.

"Please go down at once, sir. The Lieutenant Colonel has given express orders for all officers and men of the garrison to be on parade at eleven sharp. Please go straight down."

I race downstairs. Sure enough, they are all assembled in the yard, the whole garrison. I am just in time to get in line beside the regimental chaplain, and then the divisional commander appears. He strides up with a curiously slow and solemn tread, unfolds a sheet of paper, and begins in a loud, resonant voice.

"A terrible crime has been committed, instilling horror into the realm of Austria-Hungary and the entire civilised world. (What crime, I wonder in alarm, what crime? I involuntarily begin to tremble as if I had committed it myself.) "I have to announce the wicked murder"—what murder?—"of the beloved heir to the throne. His Imperial and Royal Highness Archduke Franz Ferdinand and Her Highness the Archduchess have been assassinated." (What, someone has murdered the heir to the throne? When? Oh yes, there were all those people crowding to read a bulletin pinned up in Brünn yesterday—so that's what it was about!) "This despicable act has cast the whole imperial house into deep grief and mourning. However, it is above all the imperial and royal army that must … "

I can't hear what he is saying distinctly any more, but the words "crime" and then "murder" have fallen like hammer blows on my heart. I couldn't feel more afraid if I were the assassin myself. A crime, a murder—that was what Condor said. All at once I'm not listening to the wearer of that blue plume of feathers, an officer festooned with decorations, as he addresses us in a voice like thunder. I have suddenly remembered last night's telephone call. Why didn't Condor call to give me news this morning? Without stopping to report to the Lieutenant Colonel, I use the general confusion when the announcement is over to run back to my hotel. Perhaps a call has come through by now.

The porter hands me a telegram. It arrived first thing this morning, he says, but I was in such a hurry as I ran past him that he hadn't been able to give it to me. I tear the envelope open. At first I don't understand. No signature! A text that makes no sense at all. Only then do I realise that it is simply information from the telegraph office, to say that my own telegram, handed in at Brünn at 15.58 hours yesterday, was as yet undeliverable.

Undeliverable? I stare at the word. A telegram to Edith von Kekesfalva, undeliverable? But everyone in and around the town knows her. I can't bear this suspense any longer. I immediately ask for a telephone call to be put through to Dr Condor in Vienna. "Is it urgent?" asks the porter. "Yes, urgent," I tell him.

Twenty minutes later I am connected, and—by some miracle, if a terrible one—Condor is at home and answers the telephone himself. In three minutes I know it all—there's no time in a long-distance call for tactful phasing. A diabolical chance ruined everything, and the unhappy girl never heard of my remorse, my fervent and honest decision. The Colonel's plans to hush the business up came to nothing. Ferencz and my other comrades had not gone straight home to barracks from the café, but went into the wine bar, where they met the pharmacist with a number of other people. Out of sheer friendship for me, Ferencz, that well-intentioned idiot, confronted the pharmacist and abused him roundly, calling him to account in front of everyone and accusing him of telling wicked lies about me. It caused a tremendous scandal, and next day the whole town knew about it. For the pharmacist, his honour wounded, had stormed straight off to the barracks first thing in the morning, to force me to bear witness to his veracity, and on hearing the news that I had disappeared, which struck him as suspicious, he had driven straight out to the Kekesfalva house. Here he confronted the old man in his office, shouting in such a loud voice that the windowpanes shook. The Kekesfalvas, he said accusingly, had been making him look a fool with their "stupid telephone call", and as a local citizen of good standing he wasn't taking such impudence from a bunch of military men. He knew, he added, why I had run away in such a cowardly fashion, and it was no use trying to pretend to him that the whole thing was just a silly joke. There must be some very shady dealing on my part behind it—but he was going to clear it all up even if he had to go to the Ministry of War, he wasn't having snotty-nosed young fellows call him names in a public bar.

With great difficulty, the furious man had been calmed down, and he went home. Horrified as he was, Kekesfalva only hoped that Edith would not have heard any of the pharmacist's wild accusations. But as bad luck would have it, his office windows had been open, and the pharmacist's words had carried with dreadful clarity all the way across the yard and through the window of the salon, where Edith was sitting. That was probably when she decided to carry out the plan she had made so long ago. But she dissembled cleverly; she had her new clothes brought and looked at them again, she laughed with Ilona, talked equably to her father, asked a hundred little things—was this and that ready and packed for the journey? Secretly, however, she told Josef to telephone the barracks to ask when I would be back, and whether I had left any message for her. When the orderly who took the call said truthfully that I was called away on army business, no one knew how long I would be away, and I had left no message for anyone, that will have been the last factor in her decision. In the impatience of her heart, she did not wish to wait another day, another hour. I had disappointed her too deeply, I had struck her too mortal a blow for her ever to trust me again, and my weakness made her fatally strong.

After lunch she had herself taken up to the terrace, and Ilona, who in fact was worried by Edith's striking cheerfulness, did not move from her side. It was as if she had some dark presentiment. But at half-past four—the very time when I used to visit Edith, and just quarter-of-an-hour before my delayed telegram and Condor arrived at almost the same time, she asked the faithful Ilona to fetch her a certain book, and unfortunately Ilona agreed to this apparently harmless request. That brief moment was enough for the impatient Edith, who could not master her own heart, to put her plan into practice—just as she had told me she would on that same terrace, just as I had imagined it in my nightmares, she had done the terrible deed.

Condor found her still alive. Extraordinarily, there were no major signs of external injury on her frail body, and the unconscious girl was taken to Vienna by ambulance. The doctors still hoped to save her until late into the night, and so Condor had telephoned me from the hospital at eight in the evening. However, on the night of the twenty-ninth of June, the night after the assassination of the heir to the throne, all the offices of the Austro-Hungarian monarchy were in turmoil, and the telephone lines requisitioned the whole time for the use of the civil and military authorities. Condor waited four hours before he could get a connection. Only when the doctors said, after midnight, that there was no hope left did he have the call cancelled. Half-an-hour later she was dead.

Of the hundreds of thousands of men called up to fight in the war during August 1914, I am sure that few set off for the front as gladly and even impatiently as I did. Not that I was looking forward to the ferocity of war, it was just a way out, an escape route for me. I fled to the war as a criminal runs to hide in the dark. I had spent the four weeks before the declaration of war in a state of self-loathing, confusion and despair, which I remember to this day with more horror than the worst savagery on the battlefields. For I was convinced that through my own weakness, through the pity that first attracted and then repelled me, I had murdered another human being, and moreover the one human being who loved me passionately. I did not venture out in the street any more, I reported sick, I hid away in my room. I had written to Kekesfalva to express my sincere condolences (it was my own part in his daughter's death for which I was really sorry). He did not reply. I sent Condor explanation after explanation justifying myself. He did not reply either. I did not receive a line from any of my comrades or my father—which in reality was probably because he was overworked in his ministry during hose critical weeks. However, I took this unanimous silence as a judgement passed on me by one and all. I increasingly fell prey to the delusion that they had all condemned me, just as I condemned myself, they all thought of me as a murderer because I thought myself a murderer. While the whole realm was in uproar, while the telegraph wires were hot and vibrant with terrible news all over Europe, a continent in a state of turmoil, while stock exchanges tottered, armies were mobilised, and the cautious had already packed their bags, I thought only of my craven betrayal, my guilt. So to be called up and have my mind taken off myself was liberation. The war, the millions of innocent souls it swept away, saved me, a guilty man, from despair (not that I am proud of it).

I dislike high-flown language. So I will not say that I went in search of death at the time, only that I did not fear it. Or at least, I feared it less than most of the others did, for there were many times when a return to the hinterland behind the lines, where there were people who knew about my guilt, seemed to me worse than all the horrors of the front—and where could I have returned to, who still needed me, who still loved me, for whom or what was I to live? If to be brave is nothing higher than to feel no fear, then I can say with an easy conscience, and meaning it, that I actually was brave in the field, for even what seemed to the most virile of my comrades worse than death, even the possibility of being crippled and mutilated, held no terrors for me. I would probably have regarded it as a punishment, as just revenge to be a helpless cripple myself, the object of any stranger's pity, when my own pity had proved too weak and cowardly in the past. If death did not come to meet me, then, the fault was not in myself, for dozens of times I went to meet death with cold indifference. Wherever there was some difficult task to be performed and volunteers were called for, I answered the call. I felt happiest in the thick of the fighting. After my first wound I got myself transferred first to a machine-gun company and then to the air force. Apparently I really did do all kinds of daring deeds in the rickety planes of those times. But whenever my name was mentioned in dispatches for "outstanding courage in the face of the enemy" I felt that I was a fraud. And if anyone looked too sharply at the decorations I had won, I quickly moved away.

When those four endless years were over at last, I found to my own surprise that I could go on living in the world as it then was all the same. For we who came home from Hades judged everything by new criteria. To a man who had fought in the Great War, the death of another human being no longer meant what it did to a man in peacetime. My own private guilt had been dissolved in the huge bloodbath of general guilt, for the same man, the same eyes and the same hands, had also set up the machine gun that mowed down the first wave of Russian infantry to attack our trenches at Limanova, and I had even seen, through my field glasses afterwards, the glazed eyes of the men I had killed, and the men I had wounded who lay for hours in the barbed wire, still moaning, before they perished miserably. I had brought down an aircraft outside Görz and seen it turning over three times in the air before crashing on the rocks and going up in flames, and with our own hands we had then searched the charred bodies of the airmen, still smouldering horribly, for identity discs. Thousands upon thousands of the men who marched beside me had done the same, with rifles, bayonets, flame-throwers, machine-guns and their bare hands; hundreds of thousands and millions of my generation had killed enemy soldiers in France, Russia and Germany—what was a single murder beside all that, what was a private, personal guilt within the cosmic, thousandfold guilt, the most terrible mass destruction and mass annihilation yet known to history?

And then—another relief—there were no witnesses against me left in the post-war world. No one could accuse a man decorated for outstanding courage of his former cowardice, no one was left to reproach me with my fatal weakness. Kekesfalva had survived his daughter's death by only a few days. Ilona was now the wife of a little notary in a Yugoslavian village, Colonel Bubencic had shot himself on the banks of the River Save, my comrades of the time had either fallen or had long ago forgotten one insignificant episode—everything "before the war" had become as unimportant and invalid as the old pre-war currency in those four apocalyptic years. No one could accuse or judge me now. I felt like a murderer who has buried his victim's body in a wood where snow begins to fall on it, thick, white and heavy. The protective blanket of snow, he knows, will lie over his crime for months on end, and then every trace will be lost for ever. So I plucked up my courage and began to live again. Since no one remembered me, I soon forgot my own guilt. For the heart can forget very well and very deeply what it really wants to forget.

Only once did a memory come back to me from the opposite bank of the river of Lethe. I was sitting in the stalls of the Opera House in Vienna, in a seat at the end of a row, to hear Gluck's *Orpheus* again; its pure, restrained melancholy moves me more than any other music. The overture was just ending, the lights in the dimmed auditorium did not go up in the brief pause which gave a few late arrivals a chance to take their seats in the dark. Two of these latecomers, a lady and a gentlemen, cast their shadows on my own row.

"Excuse me, please," said the man, with a civil bow to me. I stood up, without really noticing or paying any attention, to let them pass. But instead of sitting down in the seat next to mine, he first guided the lady ahead of him carefully with the touch of affectionate hands, easing the way for her, so to speak, and folded the seat down for her with care before helping her to sit down. The nature of his concern was too unusual not to strike me. Ah, a blind woman, I thought, and looked at her with instinctive sympathy. But now the rather stout gentleman was sitting down beside me, and with a pang of the heart I recognised him. It was Condor! The only man who knew the depth of my guilt was sitting close enough for me to touch him. Condor, whose pity had not been murderously weak, like mine, but was a self-sacrificing force for good, the one man before whom I must still feel ashamed was here! When the lights came up again in the interval he would be bound to recognise me at once.

I began trembling, and quickly put my hand up to shelter my face, so that I would be safe at least in the dark. My heart was hammering so hard that I did not hear another bar of the music I loved so much. The proximity of this man, the only person on earth who really knew me for what I was, troubled me deeply. As if I were sitting stark naked in the middle of all these prosperous, well-dressed people, I was already shuddering at the thought of the moment when the lights would go up and reveal me. And so in the brief moment between darkness and light in the auditorium, while the curtain began to fall on the first act, I quickly ducked my head and made my escape up the central gangway—I think quickly enough for him not to see or recognise me. But since that hour I have known that no guilt is forgotten while the conscience still remembers it.

TRANSLATOR'S AFTERWORD

Stefan Zweig's novel *Beware of Pity*, not a literal translation of the original title, *Ungeduld des Herzens* (Impatience of the Heart), was first published in German in 1939. As he was among those Jewish writers whose books were burnt by the Nazis, publication was not in Germany or Austria but in Sweden, when his publishers had moved to Stockholm for the duration of the war. It must have gone straight to its English translators Trevor and Phyllis Blewitt, since their version appeared in the same year. In his lifetime Zweig was an extremely popular author, so the swift translation is no surprise. When he wrote the book he was living in England, first in London and then in Bath; he and his second wife left the British Isles on the declaration of war in 1939, for fear of internment as enemy aliens, and went first to the United States and then to Brazil, where they committed suicide together in 1942, just after Zweig had delivered the manuscript of his memoir *The World of Yesterday* to the same temporarily Stockholm-based German publishing firm. The memoir too was quickly translated, and its first English version, by an anonymous translator, appeared in 1943.

The first translation of this, Zweig's only completed novel, is therefore over seventy years old, and as translations do tend to date (a sobering reflection for translators), after that length of time the moment seemed to have come for a new version of this very powerful work. A sense of historical period is important in the book, both now that we can look back at the twentieth century as a whole, and surely also at the time of writing, when the Second World War was about to break out. Zweig, himself a lifelong pacifist, draws a graphic picture of the extraordinary elitist world of the officer class of the Austrian army, especially the cavalry, at the time when the main narrative is set, early 1914. The note he wrote for the first English version, also included at the start of this new translation, elucidates it for English-language readers; one is tempted to reflect that its arcane rituals, baffling to the non-initiated, are reminiscent of those of the old-fashioned British boarding school. It is a telling presentation of a little world sufficient unto itself. The hapless young protagonist, Lieutenant Anton Hofmiller, idealistic but irresolute, and without the financial means of many of his young fellow officers, suffers the terror of social ostracism as he finds that he has offended against its unthinkingly arrogant ethos.

The main narrative is set inside a framework story, a device much used by Zweig. As the book opens an anonymous writer, clearly a version of Zweig himself, encounters the now older and wiser Hofmiller, who fought with distinction in the First World War, and who ranges himself on the framework narrator's side at a supper-party discussion in 1938 of the possibility of another war. The whole book, therefore, spans the imminent outbreak of the two world wars of the twentieth century.

The main part of the novel, told by Hofmiller to the framework narrator, deals with situations and characters of great emotional intensity. The disabled girl Edith, whom young Hofmiller pities and who hopes his pity will turn to sexual love, is memorable, and reminds the reader that Zweig knew Freud well, and visited him in his last illness in London as another exile from the Nazis. Freud's case histories of hysteria come to mind at times, as Edith (for whom there is every excuse) shows herself by turn pathetically self-immolating and demandingly petulant. Another notable character is the physician Dr Condor, who acts as the touchstone of good sense and right thinking. Some of his medical theories also seem tinged by the development of psychoanalysis of the time.

The main narrative also contains two stories within its own story; one long enough to be a novella on its own, the tale of how Edith's father, starting from poor Jewish beginnings, became a wealthy supposed Hungarian aristocrat; the other a shorter story, about a former member of Hofmiller's regiment who had to resign his commission for some unspecified offence, but retrieved his fortunes by a stroke of luck. Most unusually for Zweig, whose stock in trade does not include happy endings, both men appear to have made happy marriages. In translating, I have wondered whether Zweig felt that these episodes would offer some relief from the painful if fascinating development of the main plot, where flaws of character and unfortunate coincidences lead inexorably to disaster. The news of the 1914 assassination in Sarajevo of Archduke Franz Ferdinand, for instance, plays the part of a malevolent deus ex machina in preventing a reconciliation between the protagonists.

There remains, intriguingly, the question of why this is the only work that Zweig allowed to leave his hands as a complete novel. His method, as he records it in his memoir, was to cut and cut at his first draft, until he was almost always left with a narrative no longer than a novella or a short story. Many of these short works of fiction could easily have become full-length novels in another writer's hands. I think in particular of the powerful *Amok*, with its framework setting on board an ocean-going ship and its exotic Far Eastern setting for the main narrative, which strikes dark Conradian notes. And it seems very possible, although we cannot know, that the unfinished *Rausch der Verwandlung* (Intoxication of Metamorphosis), published in German after his death and recently in English as *The Post Office Girl*, might have undergone the same drastic cutting process. So why not *Beware of Pity*? After translating it, I tend to think it was because, in the circumstances of the late 1930s, Zweig wanted to get his anti-militaristic message across as quickly as possible, and he did not have much time left for writing, for cutting what he had written, or indeed for living. I am glad that he did allow the publication of this one full-length novel.

ANTHEA BELL   2011

PUSHKIN PRESS

Pushkin Press was founded in 1997, and publishes novels, essays, memoirs, children's books—everything from timeless classics to the urgent and contemporary.

Our books represent exciting, high-quality writing from around the world: we publish some of the twentieth century's most widely acclaimed, brilliant authors such as Stefan Zweig, Marcel Aymé, Antal Szerb, Paul Morand and Yasushi Inoue, as well as compelling and award-winning contemporary writers, including Andrés Neuman, Edith Pearlman and Ryu Murakami.

Pushkin Press publishes the world's best stories, to be read and read again.

*